THE LOST ORDER

THE CELESTIAL CHRONICLES
BOOK ONE

EDWARD GYE

For Elaine, an angel among us.

CONTENTS

A Letter to the Mortals

"How can I impress the particulars of reality upon you when you are a part of it? It would be as futile as trying to describe the air to a bird, or water to a fish. To truly know the existence of something, you must see it from the outside. From the perspective of somewhere else. It is a perspective I never wanted, but it was forced upon me. A perspective I alone have earned and can now provide.

I remember the first time I encountered an angel. The only certainty I've learned from all of this came in that first moment. They are not characters in a story, or convenient metaphors to provide a lesson to the dim masses. They are nothing like what I was taught. Elegant, strong, kind, and fearsome. Some are more beautiful than you can fathom, and others are more heinous than your nightmares. Angels are all these things, and demons are scarcely different. I have been broken, healed, and used by both. The only difference is their intent.

In a malign coincidence, I was torn from my life and used as a pawn in their everlasting war. It is in their world that I learned our reality is a pale facsimile of theirs. Except I never passed. I was taken alive.

They can do such things. Things we consider impossible. Miracles. Life-changing events for us exist in a single breath for them.

As I learned how to survive among the immortals, I clawed my way back to our realm. Through these struggles, I swore I would bear witness to their reality, however extraordinary it may seem. The only thing that gives me pause is that to speak of such things is a crime. It is forbidden to provide knowledge of the immortals to the living. Although, perhaps, I am their retribution. After all, it is written in their legends that the immortals will be judged by us.

As a gift, I provide to you an invocation, a promise written by the ancients, an important creed still used in the Great Library to this day. I needed it in my journey, as will you for the pages that follow:

> Let those who understand, read;
> Give those who read, voice;
> Provide those with voice, vision;
> Grant those with vision, wisdom.

With that, I give you the stories of the unseen, some of which are happening right now."

~ El-aria

CHAPTER ONE

The young postal worker halted his Royal Mail van on the verge of a country road. Today's delivery was different. He retrieved a padded manila envelope from the neatly organized box that held the post for the local area. Scrawled across the top in bold black letters: 'TO BE DELIVERED AT 10:05 AM Monday, NOVEMBER 23rd, 2026,' addressed to Alice Grey.

The envelope was addressed to a house at the end of a long tidal lane. It became an isolated island at high tide, accessible only by boat. There were no warning signs, no fences to deter the curious. Those who attempted the lane either knew the local lore or risked getting stranded.

When the house was built in the seventeenth century, people began spreading local gossip. No masons were hired to build the stone house, and residents couldn't recall any construction. It was as if it appeared one day from the mud and the trees. Residents of the small coastal village rarely spotted the inhabitants. It was such a mystery at the time, the local community accused the inhabitants of witchcraft – like many who were misunderstood in that day. Gossip has a way of becoming a legend, and over the years, consensus grew that this may be the place where the last of the witches from Pendle Hill escaped. Whenever anything tragic happened in the community, the town whispered with caution and half-truths that it was due to the ghost of the witch who was tried and burned centuries prior. The last person to survive was a young girl, Alice Grey, whom locals say was forced to live out her days in solitude on the island.

It was the first delivery to this address in living memory of the post office, and it appeared in the office in the nineteen fifties. It caused an immediate stir since it was addressed to Alice Grey. She would have had to be about two hundred seventy years old when the envelope was posted, and by the year twenty-twenty-six, she would be almost three hundred fifty years old.

As the envelope sat, carefully stored in the local post office, and the years drew near, an office betting pool began to form. During the last year, rules cropped up, so as not to allow an unscrupulous delivery person to cheat the game. One had to get a signature, and a picture of the recipient. The last thing to be delivered was during the First World War. The delivery man immediately quit thereafter and never returned, and the office was unsure if the package was even delivered. To win the pool, one must stick to the rules.

The young postman steeled himself. He was going to win this bet and deliver this package, even if he had to throw it on the porch and run like the wind. If any of them had been brave enough to open the envelope, or clumsy enough to lose it over the years, not only would the world have been saved, but all of existence as well.

"Never a bloody signal when you need one," he said as he shook his phone and aimed it forward toward the windshield in hope. "Nothing." He tossed the phone on top of the box of post to be delivered beside him and spied the long lane to the house again. The tide looked low enough. He looked through his dusty windscreen at the dead weeds and long-abandoned garden surrounding the house. It was a hot summer day and a clear blue sky above. He decided he'd make the drop as fast as possible and be gone in no time.

He began the slow, careful drive down the lane, dodging potholes and minding the steep drop-off on either side into the water. It was just big enough for his small postal van. There was not enough of a drop to cause serious injury, but certainly enough to partially submerge his vehicle and become the laughingstock of the office.

With the amount of concentration, he needed to drive the narrow lane, it would have been impossible for him to notice the figure of a person peeking through the curtains of the front window at his progress. Likewise, as he slowly drove the van along the lane toward the house, it would have taken a careful eye for him to see the water calmly rising behind him, gently cutting him off from the mainland.

As he got out of his van and walked up the steps of the back porch, his concentration was broken by the abundance of the garden. He paused to look at the surroundings. It was teeming with vibrant flowers and some of the greenest grass he had ever seen. He had never seen so many butterflies flitting about in his life. It was like a professionally maintained botanical garden in front of the sea. He looked around, astonished. He had passed the house hundreds of times. The garden was most definitely a dump. Although he thought, the backyard away from the road was a different story. As he walked up the remainder of the wide wooden staircase to the wrap-around porch, he took in the state of the building as well. He noticed the wood and the stone exterior. It was an aesthetic he had always wanted for a house of his own. Craftsman style. He couldn't understand how he never noticed from the road before. As he stepped to the door enveloped tucked under his arm and knocks. The door gently swung open from the rap of his knuckles.

"Package for Ms. Grey," he asked in a tone, unsure he had the right person.

"That would be Miss Grey. I've never been married." A woman in her early thirties peered out at him as she swept the wooden floor of the dining room. "You can call me Alice if you like."

He peeked into the room, checking for anyone else. "Perhaps this is for your mother, or grandmother, even?"

"Nope, that's me. I'm the only one who lives here. I've been waiting for this delivery for a long time. Place it on the table if you can."

"The delivery schedule is very specific. I arrived exactly as instructed," he said as he stood in the doorway, holding out a tablet and stylus for her to sign in receipt.

She doesn't look up. She continued with her duties and allowed the awkward moment to hang in the air.

"Ma'am, if you could sign here, please."

She looked at him and smiled, and then crouched to get her broom to reach underneath the table, stretching her arms. "You might as well stay until morning now."

His face couldn't hide the absurdity of her comment. He shook his head and tossed the package on her kitchen table. As he turned around, his gaze met a storm-ravaged garden. The sea pounded the shoreline as if it had been doing so for the last few hours. He wondered how this was possible. He steps to the center of the porch, and his jaw drops in disbelief. The wind blew his sunhat sideways off his head. It tumbled across the deck of the front porch and then off into the distance. He looks off the shoreline of the small island out into the bay, leading to the open sea. There was a much larger storm rolling in, this was only the beginning. Further out to sea dark clouds were pelted out sheets of rain, and the contrast with the quickly remaining sunlight made the vibrant gardens at the bottom of the stairs contrast with even more color.

"The weather can change awful quick here," she called after him from inside the house. She wasn't bothered.

He couldn't understand it, but her words soothed him. He felt like a child whose mother was calling him in when all he wanted to do was go play outside.

"Umm…" he turned back toward the front door, his eyes desperate for some kind of help in understanding what was occurring.

"It's okay," she said, coming to the doorway. "It happens all the time to newcomers. You can try to go back down the lane, but the waves will sweep you out to sea. I've seen it happen before." She shook her head and walked back in. Alice walked to the stove in the kitchen, giving the contents of a large pot a stir. "I've been working on some goulash. It'll be ready in about an hour. There is plenty here."

He ignored her passive welcome and walked to the end of the porch, and over peered around the corner of the house at the long drive. The rain pelted in from the side, drenching him as he stood near the edge of the porch roof. He could see waves, a few feet in height slide across the roadway as if it never existed. He drops his head in defeat without a word.

Hours later, the postman sat in a wooden kitchen chair facing the fireplace. He peered across the room at the window that overlooked the porch. He couldn't see the pitch blackness of the sea through the window, but he could hear the ferocity of the storm. He turned back to look at the safety of the fire, wondering in the structural integrity of the house itself would hold.

"This house has been here for centuries, don't you worry." She said looking at the fire along with him. "It's lovely, isn't it? The fireplace. I brought it over from the old house in Lancashire. The family had that house for centuries until they were driven away." She got up and wandered over to the stove, serving up the dinner she had made.

The postman glanced again toward the window and the howling wind outside.

"They say it's the water." She handed him a bowl of her goulash and a large hunk of freshly baked bread and sat back down in the wooden chair beside him.

"What do you mean, the water?" She's nice, but she speaks in riddles. Probably gone crazy from living alone in the house too long.

"It kicks up out of nowhere. Most of the time, it's a nuisance and keeps me here. Though sometimes it protects me. The weather was just like this the night I came to own the house when my sister retired. Now that it's back, I finally get to leave, too."

A calmness overcame him. So much so, that he wondered if she had drugged the goulash.

She got up out of the chair beside him and walked to the window at the other end of the house that overlooked the long drive in. "See here," she pointed out the window.

The young postman got out of his chair and walked over to stand beside her. He looked out the window to see the lane in the dark with a large group of people carrying torches at the end, near the main road. The lane is fine, he thought. There was no water, no storm, I could leave. He turned to look out the other windows and could see the storm still battering away at everything outside.

"That night was as much about the history of this place as it was about my family, and even the mortal realm," she said, pointing to the window again.

He looked back out the window to the lane again. He couldn't understand. It was like he was peering into a dream. It felt like he was watching a movie as he observed the crowd of people, all dressed in centuries-old clothing.

OCTOBER 1692

The crowd gathered in the twilight at the end of the lane, their faces each lit by the light of their torches. The leader turned around to look at his supporters. He tallied them up, making a mental note of who was and was not present – surely to be used against them later in the week at church or the village square. Some attended out of genuine anger and fear of the occupants of the stone house, and others for a show of political support, to stay in the good graces of their neighbors.

Inside the house, Alice's older sister Charlotte runs to the window overlooking the lane. She sees the lit torches and people gathered at the road.

"I knew they would come at low tide," she said in defeat. The word in town that day had reached a fever pitch after Goodwife Brewer had brought her sick child to see Charlotte. The stone house had become the not-so-secret haven for the town's women should they need specialized medical attention. However, this time it was too late. Mrs. Brewers' ten-year-old child was too ill to be saved and died several hours later. In true fashion of the time, the Brewers blamed Charlotte, and anger in the town quickly turned to calls for justice and revenge.

The man leading the group raised his torch high and began walking down the lane – the crowd obediently following close behind.

"Charlotte and Alice Grey, you are charged with the murder of young Andrew Brewer." The crowd of thirty-odd people acknowledges the charge with jeers. The women bang small iron pots with stones they found along the road. With each bang of a pot, the crowd hoped the loud noises would protect them and drive evil spirits away.

"You have been found to partake in acts of sorcery." The crowd picks up the pace, and the shouting becomes constant. "And for this, you are also charged with the act of maleficium!"

Inside the house, Charlotte runs from the window and grabs her overcoat and hat. "We've had to flee too many times. It won't happen again. On one hand, we are meant to serve the everlasting realms, but in this realm it is forbidden to defend ourselves from their precious mortals who persecute us?"

Alice begins crying and runs after Charlotte, jetting past her to block the front door. "You can't go out there!"

Charlotte pushes her aside and opens the door to the porch. She reaches into her pocket, pulling out a small pouch.

"No," Alice cries and grabs the pouch from her sister. "They'll kill you."

"They can't kill me," she said, gesturing in the direction of the crowd. "They're only mortals."

"No, not them!" Alice stopped herself. What scared her more than anything in the world were the other realms that allowed her and her sister to live. They lived by a strict covenant, serving the other realms in exchange for endless life on the mortal plane.

"We don't have time for this. Lēaf na," Charlotte shouts. The pouch suddenly reappears in Charlotte's hand. She crouches down, pouring a line of fine powder in front of the doorway, and mutters a few more words. The sand slides into the form of Latin words that span the threshold of the doorway.

"I'll be back in a minute," she says, standing up. "I love you," she said staring deeply into her young sister's eyes. She slowly dissolved into the air.

Walking down the lane, the crowd gathers in a haphazard line to avoid falling into the surrounding water. The waves calmly lapped the banks of the lane and it began to lightly rain. The leader of the group looked at the house, fearing a fight should they not come out. "Grey sisters, based on these charges and witnesses, we intend to try you for witchcraft. Show yourself!"

Charlotte materializes out of the darkness, a few feet in front of the crowd. "If I go with you now, how can I be sure of a fair trial?"

"What happened to that young child wasn't fair. What do you know of fairness?" a man's voice shouts from the crowd.

"You took that child for yourself," another voice shouts.

"Witch," several people yell. A rock is launched from the back of the crowd, hitting Charlotte in the shoulder and knocking her to the ground. Three others rocks land in the mud beside her, and then silence falls. The crowd thought this would be enough for Charlotte to give in.

Charlotte picks herself up and waves her hands across the crowd. "My family shall not be harmed. Tonight or ever!"

Screams come from the back of the crowd as the tide quickly rises and cuts everyone off from the mainland.

"You came here for a fight," Charlotte yells.

"No, we came to take you to trial," the leader says with a false reassurance. At that moment, another rock flies from the crowd and lands at her feet.

She looks down at the rock. "I'll save you the time. For I came to provide like for like. You came to reign havoc, so havoc shall be yours. I am that I am, what God and nature have intended." The rock in the mud just in front of her feet slowly drifted up from the ground. She held out her hand and it gently landed in the center of her palm. In an instant it turns into an apple. She takes a bite and lets it drop to the mud at her feet.

The crowd gasps and falls silent. Many could swear that it was never a rock that was in her hand, but an apple all along. The man who launched the projectile half-wondered if he threw a rock at all. Anything else would be impossible. It was impossible to reconcile what everyone saw, and so a few whimpers could be heard as the crowd remained stunned.

"I promise you, the Devil's got nothing on me." She stepped toward the leader of the crowd. "I scream like the wind", her voice boomed. Her words turn into a gale force wind, and knocked everyone to the ground except Charlotte. She wasn't sure she was going to be able to control the elements this time, but she had to make a stand for her family. A stinging rain began to pelt in from the side.

The leader of the crowd stood back up and held out a cross. "Demon, I compel you to show yourself."

Her voice boomed again, louder than the sound of the driving wind. "And roar like the waves." Tall waves began to crash against the road and fell upon the people, who struggled to stand up in the wind. "We are neither from this world nor the next. We are not the angelic or the hexed," her voice echoed above the force of the wind and waves. Only a few of the crowd remained as they tried to stay on their feet. "We are created, not born, forced to carry out our duties, sworn." She raised her hands by her side and then slammed them together.

Two large waves the height of twenty feet close in on either side of the lane. They crash together directly above the crowd, flinging everyone about like bowling pins. As the waves clear, the only one left was the leader, tattered and broken. He clung to the banks of the road as the waves receded back into the tide, now inches below the road.

Charlotte slowly steps toward him. He struggled to stay conscious while clinging to the tufts of muddy grass. The wind and the rain continue to howl. He wasn't sure if he was strong enough to fend off more waves. She steps closer and crouched next to him. In a voice as calm and comforting as a nursery school teacher, she explains; "This house and all who are in it will be protected from this night forward. All those who threaten it or trespass shall be damned, whether they be from this world or the next."

MODERN DAY

"And that was the last anyone saw of her," Alice said as she stared deeply at the fire.

The delivery man realized they were sitting back in their chairs, facing the fire. He didn't recall walking back across the room. He was now sure she had drugged him.

Alice continued, "The very next night, I became the property of the celestials. The angels, the ones you believe to be 'good'," she said, as she shot an angry glare toward the young man.

BACK IN 1692

Alice tossed and turned in her bed, desperately trying to get to sleep. She had never been alone before. Missing her sister, the last remaining member of her family, was all she could think about. She feared that more villagers would return to take her away. At the very least she would be tied to the chiding stone in the center of the village, and left for the weather and the crows. Frustrated, she sat up in bed to shake off the worry. As she did, her eyes caught the light of a bright star outside her bedroom window. It was brilliant, like the light of a full moon. The longer she looked at it, the brighter it became. As she slowly walked across her bedroom, entranced by the star, she realized it wasn't getting brighter, it was getting bigger. It was getting bigger because it was heading toward her house from across the sea. Within moments, she was shocked out of her trance as the bright soft light flooded in through all the windows of the house, illuminating everything.

She had to know what it was, and quickly left the room to go down stairs. Everything was glowing, even the walls that were not in direct line of a window. The wooden chairs, the metal crockery that hung in the kitchen, it all reflected and glowed the bright soft light that came in through the windows. As she opened the door and walked onto the porch, she kept trying to make out what the object was. The light, now just several yards away from the edge of the porch was too bright to discern any particular shape. As she stood on the porch in the night air, she forgot all about her fear of the villagers. She felt an immense peace emanating from the bright object floating in the air. As she became more transfixed, she could no longer discern any of her surroundings, everything turned to light around her. The porch she was standing on disappeared, she could no longer see her garden and the sea beyond, not even the twilight above. It was as if she was floating in light.

Out of its center, she could see a figure emerge. "Fear not, you shall not be harmed," the figure said in a soothing voice.

"Who are you?" young Alice asked. She shielded her eyes as best as she could.

"I am of the celestials, a realm from which you and your family descend. You are the last of the portals through which all life-force flows into the mortal realm. For this burden, we give you the gift of eternal health."

The next thing she knew, she woke up in her bed the next morning. She had to learn to fend for herself. Learn how to function among the human world that hated her, while serving the celestials who had bound her to the mortal realm.

As the years went by, Alice wondered if the price for her immortality was the hatred and fear she elicited from humanity. The only thing that eased the burden of loneliness was that, over time, witchcraft had become popularized in the modern era. She considered most in the modern era to be charlatans who were into cosplay. Though she sometimes found relief among the pure practitioners. Her solace coming from the same understanding and disconnection they experienced between themselves and the rest of humanity.

An anger steadily grew in her every day after the night Charlotte disappeared. Alice's family had not told her of the celestial burden that was about to define her existence. After the first two centuries, the heat of her anger became as hot and destructive as the coals that glowed at the base of the fire she and the postman were sitting in front of. It took two more centuries to come to terms with her cosmic role. Manifesting mortal souls according to the design and plans of the celestials was a full-time job. It took all her energy most days, leaving her with little life-force to enjoy eternity on the mortal coil. She realized that if she really wanted out from under the thumb of the celestials, she would have to be as cold and deliberate as they were.

MODERN DAY

"You were created by angels?" Even in his hypnotized state, the postman knew that was crazy.

"Not exactly. Over the centuries, I learned this to be misleading."

The young mail carrier furrowed his brow. It was a weird story. He scooped a spoonful of soup from his bowl, and as he chewed, he again tried to retrace his steps from the window to the fireplace.

"Eth is tempered by water, which is why we were told to come to this place so long ago. They thought it would protect the last two of us. Whenever someone comes to visit, it causes a rise in me so bad, a storm surrounds the island because they pierce the veil."

"What the bloody hell is eth?"

"Eth is the life force that fills every soul's existence. In order for your soul to materialize in the mortal realm, what you call 'being born', eth is the cosmic spark that gives you life. The reason you are mortal is that you are the only creature that can grow and transmit eth on its own. Outside of the mortal realm, eth is the game that everyone is in. Heaven creates it, the Etheric realm barters and manages it, and Hell craves it. Away from Heaven, the only consistent source of eth Chthoniis a mortal soul."

"You know you aren't making any sense, right?" he said in a boozy state.

The bowl he was eating from contained a drug she liked to call Adamantia, something she had spent centuries developing. It allowed the eth within a soul to slowly bleed out, without affecting the body or the integrity of the soul itself.

Alice smiled. She liked him. The last person who visited was scared out of their wits. She had to bury her out by the dock. This was to be different. She needed his eth to entice a demon from the underworld, and use it to get the cosmic ball rolling. She looked over at the package he had delivered and smirked.

"I am one of the last of a true clan. As punishment for our powers, throughout history, we have been forced to serve the spiritual realm as a portal between this world and the next. My sister came before me and tried to escape many times. The Gods would not have it, but she found a way out on that fateful night. After that, the celestials forced me to fill her role, and I have been enslaved ever since. They can't let me go, for I am the last."

"So you can't die. You mean like a vampire?"

She shot him a look of absurd pity. "That is about to change. It's not enough to escape my persecution. I want to make sure this doesn't happen to anyone else. The celestials will have to do their own work from now on. It's long overdue."

The fire popped, and the logs shifted, half crumbling to ash. She looked at the fire, gently lifted a hand – willing a group of flames to rise slightly higher than the rest. They flickered together, forming a small tornado in the fireplace. The flaming tornado rose to the top of the fireplace and then began curling out like a snake and stretched out toward the young man's face.

"They are around us all the time, you know. Some like to watch, some like to mingle or persuade you to do things. Some want to help you, others manipulate you. But I need you. You are about to become one of the few souls to exist in the unseen realms. I cannot end your life. It is not your time. So you will become a living mortal in the realm of the immortals. Your existence won't be easy. celestials will want to destroy you, and chthonics will want to enslave you. Trust no one."

The young man felt quite woozy at this point. His faculties left him faster than he could account for. "But you're a witch. What do you know of heaven?" The postman said as he became mesmerized by the small tornado of fire, now just inches from his face.

"A soul will have to be taken and the war must begin again."

The fiery tornado grew and stretched all the way into the young man's eyes. His body became rigid from the shock of the pain. He was no longer present. His body calmly sat in stunned reception of the flames. The tornado grew in strength, widening as it seemed to attach itself to the young man. His began to skin glow, and as it did it quickly turned to molten rock. Soon after, the molten rock begins to glow and pulse with energy.

Alice held out her hand and the manilla envelope the man had delivered earlier that day flies across the room, through the tornado of fire, burning the packaging away. Untouched by the fire, two golden scrolls appear. They gently land in the palm of her hand. The husk of the young man's body glows even more, and a wind begins swirling inside the room, forming a tornado out of any loose objects around the two of them.

A white light begins to crack and emanate through the molten rock. As it reaches its peak, the young man's spirit steps out of the body and stands beside himself. He looks at what used to be his body and then over at Alice. "What is happening to me?"

"Our bodies are just vessels in this life," she says without looking at him. She realized there will be no dead to welcome him. Yet another violation she didn't account for. The tornado of fire turns a much deeper orange, with black lumps traveling up from the base of the fireplace and into the molten husk. The white light turned to a deep red glow, and the molten rock swells to crimson and then black. The young man's spirit stood beside the body in amazement, unsure of what to do.

Alice turned to his spirit and held out a hand. A sheen appeared around his soul like a cloud of glass. She continued to hold her hand steady and the sheen turns a slightly milky white, and soon slides away from the young man's spirit, pooling in the palm of her hand, forming a translucent cloud of lime green energy. "I'm going to need that," she said thankfully.

"I don't feel right." The young mans soul begins to dim. He continues to stand still with the vague hope of returning to his now charred and molten body.

The molten body begins to vibrate with even more energy. Through the molten crust of the neck, a fist punches its way out. After a fist, an arm appeared, red and scarred, as if it had been dyed with blood. The arm fought it's way around to find some leverage. It pounded the exterior of the body to make the hole larger, and then another arm appeared. Finally, a creature pulled itself up out of the molten shell, as if it were pulling itself up through a hole from an underground cavern. The moment the creature cleared itself from the molten shell, the creature simply wraps an arm around the young man's spirit and throws it down into the hole to the realm below.

As soon as the young man's spirit disappeared, the wind swirling around Alice's living quarters simply stops. All the flying knick-knacks, kitchen utensils, and housewares crash to the ground.

The demon stands still, staring at Alice. Resembling a bodybuilder, it had a stocky frame, red leathery skin that seemed to be held together from layers of scars, which were only interrupted by sparse wiry hairs covering its body. Its legs had large haunches, its arms were muscular like a human but much larger, and it had piercing yellow eyes. It looked like it could have once been a human or even an angel, but the trials of hell left the demon's body twisted, hard, and vicious. It used might, sex, wit, and emotional manipulation in equal measure to succeed at one thing: tormenting whomever it wanted. The very reason Alice picked it.

Alice steeled herself, knowing exactly what she had done. She had summoned demons many times in the past, but never outside of a circle of protection, and always to fulfill a celestial task. Without a circle of protection, this demon could roam free of its own will and accord - which is what she wanted.

It looked at her, determining if it should attack. However, the surroundings of the mortal realm were off-putting to it.

Alice holds out her hand, allowing the cloud of lime-green eth to develop just above her palm. She blows the small cloud of eth toward the demon and it quickly drifts toward its chest, bursting into a soft diffusion that surrounds the demon's entire body like a bubble. It first turned a flash of milky white, then became transparent, and finally settled into the demon's skin and disappeared. Alice had just done what nobody since the beginning of creation had done. She gave a demon a small sliver of the gift of life. It would take a lot more to sustain it permanently.

The demon draws a large deep breath and exhales in a relief it didn't even know existed. It wanted more.

"As above, so below," she says, looking at the creature.

"As below, so above," it says, grunting back in a deep grumbly voice.

"You are Ganislay, are you not?"

"I am Ganislay, guardian of the sixth realm, keeper of the ashes." Ganislay's voice was so deep it rattled the windows in their panes. Alice felt the call of Ganislay's voice. It was inviting, like a dark abyss. She steeled herself once again, remembering that demons, as well as celestials were not built to function within the mortal plane.

From the depths of hell, Alice could tell it held a middle rank, which is exactly what she wanted. Nobody important wouldn't miss him, but he was strong enough to survive on his own. Since Ganislay didn't serve on the infernal council, it held no agenda other than its own survival. For Alice, this made everything easier to control, for she was about to offer the one thing that every chthonic secretly desires. Freedom.

Alice held out the scrolls. "Ganislay, thank you for answering my call." She was polite to celestial and chthonic alike. She often had to work with all spirits and various forms of creation. Ganislay attempted to pick up the scrolls from her hand, but she holds them firm. "With these, you are free to storm the gates of heaven. You will never be able to do it alone. To succeed, you need to destroy the portal of Judgement." She paused and glared at him. chthonics are classically stupid, too blinded by their own desires and usually needed constant direction. "Do this and you are free of hell forever."

Ganislay nodded. Being forced to do things was the mainstay of its existence. Ganislay was a slave to nearly everyone he came into contact with - except mortals and those beneath him in the pecking order. Like every demon, he was free to strip away any semblance of life, dignity, or personality from the souls he came across. For doing so provided Ganislay with the only solace one could have in the depths of hell. Eth. It made the existence of hell slightly more bearable. Like any chthonic, no matter the rank, any time Ganislay came within proximity or an entity or source of Eth, an irrational desire overcame him. All he wanted to do was destroy anything in his path of acquiring eth. The one thing every creature in the underworld wants is access to life again.

Alice let go of the scroll and Ganislay snatched it with a long tail that appeared from the back of his body. He opens his mouth and subsumes the scroll into his body. He smiled, hoping she would be impressed.

"Don't hang about, I release you. Be gone!" She shook her hands at him like he was an irritating child. Ganislay disappears into the air with a deep boom. A shockwave of eth shoots out in all directions from her living room, blowing open the doors and builds like a tidal wave as it travels across the surrounding geography. Alice knew that would happen. It's exactly what she wanted to happen. Giving a summoned demon free will is an act of war against the celestials. But she had many more things in place behind the scenes to escape her enslavement.

By giving a demon two keys to enter heaven, it causes a momentary disruption in the flow of eth. For two brief minutes, as Ganislay disappeared into daily life, all life-force stopped flowing to and from the mortal plane. Nearly six hundred souls were lost in between the realms while on their way to being born, and two hundred fifty mature souls are erased as they expire from their mortal bodies. Alice created a momentary spiritual vacuum. It's exactly what Alice wanted – to cause disruption throughout each realm of the spiritual planes.

Alice smiled. "That ought to piss them off," she said as she opened the back door. She didn't care if Ganislay stormed the gates of heaven or not. She just needed one big cosmic distraction while she made her escape. If everything went according to plan, heaven will blame hell, and the war wouldn't even come to her doorstep.

The morning sun streamed in through the windows. The clouds cleared, giving way to a calm morning on the sea. She propped the back door with a chair so she can let the fresh air come in. "Oh…" she clasped her hands as she looks past the lush roses in her garden toward the open water. She loved looking at the sea.

Alice walked back in front of the fireplace where the two chairs stood. She looked at the shell of what was the young man's body, now blackened and half crumbled. Nothing but burnt carbon and ash, yet perfectly forming the body that once existed. She leaned over, took a deep breath, and blew as hard as she could. The ash and burnt carbon flaked and floated off into millions of bits. As it did, each bit turned into a butterfly. Soon her living room was full of thousands of butterflys flitting about. She waves her hands again, shoeing them out the door. As the room cleared, she picked up the broom and began sweeping all the dust and fine debris from the floor again, just as she was doing the day before.

Chapter Two

Percival looked closer at the display panel of his channeling orb as he worked at his desk. The channeling orb was the main tool used by every angel in Percival's department. Made of adamantine, a metal alloy attuned to the mortal realm, each orb consisted of two dials on either side that served as handles and controlled which mortal souls Percival wanted to tune into. He turned the dial on the left to change geographic locations and then turned the dial on the right to hone in on the frequencies and vibrations the mortals in the vicinity emanated. A screen in the middle flitted through different people's lives like a television quickly changing channels. The orb was the quickest way any angel in Percival's choir can see into the circumstances of every mortal.

He had his favourite people to check in on. A slight turn of the left dial could move the signal thousands of miles. As the number of souls increased over the millenia in the mortal realm, the more sensitive the dials had become. Percival had become a master at tuning into people just a few feet from each other. He also had his favorite frequencies of eth. The vibration at which eth flows can determine the behavior and perspective of any mortal. In his experience, Percival often noticed that mortals are their own worst enemy, many times choosing to allow in energy that doesn't suit their goals or interests. If he saw one of his favorite cases attached to a conflicting frequency, he would jump into their lives for a few minutes. The simple presence of a celestial in a mortal's life often changed things – a phenomenon known as imbuing. It took him thousands of cases to realize that he often didn't need to do anything except show up. Many times he wished mortals could understand this concept. However, his favorite moments were when he could shoe off anything negative that was lurking too close to someone he was helping. If the energy or entity was particularly nasty, he would call upon a member of the Archangels to dispatch it. Percival did not enjoy working through force of will.

"Oh Sally, how are you doing today?" Percival wondered, as he dialed the channeling orb to focus in on her life. "Still getting over that broken heart. He wasn't good for you. I wish you could see that." Percival watched her as she sat at a busy cafe, too focused on her own thoughts to notice the world around her.

Suddenly the display of Percival's orb automatically zoomed out from the area he was looking at, and a warning sign appeared over the coast of the UK on his screen.

"Oh dear", Percival said standing up in shock. He didn't know what to do. Several cycles ago he created an algorithm that allowed him to see flows of eth on the mortal plane before any of his colleagues. He peered across the miles of other brightly lit workstations that the other celestials were working on, and realized that his algorithm was working. He had the edge on the rest of the office. Heaven hadn't noticed a thing, but they were about to. The large shockwave of eth that Percival watched on his screen would inevitably disrupt the entire mortal realm. Percival knew every channeling orb was about to lose connection, and when that happened, every mortal would endure a blend of insanity that hadn't existed since the dark ages.

The invisible flow of eth grew like a tidal wave as it rippled across the world from Alice's house. Suddenly, humanity found the inspiration to express the things they've long suppressed down. The energy's strength leads to simultaneous spikes in violence and acts of compassion seen across the Earth throughout the day.

Percival watched one such instance of disruption. A small imp, invisible to the eyes of mortals, was just about to interrupt a man's pleasant commute to work by having him cut off in traffic and swerve into a lamppost. Instead, as the wave of eth passed, the man saw a woman walking down the sidewalk he hadn't seen since high school. He quickly swerved his car to a haphazard stop and jumped out to declare his long-lost crush toward her. She retorted she had just made a promise to herself to never date another passive man again. Crushed, the man attempts to return to his car, only to be assaulted by two young men passing on the sidewalk. It was an opportune moment to divest him of his belongings. Now broken and battered, the woman of the man's affection promptly falls in love with him and runs to console him as the young men run away.

The Spiritual plane watched many such scenes over those brief moments. Humanity acted out in ways that contradicted individual goals. It was a spiritual earthquake, like the recoil from a gun. Heaven's ineffable plans from above, the misdeeds from below, and all those in between, all clashed simultaneously within each person. All an entity could do was sit back and watch it happen.

Central Existence, a building that sits at the center of Heaven and acts as a transceiver and control center for all of existence, certainly noticed. Every department immediately called an emergency meeting. The building sits on top of a tree-covered mountain with waterfalls of eth plunging to the rest of heaven beneath it. The building stands as a symbol for those who were once mortal, and as a central administration building for the inner workings of heaven. At the base, several departments, each as large as the next, handle different aspects of existence.

Percival continued to watch the surrounding cubicles, as his colleagues began to get their connections to the mortal interrupted. The Department of Principal Communications and Endeavors for Humanity was the size of several airplane hangars. It's been said that Heaven is a big place. In order to make sure everything runs to perfection, it takes an equally large endeavor behind the scenes. Departed mortals don't see the armies of angels and administrators backstage. They are too busy living in eternal bliss to care about the cogs required make existence run on time.

One by one, celestials of all grades stand up from their desk and peer around the room like lost prairie dogs, unsure of what just happened. "I lost signal, can't connect to anything," one celestial announces to nobody in particular. Acting almost as an invitation, one celestial after another stood up and confirmed the same. For the first time, Heaven had lost connection to the living and the dead. It was working blind.

Percival looked at the confused appearance of each of his colleagues, and at the disconnected channeling orbs that lay powerless on each of the desks.

"Ok choirs," Deacon said as he hurried into the middle of the desks. Deacon was the head of Percival's division. He was as much a tyrant as an encouraging coach. However, even when he had his coach's hat on, his tone came across quite brusque. Nobody could argue with it though, as Deacon was intentionally built for the role he was in, as most celestials are for the duties they fulfill. When Deacon stopped in the middle of the sea of desks, he immediately co-located himself - appearing in multiple locations throughout the length of the workstations, so that each of his colleagues could easily see him. "Lets get back up and running. This was just a drill to see what would happen if the real thing occurred. Reconnect with your cases, lets make sure those miracles keep happening."

"We lost connection. There doesn't seem to be a signal from our realm to theirs," one celestial explained as if Deacon was uninformed.

Deacon looked at him reassuringly. "The engineers already ran diagnostics and reacquired a signal. The next step is to initiate protocol nine. Go through your checklists. We don't want any mistakes."

Percival looked at Deacon with suspicion. They only used Protocol nine after an invasion or eth attack. It had never been used.

Deacon saw Percival's gaze out of the corner of his eye. He didn't want to look at him. To do so would be to acknowledge Percival's concern to the others. Percival was Deacon's most accomplished celestial on the floor. However, Deacon never wanted him to know this. Percival was too honest, which is what made him so efficient. It was also what made Percival the department's biggest pain in the ass. Deacon had resisted affording Percival advancement in the department for centuries. Anything above his current role would involve a lot of politics, and Percival was not suited for politics. However, decisions come quick in heaven, and this was all about to change.

The dazed looks from the pool of celestials slowly faded as Deacon's instructions seeped in to their minds. Deacon walked over to Percival's desk and picked up his orb, holding it high. "Lets get to it folks." He placed the orb back on Percival's desk and clapped his hands like a motivational coach. "Lets get these blessings rolling, miracles don't happen on their own" Deacon said with the fervor of a preacher at a travelling show.

One by one, the members of the department began to sit back down and get back to work. His multiple appearances disappeared and Deacon muttered to Percival, "My office in five. Keep it quiet."

Deacon meandered his way back out from the middle of the pool of desks, encouraging each celestial as he passes by like a politician making an appearance at a rally.

Like the hack of any network, the disruption was discovered and corrected. Percival knew those heavenly few minutes were long enough to change the course of the universe. Now he needed to figure out what the perpetrators took, then they'd figure out who the perpetrator was. The investigative skills he gathered during his time in eternity led him to realize that motive often pointed to the perpetrator. Randomness and chaos are the rarest of things. From the day he was created, Percival embraced life in the 'Higher Third' while many celestials found it unsuitable for them. He read the entire history of Heaven, its facts, the mythologies and prophesies, and when nobody was looking... even the conspiracy theories—of which there are many. He wondered which category this moment would fit into.

Percival sat down and powered up his Channeling Orb. As he held the two wheeled object with both hands, he flitted between different areas of the world. He was determined to find the breach before anyone else. Of the millions of choirs, he worked the hardest to get into this one. Everyone knew it led places. Unlike other celestials who were created specifically for the roles in his department, Percival worked his way into his current role. It didn't make him any friends, but he loved it nonetheless. The only thing better in Percival's mind was the Office of Planning & Design.

"No... no...," he said, flitting between each case that popped up in front of him. "God, no, what is he thinking?" he inquired, flitting past another.

Instead of simply having the lower choirs report back to central like in the old days, the directive came from high above that they were to roll out a new technology that instantly patched the Central Choir through to each of the lower choirs and onto their individual cases. For the first time in existence, Central had direct access to all earthly cases. A side effect of this was a celestial's favorite pastime became watching people and guessing why they do the things they do.

"Awww," Percival sighed, stopping on the scene of a kitten discovering its new house for the first time. The problem became the Great Compact – a policy created in ancient times that necessitated balance between all three realms. When the technology was developed in Heaven, they ignored the fact that according to the Compact it would eventually have to be given to the mortals. On the mortal plane, the great compact was adopted by the simple maxim of 'what happens above, also happens below', or among the dogmatic 'on earth as it is in Heaven'. And so, it didn't take long before the same technology permeated the human consciousness, giving birth to the internet in the late twentieth century. As humanity caught on to the trend and web pages could be easily shared, Percival came up with the idea to dedicate much of the content to cats, a lighthearted attempt to thwart the inevitable stream of negativity that access to constant information provides a population.

While a celestial cannot change a person's thoughts or actions because of free will, they used channeling orbs to direct the masses of celestial forces they had on the mortal plane. The hope was, by increasing the speed of communication, heaven could influence events to prevent a person from taking a dangerous path in life. Unfortunately, what Heaven knows, so does Hell. However, Hell could never organize itself enough to create such an ordered approach to its own armies. Temptation was always a much more subtle art, but unfortunately, mortals tend to be attracted to it much more often. So Hell has always had a much better conduit to the mortal world. After Hell launched the opening salvo by destroying the garden of Eden, Heaven knew it had to do something to prevent such an occurrence again. The best minds of Heaven got together and calculated the only possible solution was constant vigilance on their part.

Percival kept flitting through circumstances. "Ah ha..." he muttered in a low voice. He instinctively leaned toward his desk to focus. The display showed a bird's-eye view of the earth, from tens of thousands of feet above the British Isles. He turns the orb to reverse time to view the origin of the shockwave again. He sees the shockwave of energy as if a bomb went off - invisible to the human eye. Just as he felt moments ago. The other celestials must have felt it.

He leans back in his chair to peer over to his colleague across the aisle. "Sidnael, what do you think that was? Are you back up?"

"I don't know," he responds. "Deacon said it was some sort of drill. I'm just coming back online now."

"Did you feel anything," Percival asked trying to find out if Sidnael had any clue.

"No, what do you mean? I'm worried about losing contact with my cases."

Percival looks away. He didn't understand how Sidnael could ignore the waves of emotions coming off all of humanity. He stands up and looks across the office again. Every celestial was dutifully powering up their channeling orb. As he starts walking toward Deacon's office, he notices that not a single celestial in his pool of colleagues seemed to be affected. He had little information, but at least he found the source.

Outside of his department, the hallways of Central Existence looked like something from an old university office building. Hardwood doors and frosted glass windows. Deacon, who became Director of Operations for the Ministry of Human Affairs, preferred a certain aesthetic. Percival found this ironic, because it indeed ended up reflecting the institutions of higher education on the mortal realm.

He found these halls overly political in a way he never expected, and everything was on a need-to-know basis rather than being a fountain of knowledge.

Percival received an equal offer for the same role in the Arcturian division, but he had dedicated years to studying humans. Humans were some of the most complex creatures of the universe. He found it endlessly fascinating that despite all the invention and free will available to humans; they spend the majority of their time finding ways to make themselves miserable, yet verbalize the contrary to all within earshot. Celestials who were newer to the department usually found this frustrating, as humans will often undo a celestial's hard work. For Percival, it was all part of the fun - he often sat in an intellectual grey area that caused him to remain more objective than his colleagues.

As Percival walked down the hallway at a deliberate pace, an un-marked door suddenly swings open behind him. "Come with me please," a co-worker said, as she popped her head around the door.

Percival stopped and looks behind him. *I always thought that door led to a storage closet. It's too mundane to be anything else,* he thought.

"That's the point. You weren't supposed to know. And now you need to know," the entity responded to Percival's thoughts. "It's nice how that works."

"Yes," Percival responded. It was common for celestials of higher rank to read the thoughts of their subordinates. However, celestials consider it rude to do so with those with whom they are unacquainted. Percival paused, staring at him and waiting for the awkward moment to affect his new acquaintance. He doubted this entity had the social awareness to notice its own faux pas. The problem was, this entity wasn't a celestial. Known as Envoys, looking like mirror images of the mortals the department was in charge of, they served as mysterious liaisons between the celestials and the mortal plane.

Percival let the moment pass and walked toward his new colleague, stepping through the threshold and followed the woman down the stairs. He had heard of these folks. The giveaway being that they are immaculately dressed in charcoal gray suits, they came and went between all regions of the heavens, and Percival speculated elsewhere as well. He often wondered what it would be like to be an envoy.

Envoys were famous for bringing the wrath of the heavens when it was too unpalatable for a celestial to do so. Celestials were famous for unleashing flood and famine, but they usually gave warnings beforehand. Envoys were a special breed. No celestial would dare ever disobey a directive, well, not since the Great War, but Percival supposed it was the Director's way of taking care of the choirs. No matter how prestigious an institution is, there always needs to be someone who takes out the rubbish.

The stairs led to a single room at the bottom and as he entered, the first thing Percival noticed was the number of other doors that led into this room. A door that led to the Director of Operations' office, and other than that, Percival could imagine who else was in the room.

Deacon stood beside a table, pointing down at a book with columns of data in it. He cleared his throat. "Good, we're all here." A large hologram screen pops up from the desk and creates a screen almost like a room divider.

"Just a few minutes ago, we had all channels interrupted," Deacon announces. An image shot into the hologram of the place that Percival was looking at on his channeling orb moments prior. "The source seems to emanate from this location, thanks to our colleague." Deacon gestured toward Percival. "The problem is, when we came back online, we didn't get all the connections back. One mortal seems to have gone missing."

"This isn't a lost soul," the Envoy standing next to Deacon adds. "We have enough communication between here and the underworld to know exactly when a soul passes to them instead of us. But this one is simply gone."

The Chairman leaned over the table, slightly pushing his shoulder through a group of Celestials. "It's impossible to erase a soul and all it's eth."

"We need to figure out how that happened and where this mortal went. The longer we take, the less likely we'll get them back."

"The only way that would happen is if he were with the Lost Order," Percival blurted out from the back of the room.

The room erupted with grumbles of disbelief. Percival realized that mentioning the Lost Order was frowned upon, and that he needed to quickly explain his position otherwise he wouldn't be invited back again. "I know we aren't supposed to talk about it. But there is a trend I've been seeing over the last century. Whenever a celestial or a chthonic needs to accomplish a mission, yet they don't have the power to create a directive or a waiver needed to accomplish the task, they will simply open a portal and slip the offending entity into Dudael."

"But this is a human soul we are talking about. Erasing a conscious energy, human or otherwise, is forbidden."

"Yes, but placing something into Dudael isn't erasing it, is it? The energy source you are looking for is caused by an invocation. The tidal wave of eth was just a distraction to get us to look the other way. I bet if you look at the number of deities in the underworld you have one less. Likewise, I bet if you look at the balance of eth on the mortal plane, it will be the same as before the interruption, but you can't connect to one of them. The one you can't connect to – that will be your invoked demon."

"Yes," the envoy glares back at him interested that one from the choirs would be this savvy. The rest of the celestials including the chairman listed while also trading whispered strategies to one another.

Deacon stood in silence, waiting to weigh in after he had heard all the facts.

Percival continued, "If a mortal is going to be dim enough to conjure a chthonic, there is no way we won't know. We send out an Arch immediately. But if you want to do it with any chance of success, you'd have to possess someone here, which would throw the balance of eth off, and at the same time you'd have to swap a soul. You can't send them to hell or even here, we'd know. So you use a third option and send them to Dudael. That ability is only available to a few entities, this was no mortal who did this."

"You're telling us there is a human soul in the realm that was created specifically to punish angels and demons," one of the department heads responded.

Percival smirked, it was finally seeping in for them.

"They wouldn't survive," a celestial blurted out from the crowd.

"In the history of existence, eth has never been lost. There is always a balance," someone else said.

"Thats not true. We've messed up a good few times. Once it was so bad we had to flood the world and start again. The last time it was so bad the mortal refer to it as 'the dark ages'."

The rooms erupted in panic. Every celestial and chthonic knows that to create imbalance would be to upset the flow of the universe. The few times it happened the only way out was to create a new aeon, a sort of celestial hail mary to make everything right again. No celestial liked that, it upset the apple cart, celestials were reassigned, agendas changed – but at least existence was saved.

The chairman tried to calm the room down and gave a disapproving look toward Deacon for causing such a ruckus.

Deacon looked back at the chairman. "You told me to bring him. I warned you."

"With respect, there is a balance, and that's the point," Percival announced over the jumbled mass of debates. "They just replaced it with something else," Percival announced over the jumbled mass of debates. The room turned back to listening to him. Celestials and chthonics' ability to do this posed a threat from the beginning, and it had been growing steadily over the millennia as entities were scrubbed into Dudael to maintain the balance of eth. Maintaining balance of the life-force throughout existence was left to one entity alone. Often in the race to accomplish a mission or follow a directive, celestials probably didn't realize the real threat they were causing, which was undoing the central flow of conscious power. Heaven didn't like being seen as having loopholes in its creation. But the everyday necessity of its mission had created one.

"This means," he continued calculating in his head, "that if they can keep eth in existence but make it inactive or hide it, it eludes to the possibility that there are more of them than us."

The entire room looked at Percival like he was insane. It was blasphemy of a sort, and if true, it would be a philosophical shock to every rank and member of the choir.

"Impossible," a member of a higher order muttered through the silence.

"Even... even so, sir. There it is."

The room parted so that Percival was in clear eye-shot of the chairman and the Seraphim who just challenged Percival. "Can you back all this up?"

"Yes, sir, plenty of historical data on these types of events. It just gets ignored. I always rely on the data sirs," he said slightly bowing to the Chairman and the Seraphim. "After the data, everything else is just politics," he gestured toward the rest of the room. He then retreated out of sight behind a group of celestials in hope of escaping any further ire. The calculations were correct, but Percival wasn't built to deal with opinions - he didn't understand them.

Like the majority of celestials, out of respect Percival rarely spoke of the one who created him. Often throughout his office, colleagues would reference 'the Chairman' who it was believed to be an aspect of the Most High, secretly under cover, or possibly one of the Seraphim. Nobody except the Seraphim and above actually knew, and they weren't about to spill the beans. This was because proximity to the throne of the almighty was the currency of power throughout the choirs. Should a celestial actually directly reference the Chairman, usually they would receive a suspicious look. It was enough to make an angel be passed over for promotion, get demoted, ex-communicated or any other horrible things right down to the "cold shoulder". Sometimes in the heat of the moment when trying to accomplish a mission or directive coming from the Chair, celestials have been known to disparage the difficulty of a mission, but not usually the one who created it.

It was because of all of this, that Percival found being in the presence on the Chairman to be mind bending. He wanted to hide. Percival went deep enough into his thoughts that he lost himself. As the conversations in the room continued, he went so deep into his own thoughts that he co-located himself at Alice Grey's house – the source of the shockwave. He stared at her as she stood on her front porch, staring out at the ocean. He could hear the waves of the water in the bay and feel the breeze across his face. It was a sensation he had never experienced before, for he was feeling what she felt.

"You are not welcome here," she said as she turned to look directly at him. "And you cannot stop me."

"Percival..." an envoy said, snapping his fingers in front of Percival's face. "Focus."

The Chairman looked at Percival, seeing right through him. He knew Percival had co-located an aspect of himself. "What did you see?"

Percival was suddenly present in the room. He had never co-located before. It was an ability that was not afforded to him. His job had always been to analyze, and experiences in the mortal realm were out of the question. Percival looked at the chairman in confusion. He was experiencing a mixture of loathing and a complete lack of confidence in his own abilities. All he could think about was his inability to tackle the problems this case presented him, and all the complications to come.

The Chairman realize Percival had just come face to face with fear for the first time. Percival didn't really know what fear was. He felt the full range of emotions and a few physical sensations. These were alien to him. In that moment, Percival's existence changed forever.

The chairman knew what it meant for Percival. He walked over to Percival and placed his hand on Percival's shoulder. "Folks, I am going to need the room", he said without breaking his gaze toward Percival.

The other celestials grumbled and looked at each other.

"She's trying to release herself from her role," Percival muttered to the Chairman.

The Chairman patted Percival on the shoulder, motioning for him to hold off speaking for a moment. The Chairman went over to thank a head of department, and muttered a few niceties.

"Who?" Deacon asked as he leaned forward across the desk, trying to coax the information from Percival before the chairman returned.

Percival leaned back and sat on the edge of one of the few desks that were in the room. The flood of emotions exhausted him.

When the last Department head left the room, the Chairman walked back over. "I prefer a much smaller quorum. What just happened was momentous, but that doesn't mean we can't make quick work of it before things really get out of hand." The Chairman leaned against a desk opposite Percival, a specific move to mirror him, and he gestured for Samuel and Deacon to come in closer. "Who did you just experience?"

"The Portal."

The Chairman looked at him in confusion. "There are three. Ours - the portal of Consciousness, theirs - the portal of Mortality, and nexus of the two, the Talis Maker. The portal of mortality has served the longest of the Portals and has made several requests to stand down."

Percival looked him dead in the eye, he good still feel the reminance of her emotions flowing through his veins. "She doesn't need to have a request granted if there is no veil between life and death."

"Whoa... slow down. How do you know it is the portal of Mortality you met?" the Chairman looked at him with concern. "And how do you know she doesn't need a request?"

"I read a lot," Percival said, embarrassed. "When everyone one else is given liberty to pursue their interests, I like to keep up with current events in the Communications office, even the forms."

"I thought the only one who liked forms was Gladys," Deacon looked at him with a mixture of astonishment and pity. "We invented bureaucrats to deal with all the forms but even they refused do to the volume of work. Why would you do that to yourself?"

"I heard they tried to unionize," Samuel said slyly.

"Yeah, that's when they brought in Gladys," Deacon. There is no way she was created by celestials.

"I can't believe we create bureaucrats, never mind Gladys."

The Chairman glared at them both, amazed at how fast gossip could be spun up. He always saw it as a sign that his choir had been working too hard.

The three of them noticed the Chairman waiting for them to get back on track.

"Besides, I tracked the signal down to her location. It's why I'm here, right?" Percival looked at Deacon.

Deacon nodded and flipped his hand. A hologram of the globe popped into existence in front of them all.

"What's she's done is created enough of a disruption to pull a demon from hell? Additionally, though, and I can't prove it yet, somehow she's gotten a hold of one of the keys to heaven and given it to him."

The chairman's back stiffened. "What do you mean? How do you know?"

"I read her thoughts when I was standing next to her." Percival looked at the floor. Interfering, especially with one of the Everlasting, was strictly prohibited.

"And it's a good thing you did," Deacon said, swooping in.

"Well, not really the key. She gave him one of the bands with the inscription of authority. Once whomever it is memorizes the inscription—I'd say that's the ball game."

"Samuel... you're up. You need to intercept that key before that chthonic gets too far with it. You can have anyone you like for the task. Brief your envoy before you go – but get this done now. You don't worry yourself, Percival. I want to thank you for all that you've done thus far. Samuel and his crew of Archs are going to take it from here. Why don't you go and get some rest." The chairman gestured for everyone to leave, and then slyly asked Deacon to stay behind.

Each celestial and envoy obeyed, and disappeared in an instant to prepare for their new assignments.

"You know what this means for him, right," the chairman

"Not completely, no," Deacon said, looking back at the chairman for some guidance. Deacon realized he was going to lose Percival from his staff. The question was, how?

"I will not dis-incorporate him. He did his job better than any celestial would have. There can't be a negative consequence for a job well done—we don't work like that, at least not under my watch," the chairman reassured Deacon.

"Then it means promotion." Deacon flicked his hands and pulled up Percival's files. They floated between the two of them. One file was a video of Percival debating with Gladys over a pile of paperwork. Another showed the number of 'A+' grades he received during his academy. "He's in the angelic choir, seconded to the Third Order. He's on track to become a first triad celestial."

"I could make him an Archangel, but I don't think he's got the grit. Uriel would be fine with it, but you stand him next to Michael..." the Chairman let the statement trail off and finished it with a simple shrug of the shoulders.

"Yeah, that's not a look you want. He'd be the weak link in your starting line-up." Deacon let the moment hang in the air. He did this on purpose because Deacon himself tried to become an Archangel many times over and he was always told that it wasn't in the cards for him. Since those times, it was well known that those within Deacons department would never be allowed to be promoted to Arch status. However, he always presented it as if he was protecting his choir from the politics of promotion.

The chairman knew what Deacon was doing, so he's have to back-door him into agreeing. "We will open up an epic change to policy by setting this precedent if I were to give him anything higher. Or that leaves us with the inevitable."

"He can't go back to what he was doing. He's been in contact with a one of the Everlasting, he knows too much now." Deacon knew the Chairman knew all of this, he was simply doing the political math out loud. The angelic choir was not meant for contact outside of their knowledge of humans. It's what allows them to imbue upon humanity and maintain a balance of eth. "So what are you saying if you aren't dis-incorporating him? You aren't, are you?"

"Well, we don't want that." The Chairman knew he was about to get what he wanted.

They both kicked their feet around the floor, trying to come up with solutions.

"You know..." the chairman paused again for a moment. He knew what he was about to say was heavy. "The other side..." he said, pointing a finger discreetly downward, "they invented something in the late eighteen hundreds for cases like this. I believe they called it 'middle management'. I could create a title for him." The Chairman was introducing a veiled threat to make Percival, Deacons boss. He knew this was check mate.

Deacon's eyes grew frightened and a feather from his wings dropped to the floor. The stress he felt from just the words alone made him wonder if he would go bald. "Mr. Chairman, we'll have to be very careful. The dithering incompetence of middle management has faltered many an empire."

"You're right. I'll have to make him an Arch after all. Start training him up." The chairman turned and disappeared out of the room before Deacon to retort again.

Chapter Three

Samuel and Mako didn't speak as they walked to into the lobby of the office tower. The lobby was tremendous like an airport terminal, with the sound of hundreds of leather shoes walking across the polished marble floor. The surroundings intended to leave no doubt in any visitors mind that this was one of the largest banks in the world. Sections of the ground floor were clusters with couches, each with groups of people having meetings. It was overwhelming for any visitor, but for the people who worked there – it was normal. As they stride across the lobby floor, Samuel tried to justify to himself the murderous act they were about to unleash.

This is going to be an assassination. That's what Samuel finally settled on. He had killed many in his day, but only when ordered. This was different. Broad daylight, no orders, complete deniability by the higher choirs, but it would finish the mission once and for all. Dis-incorporating a demon while in the mortal realm was rarely done, the consequences were too great. usually they were just dispatched back to hell. But to maintain the balance of eth, he would need to find the soul that was still alive, dispatch the demon who was in possession of the souls life force – and it was doubtful a demon would give up such a sum of eth without a fight.

Samuel wanted to tell Mako many things to prepare for the next few moments. Nobody had ever attempted a job so daring. But it was far more important to make sure they hadn't been seen. Their sleek Italian suits made them blend in to the crowd of bankers, so nobody would question why they were there. The demon had set himself up quite nicely by possessing one of the department heads, a Mr. Alex Wright. They had only minutes to get to Alex's office on the 26th floor before the deadline. The timing had to be just right. Samuel looked at his watch. Instead of it displaying a regular watch face, it displayed the position of the planets throughout the cosmos. The entire mission depended on the cosmic timing, if certain celestials knew, the gig would be up, Hell would be informed. At the two o'clock hour, Hell and the Principalities experienced a cosmic blind spot. So they had to dis-incorporate the demon on time. Perhaps it was because they were so close, nobody would suspect, but he was watching the exits and people coming at him from all angles. They were far into enemy territory, and he was sure they would be discovered any second.

They passed the banks of reception desks to the fourth elevator bay and walked into the next elevator that was loading, cutting off two people as they got in.

As the elevator began its ascension, they glanced at each other. Samuel could tell Mako wanted to say something, but it was strict radio silence, and only in-character from here. Samuel discreetly checked that his sword was in the correct position beneath his coat. It didn't really matter if anyone in the elevator figured out what they were carrying, or if they suddenly began talking. It would be just as easy to stop time and wipe everyone's memory. But that would be a huge ripple, and every angel and demon from here to Paris would know. The only hope was that Percival had done his bit outside.

The bell for their floor rang, and they stepped toward the reception desk. Law offices of May Wright enshrined in steel lettering above the woman at reception.

"Masamoto here for a two o'clock with Alex Wright, please", Samuel said as he poured the most charm he could into the banal request.

The receptionist looked at Mako, who simply nodded. Mako could speak English fluently, just as he could speak any other earthly language, but he loved to play on people's biases and just nodded when she looked at him.

She glanced, almost addressing him, and then decided that he probably didn't speak English. "Thank you, please have a seat for a moment," she said to neither of them in particular.

They nodded and walked over to the bank of sofas. Looking out the window across London, Samuel cleared his mind thought about the beautiful view. This moment held a lot of firsts for him. The first time being back on Earth. The first time clothed as a mundane. The first time working off the books. If he could pull it off, it meant heavy kudos.

A different woman walks over to Samuel and Mako. "Mr. Wright will see you now. Please follow me."

"Thank you", Samuel said, still distracted by the view from the building. To anyone else, he seemed in awe of the spectacular view of the Thames and the surrounding buildings of Canary Wharf, but he was bricking it. Mako fell in behind him, just as they had planned. As they walked, Mako made sure to stay 5 paces behind, pretending he was a slow walker. It was a style of attack formation, but Mako was focusing on the moment, the enjoyment of being in the office environment. It had its own kind of peace. Something only found on the mortal plane.

The secretary presented Alex's office door to them so they could enter.

"Good to meet you," Samuel said, entering the room and approaching Alex. Alex stood up from behind his desk, "And you." He stretched out his hand and provided a firm shake.

Alex immediately knew something was wrong. He tried to pull his hand away. A shudder ran through his body like an uncontrollable shock-wave.

Mako walks into the office without breaking stride. "Um zam-ran," he announced.

Alex glared at him like the long-lost enemy he was. "Ganislay," he announced in three different voices at once.

Mako lunges toward Alex, four wings appearing on his back that propel him faster toward his target.

Samuel pulls Alex in closer, and a portal opens behind them, revealing a battlefield. Two people remain frozen in hand-to-hand combat on the other side. Mako tackles Alex and Samuel, shoving them through the portal. As they fall through, the action on the battlefield speeds up, while the reality of earth slows to a halt.

As they fall through the portal toward the battlefield, the horrified secretary can't calculate what she is seeing. Samuel flings his free arm towards her, throwing a small orb of soft light that ends up surrounding her, wiping her memory. She closes the door to the office, content that nothing has happened despite the portal still being opened. Samuel planned to be back and gone before the ripples of what they have done get too wide.

All three of them fall onto the battlefield, rolling in front of the two demons locked in combat with one another. Samuel brandishes his sword, slaying both demons in one swoop, and then rolled to a standing position.

Ganislay, knowing that he is revealed, extends his arms around Mako, who is holding him by the neck, grabs him by the back and throws him like a sack of potatoes to the ground.

"Where is the key?" Samuel demanded.

This stops Ganislay, as all demons and creatures are compelled to answer when a Celestial addresses them. Ganislay looked at him with all the hatred in the world, eyes white as milk, unable to discern the light of the world. A tail appears from behind Ganislay and it curls around two scrolls, pulling them out of his own body, lifting them high in the air to tease Samuel.

Mako stabs Ganislay with a thorn on the edge of one of his wings. Ganislay falls backward and drops the keys behind him.

The appearance of the keys glimmered like a beacon to all within Dudael. It was like a glistening of water to someone enduring a desert for a thousand years. Eth and especially life, doesn't exist in Dudael. The shimmer of Eth flashed through the realm, sending every celestial and demon into a frenzy of desperation. Tens of thousands clammer and fight over each other toward Samuel and Mako. In one great mob they charge across the hills and valleys toward Samuel. Hungry from being frozen in the same battle for millennia. Any celestial who could present the key would be able to return to Heaven, and any demon could escape with it back to Hell and be would be crowned.

"The dogs of Hell will be on us in moments. But this," Ganislay announced holding the scrolls closer, "this is mine. I will lead an army of my own out of the gates of Hell."

He grabs Mako, wrapping his tail around his neck and wings several times. The tip of his tail pierces Mako's neck like a large snake and begins draining the celestial of all his life force.

Samuel looked on in horror, stunned by this demon's brutality. He quickly realized, in Dudael, celestials and chthonics were equal.

"Looks like only two of us are getting out of here," Ganislay chuckles. He flung Mako's drained body onto the hardened dirt. Mako looked gaunt and withered, almost un-angelic. "I don't think that one has a chance."

"No," Samuel screams. He can hear the thunder of the thousands of celestials and demons behind him, battling and clawing up the last hill to get to them. Samuel turns into a beam of light that zips straight toward Ganislay's chest. Samuel tries to split him in half and instead, the light bounces off of him, and Samuel returns to his usual form as he tumbled across the ground. Ganislay stumbled and loses one of the scrolls.

Ganislay looks at where he was hit, "Looks like I just got an upgrade thanks to your friend."

The mob of battling Celestials and Angels thunder toward the scroll as it lands on the ground.

"I'll come back for you," Samuel shouts toward Mako as he turns into another spear of light. He snatches up the scroll as he streaks by and pierces the mob, rocketing into the distance with a boom that shudders the entire realm.

Samuel falls back onto the office floor and glances backward in time to see the portal he just came through closing behind him. He knew Mako was stuck, perhaps for eternity. He also knew Ganislay wasn't going to waste any time trying to get out of there. The bigger problem was a million Chthonics and Fallen Angels had access to getting out of their own eternal hell. It might not stay in Ganislay's possession for very long. Who knows

Samuel watches the portal close like a circular lightning bolt. He looks at the one scroll he does have and tucks it into his inside pocket. He had to move quickly. It wouldn't be long before the energy of the scroll was felt around the world. He looked over at the windowsill. A ray of sunshine reflected off the mental window casing. He leaps into the brightest spot and disappeared.

Chapter Four

P ercival tidied up his desk for the day. It was a ceremony he did every day. Pen stationed parallel to the top of his writing pad. 2 mechanical pencils placed to the right of the work area, and the stamp inside the top drawer. Even though he was left-handed, that area needed to remain clear for coffee or tea, which he drank in equal amounts and interchanged randomly so neither one could become a vice.

"Ah..." he sighs with a smile, looking at his tidied work. Even though angels' scribe by merely thinking of their script, he still found joy in roughing it through some of the more important orders that came from head office. Every celestial has a vice, and while he needed none of these things, after years of watching humans, he would try and build the surroundings that he could, so he could better understand them. Only the Chairman and the Most High had endless knowledge. While he could remember infinitely more than any human, it was difficult for him to understand that humans were much more limited. He wanted to know what this felt like, so he would drink tea and write his thoughts or doodles, simply because that's what he saw humans doing. Though for he was no closer to understanding the in's and out's of why his cases did the things they do. He could just foresee what would happen.

"Percival, could you be a lamb and take these up for processing on your way out?" one celestial asked on their way past.

"Yes, of course," Percival responded. Before he could barely finish the sentence, a heavy pile of files landed in his arms. Celestials took advantage of him all the time, but Percival always felt that since he volunteered, there was no use in complaining. The trick was not volunteering, a habit he was trying to break.

Percival began the long trek up the staircase that stretched up the side of the large picture window in their office. He lumbered along with the files underneath his arms. It was his favourite walk through the building. As he got midway up the staircase, he stopped, it was the same place he stopped every time, the large landing midway up the staircase. The staircase sat adjacent to the large picture window that looked out over the lake where all new souls gathered when they entered heaven. When he had extra time, he would take a longer walk to the lanai just outside the large window. It led to the outer veranda where he could watch the entry pool at the bottom of the waterfall beneath their building. Some souls were meeting for the first time since their passing.

Most celestials didn't bother to walk, instead they would teleport to their destination. Unless they were assigned to do so, many celestials didn't bother to watch the joys of the new souls at the lake. To Percival, it felt like they all missed the point. Eternity may be endless, but he wanted to enjoy every moment of it.

Percival was never sure whether it was better to serve in heaven or be a spirit. It was something he contemplated often, not out of lament, but out of wonder for life on the other side. His work was detailed, and sometimes his shifts felt like an eternity of their won, but they had their benefits. In the end, he reached the same conclusion he did every time he pondered this; 'He was glad for what he had.'

"Percy, I'm on my way in. You did great buddy, we had some snags, but mission accomplished. You were able to keep a location on that demons eth with no problem," Sam communicated with him.

Percival looked up to the sky, far above the structure. Streaks of light darted in and out of the realm like glints of lightning across the sky, signifying traffic patterns of Angels and Archs departing and returning from their assignments. While newly welcomed souls entered through the main gate, Angels and Archs traversed from the gateway at the top of the building, and the portal at the center of a stream of eth that flowed out of this realm to each of the other planes.

"Excellent to hear. Once you get in, let's see how we can straighten out those snags. And stop calling me Percy." Percival knew he needed to get this task done faster. He levitated up from the floor and closed his eyes. He kept his eyes closed for only a moment, and opened them as he appeared before the office door for the ICCO. Gladys was at the reception desk. She saw Percival and got her rejection stamp out. She loved rejecting his filings, not because his work was sloppy–but because it put him in such a tizzy. There was no law against winding someone up in heaven, as long as things didn't get out of hand.

"Hiya Gladys."

She sneered.

These came from my head of team, I'm just here to deliver them.

She put her stamp down, slightly disappointed, and pointed to the in-basket. He looked confused. She was never this inviting. The inter-choir communications office, the ICCO, looked like a cross between a county clerk's office and a high school administrative counter. Papers were stacked everywhere in small piles across the office, giving it an appearance of ordered chaos, but Gladys had a keen sense of which pile was meant for which region, choir, or realm.

"Is that Percy?" a voice came over a small intercom on her desk.

"Yes sir", she stated, still unimpressed.

"Please send him in here."

Percival's eyes lit up. He had never met the head of the ICCO before. Gladys waved a ceremonial arm toward the open doorway of her boss's office, remaining unimpressed.

Percival nearly skipped past her in his joy to meet the head of communications. Te office was unimpressive, exactly like the main reception area, filled with stacks of papers.

"Percival, do you know what we do here?", the head of the ICCO announced from behind a stack of forms.

"Yes," he said, sitting down in the visitors chair.

"Everything. Celestials like to think they are omnipotent, but they only know what they know, just like the souls out there in heaven. Aside from sitting in the Big Chair itself, and I wouldn't want that responsibility, this is the next best thing. We know everything. Which is why my receptionist is so bloomin' unimpressed by all of it." He shot an irritated look in the direction of where she sat.

Percival squinted a little. He was sure the ICCO director had just attempted to swear. "How can I help you, sir?"

"I've only handed out two of these in my time here. But whatever is going on, I can tell you—even we don't know here at the ICCO." Kevin narrowed his eyes toward Percival, feigning suspicion in order to disguise his utter confusion of why this was happening. He reached into his inside breast pocket and revealed an envelope. "This just came from above, requiring your immediate attention." The envelope, inlaid with mother-of-pearl, glistened as he handed it to Percival. "I can't know what's in it, only the parties involved can. If anything were to go wrong, this is your get out of jail free card."

"Get out of jail," Percival shuddered at the implication. He opened the envelope, which revealed a folded letter in golden writing.

Percival of the Archs:

You are to report to Section 2 for the sole purpose of assisting Archangel Samuel with the task of 'The protection of Judgement'. No other choir may know of this project. You may recruit as needed.

You are being given special dispensation to use any and all means to accomplish this task. Please report to section two immediately to begin your strategy session.

Gratefully,

Director First Class - Dominions

Percival's arms fell to his lap. This meant there really were snags with Samuel's mission.

Kevin looked at him with a hint of contempt. "Such a thing has never happened, to my knowledge."

Percival was confused. *How did he know what was in this letter?* He didn't know what to say, so it was best to say nothing.

"A celestial of your rank getting such a memo," Kevin goaded again.

"Oh," Percival said with relief. He thought he had already somehow spilled the beans. Then he caught on to Kevin's tone of voice. If there were two common sins within members of the choirs, they were envy, and pride. However, after the Great War, authorities heavily policed members of the choir regarding these sins. Percival stared at him suspiciously, as he did not abide such fundamental rules being broken. He couldn't figure out for the life of him where this conversation was going next. Instead, he chose to ward Kevin off the only way he knew how, by mustering a childlike scowl.

Kevin had seen many special assignments in his day. Special assignments often involved converting the worst cases before their souls were lost forever to the underworld. The higher-ups assigned such cases to Celestials as busy work, or to test them. Kevin always felt sorry for the recipient. The higher ranks dangled these cases like sweets, because nobody else wanted to take the time. They always came with the promise of promotion of accolade, but were impossible to accomplish. However, an assignment like this had never been given to a celestial seconded to the Principalities. According to inter-office policy, any communication about special assignments above the Archs too sensitive, so they typically delivered such messages individually. An envelope made of mother-of-pearl only came from one place, the Dominions. Something about it all was very strange. He was going to have to do his best to look into it. Quietly.

Kevin leaned back in his chair, growing uneasy by Percival's odd attempt at staring him down. After a moment, he waved him off. "I really can't know. Is there anything you need from me to get started?"

Percival stood up, "No sir. I shall be on my way. If I need anything, I shall let you know."

Percival had never received a promotion. He had worked as a scribe in the Principalities for eons. He'd watched angels come and go from the choir. Most transferred out of the secondment to their original choir. They couldn't take the politics. Percival waited ages, and when he was tired and disgusted by his superiors–he waited some more, always putting in extra effort.

He floated out of the room, or so he thought. Gliding past the reception counter, "Bye Gladys, have a nice day."

She looked at him out of the corner of her eye and sneered. "We don't have, <u>days</u>."

He didn't mind her curt behaviour. He'd win her over eventually. Closing the door behind him, he started down the steps and stopped to look out the large window again. All watched the arrival of souls being carried by the celestials who streaked in. He was proud to serve each one of them. The thought of Section Two entered his mind. He'd heard of it. It carried the mystique of a secret agency. A place where careers were built. Section Two was made famous by Michael. It was where he planned all his major campaigns. Percival thought it strange that he had been assigned there.

"Oh dear," he said outloud, realizing that Sam was on his way in. "Sam," he said, looking up at the path of angels flying in and out.

"Yeah, I'm almost there. About to hit the atrium in about a few moments."

"Ok, yes, I need to change where I am meeting you. Meet me in Section Two, room three-b."

"Umm... section two. Are you sure?" Sam said as he was making his landing in the top atrium. He had to go through processing. There was a long queue of Celestials on their way back from tasks in other realms. He looked around for a shorter lines at the check-in. The lines had gotten longer given the circumstances. The order had come from high above to increase security.

"Yes. to be honest, I've never heard of it before," Percival responded. "You're an angelic choir... I'm not surprised."

Once he made his way through processing, Samuel teleported down to three-b and strode into the meeting room with a mixture of confidence and loathing. "Where is everybody," he said looking around, finding only percival. Sam knew the history of three-b, it was obvious to him that Percival didn't.

The room was stark, save for one long rectangulae table and four chairs. It looked disused, like a cross between a storage closet and an interrogatin room. Whenever an angel was going to be demoted or permanently discarded, upper management would use this room. Celestials spun many a fantastical story about three-b as grade school students do about the principal's office.

Sam loosened up a bit realizing the only entity there was Percival. If it were serious, there would be an entire committee. "It's just you and I?"

"I was given this a few moments ago in Kevin's office." Percival noticed Samuel was very tense. "Are you okay?" he asked as he handed Samuel the note.

"Honestly, it's all a little weird. We're in a room that nobody can go in unless invited, in a section that doesn't officially exist. I thought I was being dis-incorporated"

"Heavens no," Percival conciliated.

"That's... what they do here," Samuel said, as he looked at Percival in disbelief.

Percival began to worry. "We were given this room. I'm pretty sure because of what you are carrying with you. At least I think so." He looked around at the table and chairs. He looked underneath the table for anything suspicious.

"What are you doing?"

"I don't know, looking for scary things. Isn't this how you do it?"

Samuel looked at him with disbelief.

"Hello Celestials," an envoy said, appearing out of nowhere.

"Good heavens," Percival jumped.

The envoy looked at him as if he were ill.

Samuel looked at Percival in pity. "I don't know. He's got a whole vibe going on right now," Samuel said, reassuring the Envoy. "He's been worried ever since we got here."

"Yeah," the Envoy said, sitting in the chair. "The reason you are here is that... I'm guessing... the last task didn't go so well."

"But you... I thought you said you retrieved the key," Percival said looking at Samuel in disbelief.

Sam looked proudly at Percival and the Envoy as if he were being watched by a hundred others. "Indeed, my friend," he smiled. He revealed a large scroll embossed with platinum inscriptions in the angelic language. He plunked it on the table with a heavy metal thud.

Percival became stiff as a board with fear. If he were mortal, he may have gone pale, possibly fainted. "Oh dear."

Samuel stiffened as well. He had known Percival for eons, he knew that 'Oh dear' was about as close to swearing as Percival ever got. Percival couldn't say the word 'shit' even if he had a mouthful of it. In a way, Samuel respected him for it.

"What do we have here?" the envoy eyed the scroll. It took both hands and significant muscle to lift it so he could turn the scroll and read the inscription.

"How long did he have this in his possession?"

"Probably since the blast," quipped Samuel.

"So a probable." The envoy began adding up all the possible scenarios in his head.

"And were you able to dispatch him?"

"No, that is the wrinkle. When we went in for the attack, I tried to open a portal to the underworld where to dispatch him. However, we ended up somewhere else. I don't know how"

The envoy placed the key on the table and looked at Samuel for more information.

"I think we were in Dudael", Samuel said cautiously.

"Ah-huh," The envoy said looking at him up and down. He was used to the weird. The envoy revelled in dealing with the darkest and most arcane energies and entities. But he was sure Dudael was Heavens own ghost story.

Samuel continued, unsure of the reception of his statement. "That's when we ran into complications. Hoards. And I mean legions upon legions of chthonic and celestials in a gruesome battle. They were all trying to reach a beacon on top of a cliff, that is until they saw our portal. Mako survived, but he's stuck there with Ganislay."

"OK, we'll have to put a hold on that for now," the envoy noted.

"We are going to have to get them back. You said on the top of the cliff was a beacon of light that everyone was battling to reach", Percival interjected. He had no doubt in his mind that Dudael existed.

Samuel knew Percival was on to something. "Yes, a beacon of light."

"I don't know how much you two read. If you read the literature of the humans, they often describe us as beacons of light whenever we present ourselves with a message. It only appears this way because we are connected to a more concentrated level of consciousness that they are."

Samuel and the envoy look at him with veiled frustration. "Ok, where are you going with this?" the envoy asked.

"Dudael is a place that imprisons celestials and chthonics, cutting them off from the rest of existence. If the a living mortal was indeed hidden in Dudael, they would still have all their mortal energy. Their eth may have been portioned out, but without going through the gateway of death, it would only regenerate. That's why we have humans, to transmit the energy of life force. But Dudael isn't built for them, everything in Dudeal is at a lower frequency. To a Celestial suffering from diminished capacity, the human would most likely appear as a beam or beacon of light."

"Ok, but the problem with your theory is that Dudael is basically the realm of the undead. That means this mortal is now undead as well."

Percival decided not to answer right away and instead look up at Samuel.

"Why would the mortal still be alive?" he asked rhetorically. Percival didn't just need someone on his side. He needed them both to fully understand how bad the predicament was – and for this, they needed to begin to think things through themselves.

"Judgement," Samuel said vacantly, as he was deep in thought. "She may have been touched by mortality, but this being didn't pass through judgement. Shit... that means –"

"Yep," Percival interrupted.

"Well, if that's true, it also means that the Portal's next move is–"

"Yep," Percival interrupted again with a grave tone.

"Do either of you want to fill me in," the envoy interrupted. "I have no clue what you're talking about,"

Percival looked at him with surprise. This was the second time emotions were expressed in so many hours. It struck him as odd. Celestials and even envoys were devoid of most emotion. Something was going on that was bigger than the three of them. He put it to the back of his mind and responded to the question. "For a mortal to truly pass, they must go through judgement. In order to pass to universal consciousness one has to have the ability of discernment and that comes from the skill of judgment. For the uninitiated souls, judgement is a fierce character, to others it's a type of agreement, or cooperation."

"That's great. It means they aren't connected to the universal con- sciousness," the Envoy jumped in.

"Yes, that's true. But it also means we have a living being in the realm of the Celestial undead that is still connected to the rest of mortality. It could lead to all of those within Dudael controlling mortality. So the entire realm will be chasing after this person in order to control them. Any desperate Celestial or Chthonic who controls them can create a portal to the mortal realm, or Hell or where ever they want to go," Percival impressed.

Samuel's gaze remained vacant. He knew Percival was right. Percival didn't push ideas on to others like this unless he had a lot of hard research to back up his claim. "All of existence is about to get messy", he said in a fearful tone.

The Envoy wasn't sure which was more disturbing, the idea that something actually could frighten Samuel, or that all of Heaven and Hell's misdeeds could be unleashed throughout existence. "The worst thing in the world is the unimagined hell. Let's hope one of ours gets there first."

"I don't think you want that to happen either. We're talking about the fallen, and any Celestial that sat in a grey area during the Great War in Heaven. They've been locked up for mor eons than most of us have aged. They're gonna be..."

"Pissed off," Samuel interjected.

"Yeah... that. A Celestial is likely to bring the war to us. A Chthonic is likely to take their grievances to face off the kings and princes in Hell."

"This will make Armageddon look tame... at least one of us has control of that," Samuel admitted.

"But without the Key, there is no way for Chthonics to enter Heaven."

"Not necessarily true," Percival admitted.

"You mean it gets worse," Samuel said, looking for some sort of silver lining.

"To release herself from her role, Alice Grey's next move will be to kill the Portal of Judgement. Once that happens, all they need to do is kill one mortal, and they have a gateway here. They've got about seven billion gateways to choose from." Percival looked at them, he knew he had finally gotten them to understand, mostly because of the grave looks on their faces.

The Envoy stood up and paced the floor. The Envoy held up his hand for Percival to stop. "Before we go any further with this, I'm trying to decide if I like having you around."

"What does enjoyment have anything to do with this," Percival wondered outloud.

"He's kidding," Samuel reassured him.

"Okay," the Envoy said, stopping. "All we have to do is stop a centuries old witch from killing Judgement and unleashing all of Hell upon earth, while also save a mortal from the depth of the most epic battle that neither Heaven nor Hell wants to recognize is actually happening?"

"Yeah, but I was told that I could recruit whomever I needed for the task."

The Envoy raised his arms and glanced around the room. "Well, where are they? We're in this room because the Chairman wants this off the books. The Choirs can't know. If the Choirs know, then the Divine Council knows – and you don't want that. The moment this goes to the Council, we've got a war on our hands. Either an all out war with Hell, or another Great War here. So we're it!"

Samuel leaned down slightly in the vague hope that maybe someone was under the table to assist them. The other two look at him. "I'm kidding..."

"Yeah... its time to see what the other side knows," the Envoy flatly announced.

"Really? You're going to travel down there," Samuel said, slightly impressed.

"I try to avoid it as much as possible. I'd rather send a Power or create a temporary aspect, but sometimes you gotta do a job yourself. Mostly I hate the smell."

"I'm going to try to stop this crafty bastard before it all gets too far. We don't want to have to tangle with the portals any more than we have to."

"Good point," the Envoy agreed.

"You're going to go slay a demon," Percival asked. "How... how does one do that?"

He pulled his sword out from its sheath and quickly whisked it toward Percival. It lit on fire as it stopped just in front of Percival's face. "Sometimes, it gets messy – you never know until you're in the moment."

Percival couldn't imagine needing to strike anyone. In his mind nearly everyone can be reasoned with or at most, gently persuaded by altering a situation.

"I'll let you know how it goes," Samuel said as he disappeared from the room.

The Envoy looked at Percival with a mixture of mild pity and concern.

"Is there anything I can help with," Percival asked.

"Oh God no," he chuckled. "I'm just pissed this trip is going to ruin my suit," he said, disappearing.

The wisps of smoke drifted away from where Samuel was just standing and the silence of Percival's own drifted in. Just an hour before, he thought he had seen most of the inner workings on Central Existence. His choir was always taught that everything in Central Existence works on transparency, so orders can be tracked from creation to execution and back. Now he realized there was so much he didn't know. He had never heard of this room before he arrived in it.

How was this transparency? He couldn't account for it. He assumed something was missing from what he had researched. The thought of existence making a mistake just didn't calculate in his mind. He was going to find out.

CHAPTER FIVE

Percival walked into his favorite section of the Great Library. He stopped and looked at the pedestal where the Book of Life resided when not in use. Peter was most certainly at his post right now. Even Saint Peter needed a break from time to time. This surprised Percival when he first learned this. There were many quirks about the day-to-day runnings of heaven that surprised him. Many of these surprises came crashing in during his visits to the library. Working at the gates with Peter was Percival's first assignment. Little did Percival know that the day he came here, he was being promoted.

"This is the Great Library," Peter said as he led Percival through the doorway entrance into the library. It was odd for a Celestial to mix with departed mortals, though the saints and great prophets were of special rank and often volunteered to mentor newly created Celestials. "The history, mysteries and legends of everything are in here. If you want to become proficient, you need to study the works of the Celestials, the mortals, and what sense you can make of the Chthonic literature. The mortals are interesting. They split hairs and categorize their own people to prove righteousness to one another, and they pontificate and debate one another about whether we exist at all."

Percival looked a little upset. He thought it odd that he was created to protect mortals, including the mortals who doubted the existence of Celestials altogether.

Saint Peter saw the look on Percivals face and interjected. "Don't let it bother you. I find it all very funny, because even the believers often miss the message. Besides, they are missing out on this," Saint Peter said lifting an arm to introduce Percival to the grandeur of the library.

Percival was slack-jawed as he looked around. He instantly forgot what Peter had said and focused on the sheer beauty of the room. It didn't look like anything else in Central Existence. He could feel the energy of the information as it wanted to pour into him. He didn't know where to start.

Enormous columns carved from luminescent crystal supported the vast, vaulted ceilings. The ceiling sparkled from the reflected lights that dotted the floor of the library. Peter noticed Percival was transfixed on this, so he dimmed the floor lights for the proper show. The vaulted glass ceiling stopped reflecting the light below from the library and as the lights dimmed Percival could see the cosmos. Percival instantly knew he could simply allow space to drift in it's natural way, or shift and chang the constellations according to his thoughts.

"It's a map that focuses in on whatever you are studying or should study at the moment. The universe has its way of telling us things all the time, even Celestials," Peter said in admiration.

Percival turned his attention to the endless rows of shelves that lined the library. The aisles of shelving were so tall, they looked like they supported the structure on the building. Each shelf in the library was carved from a material that blended light and substance, shifting between transparency and opacity. The shelves held an immeasurable number of books and scrolls, each unique in size, shape, and hue. Some books were bound in ancient leather and embossed with pre-

cious metals, while others were scrolls of delicate silk. On many, the
text on the covers glowed with a golden hue.

Even though angels are created, their creation only provides them
with a limited amount of information. They learn the rest based on
the function they are to perform, just like any other entity or mortal. The problem was, Percival was good at everything, at least with
knowledge-based activities. When he was first scribing at the gates,
Peter used to read off the names in the Great Book as fast as he could,
while Percival tried to recite them from memory. It wasn't long before
Percival could beat him in the race. That's when Peter realized it was
time to introduce Percival to the Library.

Peter put a proud hand on Percival's shoulder. "There are a few
rules you must always abide. He said as they approached the beginning
of the aisles of knowledge. "You may not borrow any books, which
is why there is no registration desk. I think this is why visitations
have dwindled over the millennia. Celestials would rather gain their
knowledge through experiencing the other planes or observing the
mortals. Mortals may not enter except for limited invitation - but that
decision is above your grade."

Percival was barely listening. The aisles of books stretched as wide,
as deep, and as tall as his eyes could see. "It's tremendous," he said,
interrupting Peter. "It would take several cycles just to get to the right
book."

"Oh, don't be silly, this isn't the library of Alexandria. You've been
spending too much time watching the mortals." Peter walked him to
the edge of the closest aisles. "You can order this library any way you
would like it. Of course naturally it is done by the broadest topics, but
perhaps you would like everything in chronological order by when it
was written."

"Oooo, that's interesting. Who wrote the first complete work," Percival asked. His eyes conveyed how hungry he was for the knowledge in any one of the aisles.

Peter looked at him slyly, "It's not who you think."

"It also depends on what you mean by complete," another voice appeared out of nowhere. A tall woman glided toward them. Her vibrant platinum hair perfectly framed electric green eyes. "Do you mean fiction, philosophy, or science?" She eyed Percival with a welcoming, but inquisitive look.

Percival looked back at her, and though it best to simply state what he thought of all types of literary discourse. "I've always found many philosophies to be quite fictitious, many fictions to be scientific, and doesn't science, especially mathematics, eventually lead to philosophy anyway," Percival asked.

"Where did you dig this one up?" the librarian asked Peter.

"He's young, but you wanted to be notified should anyone ever pique my curiosity."

"I did. So yes, Peter is correct." She raised her arms toward the aisles, "You can arrange everything by date of completion," every book disappeared and then reappeared in an instant. She walked toward the first aisle and picked up a scroll to show him, and placed it back down. "Or according to the greatest works ever written." The aisles reordered themselves. "If you ask the mortals, many would say the greatest work is by Fitzgerald, Rumi, or even us."

"So, which is the greatest work?" Percival asked.

"We have a competition every cycle, and the reigning champion has been Steven Parker's tenth grade history paper written in 1968 at Red River High School in Grand Forks, North Dakota. How he got a passing grade, one will never know." She suddenly whispered, "I think he had a little help," she said, pointing toward the floor.

"So, does that make it history or fiction?" Percival asked.

"He would like to think it falls under History," she said, shooting a disapproving eye toward the paper. "But it is the greatest works of fiction every written. Anyway, moving on... The most interesting way to tackle this room is to order the books in the order of what the Universe wants you to know next."

The books reappeared in yet another order and the librarian took the first book off the shelf. It was titled "Principal Factors Of The Etheric Body".

Percival looked at her confused. "What the Universe wants me to know? What do you mean?"

"The Universe is a living entity as well. It tries to speak to us all the time. Sadly, even many Celestials are too busy to stop and listen. The archs are the best, they can feel a faint pulse of what is to come from miles away. "

"What's this about?" Percival asked as he carefully took the book she held out for him and opened it.

"Don't worry, you can't damage it." She smiled, reassuring him. "Everything in heaven is protected, no matter how fragile, slight, or dainty. Harm has no power here." She smiled, enjoying his quaint efforts to be respectful. "The book is about the process of how the soul and the force of life flows in and out of the mortal body."

"It's the bridge to the other planes for the mortals."

"Very astute."

"Can I read them all?" he asked, looking at the aisle.

"I don't think anybody has ever tried. You may visit as often as you like, and stay for as long as you like, however books do not leave the Great Library."

Over the next millennia, Percival spent every spare moment he had reading the texts. First continuing with the theme of what the Universe wanted him to know, and when he felt he had exhausted a topic as the books became repetitive, he would change to something more stimulating. What always amazed the Librarian was that he would sit, as if on a chair, while he floated among the aisles, whith a book in his lap. He would never use a table. It was as if he didn't want to waste time with the ceremony of using a reading spot, but would rather begin studying right there in the aisles. As if time mattered to a celestial. As she would go about her own research duties, she hardly ever noticed his presence.

It was sometime into the second millennia of humankind, after Percival had devoured the mythologies of the celestials, as well as those of the mortals from every planetary system, that he finally posed his first question. The librarian was at her desk, a large table with two elevated platforms on them. On one lay an opened scroll showing an ancient prophecy written in Aramaic, and on the other, a historical timeline. In front of her sat a large ledger that she was meticulously filling out, based on the accuracy of what she found in the prophecy and what the historical record showed.

"It's like we've set up a great system of irony," he started. The more time he spent in the Great library, the less time he was giving others to catch up. The amount of information had to go somewhere, and sometimes it came bursting out of Percival mid thought. It was up to the celestial he was speaking with, to keep up. In this way, Percival was becoming unforgiving. If the Great Library was available for all celestials to read, he felt it was their responsibility to read it in order to fulfill their duties. Unfortunately, most of the time, this left Percival feeling frustrated, as many of his colleagues couldn't understand the context from which he was speaking. He was learning the fine art of celestial arrogance and didn't know it.

The librarian looked up at him, unphased – welcoming him to continue with his thought. As if she had been waiting for this moment for a long time.

"Central Existence has all the power, but we feel the need to create mortal entities with free will. Those born onto the mortal plane are convinced their free will give them complete agency over everything in their life, yet choose to be blinded by the agency that others have as well. Thus setting up a crazy system of physical reality that is stacked against them, yet the mortals get all the blame. All the while being convinced that there is nothing beyond their physical body. Even though they are a reflection of us, in a sense. Which is also ironic, because they don't think we exist."

"Uh oh, I feel a question coming on here."

"Well yeah. I'm not sure if the joke is on us, or them, but the real question is, what's the point?"

"Well, in the grand scheme of things – that's all part of the ineffable plan. Only the Most High knows the answer to that."

Percival looked at her with frustration. It felt like she was evading his question. The first of many, as he would eventually come to her with many more questions over the millennia that he spent in the aisles of the Great Library.

Percival now looked at the librarian's research desk with fondness. The questions he used to ask seemed so simple. Just in the last hour, he had so many more that made little sense, despite all the research he had done in here.

"I wouldn't say they were simple questions, just sophomoric. Without regard for all the subtle contexts that make a moment," the Librarian said appearing out of the nearest stack of books. The books she was holding in her arms to levitated and floated ahead of her, settling on the desk beside where Percival was standing. Each book opened to the pages that she required, and came to rest, waiting for her to study them. "The question you have now is much more interesting. When you build a system as complex as this one, there will always be contradictions, parallel truths, and because of it, many injustices. The universe has competing interests, which issue do you attend to first?"

Percival nodded. "How did you know." He thought it strange the way she talked about building the system, as if she had a hand in its design. Everyone knows the Son of Man appeared in, and every celestial knows the leader of the Sons and Daughters of Light, but only a select few in central existence who sit next to the throne actually knew who the Most High was. In a moment of pure speculation, Percival's mind wandered toward the possibility that the Most High could spend time as a librarian.

The Librarian, reading every thought as it passed through his mind, smirked at the whimsy. Then she looked at him to impress the simplicity of the point he had missed. "Have you not spent time in the Design and Planning section yet?"

"No, not yet. I got too enthralled with leaning the Ana'kh language. I wanted to be able to translate Anunnaki prophesies myself from the primary sources."

She gave an impressed nod. "Not something I had considered. They were very successful in detailing how to direct Eth during their heyday. In exchange for putting in the hard work on this, they were given a place on the Council." She pulled out one of the side drawers in her desk and hunted through it, looking for her favorite stylus. While it was impossible to ruin and of the books or manuscripts in the Great Library, they preferred sticking to a specific style. She liked using the long stylus, as if she were a medieval scribe from the mortal realm. She enjoyed the kinesthetic tone it provided every moment. Despite her eccentricities, she had her own unique charm. "Which is why I think you are here. You are worried about the Council."

"How did you know?"

"You are the only real apprentice I've ever had. Maybe the only one I ever will. Which means I know you better than you know yourself. You are dealing with some sort of issue that you need to capture or kill a Chthonic, which is connected to that immense explosion of eth everyone is speaking of. With such high stakes, it's natural to be worried about steering clear of the council."

Percival looked bereft. There was still so much he didn't know. She could calculate exactly what he was thinking, as if he was on some sort of predetermined path.

"What are you stuck on?" she asked, finally settling in her seat, stylus in hand.

"I'm not even sure. I just wanted to go somewhere that made sense. Objectives for this mission are piling up. How do you prioritize things when they are all critical?"

"You don't," she replied. "It's the same with any fast moving situation. While we have unlimited resources here, using them comes at a price. That price is an all-out war. We have to maintain balance and the agreements we have made. So you achieve what you can, the most you can, with whatever moment you are presented with. Just like any other time. Just because you are in an acute situation, it doesn't change the rules of the universe. What you really mean is. How do I prioritize the things that evade the notice of the Divine Council?"

"Yes," he said, looking away.

"You were picked for this role, because the Most High needed someone new, a neutral observer. That's just a reality of how existence works. It's partly political because you are inexperienced, and because this will most likely create trust within the Council should they have to get involved. We may be divine and our mission may be pure. However, within our ranks, celestials are very political. That isn't the healthiest thing for the Choirs. My advice, make it your business to figure out what the political reason is for your involvement."

In a quick golden flash, a small envelope appeared on the Librarian's desk. The librarian "Hmm... an interoffice memo just arrived for you," she said, looking at the envelope. She slid the envelope across the desktop toward Percival.

Percival dreaded what it said. Since his involvement with this project, each letter he had received has caused an ever-increasing amount of ire.

"Mission failed. It's time we go see a witch about a demon," Percival muttered out loud.

The Librarian winced, "Let's keep the sensitive business of Central Existence to ourselves." She quickly changed her wince to a look of encouragement just in time for Percival to see.

"Oh yes. Apologies. I suppose I should attend to this," he said as he turned away.

She smiled. "Yes. Good luck."

CHAPTER SIX

Percival and Samuel stood at the beginning of the lane looking at Alice Grey's house. Percival looked at the craggy mounds of smooth eroded rocks covered in tufts of grasses rising out of the mud flats. He couldn't tell which way the tide was heading, as some grasses were slightly immersed. He liked the rugged beauty of the tidal bay that surrounded the house. He could feel the residue from the immense wave of Eth that originated from here. To Percival the residue felt like echoes from someone who had just screamed. Likewise, he could feel her stare from the house as they stood at the end of the lane. She already knew they were there, not that she was physically looking at them. Like any other celestial, he could always feel when a mortal or anyone visiting the mortal plane was looking at him. Since attention directs intention, even directing one's attention changes the flow of Eth on the mortal plane. To a celestial, such changes are as common as breathing is to a mortal.

"You know, the last time I saw the portal, she promised to turn me into a chicken and roast me for dinner," Samuel announced. He knew there was a fight coming. He could feel her ire toward him. "I don't even know what chicken tastes like."

"I thought they turned people into toads," Percival said as they strolled down the lane.

"She said there would be brussels sprouts and gravy."

Percival looked horrified. "Really... with sprouts?"

"Uh-huh," he nodded. "I don't know what they are, but I haven't heard good things."

"That's just mean," Percival said, feigning concern. In all his time he had read about some fairly horrific things, and he had since learned that witches are no joke. However, they were rare, and the legitimate sorcerers were occupied with far more important matters than turning people into roast dinners, even if there was the added threat of sprouts. "Let's just double check what we are getting into," he said, changing the subject.

As they walked down the lane, Percival reversed time to see what had occurred. The tide rose and fell and the sun sunk into the East. They saw the wind from the storm that Miss Grey kicked up in her disturbance. As time continued to reverse, they remained undisturbed by everything around them, as if they were in a bubble. As the sunset reversed back into daylight the day before, Percival slowed the reversal of time down when they got to midday, and saw the postal truck driving down the lane to the house. "I believe this is our victim here," he said, donning the voice of a cheesy TV detective. Percival stood right next to the postal van, frozen in time as it passed him. He reached in and shot a light toward the young man, taking a copy of his Eth signature. A copy of his Eth signature floated in the air, looking like a medallion of energy, with symbols in a circle, much like a zodiac chart. "We are going to need that."

Percival pulls a small pouch that sparkles with brass from his robes, opens it, and slides the Eth signature in. The pouch was actually a portal to his desk drawer, a trick he used when he was in meetings at Central Existence and didn't want to carry a load of files with him.

Samuel nodded. "If you think he really is in Dudael, we'll have a better chance of finding him now that we have his signature. Good thinking."

Percival returned time back into its natural forward motion, and sped it back up to the current moment. They continued down the lane, this time appearing as two Police Officers checking on the resident.

As they approached the house, they were both hit with a wave of Eth that made them back off like a terrible stench in the air.

"Oh, this guy never stood a chance," Samuel said, looking around. "She's got a ward around the entire property. From the road, the whole place looks like dog shit, but if you're brave enough, or stupid enough to continue on, it draws you in by showing you whatever surroundings you find to be the most attractive." It wasn't the most innovative spell Samuel had ever seen, but it was one of the strongest.

"Diabolical." Percival said vacantly. As they got to the end of the lane and rounded the corner of the building, they could see hundreds of small glints of light flitting about like shards of glass in the air. The butterflies that live within Alice's back garden appeared as they actually are to Percival and Samuel. That is, fractured Eth from the souls she had destroyed over the years. It was worse than murder, for these souls can never be returned. Dis-incorporating mortals violated many rules of existence. Such a thing would upset the highest of chthonic princes, for it prevented them from collecting Eth.

Percival had a tapestry of emotions flood into him all at once. He experienced the moment of their mortal deaths, as well as the moment of their spiritual dis-incorporation. Sorrow and compassion ached throughout his celestial body, flooding into the depths of his own ichor and expanded out through his own flow of Eth. Confusion overcame him. He didn't know what to do. He wanted to gather them up and somehow reconstruct them back into the normal flows of Eth. But they were permanently separated from all of existence. He could see them, but it was impossible to communicate with them. They were torn from the fabric of existence. Percival grabbed Samuel's shoulder, and Samuel's attention immediately shifted to what Percival was looking at.

Samuel immediately received the same flood of emotions that Percival was having. After a moment of being stunned, they reflected on the purpose of it all. Connection. Knowing that the fractions of Eth flitting about the garden, and the souls that originally contained them, would never be returned to the flow of existence. It put everything into perspective for Samuel and Percival.

"We can't help them, but knowing this, we can prevent it from happening again," Samuel said in hopes of reassuring Percival. Samuel had seen this only a few times before. It galled him that he felt so helpless when his duty was to protect souls.

Percival felt angry for the first time. "Tell me, as we stand here, as this horrible entity watches us from inside her house, are we being stupid or brave?"

Samuel nodded his head. "Probably a little of both," he said staring at all the fractured Eth. "Let's do this."

They teleport to her front door and knock. As they do, the water around the island begins stirring into waves several feet high.

"What do you want, I'm too busy for visitors," she boomed as she opened the door.

Samuel glanced at Percival to take over.

"Such a lovely garden you have. Is that Camellia? They bloom for such a short period." Percival loved flowers.

Alice looked at Percival suspiciously. There was only one way Percival could see past the spell that prevented everyone from seeing her true home. The camellia beside the doorstep could only be seen by her and other immortals. Luckily, this celestial was naïve enough to give up his own game. Though Samuel and Percival didn't know it, she could now see past their disguises and see that they were celestials. Of course, she could have guessed. Celestials appear either through polite inquiry or by announcing powerful commands. Alternatively, chthonics simply barrel their way into her day, disrupting every inch of eth along the way. She had hoped, given her dealings with him in the past, that Samuel had been cast out of the choirs. It was obvious that he hadn't been, so she could not harm him in the way she would like.

As they stood at her doorway, Alice could feel a draw on her power. Eth moves from dark to light, but since she was neither, and was instead a portal for Eth, anything dark nearby was gently passing through her and heading to them – drawing a bit of Eth from her as it passed through. The draw of her energy irritating her. She tries the slam the door in their face but she couldn't move it more than an inch.

"We are just meeting up with all the residents in the area. There was a heck of a storm last night and wanted to make sure you are alright, way out here on your own."

She realized they would not give up the game and leave. "You know your flowers. Shame that my camelia hasn't bloomed yet," she said.

"What do you mean?" Percival said, looking directly at the fully blooming flower.

Samuel didn't understand what Percival was seeing, and just before he could reach out to stop him, Percival touched the flower. As soon as he did, the spell that Miss Grey had cast completely exposed them both and forced them to appear in full celestial form.

Samuel stood tall before Alice, with an aura of serene authority. She knew it could turn to a rage of violence at nay moment – she could feel his desire to do her harm. His wings were vast, extending gracefully from his shoulders and shimmering with a soft, ethereal glow. Each feather catches the daylight differently, creating a subtle rainbow effect that dances with his slightest movement. Percival appeared as a softer, more nurturing presence. His wings, though equally impressive, were slightly smaller, adorned with feathers that were translucent, catching and reflecting the light in a delicate, magical manner and cast an ice blue hue around him.

She sees this as nothing more than what they both are, the essence of Eth. "I've had too many visitors already this week. I thought I told you never to come back, Samuel," Alice demanded.

Samuel hadn't prepared Percival for all the tricks they could encounter with Miss Grey. In their distress at seeing so much fragmented Eth from the different lost souls, Samuel hadn't thought that Alice may have laid a protection spell in addition to the ward. She had set up a type of protection spell that revealed all who came to her door. Any unexpected visitors who could see her garden in bloom were there to intend her harm. If they couldn't see the garden, anyone well intentioned was usually frightened away by the state of the garden's circumstances. Of course, if they were welcome, she laid out a scene so enticing they felt safe enough to continue to the door.

"Why don't you invite us in?" Percival gestured. He had the power to compel without speech. While all angels can compel a demon, Percival could compel anything through his will.

The woman walked into the house, throwing an arm out in an awkward wave, recommending that they follow her. "You can sit down if you want," she said, sitting in her favourite chair. She looked Samuel over, determining what she was going to do with him. Unsure of her abilities, she questioned if she could cast a spell over a celestial to change their existence. She didn't have the power to compel them like she did chthonics, but there was no harm in trying.

They stayed standing, and Samuel looked around the room. He was feeling a block over some of his powers, but he didn't know why. He wondered if Percival had noticed the same within himself.

"You had a visitor yesterday, and it seems he's disappeared," Samuel said directly toward her.

"Yep," she says flatly. She knew there was little they could do about it. "He's passed on now."

"How can you be sure about that?" asked Percival.

Samuel realized Percival was under some sort of spell. She got up, walked to the kitchen, and brought back a tray of tea and cookies, plunking it down on her table with an awkward clatter.

"Oh yes, thank you." Percival grabbed a chocolate chip cookie and took a bite. "This is wonderful. You are going to have to give me this recipe."

Samuel realized it was worse than he thought. Percival shouldn't be able to taste anything, or feel or otherwise be able to have sensation from the surrounding environment. He was beginning to have mortal tendencies without even realizing it. Many of them were as much reflex as they are choice.

"The time has come. Us Endorian women have been fated to live in obscurity for centuries, ever since magic was forbidden in the time of Saul."

"What do you mean?" Percival inquired as he finished the biscuit. "What happens now?"

Samuel drew his sword and thrust her against the wall. He places the blade at the base of her neck. Time stopped, the world turned gray, and what natural shadows that were present in the room before, suddenly turned to small creatures that slowly crept out and surrounded the three of them. They waited for a command from Alice, revelling in the violence to come.

"You would destroy the portal of mortality," her voice thunders throughout the room without actually speaking. "Please do, release me."

Samuel looked down at Percival, who was now frozen in time.

"He is now as much mortal as he is celestial."

Samuel looked at Percival. He pounded the woman's head against the wall and then releases his grip, allowing her to drop to the floor. She stood up immediately and blue flames shot out of her eyes, engulfing the room and setting it on fire. The shadow animals turn the wraiths, lunging through the air directly at Samuel.

Samuel fights them off, and as he does, each disappears into a plume of smoke.

As the fire rages across the room, suddenly Ganislay falls out of the flames and tumbles across the floor, destroying all the furniture in his body's path. He immediately flings out his long tail, propelling Percival into the far wall and wrapping the end of his tail around Samuel's neck several times like the end of a whip. Ganislays tail thrusts Samuel into the ground several times like a chimpanzee pummeling a rag doll.

Alice's voice thunders again. "The prophecy is fulfilled, the bridge between two worlds has been created. The time of the seen and unseen has begun." Alice scurries across the room out of the way as she watches Ganislay pound Samuel on the floor several more times. She stands to her feet and stares at them. Celestials and chthonics were now fighting in the open on the mortal plane.

Percival tries to gain his faculties from being hit by Ganislay. Percival looked at a metal object in Alice's hand. It was a large disk, a type of talisman. He couldn't believe what he was seeing. In an instant, he shook off the spell that had entranced him. He struggled to comprehend what he was seeing. He thought it was a myth of the mortals.

The fire now had engulfed the entirety of the room, and began to eat through the ceiling to the second floor. As Ganislay has successfully defended Alice from the celestials, the fire begins beckoning Ganislay, and a great pressure forms as a portal to Dudael opens to pull him back to realm Alice intends him to be in. Ganislay tries to resist, but is sucked through the flames back through the portal. Samuel and Percival begin to be pulled in as well. They turn into rotating blades of light and speed away from the trap. They drift up through the ceiling and hover over the house, watching the destruction unfold. The entire house explodes, quickly parting the trees on the small island as the gas services ignite. An orb of light zips between Samuel and Percival and zips to the horizon faster than they can realize it.

The blades of light drift back down to earth and begin speaking to one another. "Do you know what that was?" Samuel asks as he morphs back into his celestial form. They settle on the dock light as feathers. Percival's orb morphs back into his celestial body as well.

"That was the Talisman of Endor," Percival responded with wonder. "It gives the holder the power to not just commune with the living and the dead, but to summon and command them at will, as well as immortals." He peered off the edge of the dock to see his reflection in the water's surface. He noticed he could not see Samuels. "I thought it was just a story, but I guess not."

Samuel wondered what he was looking at and then noticed Percivals reflection. He somehow had turned mortal. "There is way more to this than you and I have been led to believe." Samuel begins walking off the dock toward the burning house.

"Where are you going," Percival called after him.

"Where do you think?" Samuel asked rhetorically, walking through some flames toward the main road. "To the hidden kingdom. Her next move is to kill judgement."

Percival follows him as fast as he can. However, he notices that he now has to avoid the clumps of flames on the ground. The proximity to the heat was hurting his skin. As soon as he clears most of the flaming obstacles, he catches up to Samuel. "We can't do that, celestials are forbidden from the Etheric plane without specific orders."

Samuel bounces his head in agreement. "Yep, but this is why they gave you that 'get out of jail free' card. Isn't it?" Samuel stopped and levied a challenging stare. "I don't see any other way."

Percival didn't know how Samuel knew about that. "This is suicide. This assignment is only just beginning and so far we've battled an Endorian witch, come in contact with the keys to Kingdom of Heaven, and flirted with the eternal prison for immortals. This is either the bravest assignment ever bestowed upon celestials, or the most insane! I can't decide."

Samuel stopped and looked at Percival. "In my experience, the bravery and insanity are well connected. C'mon, let's go."

As they walked down the path away from Old Widow Grey's burning cottage, Samuel waved his arm, and a rush of sound filled the air. In an instant they teleported, this time to the middle of Trafalgar Square.

CHAPTER SEVEN

Ganislay suddenly appeared on the edge of a cliff back in Dudael. Before he could get his bearings, he began tumbling down the rocky edge. He slows himself down and grabs a steady piece of rock by chance, more out of accident than skill. As he layed on the steep slope, he looked beneath. The hoards of angels and chthonics battling one another was far below.

The first time he was here, he realized that there was no winning this war. Every time he slayed a chthonic that was attacking him, and the lucky few blows he got in on a celestial, they would only be maimed or stunned for a few minutes. After spending his life in hell, Ganislay realized that this place was a hell of its own. Its inhabitants were destined to fight each other for eternity without realizing the length of time they had been here.

Ganislay claws his way to the top of the cliff side again. He gasped for breath and dragged himself onto the level ground. He could rest for the moment as he could hear the roar of the fighting down below. It wasn't getting closer, and as long as it remained at a distance below him, he was safe. Being pulled from one realm to the next exhausted him like never before. He was sure he had spent some Eth, or at least someone had stolen it from him as penance. He wasn't fully sure how portals worked. In Ganislay's experience, that's what hell is - being a slave to another's bidding with no chance for rest or comfort. He became accustomed to being used as a weapon. If he didn't fight or exert his will on another, he would become a slave to another entity who would.

When he was summoned from hell by Alice, he thought he found a way out. Instead, he became a slave to two masters, Alice and the Prince of Darkness. However, there was no advantage to fighting here. For him, Dudael was quickly becoming a safe little cove on the side of a roaring river. For the first time in his existence, fighting didn't advance his status. It was a kind of peace he had never known. Pain was still pain. Eons in hell taught him how to function through that. This was still pain, and the pressure of being trapped and possibly snuffed out at any moment carried it's own burden, but was nothing new.

He spotted a cave which had a light streaming from it. Whatever it was, he could easily snuff it out in order to use the cave as additional cover. If this battle was going to last millennia, he was going to need some cover. What seemed strange to him was the fight was only down in the valley. Although celestials can fly, and his chthonic clan were strong enough to claw and pull their way up the craggy cliff side, none attempted. He stayed on edge, there had to be a dangerous reason that he was the only soul up here.

Ganislay struggled to get to his feet. Once he did, he stumbled into each step. The fight he just had back at the Portals home thrashed his body. Getting a beat-down from a Celestial creature whose sole purpose is to destroy your very existence is never a healthy endeavor – even when you do win. He stumbled again, kicking a loose rock off the side of a cliff... and it fell. He didn't realize at first, and then he stopped after his next step.

"That's why they are fighting," he said, looking back at the rock as it slowly drifted lower and lower down the cliff. Not much falls in hell, even those who feel like they are falling when they arrive in hell are actually being attracted to the fall either by their own doing or they are being compelled to fall through the will of another. Things don't fall due to physical force. The rock has no Eth. It could not have done anything wrong–so it could not be compelled to fall, yet it was. It meant there is gravity here, space-time, which meant they were on the edge of mortal existence.

Ganislay fell to the ground out of relief. He watched the beauty of gravity. It was less than the pull of gravity he had felt on Earth. As it approached the hoard of battle it stopped. It no longer fell, and instead remained floating above the heaving battle. The fighting was fierce and chaotic, nobody noticed. Ganislay looked up and gazed across the expanse of the valley. If there was gravity, it means there is the passage of time. In Hell, there is very little passage of time, which is one of the reasons it is very difficult for things to change. One day in hell feels like an entire millennium to a soul. Time is the real gift that souls receive, for it allows them to change things. The souls who don't believe circumstances can change have fallen into chthonic traps, so that their Eth may be collected. Ganislay had set more than his fair share of eth traps in his day, both on earth and in the underworld.

He craved rest for the first time in his existence. Chthonics aren't born, they are created and forced to do one thing – deliver vengeance. Now that he was within the field of space-time but not under some-ones direct command, those years of delivering vengeance were catching up to him.

As he entered the cave, the light shining out of it began to dim. He walked around a sharp bend of rock and stopped when he saw a purple fire smouldering in the center. Fire in Hell burned because it fed off the will of a soul, not chemistry. Ganislay noticed that this purple fire burned like a mortal fire, there was a fuel that was not based on Eth.

For the size of the fire, it did not put out as much heat, but it was out of the driving dust and winds of the canyon and valley below. Ganislay was ignoring the obvious. Opposite him, leaning against the wall, was a cloaked figure whose face was obscured by a large hood. Ganislay could not see a figure because of the light shining from beneath the robe, which was just as bright as the fire. The only thing he could make out as the light shimmered, appeared to look like glistening diamonds or quartz. Strange creatures did not bother him, for the mortal realm was as wide and deep as the spiritual. However, without more knowledge of what this creature was, Ganislay wasn't about to attack it.

He stared into the fire. Even the fires of hell were mesmerizing to him. If he had any kind of consciousness, he might have felt nostalgic. Instead, he just enjoyed the roar of the wind outside the cave and the peace he was finally experiencing inside.

"Where did you come from?" the cloaked creature asked. The deep voice bounced off the cave walls and sounded like several voices garbled together.

"From out there," Ganislay slyly gestured toward the outside. He wasn't going to give this creature anything for free. "You have nothing to fear from me."

The creature appeared to be staring at the purple fire, just the same as Ganislay. The flames would raise and lower, as if it were getting more fuel from something, but there were no logs, nothing it was feeding upon. Ganislay was beginning to feel strangely better. He didn't have the constant pit of hunger and anger in his stomach, the longing for Eth that drove him to insanity. He wondered where that constant companion had gone, for it was such a part of him. However, its absence caused him to fall asleep for the first time in his existence.

Moments later, the creature was on top of Ganislay, shoving him to wake him up. "C'mon you damn fool!"

Ganislay jumped to his feet, grabbing the creature by one of its shoulders and pinning it to the wall.

"You've been asleep for days. Something is wrong outside," the creature said in a stressed voice. The light from the beneath the cloak was still too much for Ganislay to handle and he dropped it to the ground, trying to focus his eyes.

"Apologies for startling you," the creature said.

The words had no impact. He had never had an apology directed to him before in any kind of honesty. Apologies were always used as a tactic for manipulation. He was sure this was no different. "What is diff..." Ganislay trailed off and then turned his head as he realized he couldn't hear the roar of the battle.

He ran to the entrance of the cave and carefully looked out. He crouched down very low, getting on all fours. He was just as powerful on his arms and legs as he was walking upright, but he could run much faster. He peered around the corner to see if anyone was close by. There was nothing on the plateau, just as he had left it. He stepped out on the plateau, still keeping himself low so that nobody could see, and looked the several hundred feet down upon the valley. The battle had stopped. Celestials and chthonics had separated themselves. The celestials entrenched themselves at one end of the canyon, clustered in their choirs, while his clan huddled at the other end. In between were several battle-torn warriors from either side. They each were heavily wounded, and it would be a mercy if someone were to disincorporate them. Though there was no advantage for either side to do so. So there they remained.

Ganislay crawled back into the cave and stood up. "How long have they been fighting?" he asked, sitting back down near the purple fire.

"For as long as I can remember."

"And how long is that?"

The creature stared at the fire for a few moments, and then up at Ganislay. "I lost count after a while. It seems time doesn't exist here. Every day and night since I got here, listening to the wretched screams and cries that pierce through the roar of the battle."

Ganislay knew the creature wasn't a chthonic, for such a thing would not bother a chthonic. It wasn't any type of celestial that he had ever seen, which in Dudael left an Etheric, possibly even one of the Everlasting. He needed a lot more information before he could decide how to use this creature.

"It has never stopped until you showed up a few days ago."

Ganislay grunted. He could only imagine a battle finishing because either he finished it, or it finished him. "We'll see about that."

The two stayed up late into the night watching the fire. There was no hunger, no food to eat, nothing to busy them, or distract them. It was a prison in its own right. Ganislay watched the creature through the flames, and as soon as it solidly drifted off for the night, and then he made his move.

He sat on his haunches like a dog, and sniffed the air, getting closer to the fire. He was not afraid of fire, his ichor was forged from it. This made him wonder further if the creature was some sort of celestial. He stuck his nose close enough to the flames that they were lapping against the edge of his face. The heat did not intensify the closer he got to the flames. He took his giant clawed hand and put it into the flames. It didn't affect him. He still could not understand what fuelled the fire, so he reached further down into the fire, to the white hot purple center, but felt nothing. There was no floor. It was a bottomless pit.

He grunted and sniffed with enthusiasm, much like a gorilla. He then realized he may have been a bit too loud and awoken the creature.

It moved a bit, and Ganislay made a short hop back to the wall where he was originally sitting. The creature's sleep was only slightly disturbed. It shifted position, found a comfortable position and drifted off again. Ganislay waited another good few minutes, making sure it was well asleep again. Once he was sure, he crawled back to the edge of the fire, and this time stuffed his face into the base of it.

His head popped up through the base of another fire, inside the fireplace of a small cottage. From the base of the fireplace, he could see an older creature creating a meal in a small kitchen several feet away. It was a modest cottage, with a small living space, and a kitchen. It was not a palace, certainly not anywhere in Hell. The atmosphere seemed calm – and a light streamed in through the windows, the same purple hue as the fire, which meant it certainly wasn't the place of the mortals. The creature in the kitchen turned slightly as it worked. It was some sort of etheric. Ganislay's eyes widened, and he pulled his head out of the fire. He was back in the cave, the other creature still sound asleep. Why hadn't the sleeping creature ever bothered to check the fire? Ganislay looked at it, such a strange thing to trap one's self in a circumstance for eons. It was definitely something the mortals often do to themselves. But this was not like any mortal he had ever seen.

Ganislay reckoned the place on the other side of the fire was the land of the Etherics. Every creature comes from somewhere, but few had ever seen the world of the Etherics. Most entities had never seen any of the other realms until they are summoned to do so. To do so, mortals of all types would need technology, Celestials had the power of consciousness, and chthonics, the technology of fire and collections of Eth to score a ride. Nobody really knew how Etherics serve the mortal coil or how they even get there to do it. But somehow, this Etheric had created a permanent portal into Dudael. Why, he wondered. It would have to be a puzzle he figured out later, because the next thing he needed to find out was why the battle had stopped.

He needed to be fast. He hated going fast in gravity; it tired him out, unlike in the underworld. But he felt incensed and better after his slumber. He crouched to his feet again and ran out of the cave, keeping close to the ground. As he ran across the plateau, he felt a kind of freedom he had never had. He had wind in face, much like the mortal worlds, and the bright light of three moons to show him the way. They were each different colors, a pale blue, violet, and a dusty red. It no longer felt like a prison to him. Maybe it was for others, but not for him, and probably not for his clan.

He crawled downs the cracks and spines of rock columns that made the canyon. It was going to be an exhausting mission to get back up. As he made his way down, he placed himself around the last outcropping of rock that separated him from the edge of his clan. He waited to build up his energy and watched.

It was different down here. Within moments, he realized that he wasn't tired, and that gravity didn't exist any longer. Time stopped down here. It must be an endless night, he imagined. The three moons would never set for those at the bottom of the canyon.

He walked up to one of the first chthonics he encountered and nudged them. "Why have you stopped fighting? We can surprise the enemy," he said, pushing them with his foot.

"We've only just stopped moments ago. We've been fighting all day," the chthonic replied.

Ganislay grunted and sniffed. This was different than what the creature told him at the top of the Canyon. This one must be crazy. He walked along deeper into the crowd and nudged another chthonic. "You, let's go surprise the enemy and grab a celestial for ourselves."

The chthonic burst from its sleep and stood up, being about twice as tall as Ganislay. "If you have the will and the might," it shoved Ganislay into a nearby rock wall without even trying, "Then you do it yourself. The rest of us will fight again tomorrow."

Ganislay made his way out of the crowd, and back to where he first came down the canyon wall. None of this made sense. They were doomed to stay in the same moment, only this time, that moment was an eternal slumber instead of fighting.

By the time Ganislay reached the plateau again, it was an equivalent of several hours. The higher he climbed, the more gravity tried to pull him to the valley below. At the top of the canyon, the sun was rising, the two suns were beaming new daylight across the plateau. He still was not used to sunlight. As and he looked down below he could see that it was still firmly night time. The canyon walls created such a shadow that no sunlight was able to penetrate. There was still no fighting, nothing to be heard.

Ganislay walked back into the cave and the creature hadn't moved much, simply shifting position in its sleep. He sits back against the wall, still wondering about the circumstances at the base of the valley. Ganislay began to drift away before his curiosity caught him again. Why hadn't the creature tried to leave through the fire? It can't be chthonic, a chthonic wouldn't be afraid. Ganislay was tired of being a slave to other creatures' whims, even sticking to something else's timetable. Now that he was away from the reaches of Princes of Hell – planning the siege of Heaven was going to have to wait. This creature, whatever it is, wasn't going to stand in his way. He got up and walked over to the creature, and grabbed it.

"Wake up," he said, throwing it across the fire and onto the ground.

"What is wrong with you?" the creature yelled, startled.

"Why haven't you left here? Why do you stay in this cave?"

"Leave... how can we leave? It's impossible."

Ganislay snorted. He thought he smelled a lie. It incensed him, like a shark smelling blood. He ran over and picked the creature up. As he carried it toward the cave entrance, he got a transfer of energy; he saw the creatures past. An image of a human boy in a room late at night approaching an older man at a desk, then suddenly the middle-aged man picks up the boy and tosses him toward a wall.

The creature began to throw punches into Ganislay's chest, doing the best it could from its awkward position. The creature may as well be a baby trying to fend off a wolf. Ganislay liked it. He liked the position of authority, and being much bigger than the creature. Being down in the valley the evening before made him realize home much power he really had. He had never seen power stripped away from a celestial or chthonic before. They looked like puppets down there. He dragged the creature out onto the plateau and held it out over the edge.

"What did I do? What do you want?" The flow of energy came from the creature as it flailed in the empty space.

Ganislay was unsure if he could kill it. He stood staring at the bright light reflecting out from the tattered clothing. He could see in the light of the morning that it was wearing the cloak of a celestial. But it was unlike any celestial he had ever seen. The tattered emerald cloak had a relief pattern in an offset green that Ganislay hadn't noticed before. Now, in the light of day, he could see everything. He also noticed that the symbols on the cloak were slowly moving.

"Who are you?" Ganislay asked. He noticed that either his arm was getting tired, or that the creature was somehow getting heavier.

All the symbols on the cloak moved to the creature's sleeves and as the creature tried to grab Ganislay's arm this time, Ganislay was hit by a powerful force of pressure. In his shock, he released the creature as he was shoved back to the ground.

The creature flailed about as it floated in the air off the edge of the plateau.

Ganislay laughed. He thought it was possibly human, but they can't fly, not even here. It wasn't quite a celestial... it was far too small. He stood back up and walked back over, grabbing it and throwing it against the canyon wall that rose above the plateau. "What the fuck are you?" He picked the creature back up and ripped the cloak off. A light shined so brightly it made the morning light of the suns seem dim. Ganislay had to shield his face. The light hurt everything inside him.

The creature stood back up, dusting itself off and nursing its arm. It was bipedal, but that is all Ganislay could tell through the brightness of the light. It looked like it was constructed of millions of shimmering diamonds.

In the valley below, it was suddenly daylight and screams began drifting up. The hoard of chthonics raced toward the base of the canyon beneath the plateau, trying to hack their way through the celestials as they went. Ganislay peered off the side of the cliff to the battle below. He forgot how fierce these battles could get. He was glad that he wasn't stuck in the moment of time down below, being consumed by one thought.

"Give it here..." Ganislay was suddenly tackled from behind by a chthonic. An axe handle was choking him out as he was being dragged to the cliff side. Ganislay went limp so all his weight would pull the other chthonic down with him. He didn't wait to grab the axe and instead plunged his teeth as deep as he could into the side of the chthonics neck and pulled. The chthonic gave out a gurgled screech.

Ganislay got on top of the chthonic, pinning it to the ground. "What are you after, and maybe I will let you live." He placed his clawed hand over the wound on the chthonics neck. The pressure gave the chthonic a slightly better chance at talking – but Ganislay knew it was either going to drown in its own blood if he kept the pressure on, or it was going to bleed out if he let go.

"The light," it said, reaching for the creature beside Ganislay. "Kill the light and we win. The realm is ours." Even dying, its last gestures were to complete the task of its desires. Chthonics were so materialistic they never even realize that it causes their downfall.

Ganislay snapped a look over at the creature. It began backing away and putting its cloak back on. Ganislay looked back at the chthonic and let go of the wound. "No, the realm is mine." He stood up and kicked the chthonic off the side of the cliff. It began to fall slowly in the slightness of the gravity. He ran back to the creature and grabbed it again before it could put the robe on.

The second he grabbed it, he felt a charge like never before. It was stronger than when he was reigning in hell.

The battle raged below. Mako, who was about to get hit by a chthonic wielding a large mace, was saved by the falling chthonic crushing his assailant. He was knocked to the ground by the force of the body exploding beneath the falling chthonic. A loud roar came through the crowd that stopped both celestial and chthonic alike. Mako looked up at the top of the canyon to see a figure holding out a beam of light.

Ganislay stood at the edge of the cliff, holding out the creature like a trophy he had won. He roared again, this time to make sure it was really him doing it. Instead of his normal snorted growl, it had the added timbre like that of several trumpets. It shot across the valley, rumbling everything in its path.

The fighting stopped. It became clear to Ganislay then that the celestials were preventing the chthonic hoard from advancing up the canyon wall, rather than simply fighting for the overall cause. Every celestial took flight above the hoard, for there was nothing left to defend on the ground.

It was only moments before the first of the celestials was upon him. The first one swooped down and landed right in front of him, immediately throwing a punch. Ganislay roared out of reflex, only this time the pressure blasted the Celestial off of the cliff side. Ganislay began running for the cave. A loud hum, equal to the level of his roar, began to form. The celestials in their thousands formed a circle far above him. They were singing, and the longer they did, the louder the vibration became. The entire canyon began to vibrate and the cliff sides began to crumble.

Ganislay swiped away at each of the celestials as they swooped down upon him. He barely made it into the cave, never letting go of the glowing creature – sometimes even using it as a weapon to bludgeon the celestials away. Ganislay stood at the cave entrance, defending himself from the multiple choirs outside. It was the singing. It pierced his ears and rang throughout his mind. He felt like he was about to have a stroke. He roared again, this time as a reflex of frustration. It did no good. The sound from the choirs was far too much.

The cave walls groaned from the power of the sonic waves. Ganislay couldn't bear to even look the celestials in the face, they horrified him. Most chthonics are formed in the image of fallen mortals. They have a familiar form, even when it is grotesque. Celestials however, were often made of heinous things, sometimes resembling humans... sometimes looking like objects one could never conceive of. He couldn't imagine why the mortals prayed to them for assistance. He grabbed one that looked like a whirring mass of concentric circles with wings and used it as a weapon to crush a much larger celestial. He knew this method wouldn't work for long.

Ganislay remembered the fire. He breathed in and let out the largest roar he ever thought he could muster. It sounded like the cross between a hundred bulls and angry dinosaurs. The smaller celestials simply melted into liquid, showering those around them. There was stunned silence among all of them. It weakened Ganislay, and each celestial felt a mixture of pain and fear that they didn't know this was possible. They backed away for a moment.

Ganislay took this as his chance.

"What are you doing?" Ganislay could hear the creature in his hands through the rumbling and groans of the cave and mountain above them.

"Saving our skins," he said, running as fast as he could toward the fire. He dove straight toward it head first, like a swan dive. They burst out through the bottom of the fireplace inside the small cottage and onto the living room floor.

Ganislay lay across the entirety of the living room floor, smouldering from the heat of the transition between dimensions. One of his legs lay draped over a strange-looking chair. It groaned from the weight of his leg and then crumbled to pieces. As he twisted his body to gain some sort of leverage to stand up, he locked eyes with a large etheric sitting on a settee. He froze.

The etheric, stared down at him, trying to hold back his shock as he took another sip from a mug it was holding. He had only seen a few chthonics in his existence, but never a human. He knew this had to be a sign that the veil between the four realms was beginning to crumble.

CHAPTER EIGHT

The eth portal closed behind Samuel and Percival after they walk through it, sending another ripple of eth throughout the center of London.

"Why did you do that?" Percival asked in amazement.

"You didn't expect us to take the time to travel here, did you?" Samuel was becoming irritated with Percival's by-the-book approach.

"But everyone will know we're here because of the size of the eth wave you just made."

"It's a perk I've accumulated over the years of working this job." They walked up the steps to the National Gallery and into the main hall. "You've been used to things pretty much from the standpoint of the Central Existence, you're too sentimental toward mortals. There are many tricks here in the field."

Percival saw a woman standing at the entrance of the museum dealing with her young toddler. The woman tried to bundle her daughter in a coat as she was midway through a tantrum. Percival quickened his pace and simply stood next to the woman and child, and smiled. He glowed a little more, forcing his eth out like a haze the surrounded everyone close by. This allowed his energy to imbue upon the mother and her daughter. The young girl stopped crying as its attention changed to an street performer was was walking up the steps, carrying a large bundle of balloons.

"See what I mean?" Samuel smirked as he caught up with Percival.

"I suppose I am a creature of habit," Percival agreed.

"They're not even sure we exist," Samuel said, as he watched all the people in the middle of the square. "Some don't care, others think we're the fairy tale section of the Bible, and then the misguided who think we're cute little babies with wings – they're the most troubled ones. I often want to slap them around just as much as I want to protect them. I think mortals, especially humans, are more committed to their own misery that the underworld is."

Percival, "Okay, I get it you grump. But life on earth is one of the toughest lessons ever created by Central Existence. Mortals are the few who can transmute ideas into material existence. We're not them, so let's not say something we might regret."

Samuel motions for Percival to follow. They walk into the building and Samuel leads them to the busy cafe in the museum. Samuel grabbed a spot at one of the tables that a couple just vacated moments prior. A miracle of its own for the amount of people visiting. Samuel waves his hand, and a server happens by and clears the table without a word. Samuel peers over at Percival with pride.

"Yes, you influenced one of the staff to come and clear the table. It's the same thing we do up there every day," Percival said to refute Samuel's pride.

"Correct, but what you don't see is the entire team working behind the scenes to ensure what we would like to happen does actually happen. It's like a watch with many gears. You might wind it up, but it goes through several gears before your work hits the spring. Watch that table." Percival noticed the several tables of spent crockery waiting to be dealt with. He looked at the table that Samuel was pointing at and it was like a veil melted away, revealing another layer of the world.

Suddenly, the population of the room quadrupled. There were small creatures everywhere. Some were sitting on tables, some small enough to be sitting on mortals shoulders. A pair of the strange creatures scurried on top of a person's hand as they picked up a biscuit and fought one another for it – only for the biscuit to fall onto the floor before the small creatures chased after it. Samuel waved his hand and Percival watched as a wave of eth, like a wave of pressure, roll from Samuels hand across the room. The wave scooped up the creatures that weren't enthralled with what they were doing and carried them out of the room. All the while, the creatures were hooting and hollering like they were surfing a wave at the beach.

Moments later a server walked into room, surrounded by all the creatures that rode the wave Samuel had created. They were nipping at his heels, guiding him in, making a B-line directly toward the table Samuel pointed at. The server took the crockery off the table, wiped it down, and left the room. Not attending to any other table in the room.

"Wow... I never knew."

"You wouldn't. It's not a part of your role. No different from a human, it's not part of their role to know about us. As long as everyone plays their part, it doesn't really matter."

Suddenly a large etheric, different from all the rest, who looked like a cross between a dog and a six-legged gazelle, walked in and shouted something in Etheric. The smaller etherics stopped what they were doing and the volume of the conversation in the cafe that the mortals were having fell to a hush. Each creature jumped off of what they were doing and formed an orderly queue passing by the feet of Samuel and Percival.

"What's this," Percival asked.

"They've reached the end of their shift. etherics are only allowed to attend to mortal matters for twenty minutes. They are governed by the planetary hours and the Regents. They are simply moving on to another group of mortals, that way they don't become too attached to any one mortal. It creates this strange by-product, where the mortals usually fall to a hushed tones during these times since there is less of a flow of eth."

In a sign of respect, each etheric, young, old, of every race, gave the two celestials a nod or a small cheer as they walked by and out of the room.

For a moment, everything was silent. Percival enjoyed it.

"This is my favorite part," Samuel gestured for Percival to look toward the kitchen.

The other room echoed with a small battle cry, and hundreds of small etherics charged into the room like a pile of lemmings. Suddenly, a restaurant patron dropped a cup of coffee as one etheric swung from the lip of the ceramic cup. The volume of the cafe returned to a loud level as the etherics brought a new wave of energy in.

"And on it goes my friend," Samuel said as he looked around at the mayhem.

Percival had never seen Samuel pleased before. He had heard of the etheric dimension. Before entering the realm, authorities heavily police and vet celestial and chthonic. It was part of the agreement at the dawn of time. If etherics had to tend to the whims of the heavens at all times, then the heavens were not to interfere. It was part of the rights created by the responsibilities given to them. So Percival assumed they had permission to be there.

"So how do we find Judgement," Percival asked through the clammer of etheric noise and mortal conversations.

Samuel gestured for Percival to keep quiet. "Not here," he said as he leaned toward Percival. "There are eyes and ears everywhere," Samuel said as he brushed an etheric away that was trying to listen in. Samuel stood up and gestured for Percival to follow him. They walked over to one of the taller etherics, who was standing next to a table and eyeing a pastry sitting on someone's plate. As the restaurant patron lowered her hand to pick up the pastry, the etheric opened its mouth, hoping she would drop it.

Samuel nudged it, and it bickered back at him without looking. Samuel nudged it again with his foot, and then spoke to him in perfect etheric.

Percival shot a look at him. Speaking etheric was forbidden.

The etheric looked at Samuel, irritated. Even upon recognizing that Samuel was a celestial, the etheric did not seem impressed. An etheric of this ranking might come in contact with a celestial or chthonic possibly once in its lifetime, if the conditions were right. Such an occasion had altered many of an etherics' life trajectory in the past. However, this fellow was far too enthralled with the pastries that surrounded it and did not appreciate the interruption.

"How do you speak the language," the etheric asked Samuel without looking at him.

"I have worked within the realm many times. It would be rude not to learn. If above is to be below, etherics ensure the flow."

"Hurrah," all the etherics in the room shouted.

The etheric looked Samuel up and down. Not sure what he thought about Samuel uttering the etheric motto. "What do you want?"

"I need passage to an Elder."

"Oh," he chuckled. He turned back to the table just in time for one patron to drop half of her cinnamon roll onto the floor. The etheric jumped to the floor and gobbled it up.

The woman who dropped the pastry bent down to pick up her mess. "Where did it go?" She looked around under her chair and glanced around the table. "It must have rolled away." Etherics excel at making things disappear the moment they are dropped. Thoroughly satisfied, the etheric plopped to the ground right at Samuel's feet and began licking its hands clean of any icing he could find.

Samuel picked this spot because he knew it wasn't far from an elder. It wouldn't be much of a passage, but they still needed permission, otherwise he would cause a war. "What if I could give you three pastries... all to yourself?"

The etheric grunted with interest and looked up at Samuel. "Hmm," it grinned. He got to his feet and walked away.

"Five... and I want you to take me to see Alndvod."

The etheric turned to him, giving him a grumpy look. It was rare for a celestial to know the name of an Elder. Despite them working more closely with the choirs than the rest of the etherics. The pastry-loving etheric now knew this was no ordinary celestial he was dealing with. "Ten," he demanded, glaring back at Samuel.

Samuel scowled. Making it look like coming up with ten pastries was the most difficult thing in the world for him. What is precious to one might be mundane to another – it wasn't for him to judge. "My friend comes with us and you got a deal."

The etheric pulled out a small notepad and began scribbling a sigil on the top piece of paper. He ripped the page off and threw it at them. As it flew through the air, the paper turned into a ball of energy and expanded as a large net, wrapping itself around Samuel and Percival. As soon as it did, the etheric turned and trew a wave for them to follow.

As they left the building, Percival looked around at a very transformed Trafalgar square. Etherics tended to pigeons, cab drivers, and dozens rode the jets of water in the fountain, besides tending to the mortals they were assigned to that hour. Percival had trouble stepping through the crowds of etherics, trying not to tread on one and killing it.

"Where are we going?"

"To see the elder of the North," Samuel shouted over the bustle of the streets.

"Why do we need to seek permission to do this, when we have already been granted special privileges?"

"Yes, but this is a different realm and a different council applies. If we had walked even twenty feet in their realm, every etheric you see would have attacked us. They have the power to dis-incorporate if enough of them gang up. And as you can see, there are about a billion of the damned things every five feet. Being here without permission violates the treaty."

"What treaty?" Percival asked, dodging a woman on the way to an interview. There were etherics all around her cheering her on. He was sure she was going to get the job.

"The Treaty of Councils... well, that's what we call it, or what the etherics call the Treaty of Elders."

"I've never heard of such a thing," Percival said with a hint of accusation.

"If you haven't noticed, etherics are a funny bunch. Pretty self absorbed. Back in the day, the chairperson tried to make the world run on time, first with the giants... we all know how that worked out. So after the flood, he created the Etherics, a million little workers behind the scenes. The role is quite mundane, so they spend most of their time trying to entertain themselves. After a while, the choirs noticed nothing got done. We were going to scrap the entire realm and try something different. That was until several etherics stepped forward and asked if they could promise to keep the trains running on time, so to speak. Could they please keep the job? The twenty-four elders were created throughout the world divided into four sections, thus became known to the mortals 'the four corners of the earth'. They think it is the direction of their star system, but it's more about the roles of each of the Watchtowers."

Percival had no idea what he was talking about. He had been to the Great Library many times to read up on the history and laws of celestial beings and their duties. He even went beyond his duties and read all the case studies on the mortals that he could.

"Yeah.. about that," Samuel said, reading Percival's mind. "You should have spent a bit more time in the mythology section. It really would have helped you out today." Samuel gestured for Percival to turn right at the next street. He knew exactly where the etheric was leading him.

They began walking down a lane full of expensive antique shops and art dealers until they came upon a rare book dealer.

The etheric looked up at Samuel. "This is as far as I can take you," he said. "What you want is inside. She knows you are coming."

Samuel opens the door to enter the bookshop.

"My payment, or you aren't getting much further."

Ten cinnamon buns materialize just above the etheric and the tumble down upon him, knocking him to the ground.

Percival looked at him, astounded. "Did you just use a miracle to create a load of pastries?"

"You could look at it that way, or you could say I performed a miracle to prevent the loss of all humanity."

"Well, when you put it that way–it sounds like a worthy gesture," Percival admitted. This mission was really beginning to challenge his viewpoint.

As they entered the bookstore, Percival felt a calm overcome him. Books were one of the things he loved most because they were neutral territory between all realms. However, what one realm wrote, another often mistranslated. He always thought it interesting that what celestials thought was a kindly gesture to humanity by providing literary workings, mankind was able to turn into a reason to fight over. Likewise, chthonics were free to write as many grimoires as they liked, although they weren't organized enough to do so. The etherics were welcome to write as well, they just didn't. Perhaps there was something to be learned from the tendency of the etherics to abstain from most of the cosmic order.

His thought about this abstention echoed in Percival's thoughts as he explored the stuffed bookshelves. He thought it curious that only mortals were present at the bookshop, but it was clear that none of them could see Percival. However, as he rounded a corner, he accidentally bumped into a chthonic. The chthonic hissed and immediately tried to throw a punch at Percival's face, but a force prevented its arm from gaining any momentum.

"There will be none of that here," a mortal said stepping in between the two of them. "It's nice to see chthonic and celestial standing side by side. Two ends of the same coin and you don't even realize it." Percival and the demon looked at each other and then at the thin man carrying books back to wherever he was going. "Yes, of course I can see you. One cannot work here unless they are attuned to the other side."

"You can see me," Percival said rushing past the chthonic over toward the bookstore clerk.

"Apparently so," the clerk said continuing to walk away.

Percival wasn't used to mortals looking at him with pity, but he realized the obvious answer to the question he just blurted out. He stepped in front of the man, blocking his path.

The bookstore clerk rolled his eyes in disgust. Percival was just another obstacle in his day. "I am the elders' assistant. I believe we have what you are looking for, if you follow me," the man slyly eyes Percival to follow him.

"Oh yes," he says, following the assistant. They leave the chthonic behind as it stands in frustration. It continually tries to figure out why it can't throw any punches as it attempts to practice on the bookshelf directly in front of it.

"They aren't the brightest lot," the clerk said glancing over at the chthonic. "I don't know why it keeps coming in here. Perhaps it's attracted to the energy, I guess." The assistant led Percival down some stairs to a room that proclaimed:

'Antiquarian Books and Items'.

"Upstairs is full of commercial items. Anything worth reading is down here. Plenty of mortal materials to choose from. I don't know why we are so fascinated by you. Mortals are always in such a big damn hurry to die. Your friend is over there," the clerk said pointing to Samuel, who had stuffed himself in the back corner of a long aisle. He was staring down, talking to a woman sitting in a chair in an office the size of a small ticket booth. She had a small roll-top desk and a small tiffany lamp lighting her work. "Ah Percival, come... come..." she gestured with excitement. "Don't mind the paperwork. Everyone thinks they want to be an Elder until they realize the amount of paperwork involved."

"Oh, I understand. It's the reason I don't want to go any higher in choirs," Percival said walking up to them.

"So this is the fellow who discovered it all," the Elder said, looking at Samuel.

"Yes. Percival," Samuel said, motioning toward the Elder. "This is Alndvod, Elder of the North, Keepers of things from East to West."

Percival nods. He felt as though all three of them were stuffed into the corner of the building. There were now two large celestials taking up the entire aisle of the bookstore. He couldn't stand up straight, he could barely turn around without knocking reams of books onto the floor and creating a colossal mess.

"I need you to tell her what you saw," Samuel impressed.

Percival looked at the Elder as best he could from the scrunched position he was in. She was giving off the appropriate energy to tell such a sensitive thing to. "As you probably felt," Percival began with hesitance, "there was an enormous wave of eth that disrupted every-thing several days ago. I found the source of the location, and it didn't come from a celestial or a chthonic. However, what happened, at the same time as the point of origin, a chthonic was summoned to the mortal plane and swapped with a soul. This soul was not replaced in the underworld, it simply disappeared."

"I got the key back, so I thought it was pretty much done."

Percival clears his throat audibly.

"OK, I got one of the keys back."

Percival glares at him.

"And Percival thinks we have a bigger problem."

"And he would be right. A chthonic with a key to heaven in it's possession," the Elder looked at Samuel like he had two heads. "On top of that, if you have a mortal soul in Dudael who hasn't passed judgement, the first entity to control the mortal has a way out, and all of its kind may follow - if the victor chooses. With the key to heaven, they can march straight on to the throne."

"So what do we do?"

It depends on what you want.

"Just the usual. Keep everything on track, according to plan."

"Are you talking about the ineffable plan or the celestial objective?"

"OK, I don't even think the creator knows what the plan is from day to day, more like the latter. "

"He can't say that, can he," the Alndvod said, looking at Percival.

Percival shook his head in staunch disapproval. "No, he really shouldn't."

"The smart one agrees with me," the Elder glared back at Samuel. "You can't say that," Alndvod said, as if she had a pair of spectacles to peer over in disapproval. She enjoyed keeping both celestials and chthonics in line and holding them to account – even in the most joking manner. Alndvod sat at a strange crossroads, essentially being a guide for any chthonic or celestial whenever they needed direct access to the etheric realm. It was in her best interest to make sure both sides could function so that the etherics could function. Balance kept everyone in business, and alive.

Samuel looked at them both and the strange little alliance that was forming against him. "We are what we are."

"Too right," Alndvod agreed. "Well... if you truly have an unjudged mortal in the place of celestials and chthonics, it's only a matter of time before that mortal is discovered. One wouldn't want to kill it. In fact, even the most dim chthonic in all of God's creation couldn't kill a mortal in Dudael, because the realm was created to punish them, not mortals. A mortal would be invincible there. If a chthonic is smart enough to get out of that realm, I don't see why they would suddenly kill it. But you never know with them and their perverse appetites."

"How would a chthonic be able to get out of Dudael when no others have been able to for millennia?" Samuel asked.

"A mortal being in Dudael isn't just odd, it will cause a disruption between the realms and a rift between dimensions. The longer it is there, the larger the disruption. Eventually, things will bleed over from the mortal world. Beyond that, the only other thing would be the breaking of the seven seals and the return of the Most High to the mortal plane. Let's try to avoid that, shall we?"

Alvanod began searching through a pile of paperwork to find the correct travel documents to allow them passage throughout the rest of the Etheric plane.

"Yeah, but wouldn't it affect the etheric world first?" Percival nervously interjects.

Alndvod paused, looking at him with concern. "I hadn't thought of that. Yes."

Samuel looked at him with concern. "That could be just as bad. What if the Watchers are released? They've been stuck in Dudael from the beginning. To suddenly get out and then they discover etherics are running the joint. They're gonna be pissed off! It'll be a war we can't even imagine."

Alndvod looked away, visibly upset. Dudael and the exile of the Watchers were in the past for celestials, but the etherics lived the consequences every day. There was a bitterness to everything in an etheric's life. Beginning life when there is already a historical dispute is something many don't understand, unless they are born or created during a war or under an oppressor. Alndvod didn't consider the celestials oppressors, though many etherics did. The Watchers, the first group of angels the Creator sent down to protect humanity, failed and ended up falling in love with the mortals. When the Most High punished the mortal plane, the remaining angels who survived the Great Flood were bound to the mortal plane and became the Etherics. To prevent a recurrence of this incident and to ensure the execution of celestial plans in day-to-day operations, the Creator programmed etherics to influence everything on the mortal plane. However, they are strictly forbidden from direct interaction with the mortal plane except in the most dire circumstances. Centuries after the Creator began the etheric realm, chthonics made contact. Over time, the Elders realized their realm was more of a pivot between the mortal plane, and what is above and below. One thing Alndvod knew for sure was that all the realms worked together like a system, and sitting in the middle of it all allowed her and the other elders to ensure that a balance is maintained. Without that balance, existence itself ended.

"Do you think this chthonic is getting help?"

"Yes, from the Portal," Percival jumped in before Samuel could remark.

"So it was her that disposed of the mortal. But she can not determine the mortals frequency, which means we have an ascended mortal. That's only happened one other time, and you know how much that pissed the Creator off."

"That's why you feel like this has been too easy," Alndvod said, looking at Samuel.

Samuel gave Alndvod an unappreciated look. That statement was a manipulation, a tactic. Samuel wasn't used to the etheric world where they could read him. It was one of the many reasons he avoided this dimension. "Yes. I got the key back – but I think this mission helps her out more than it does us, but I can't be sure."

"She played you. The portal knew what she was doing. I'm sure you send demons back to Hell all the time. Except that the keys can never tread near the underworld. There is no way you two could have known this – it was a precaution when they were created. So when you tried to send your chthonic back to hell, the key protected itself and sent you both to Dudael. She doesn't have a protective spell on the chthonic, she's using Heavens own rules against itself."

"I don't follow."

"Samuel, do you see this," she said pointing at her own blank face. "This is my shocked face. I'm not surprised you don't get it. Our Alice Grey, the Portal of Mortality, was counting on your impulsiveness." She leaned back in her chair, half thinking about how to prepare herself for the worst, and half making sure she tells Samuel what he needs to know. "To unleash the armies of the Lost Order, if that chthonic really is under her control, it will escape with the mortal and try to kill the Portal of Judgement. All it needs to do is trick the Portal of Judgement into allowing an ascended mortal to pass through. Even if they don't kill Judgement, the Lost Order and any chthonic within the realm will spill over on the mortal plane. It's a perfect plan."

"The plan for what?"

"To end mortality, to close the Portal. For her it's just retirement."

Percival walked away to another corner of the bookstore. He didn't want to think about this anymore. He had heard of the time before mortality. Without the mortal plane, nothing is created. Nothing grows, nothing is learned. Celestials will be stuck as they are forever. The mortal plane was created in the first place so that existence could learn about itself. Humans were only a part of the solution, but it didn't surprise him that it would be something to do with humans that would cause detriment – for they were the first species in the Universe to be given access to consciousness. Not that they use it very often. He walked around the corner from the aisle they were standing in to the glass case that held the antiquarian books. He noticed one of the patrons admiring them as well, and then realized it was the Envoy from the meeting room.

The Envoy looked at him and raised one finger for Percival to be quiet. He gestured for Percival to walk toward him, as there was nobody else around.

Percival complied.

"Don't worry, it's a shitty situation all the way around. I want you to ask her for permission to seek Judgement. She'll resist, but it's your best chance of intercepting that chthonic."

Percival nodded. "Wait... how did you find me?"

"My cosmic powers," he said with a straight face.

Percival thought about it for a minute, considering all the possibilities.

"I dropped a tracer on you, dope," he whispered. The Envoy gestured for Percival to get back to the Conversation.

Percival obliged and strolled back beside Samuel. "Apologies. I needed a moment to collect my thoughts. At this point I think it is best if we attempt to head off any chances of assassinating Judgement. May we have your blessing to meet the Portal of Judgement?"

Alndvod considered the suggestion. There was nothing for the celestials to gain by destroying Judgement, but there is a tremendous amount to be lost should the chthonic introduce the ascended mortal. "My goodly friends, it's important to realize that we are at war. What we are about to do will violate the Treaty of Elders. I can't promise success because you are about to go deeper into our world than any other celestial in the history of the realms. By doing this, we are going against the standards the Elders before me set up with your choirs. I'm not even sure you are going to be able to withstand the forces and energies put upon you. It's possible that you might fall into mortality—because celestials aren't supposed to tread here. You're going to need this." Alndvod dug through one of the cubbies on her roll-top desk and pulled out a small suede pouch, handing it to Samuel. Samuel passed it on to Percival. "It's going to be difficult, especially for that one," she said, gesturing to Percival.

"You're going to need to get to the central city. It is the nexus of the etheric dimension. This is where Judgement resides where it determines where a soul is to head after its mortality. That sachet of sigils will help your grease some wheels. But again... I can't promise anything."

Percival dug into the small bag that he was carrying. He pulled out the sigils Alndvod spoke of. They looked like gold coins, but they were not uniform like minted coins. Each had a face that had different inscriptions on them. "How do we know what to-"

"It's best you be getting on now," Alndvod said, eyeing them. She shoed them away with her hands.

They obliged and began to make their way back upstairs.

"Where do we go from here," Percival asked as he let the door to the bookstore close behind them.

"We'll, we have to go through the first gateway."

CHAPTER NINE

Moloch stood on the private balcony outside his council chamber that overlooked the river of fire surrounding Pandemonia. A hulking body, with broad shoulders and a bull-like neck and head. His large hands wrap around the broad balustrade of the balcony, wide enough for a human to sit upon. He enjoyed having the best seat in the house, overlooking the pits of Hell.

Moloch despised every entity under his command. He believed that the demons and Princes of hell could always work harder at torturing souls. Ironically, he despised doing the work himself even more. Unlike other demonic princes and kings who seek power, knowledge, or corruption, Moloch's primary desire was always physical destruction. He requested fresh souls brought to him daily. The darker and more twisted the soul, the better. The only thing better than a cold-blooded killer without a conscience, was a pure soul. However, in hell, such a thing didn't exist.

His singular focus on all of this sacrifice and consumption, was the harvesting of eth. It made him both celebrated and feared by every demon in Hell. He was not driven by the same ambitions or nuanced desires as other demons. The simple goal of devouring eth was good enough for him. Because of this, since the beginning of Moloch's reign, the underworld had become a soul-eating machine.

Hellfire demons became as tortured as the mortal souls who came into their grasp. From Moloch's perspective, the more tortured his demons were, the more they would pass this displeasure on to their own victims. Those who escaped to the mortal plane, either physically or by possessing a live soul, were given additional leeway to persuade or force mortals to act in heinous ways. Early corruption of a mortal's life increases underworld power – as the eth is more abundant.

After the many failed attempts by Lucifer to hatch a viable strategy to return the fallen to their former glory, Hell grew tired of the false promises. Lucifer's time as Satan had come to a violent end long ago, led by the brute force of Moloch. Of course, the rest of Hell thought Moloch would continue his momentum of destruction and use it to lead an army against the Heavens. After a time, ferocity proved just as crucial as having a strategy. It took the minions of Hell time to realize that they needed a leader who was both ferocious and cunning. Moloch did not possess the latter. Nor would he ever. It was a realization Moloch learned after his own attempt to storm an army out of Hell. One failure was enough for him, he did not want to continue the same trend as Lucifer. Saddled with the heavy realization of his own limitations, Moloch settled into his post centuries ago, ensuring that Hell became as obsessed with stripping souls of what eth they had left when they arrived.

He gazed upon the vastness of his hellscape. Amidst the heat and flames, he heard newcomers falling into cages, gasping and screaming, struggling to breathe in the scorching sulfur. Their lungs blistered and bubbled as they choked through their own vomit and pain, trying the gasp for air. They would only get a wisp of breathable air. Enough to keep their bodies searching, hoping for more. The celestials banked much of their relationship on the mortals through faith and hope –

however, Moloch and the rest of the Council of the Fallen saw hope as an equally useful tool, as long as it was just out of reach.

The fresh souls belonging to those screams were just beginning their journey. Some last minute losses to celestials were inevitable, but Moloch accepted it as part of the business. He considered it 'spillage', like the inevitable loss of a product in a brewery. In his early days, spillage used to drive him crazy. However, over millennia, he learned how to use the celestials to his advantage. The demons clustered the souls who were sent to this level of hell. They were purposefully organized within eye shot of one another. For every soul Moloch lost in spillage, he made up for it in the anguish that those nearest to the saved souls endured when they realized a celestial wasn't coming for them.

The most amusing thing to Moloch was how leaving Hell was surprisingly as easy as entering - at least for humans. Support each other, both in word and deed. It was what made each of these souls so wretched. For they would no more help their neighbor than they would themselves. Which is what made each inhabitant so easily corruptible. From the most fractured soul all the way to the reigning throne of Satan that Moloch sat upon, Hell was one giant crab pot, where everyone did their best to keep the other down.

It had been over a thousand cycles since the upheaval that locked the Morning Star away. Moloch fought hard for the role, and even harder to make sure that the Morning Star's rules remained in place. The number one rule, there was no solace of any kind for those brought to this realm. The higher up the chain of command, the less one had to do. This concept was, of course, eventually leaked to the mortal world so that it would cause maximum corruption.

Of the mortals, Moloch and the rest of the Council of the Fallen hated humans the most. This is because humans were the first mortals to have the capacity to achieve consciousness, even though the majority of them don't look beyond themselves. However, this ability eventually transpired to all mortals, and created a lot more work for those in the underworld. It is also what sparked the Great War. This is because it meant things were up for grabs. After the gathering of the First Infernal Council, the Princes of Hell realized that humans who were less favoured by God were cast aside to the same place as them. The Princes discovered they could exploit the evil of their actions to corrupt their souls. This increased the collection of eth and continued to build the armies of Hell.

Upon arrival, no soul ever believes they belong in Hell. It is Hell's minions that manage to persuade a soul otherwise. If Hell's minions convince a soul of the recently departed, through pain or persuasion that they belong here, to the victor goes the spoils. While many in the hierarchy despised Moloch, they all grew wealthy with eth because of him. And so the business of hell was born.

Moloch watched from the balcony as an entity made it through the river of fire just outside the walls of the council building. It seemed proud as it stood up on the cracked dry shores that led to the building Moloch stood in. Its skin, which used to be human, now turned to leather and hardened ash, stiffened and prevented the creature from moving very fast. It had obviously been a resident for a few centuries, though it still had a long way to go before it approached any chance of being a demon. Joining the heirarchy was it's only chance of relieving the pain inflicted by the fury of the underworld. Moloch smiled at the entity's success.

As Moloch watched this minor victory far below the balcony, behind him, Belial appeared in the doorway from the council chamber. Belial was strikingly handsome, with a chiseled jaw-line, electric mustard colored eyes that stood in contrast to his taught black skin. They pierced through his surroundings. He was King of the Eighty Legions, a role he found easy to embody. Unlike Moloch, Belial didn't need to try to keep his role, he was naturally suited for it. As he stepped out onto the balcony, he wondered if he could easily dethrone Moloch just by throwing him over the side right then and there.

Moloch kept Belial around because he understood all the things that Moloch couldn't grasp. In the council, Belial held significant sway. Belial assisted Moloch in creating his reign, only because it brought himself closer to the throne. He knew one day the council would grow tired of Moloch's brutishness. Being in such proximity to the throne, and with such charisma, gained him the legacy of being a master of lies and deceit, specializing in political corruption and moral subversion. His influence was pervasive right from the beginning, infiltrating the highest echelons of power across the Etheric and Mortal realm, and of course, Hell. His secret passion was infiltrating sacred institutions. Belial's stock in trade all centered on sowing discord, fostering mistrust, and undermining the fabric of order and justice.

"Still keeping hope alive," Belial joked as he walked up beside Moloch. They both watched as a Sentry came into view, heading toward the new entity that made it to the shores of the Council.

"Always," Moloch said in a deep, craggy voice.

They both knew what came next. A Sentry jogged toward the entity with effortless speed. It tackled the entity, then quickly pulled it up from the ground and punched it in the stomach. The Sentry's fist bursts straight through the abdomen. Thick black ooze and specks of ichor, the fluid of the immortals, gushes, and the entity falls to the ground.

Moloch doesn't dare tear his eyes away. It is so rare that he gets an honest show.

The Sentry, much larger than its victim, continually kicks the fallen, broken body until it tumbles awkwardly from the shore and back into the river of fire. The rush of the river of fire immediately whisks the body away. It will spend the next few decades piecing itself back together, and torturing other souls for their eth before it builds back up to the same strength again.

Belial pondered what it was about such displays that always enthralled the both of them. "They say it's important to have a hobby. It adds to personal growth."

"Didn't you make that up to distract the mortals? What do you call it?"

"I believe you are thinking of multi-tasking. Yes, we had our best on that one. A hobby is different, though."

Moloch turned and stared him down. Facing Moloch directly intimidated Belial every time, and Moloch knew it. He stared him down, determining how much of a slight Belial had just barbed him with. Instead, he thrusts a large snort through his bullish nostrils at Belial and then turns, heading back into the main chamber. "We have a problem. Follow me."

They enter the dark majesty of the great hall. The throne room of all of Hell itself. The flickering glow of hellfire from outside illuminates the vast chamber, casting eerie shadows that dance across the obsidian walls, etched with ancient runes and malevolent symbols. The shadows in the darkened corners writhe and slither – echoes of lost souls trapped in eternal service, waiting to be released as Shadow Wraiths to the mortal realm to taunt the living. At the center of the room stood a massive, intricately carved black stone dais, rising halfway up the height of the council amphitheatre that surrounded it.

As Moloch led Belial up the steps, Belial looked down at the paved mosaic of each of the steps. As they took each step, they tread on the tormented faces of mortals, eternally frozen in silent agony. The entire facility drew in rivers of eth, the remainder of what little life force could be wrenched loose from the damned souls throughout the underworld.

At the top of the dais sat the throne of Satan, the ruler of the infernal hierarchy, where Moloch served. The throne, adorned with jagged spikes, is encrusted with dark gemstones that pulse with the dark eth of the first souls they captured. All those who serve in hell have something to pay penance for. Moloch's penance for being Satan was that he could never leave the council chambers. Beside the throne was a stone pillar, exactly in the center of the room, andon that pillar lay a book. The complete grimoire of all the guidelines and laws of Pandemonia, and a ledger of all the souls that should be there.

Belial was hesitant. He didn't know what sort of trick Moloch was about to unleash. As far as he knew, Moloch had never taken anyone to the top of the throne, above the lower seats of the council. However, Moloch wasn't one for being clever. A mighty warrior, yes, but cunning, no.

Moloch stopped at the top and walked to the edge of the platform. "The impossible has happened – we have a compelled demon in Dudael."

Belial's jaw almost fell to the floor. This was everything – like winning the lottery. He didn't dare say a word, though his rugged, beaten wings from the day he fell stretched with excitement. He couldn't help it.

"Yes, my friend. I share your excitement. In the years since Lucifer's last attempt, I have fought hard to lead this realm. After all this time, we have never been able to get in contact with our fallen in Dudael. I want to play this right. It could be a trap to destroy us once and for all. They could be trying to reignite the War."

Belial didn't believe that. "Duplicity is not their way. If they wanted to restart the war – we would have an army of celestials on our backs right now. Or they would simply starve us of eth."

"That is what I thought as well. Until I saw this."

A large orb appears behind Moloch and displays an image like a television screen. A portal, as if the viewer were looking out from a sewer drain, showed Percival and Samuel battling Ganislay at Alice Grey's house.

"They spoke in the language of the mortals, so we cannot understand. But watch closely." The orb showed the fire in Alice's house pulling Ganislay back into Dudael. "That isn't all." The orb shifted and swirled, changing the scene to when Ganislay first was summoned from hell by Alice and the young man's soul was sent into Dudael. Suddenly, the orb collapses into a tiny dust particle before them. "His eth print is still strong. He could be ours. Is there any reference to his passing in the Akashics?"

"I shall find out right away and report back."

"No," his voice boomed. It echoed so loud it felt like a shock from an earthquake. "Look now," his words rumbled and bounded off the chamber walls in several echoes.

Belial looked at him. Moloch had changed from the days of the First Council. He was like a field general, experienced and merciless in the ways of war. His anger won him the throne and froze Lucifer in time. But the millennia of building the tools and armies of the underworld and the savvy that it took - he was now much better at strategy. It had brought a wisdom that Belial hadn't expected. Belial opens an orb. Hundreds of words and short phrases hovered in the air in the language of Harrow. He whisked through them with the flick of the wrist and then pointed to one, highlighting it, and opened a new chapter.

"No, this mortal has not passed. It is not its time yet. His signature is also particularly strong in the Vein of Cocytus"

"As I thought. He does belong here, perhaps because of a generational curse." Moloch walked over to the pedestal that stood in front of the throne, looked fondly upon a book that was placed on top. The cover is blank. However, upon touching it, the title appeared in Harrow. "The Book of Feasts – Prophesies and Laws."

"What you may not know, brother, is that another's transgression often coerces the sins of the horde." He opened the first few pages and gently placed his scaled hands on its pages. "I have spent millennia studying this grimoire as it grows. You have to know it, feel it, for it is us. Each souls fall from grace into the pits out there, their thirst for life, is ours."

Belial takes a step closer to look at the page that the book is open to. In ancient Harrow, it read:

"Wherefore shall the lost and the forgotten, place their despair? Nowhere but here, in these rivers and depths, forged and neglected by the Creator. Cast aside for whimsey and folly in the name of Creation, anguish and pain prevail."

"We have weaknesses. It was written here and later confirmed." Moloch turned a thick block of pages to the middle of the book. "Read for yourself. We are now in the days of prophesy."

Belial placed his hand on the blank page and the writing scrawls across the page as if it is being written as he read it:

'Upon my release from these bonds, I came upon nine gates, each more formidable than the last. The first was wrought of iron, its surface etched with runes I could not decipher but felt within my soul. It repelled the unworthy, though I felt no force. The second gate stood taller, woven of thick vines that pulsed with life, as though the earth itself held the barrier in place. As I approached the third gate, fashioned from glass so dark it reflected no light, a shiver coursed through me, for behind it stirred shadows of forgotten souls—those who had come before me, those who had failed. Their whispers clawed at my mind, yet I pressed on. And so I stood before the nine, knowing each would demand a sacrifice greater than the last. What lay beyond them was not merely freedom, but my children, both sin and death. Then finally a reckoning with the Celestials of the Most High, the powers that had bound me forever to my fate.'

"The Morning Star's words upon his first attempt out of hell," Moloch stated with reverence.

They both fell quiet in a moment of respect, thinking back to the days when the Princes and Kings were still full of hope. Mentioning the Morning Star out loud was forbidden, and Moloch swore to the Council he would not repeat it until they rise against the heavens again.

"The War has come to us," Moloch said, cutting through the distant rumble of the underworld outside. "Our compelled demon was sent to Dudael, a place without gates of iron."

"Why would heaven want to bring war upon the depths?" Belial asked.

"Did you think they forgot? They work on the free will of humankind the same as we do. The celestials needed to wait for the correct moment to offer itself. That time is now."

"They'll come for our armies," Belial said egging him on. Belial knew Moloch had the wrong end of the stick on this one.

Moloch held up his hand announcing, "I received notice from the etheric realm. Our compelled demon made it out of Dudael with quite the treasure – an ascended mortal. Now, because he is in the etheric realm, our compelled demon is also ascended and can lead our army through gates of Adamantine instead of the nine gates. The portal of Mortality has already fallen, no doubt the portal of Judgement is next. This means we can finally use the gates of the mortals to leave the underworld."

"Is it written," Belial said hopefully.

"We have found this opportunity in time." Moloch said. He respected Belial for sticking by him all these years. Belial's behavior often confused Moloch. He was slow to anger and action, but once it was decided, he would often go farther and be more imaginative than Moloch's brute force.

Moloch turned another block of pages farther into the book. He placed his hand on the page, and this time, no writing appeared. "It is not written what is to come, it is now our time as much as it is theirs. If they were to succeed, they would take more than our armies. They would take away our connection to the mortal coil. They would take away sin and death altogether, so we may suffer in silence, alone for eternity. These depths were intended to be just that - for our eth to slowly fade away, with no way out."

"Yes... that is most definitely an opening to a new war," Belial said egging him on. The only opportunity Belial saw right now was directing Moloch toward being a useful idiot. While Moloch was correct in theory, it didn't work in practicality because launching a pre-emptive war was out of character for those in Heaven. If there is one thing he could count on through all his experience, it's that entities always act within the confines of their basic nature.

Moloch grumbled with happiness. Demons and devils were prone to gossip, so he knew he had to dispatch Belial right away. He knew the book was right, he knew this was the most opportune time. It is going to be all the more useful that he wouldn't have to convince Belial.

"Ganislay will seek vengeance, and that is good enough for this purpose. Get to him, have him get to Adamantine before them. Make sure he keeps the human alive. If we can collect a mortal soul that has not passed, then we can breach the Kingdom of Heaven and bring the war to them instead. I'm counting on you to lead the charge."

"Yes, Lord." Belial stepped away, bowing.

"I sense your Harrow is slipping. I will not have Impish spoken within these walls. It is for demons and those in the Depths."

"Yes, my lord." Belial bowed again as he stepped further away.

As he left the chamber, Belial slipped into an adjacent corridor and down a darkened staircase just outside the council chamber. Only the council knew it existed. However, he hadn't been into the chambers in a few millennia and it was time to pay homage.

The pain and anguish of others were the foundation of the lavish depths in the underworld. When a soul accepts that the Creator has forgotten or rejected them, it becomes the greatest pain of all. The Council chambers were the farthest a soul could get from God. The Alter itself, on which Moloch stood, was built atop Lucifer in the center of the chamber. Belial never liked to refer to Lucifer as Satan, for he did not want to give any sort of credence to the Creator's punishment upon themselves or anyone else cast to the depths. Belial was a staunch believer in all of it and could see all perspectives. He rejected the reason the Creator had punished them, and he embraced the day of the Fall. Sometimes, he believed that others in the Council regretted the day of the Fall, wishing they could undo everything.

He came to a doorway blocked by a smooth monolith of obsidian. Belial uttered some words, and the obsidian stone melted away giving way to a pale blue shimmering light. This was the only part he hated. He walked in to the room, which was a frozen wasteland. Lucifer stood frozen in time. First, Heaven cast him out for his revolution, and then after arguing with the First Council, even Hell had forgotten him. He stood, pale, leathery, so new compared to what the council looked like now. One wing was naked and turning to leather, the other still with half of its mangled feathers attached. A reminder of where they had all come from. Lucifer didn't want to make a kingdom in the depths. He wanted to obstruct and harass Heaven and the favored race of the Creator. He did not want to expand his rule. This is because, as he originally tried, he wanted Heaven intact enough so that he could try to overthrow it once again. Such an idea would never win over the narcissism and ego of those in the depths. The Fallen and their first generation of demons had everything they needed to create a kingdom strong enough to stand in opposition to heaven. Politically, Lucifer never stood a chance with the Council to remain on the throne of Satan.

Belial thought different. He understood Lucifer wanted to climb back to the throne of heaven and hold up a mirror for all to see the hypocrisy he had called out. It was the only throne worth taking. However, in his absence, Lucifer hadn't seen what the Throne of hell had become. If Moloch has his way, Lucifer never will. If Moloch can storm the gates of Heaven, he will have done what Lucifer could never do, and it would be impossible to get the rest of Hell on their side again.

"My Lord," he says, kneeling. "The time is almost near. Your throne awaits your return and the kingdom of Heaven will be yours." The cold was getting to him. In actuality, what was happening was that the curse was taking effect on him as well. He had to be careful. Even several minutes of exposure would take hold and hell would forget him. Erased from existence and never spoken of again.

In the shadows, Moloch watched Belial kneel. He could not hear him, but he didn't like what he was seeing. Nobody visited the Frozen Prince. All of hell had long forgotten Lucifer. Moloch was Satan now. He quickly scurried up through the rocky staircase, back to the main chamber, making sure he wasn't seen. He always had his suspicions of Belial, but he was never certain until now. Years on the throne had taught him to suspect everyone. He thought about immediately trapping Belial in Lucifer's spell as well, or even casting a new one. But he needed him. Moloch set his intention and a large portal opened up behind Belial. Nobody resists a free pass out of hell.

Moloch walked back onto the balcony overlooking the river of fire. He watched as the Sentry did its duty once again, throwing another soul back into the fire. He smiled and waved his hand to summon them. The Sentry and the soul who was just thrown into the fire appeared before him on the balcony.

The Sentry stood tall and at attention. "My lord." The entity stood beside the Sentry, still alight with flames and doing its best not to crumble to pieces. The Sentry raised its staff to knock the entity down to a kneeling position.

Moloch raises his hand for the Sentry to cease. It does so and returns to attention. "I enjoy your determination," Moloch said to the entity. "You will make a fine Sentry." The flames around the entity ceased and a circle of smoke whispered around the entity, immediately turning it into a Sentry, a near exact copy of the original standing beside it.

The original Sentry remained still, awaiting to be dis-incorporated.

Moloch stepped in front of him. "And to you, I send you to stand as my shadow. Watch over Belial, see that he completes my bidding." The Sentry nodded and immediately disappeared out of hell through a portal.

***

Moments later the Sentry appeared in the cool grass of a field behind a carnival tent. As he looked himself over, he realized he had never been outside of hell since he was cast into it. He was one of the first inhabitants as a previous mortal and hoped he would be returned to his former mortal self. He looked around to see several creatures scurry into the large circus tent. There was a crowd shouting. Judging from the look of his toughened skin, he did not want to know where he was. He could tell he was in the body of an ork. Which made sense because their etheric minds are the easiest to possess.

He saw a rustle in the shadows behind a nearby tent and he instinctually crouched to the ground. Belial stepped out of the shadows into the light of the three moons. He was as tall as a nordic elf, very common in the etheric realm. Belial strolled along the edge of the shadows, comfortable with the form he was given. Moloch had summoned him out of hell many times before on missions. Breathing in the freedom of being away, a feeling of contentment flowed into him. He looked around and saw the glow of the central city in the distance and headed toward a field that led to it.

The field was vast and dimly lit by the light of the Sendai, the famous violet bladed grasses that glowed in the light of the three moons.

He stayed on the pathway that surrounded the field so that the glow didn't illuminate his movements.

The sentry stayed low and followed along the pathway, just inside the Sendai, to provide cover. He wasn't used to the clumsiness of this body. It didn't move fast. His joints were huge and low to the ground. He could easily stay low, but he couldn't keep up. It didn't take long for him to begin laboring under his breath. In order to avoid coughing, he had to stop. With his eyes fixed on where Belial was walking, he lay on the ground. Though it wasn't long before he lost sight of Belial. The sentry waited, trying to see if he could spot movement between the shadows and moonlight.

Suddenly, a snarl like a lion came from above. The sentry looked up in time to see Belial's lanky body swooping down and picking him up like an eagle. He brought the ork effortlessly several hundred feet up into the air. "I could smell your fat pig's breath from the moment we left the tents."

The sentry flailed about. He felt the weight of his body – it wanted to fall.

Belial jostled him in his hands as if he was about to drop him. "Why are you following me?"

The sentry couldn't think of anything. It had been millennia since he had been out of hell. He wasn't used to social customs, he wasn't used to even speaking to anyone, much less lying on the spot..

"Moloch sent you."

"No, no. Ork."

"Are you now?" he said, drifting slowly down to earth. "An ork, in a field of Sendai. How precious. What does Moloch want you to do with me?"

The sentry looked away. He enjoyed the small amount of freedom he had breathed. It reminded him of home, long ago when he used to tend the fields for his family. He couldn't tell the truth. Moloch compelled him not to. He knew he was trapped. "No Moloch, Ork," he whimpered through clumsy words as tears welled up.

"You are in a field of Sendai that is poisonous to all known creatures living and dead, except Chthonics," Moloch impressed upon him.

Belial punched through the ork's chest, and pulled out the Sentry from the body of the Ork, like he was pulling out a soul. The Ork-body slumped to the ground like a dispensed suit, and Belial held the sentry by the neck.

The sentry looked at him with the cold white eyes of hell. "No mercy"

"You are a good soldier," Belial said, dropping him to the ground. He punched the Sentry across the face, knocking him to the ground.

The Sentry could not fight. Since Belial was a higher rank, the Sentry simply did not have the power to fight him even though he would like to. Someone of a higher rank can simply physically overpower another – so it was not worth the fight. When a soul resides in the underworld, its first experience is the loss of the ability to think individually. Therefore, the first physical change comes as the eyes of the new inhabitant turn completely white, preventing individual vision. This way, the afflicted only see what hell wants it to see. The sentry remembered this day, for it was the last moment he felt something of himself. Being here in the Etheric world was overwhelming, as it is for all Chthonics when they are released.

Belial looked down at the Sentry. "You are of the First Order, no?"

"Yes," the Sentry answered.

"We are not in hell anymore, so the prime rule does not apply." Belial reached down and helped the Sentry to his feet. "You won't understand this, but we are at war. The millennia of suffering you have been through was first caused and created by our enemies. Your enemies. If we win this..." Belial paused. The prize was so great he dared not speak it. He turned and looked at the three moons.

The sentry stared at the ground. "You shouldn't be telling me this." The Sentry began walking away toward the town.

"I need a good soldier," Belial said, continuing to look at the moons. "Moloch will not be the Satan for much longer and he knows it."

The Sentry stopped. He had heard of promotions but thought they were just myths. Then he supposed the mission was the promotion. Hell has its ways.

"Moloch is not cunning enough to take on the Creator. We will assist our brother in this pursuit, but when the time comes – we will release the Morning Star."

"Who is going to be doing this?" The return of Lucifer was often dreamt about and many longed for it, but the Sentry had not come across any active attempts to do so. Hell had style back then, souls were captured in the most subtle way. These days it's just about brutality in order to collect eth.

"We are. We are the beginning of this," Belial said persuading him.

"Lead a revolution... in Hell?" The Sentry was hoping to escape by the time the Chthonic Army gained enough stupidity to launch the opening salvo against Heaven. It's better to be mortal fodder than to try to lead a revolution against Moloch. If they lose, the Sentry would be enslaved in the pits of hell. Moloch would create a special place for those who move against him. If they were to succeed, then he would have to lead an army against the Creator. That would end in a punishment he couldn't fathom. He thought about killing Belial from behind and escaping. Maybe since they were not in hell any longer... maybe he could.

"Do you understand?" Belial roared.

"Yes," the responded out of reflex. The Sentry resigned in his mind that this was his lot to live.

Belial walked back and glared at him. "Do anything other than my bidding and I will have all your Eth. Now lets go."

CHAPTER TE

Samuel and Percival walked through the etheric world of London. Percival was amazed by the intricate involvement required for the mortal realm to function. He'd seen this look on the faces of the mortals before. When a student finally understands what a teacher is instructing in a class, or when an engineering student first sees the inner workings of a watch or a microchip. Layers upon layers of functionality. Percival could see waves of eth coming off of each etheric he saw as they accompanied the objects and people they were bound to. The eth looked like flames of light swooping off one person or object and crashing in to another. Waves occasionally intersected, nullifying one another. There were thousands of little etherics all doing their part in whatever direction he turned.

Samuel walked up the steps to The Shard in central London. "Come on, this is nothin' yet. I like this city, it truly is a gateway."

Percival was used to the grandiosity of Heaven, but it didn't come with such tactile information like he was experiencing. Everything felt so fast-paced. He looked around, the ground floor reminded him of the central office he worked in. He couldn't get over the sounds, above all, the sound of space. He quickly realized empty space had its own sound simply because it held pools of relatively undisturbed eth that had built up over time. As they walked through the foyer, Percival stopped, just too overwhelmed to go on.

Samuel was several paces ahead, and he looked back, doing a double-take. It became apparent to him that Percival needed to be better prepared for the realm. He knew that without this, they were not going to achieve much more. He stopped and dropped his head in frustration. He recalled his initial entry into the etheric realm. However, he had no prior experience mentoring apprentices. That's when it occurred to him that he may be up for a promotion. Or did they know? Did they have knowledge of his true intentions? Had the higher triad caught on and sent Percival as a spy? This is how the choirs worked. Everything was on the line. He was always unsure if something was genuinely occuring or if things were being orchestrated to appear certain ways. Samuel found the choirs manipulative in this manner. They ran a perfect strategy where one couldn't predict the correct strategy until the last critical moment. For a moment, he let his mind run wild, and he attracted fear. However, none of that mattered. What did matter at that moment was that Percival needed a proper introduction to the etheric realm from a celestial perspective.

Samuel sauntered back toward Percival and gently grabbed him by the arm. "The mission can wait. C'mon." They dissolved into the air and moments later, Samuel had transported them to a much more comfortable place at the top of a nearby building. Percival breathed in the cool air.

"It's much easier in the open air," Samuel said crouching down, looking off the edge of the building.

Percival kept his eyes closed, enjoying the sweet breeze.

"Some mortals have the same issue that you just experienced. They consider it feeling another's emotions," Samuel said, looking out at the view of London. "Unfortunately, they can't transmit eth as well as we can. They aren't meant to be open to the flows of eth. The ones who are, find it even more debilitating than we do in large closed spaces."

Samuel had taken them to his favourite spot in London – the top of the tower at Bishopsgate. All of London was visible from there. It didn't matter to Samuel whether it was rain or shine, since celestials don't feel temperature or other physical sensations of the mortal realm. However, they had extensive theories. This caused many a Celestial to become curious and sometimes attached to mortals or even some etherics.

Percival opened his eyes. He looked over the city. The sight of so many trees and green spaces from up there surprised him.

Samuel sat on the edge of the building, his legs dangling off the side. "One thing you have to learn is to control the flow of mortal existence around you. Otherwise, existence has a way of eating away at you."

The etheric realm was the closest Percival had been to the mortal world. He found it all very overwhelming. It was a cloudy day, but he could still sense the sun. He did not know about temperature, as celestials do not have a mortal body, but the energy pouring in from the sun and the other cosmic bodies in the solar system infused energy throughout the atmosphere.

Samuel gazed at Percival as he approached the building's edge nearby. He had been here so many times, he had forgotten what it was like the first time a Celestial experiences the lower realm, or even the thin veil of the etheric world that wraps around it.

"Can mortals feel this?" Percival asked, squinting his eyes like a dog, as if he were exploring the nuances of a breeze.

"Not really. A few can, but most mortals are too closed off. It's not their way or their purpose to sense the cosmos."

"That's too bad," Perciva said, exhaling. He opened his eyes and watched the sounds as their vibrations rose from the streets below and were carried in the wind. Larger waves from larger sounds swallowed smaller waves whole. Mostly, the waves of sound bounced off one another. In a few moments, Percival could discern sounds by looking at the wave pattern. He gazed into the distant skyline. From an apartment window, a small tinny speaker of a cheap radio emitted the sound of a radio announcer, flowed up into the atmosphere. He could also see the sound of a couple quietly chatting about their plans to elope. He could read them like reading a distant traffic sign.

"You'll get good at that," Samuel said fondly. He forgot how often he read wave signatures to navigate around.

Percival was used to being captivated by Central Existence, but here in the etheric realm, what got him was the value of a moment. It was intense. Celestials in Central Existence who never leave, often lack an understanding of a moment. Looking out over the expanse of London, Percival realized his ability to express this much appreciation, was part of the reason he was picked for this mission. Percival had already seen that being away from Central Existence created a new burden upon him. He had sensed this in Samuel, the trappings of Central Existence acted as a filter that the Archangels were required to deal with head on.

"About the etherics, there are a few things you need to understand," Samuel said looking down to the streets below. They appear cheerful and carefree, yet they have some tremendous limitations.

Percival finished letting the vibrations wash over him. He glanced at Samuel, then walked over and joined him at the building's edge.

Samuel continued, "Six principles hold etherics accountable for maintaining the integrity of existence. After the Great War, there needed to be something that kept existence in balance between the continual chthonic attempts to disrupt the flow of existence. That is when Central Existence created the etheric realm."

The first principle is the etheric Law of Obedience. Etherics must follow the commands of the immortals. It is important to note; it includes all immortals - not just us. In this sense, etherics are neutral. That doesn't mean they like it. No matter what an etheric says, they hold you in no higher esteem than any chthonic, entity, or even lost souls. This ensures that rebellion and war don't break out.

"Okay," Percival said, nodding.

"Trust me, don't put all your eggs in one basket based on what any etheric says. They continually shop around and play Celestials off of Chthonics and vice versa. Because we have our own agenda, they get caught in the middle. Most of the time it's a problem for them, but many times they also use it to their advantage. It's impossible to tell until it's late. "

"Sounds harsh, but ok."

"The next principle is Secrecy. It is forbidden for etherics to disclose the secrets of the etheric Realm or the true nature of the immortals."

"No big deal. We don't give our secrets to the mortals either."

Samuel shoots Percival a look of disbelief.

"Of course, there have been exceptions," Percival admits.

"Yeah... just a few here and there. We're about as secretive as a fart during church service, but that's not what I meant. The etheric realm is like the dark corner of heaven that nobody sees. It provides everybody with a level of deniability."

Percival's eyes widened.

"Yeah, shocking isn't it? You'd never considered that Heaven would need deniability for anything. Why do you think we have Envoys, or even Archs? We Archs take a lot of the stick for when things go wrong. Blow-back never goes up the hierarchy of the choirs. It's our sole responsibility."

"Well, that's nonsense, because we know everything that goes on."

"We, what do you mean we? You've been doing your best up in Central Existence since you were assigned there. Are you aware of everything that happens there?"

"Ok, no, I meant... well..." Percival said, point toward the heavens.

"Of course, the Most High knows, and the rest of us have responsibilities and the hierarchy to report to in the best way we can."

Percival looked at him. "I guess I don't really know what it's like being here." He looked at the waves of sound signatures bouncing around and colliding with one another. "It obviously gets a lot more complicated down here. It must be difficult to get things done," he said, looking back toward Samuel.

Samuel knew he was getting through to him now. He didn't want pity, or even understanding. His intention was not to be heard or to express himself, but solely to ensure Percival's awareness of the situation. "The next principle is that of passage. They control the comings and goings of every immortal to the mortal plane. This includes themselves. While alternatively, it is we who control the passage of mortals to and from the immortal realm. We can get as far as the etheric plane, beyond here - we need their permission."

"Okay," Percival said with a concerned look. This was a whole layer of control he had never seen. He thought Central Existence only had to contend with the underworld. "What is their determination for letting us pass to the mortal plane? Should we need?"

"I knew you were smart. That is the principle of balance. You know about this. We know which souls and which immortals come and go from the mortal plane because the etherics provide Central Existence with the data and context."

Percival began calculating in his mind all the things Samuel had just told him. "That's what this is all about! It's not just that the Portal summoned a demon and fractured souls, she's operated outside of the laws of existence all together. She's threatening the entire system!

Samuel nodded and waved a finger in the air as if to say 'bingo'.

Percival waved his hand in the air to interrupt with a question. "Why, in the name of everything Holy, did they send me on a mission like this?"

"Most Celestials are not fully aware of all the implications of the etheric plane. We needed to find someone who knew how Central Existence functions so that they could use the knowledge down here. This is just your first trip. It won't be long before you are running circles around me."

"I'm never going to be a demon slayer. I know that."

"You'll be surprised. It ends up being necessary to dis-incorporate them. It becomes a 'you-versus-them' sort of thing." Samuel gets up and starts walking toward the rooftop entrance for the building.

As Percival stands up, Samuel teleports them to the viewing floor of the building which is scattered with tourists. The clean floor reflects the panoramic view of the city far below, as people admire how far they can see.

"I like this space because it's perfect for training Celestials on their first trip."

Percival noticed that the architecture of the room protected those inside from most of the wave signatures emanating from the rest of the city. He watched several etherics mill about waiting on their human counterparts.

Samuel pointed toward one of the large viewing windows. "Now that you can recognize what wave signatures are, you need to see the effect architecture has on them," while pointing outside. "Remember all those wonderful secrets we are so good at keeping?"

"Yeah," Percival snickers as he envisions a church packed with captivated parishioners and a priest who is suddenly interrupted by a loud fart. "Thanks for the imagery."

Samuel smirks as he casts his arm over the view of the tourists looking out of the floor to ceiling windows. Suddenly, the etherics disappeared. "Much of what any entity experiences is based on perspective."

"Okay, where did they all go?" Percival glances around the room, trying to figure out where the etherics disappeared to.

"Think of it like focusing. They are still here. We are just concentrating on something else right now. For instance, watch the woman in the red coat, standing over there at the window. I'll refocus slowly this time."

Percival watched the woman and her family as Samuel slowly cast his arm over the scene again. As he did, Percival could see the wave patterns emanating from her. Slowly, a tiny figure beside her came into view, blurry at first, as if molecules out of nowhere appeared and congealed together to form an entity. Within a moment, Percival witnessed a small etheric figure standing next to her, no higher than her knees, and observed how its presence was drawn to the wave signatures emanating from her. "Wow, that's interesting."

"What you see is a matter of what you focus on. The same is for the mortals as well, but the effect is different." Samuel reversed everything back again, and the etherics disappeared again. "Now, without the interference of the etherics, and notice what else interferes with wave signatures."

Percival concentrated, watching the wave signatures coming off of the woman and the people surrounding her. He noticed the energy from the people inside the room as each wave bounced off the other and into every person around it. Then he noticed how the architecture of the building canceled out all the energy, regardless of its size, just as it prevented all the wave signatures from outside coming in. "Oh, oh wow. They used Eternal Symmetry to build this!" He hurried toward the side of the building where the family stood, giddy that he knew so much about something the mortals had used in their own world.

"It's not just here, it's in all of their buildings. The mortals call it Euclidean Geometry, but it is based on our laws of Eternal Symmetry."

Percival remembered studying Eternal Symmetry, its part of the fundamental information that all Celestials receive. He knew what it was, but he didn't know how to create it. Eternal Symmetry forms the basis for creating structures in the celestial realm. The existence of right angles, and every angle based upon it, changed the way wave signatures transmit. "This revolutionized the balance of Eth in the mortal realm."

"Yes, which is why we leaked it long ago. It really pissed off the chthonics as well. When used repeatedly, like when creating a building, notice how the structure gives off its own wave signature. It's pretty slight, though."

Percival turned and looked at Samuel. He was all the way on the other side of the floor of the building. He noticed wave signatures were not flowing off of him or Samuel when either of them spoke. "Why can't I see yours or my own?"

"It's a cruel irony. You can't see your own. But it's also because we are part of the same consciousness. We are connected at a similar spiritual point." Samuel turned around and walked toward the opposite side of the building and looked out of the windows viewing the opposite direction. "It will feel like I'm reading your mind or communicating with you telepathically, but what we are doing right now is only possible because we are bound together. It happens when you spend too much time with someone, or in our case, because we came to the etheric realm together. No matter how far apart we are, we can communicate just like this."

"Wow", Percival said, listening to Samuel's voice. It was as if he were standing right next to him. His voice drowned out everyone around him, even the people who were standing close to him.

"The more you imbue upon a mortal, the more you are bound to them. So be careful." Percival enjoyed the moment. It was like he could be anywhere and still be with friends.

"What I want you to do next is something very different. I want you to look at someone next to you, and when you see a wave signature that interests you, I want you to reach out and grab it."

"Does it matter which one?"

"Read them first. Make sure you pick something you can stomach."

Percival looked back at the woman in red. A slow wave of energy emanated from her. It grew and floated all around her, rising into the air, almost undisturbed by anything else. Percival walked toward it as some of it dropped like the ribbon of a thin cloud across the floor. He held out his hand and scooped it up.

Within an instant, he teleported somewhere else. Percival stepped into her consciousness, viewing everything from her memory, but also understanding how she processed emotions and why she felt the things that she did. She was viewing a memory of the death of her father just a few weeks prior. They were on a trip to London from their small family home in Devon. There was no agenda, just the need to get away and change up the dynamic within the family.

As Percival viewed her memory, he focused in on her dying father. Within a flash, Percival was in his consciousness as well. He again could see all of his memories, the sensations of his experiences and how they formed who he became, and even where he was currently. The moment startled him so much he lost focus, and for a brief few moments, he saw everything from both of their perspectives. The fight she had with her father when she wanted to leave home to go to school in London in her twenties. How proud he was when she gave birth to his first grandchild.

Suddenly Percival was back in the room, watching another wave signature emanate from her as she remembered the last few weeks. It took him a moment to realize that Samuel was right next to him with his hand on Percival's shoulder.

"Be careful not to get too lost in there."

"I could feel it all."

"A bit different from a channeling orb, isn't it?"

"Considerably." Percival needed some air.

"They can imbue on you as much as you can them. It's only happened because it's your first time around."

"I need some air," Percival said vacantly. He made a vague shuffle toward the window and passed through to the outside, floating in midair outside the building. He breathed in the vibrations from the large space outside.

"Those are the building blocks. You have yet to bump into a chthonic, but I don't think you are ready for that yet."

Percival kept his eyes closed, like he did before, enjoying the exhale of the air.

"We can experience up to five different consciousnesses at the same time. It's not something I normally do, but it helps with understanding how the Ineffable Plan is playing out down here."

"So we can completely inhabit them? Control them even?"

"That's possession... very different thing. We don't do that. Don't need to because we have empathy on our side. C'mon, it's time to get going."

As Samuel led him toward the elevators, Percival fell in love with the large vacant echoes of the hall. He was amazed at the way the sound would echo, and how they differed from the way the sound moved back into the bookstore where they had met Alndvod.

Samuel led them into an elevator with two other mortals. He looked down at a medium-sized etheric, about the size of a large puppy, and nodded. The etheric widened its gills and flapped its webbed ears to say hello back. "We're going to need that small bag Alndvod gave to you earlier," he said to Percival while still looking at the etheric.

"Oh, right?" Percival materialized it and gave to Samuel.

Samuel began hunting through the gold sigils in the bag. The moment the etheric heard the chink of the metal it became curious. It climbed up Samuel's body and sat on his shoulder to peer down into the bag Samuel was hunting through.

"This one," Samuel asked, pulling the sigil coin out.

The etheric grunted in slight disapproval. It would gladly take all the sigils from him, but only needed a specific one to enact the duty Samuel was looking for. Samuel slightly held up each one, just enough for the etheric to see it, never taking it out of the bag for fear that it would snatch it away like a monkey eyeing a picnic basket. The etheric grunted through a few more candidates until the correct one appeared. "Ohhh," it squealed as Samuel handed it to him. The etheric climbed down to the floor, sniffing the sigil and scrutinizing it. It looked at one side of the coin with the full sigil on it, running its fingers over it, and then halted. It looked up at Samuel with suspicion – then pointed at the row of floor options on the elevator key pad.

"Yes, we need access to section A."

The etheric grumbled, looking at the sigil again in disbelief. It was the sigil of the Elders. The sigil was plastered everywhere in the etheric world, so every etheric knew it, but holding the sigil in one's hands rarely happened. Those who passed the sigil were saying they were acting under the direction of the Elders themselves. It was the ultimate hall pass. The etheric could not deny Samuel's request. It turned to the elevator keypad and pressed the back of the coin against the bottom of the aluminum plate of the keypad. In the blink of an eye, the numbering of keys changed. There were options for other planets, all seven dimensions, and each section of the etheric world. The etheric pressed the option for 'Section A'. The moment he did, mortal time stopped. The two mortals in the elevator stood frozen while the elevator continued to move. The elevator slowed to a stop and the bell for their the floor rang.

The next thing Percival knew, he was standing in a large meadow of purple grass under the three moons of Etheria. "How did we get here?"

Samuel stood looking at the surroundings as well. "We have been granted permission to come here."

"Yes, but how did we physically get here? Neither of us flew or used a portal."

"You sound like a mortal. They have different methods than we do, some of which we aren't privy to, but it's all part of the God's kingdom. Just enjoy it. It's very different away from the power of the central office. Not so much is in your control."

Percival turned away from Samuel and put his hands on his hips in protest. He didn't like not being in the loop on things.

"You thought it was just us, didn't you? Just like the mortals, we only know what the Most High wants us to. It might be a lot, but even we don't know everything."

Percival dropped his head and then nodded.

Samuel walked through the purple grass and looked up at the night sky. "Those are the three etheric moons. They don't appear like that because there are three hunks of rock in space around the etheric planet. There are three moons because they serve three other dimensions. They serve the spiritual world, both chthonic and celestial, and the mortals. But it's important to focus not that etherics are different, but that they serve. They lack free will and are confined in a space where they are obligated to deliver whatever the spiritual world wants for the mortals."

"But why do they serve the Chthonics?"

"Etherics are based on the fallen. Of course, some of them naturally rebelled against the Underworld, but because they are not of the Creator, they can never enter Heaven either. They create a thin layer between the physical and spiritual world. They are the transition itself. It's unfortunate because there are many etherics that are far more supportive of the ineffable plan than the best of the Fallen in their original form."

"That's more complicated than I thought." Percival looked at him in thanks for the support.

"A frustrated angel is a dangerous thing. But as you know, it's not ours to question."

Percival nodded.

"Mortals, human or otherwise, are not aware of the war being waged against them. The humans especially are always troubled because of their attachment to ego and the physical world. All we can do is our best to keep the world on track. Only the Creator knows what the path to success is." Samuel stepped closer to Percival and threw him to the ground. Percival lands with a thud, and a small cloud of purple pollen flies up like fine powder and settles all over him. Samuel reaches underneath Percival and flips him like a pancake to make sure he gets both sides. "We'll shine like a beacon here. These grasses will provide some cover for you."

Samuel took a tumble for himself. Rolling around a few times, he liked the etheric plane. It was much like the mortal realm, although a bit strange. It has the tone of forgotten feelings. As the realm serves as a transition, the idea of permanence is foreign. Everything had a veneer of potential or the tone of sentimentality. The legions upon legions of souls that had traversed this Eth had left their mark. Even the most hardened souls destined to suffer under the Chthonics expressed their last ounces of grief and regret here–even if for a moment. The entire realm is composed of meadows and grasses, whether in the fields or under a grove of trees.

Samuel knew this would be tough, for many a celestial has felt in the past. It is common knowledge among the choirs that all who serve the Creator feel. It is always what one does with those feelings that really matters. It was fine to have a doubt in the Creator's plan, as long as it is accompanied by an action born out of faith and hope. It was going to be especially difficult for Percival, for he had already been changed by the Portal. This could be his downfall, but like everything–it will depend on how Percival plays it. Seeing that Percival was now half mortal and Samuel was in the closest proximity when it happened, it also meant that he was his Guardian. He could feel the lack of connection between himself and Percival. Perhaps this was part of the sorrow he was feeling. The feeling of losing a family member. But it was also because deep down, Samuel preferred the choirs to the humans. Even though he spent most of his time with the mortals, he could get around his distaste by knowing he was serving the higher realm. His biggest concern right now is whether he could keep Percival within the confines of his plan.

CHAPTER ELEVEN

S amuel and Percival walk through the main gates of Etheria. It looked like Vegas on steroids. Everything shined with the glow of eth. Etherics hung from the eves as they partied on the rooftops. Some drove convertible vehicles. Droves of etherics sauntered down the sidewalks and alleys in jovial groups, not going anywhere in particular. The entire city glowed with a fine haze of the eth that flowed through its center. Percival was immediately enthralled by the continual parade of revelry.

"Hey, hey," Samuel grabbed Percival by both of his shoulders and stared into his eyes. "We need to keep focused. I know you've never seen this before, but we can't let anything sway us from getting to the Portal.

"Why are they so happy?"

"Because this is Etheria. Most of these etherics live here full time. They certainly never want to leave. If you live here, you are swimming in eth, they have more than we do."

"Wow," Percival said, looking at a small group standing outside of a building. They had gathered around in a circle and were betting each other on two etherics who were lining up to fight each other in the center of the group. "They are trading eth. I didn't know you could do that."

"This realm is a complete middleman," Samuel said wading through the crowd. After the Great War, Central Existence needed to manage things in the mortal realm. So instead of creating more choirs, he allowed the choirs he had left to become part of the etheric realm. Over the millennia, it was realized that they were transporting so much eth from Central Existence, and they were putting up with so much disruption from Pandemonia, they could collect eth from both sides for the burden of their efforts. Anyone who lives in Etheria doesn't have to lift a finger. They all live in the extravagance of pure life force."

The central core of eth flowing between the Celestial and Chthonic worlds powered Etheria. While Samuel had never been to Etheria before, he had heard much about it during his time.

They walked through the city, taking in all the sights. It struck Samuel as more like a carnival than an actual city.

"What about the etherics who live outside the city?"

"They have to struggle and shoulder the burden of the duties of the realm." Samuel stopped in the middle of the street. He was lost. The vehicles and parades of etherics filtered around him as if he were a rock in the middle of a river.

"What's wrong?" Percival asked, standing close to him so the commotion can go around them both.

"I can't remember how to get there. I only know it from legend." Samuel reached down and grabbed one of the etherics from a passing vehicle. He plucked it out of a convertible as if he were plucking a blossom off of a bush. As he picked it up, the eth drained from the etheric and the creature's drunkenness turned to sullenness. It had never lived in a true moment before. It had only known over-stimulation throughout its existence. The noise of the crowd suddenly dulled, and the three of them were standing in the middle of a beachfront promenade in Barecelona. Samuel had ripped the etheric into the mortal world to get its attention. "I need you to tell me where to find the Portal of Judgement," Samuel demanded.

The etheric, scared out of its skin, points its arm in the direction of the spires of the La Sagrada Familia. "In the shadow of the Council of Elders," the etheric answered like a schoolboy reciting a lesson.

Samuel looked down the promenade toward the spires. As he did, he saw a person in the crowd walking toward them with a dark cloud swarming around her. He immediately knew it was Ganislay. "Shit," he said dropping the etheric. They were immediately back in the center of Etheria. Samuel grabbed Percival and dragged him into the entrance of a side street.

Percival fought back as Samuel dropped him to the ground next to a building. "Hey, you have to stop man-handling people. You can't just pick up an etheric or any entity you like and demand something from them. They have free will. You certainly can't do that with me."

Samuel grabbed Percival by the shoulders again and shook him. "I just saved our skins. You have to understand, we are at war. The faster you get that in your mind, the farther we are going to get."

"Let me go," Percival squirmed, shaking himself from Samuel's grip. "What War? The War was over centuries ago. Maybe you need to understand that it's time you let that go." Percival dusted himself off and straightened himself out. "You run around like you are forever trying to duck and dive under some sinister force. Nothing is going to happen. We are going to march in to the portal and get what we need. We are Celestials."

Samuel stared at him for a moment. This was certainly not like the Percival he had known. Maybe he had grown too accustomed to winning. Maybe he had been too sheltered. Either way, he figured it was time Percival learned how to stand up for himself. With one swift kick, Samuel booted Percival backwards into the main street where they had just run from.

Percival flies backward and steadies himself on his feet just before he loses his balance, like a cat saving itself from an awkward fall.

Ganislay sees Percival's eth signature through the crowds. Percivals eth emanated from him in a much larger amplitude than the rest of the glow of the city. His eyes snap to the glow of eth like a fish seeing the glint of a metal lure under water. Nothing shines like a Celestial, even in Etheria.

Percival straightened himself out again, proud of saving himself from public embarrassment. Not that the etherics would have paid him any mind no matter what had happened to him. As he was paying attention to his appearance, suddenly the shouts of revelry change to screams and Percival could hear the stampede of feet as hundreds of etherics began to scatter. Percival looked up just in time to see Ganislay rushing toward him.

Ganislay's teeth snarled and he leapt into the air, extending out his tail like a long whip. Ganislay could immediately tell he would have Percival's eth in no time. He whipped his tail and it wrapped around Percival's neck several times. Ganislay landed right beside him, crushing several etherics beneath his feet.

"Fuck, he's a hungry bastard," Samuel said, standing at the corner of a building. "C'mon kid, fight back."

The end of Ganislay's tail pierced Percival's neck like a snake burrowing into a hole.

Percival immediately felt sick and weak. He could barely hink much less fight. His thoughts became a dizzy whirl of confusion. He could still see what Ganislay was doing to him, but the visual was making no cognitive impact. Percival thought about the library back at Central Existence and all the theories he learned about demons and how to fight them. It never occurred to him he would actually need to do it one day.

Ganislay thought this was too easy, a gift. "What is a little celestial like you doing out here? You should know better." He raised his tail, raising Percival higher above his head, and then slammed Percival's body in the ground several times. "I am going to take every bit of eth. I don't care who witnesses."

Samuel snuck out into the crowd behind Ganislay. Ganislay was having too much fun, and the crowd was too loud that he didn't hear Samuel walking up behind him. The etherics continued to run in their thousands in frenzied directions, not really having a plan of what to do. The crowd got louder and more frantic the closer Samuel got to Ganislay, for they knew a severe battle was about to ensue. A demon in Etheria had only happened one other time, and it took all they could muster to rid it from the realm. They had no power over Celestials, so the prospect of an epic fight between the two on their own streets was catastrophic.

Samuel drew a sword from the top of his shoulder. As he placed both hands on the grip, it flamed. He raised it, almost joyous in his luck that was going to dispatch a demon this easily. He pulled the sword down in one large plunging motion, wedging itself between his shoulder and neck, lodging in his body.

Ganislay let out a scream like a wounded bull. He dropped Percival to the ground as his tail retracted in shock.

To Samuel's surprise, Ganislay immediately reached around and grabbed Samuel by the top of his head, flipping him over and onto the ground in front of him. Ganislay morphed into a being with the body of a giant man and the head of a bull. He screamed and snorted at Samuel, who lay on the ground in shock. Ganislay reached up with his left hand and pulled Samuel's sword out from his shoulder. He began running toward Samuel, screaming and brandishing the sword with each step. The blood of etherics sprayed as he sliced through the crowd.

Samuel couldn't understand it. That blow would have dispatched nearly any entity, except maybe Satan himself. He jumped into the air, flying over Ganislay, and as he did, he reached down and picked him up and then dropping to the ground and landing on top of Ganislay. He dug his knee into Ganislay's wounded shoulder and grabbed the sword from Ganislay, holding to his neck. "You aren't going anywhere except straight back to hell."

"Good luck. I am bound to this realm."

Samuel tried to plunge the blade of the sword into the demon's neck again, simply by leaning on the blade this time. The amount of pressure he was using should have cut completely through Ganislay's neck, but it was like Ganislay was made of iron.

Ganislay knew this was turning into a stalemate. He was stronger from the eth he had stolen from Percival, and he didn't want to lose it. He let out a growl deep enough to shake the surrounding buildings. The crowd tumbled to the ground as if trying to run during an earthquake. Ganislay's growl turned to a loud trumpet that boomed everywhere throughout the realm and then he disappeared into a streak of light from beneath Samuel.

The loud trumpets stopped and Samuel got to his feet.

"I didn't know they could do that," one of the etherics said, looking at Samuel.

"No," Samuel said looking at the horizon. "Neither did I."

Samuel walked over to Percival and picked him up. He carried him back to the side alley, and gently placed him on the ground. "Well, they know we're here now, that's for sure."

"What is this feeling?"

Samuel looked at him with care for the first time. He didn't think the consequences would have been this high for throwing Percival out into the open like that. "My friend, this is having your eth taken. A bit like mortal death." Samuel held his hands over Percivals chest, and allowed the surrounding eth from buildings to flow through him and into Percival. "Let that be a lesson learned. Chthonics crave the force of life like no other because they are cut off from it. With mortals, they have it easy. Since the Fall chthonics study humans as much as we do, but humans pretty much serve themselves up simply through curiosity or pride. With us and etherics, they have to attack us, because we are not so easily beguiled. They will betray their own kind, they will kill any entity in their way of achieving more eth. You, me, humans, God herself if they had to."

Percival lay on the ground while the eth flowed back into him from Samuel's hands. He struggled to concentrate, to function at all, as if he had been poisoned.

"Now do you understand?"

Percival did his best to nod as he continued to lay on the ground. The parades of etherics continued on as if nothing had ever happened. They flowed around the six etherics that were killed in the scuffle. The etherics attending to the scene had difficulty keeping the river of vehicles and those walking from trampling on the victims. "They don't even care," Percival said, looking at the street.

Samuel stood Percival up. etherics are no different. You need to get a different view of the world. We don't care about eth because we create it, etherics revel in it because they control it, and Chthonics will do anything for eth because they are cut off from it. It's the one thing that those in Central Existence don't seem to understand.

"What would have happened if you hadn't stopped him?"

"That sort of depends. A celestial without eth can be a horrible thing. He could have dis-incorporated you if he really wanted. Or he could have just left you there like a shell, and then that depends on what you do from that point. You'd either begin doing something desperate and you would be excommunicated, unless someone kind helps you and provides you with eth. The problem is, celestial's require more eth than most have to give. A morsel to you would almost kill an etheric. It definitely would kill any mortal."

"I would never become one of the fallen," Percival said in a much louder voice. Incensed, Percival gets to his feet and begins walking down the alley away from the street.

Samuel catches up to him and shoves him into the side of the building. Percival flinches, thinking he was about to get another beating. "The next biggest lesson. Get a grip on your own pride. Being in Central Existence is a privilege, something that most entities can't fathom. Such an environment never lets you see desperation. You never know what someone is going to do in a desperate situation, and it can be a quick trip from decadence to destitution. I've seen it many times. "

Samuel walks off in the direction Percival was heading. He was getting concerned with Percival. He was acting more and more unlike himself. For all the management of humans and watching how they interact, Samuel didn't think Percival would be this naive, or this full of expectation. He would have to keep a closer eye on him. "C'mon, we don't have eternity."

CHAPTER TWELVE

S amuel stood at the corner of a building just down the street from where the portal was supposed to be. The building was enormous, the second largest in Etheria. Only the Council of Elders was larger, which dwarfed this. The building resembled a large glass flower blossom, with some parts reaching towards the sky and other petals extending down to the ground, where a large public garden led to the Council of Elders. It struck Samuel that it looked like a large lily slanted to one side.

The function of the building sat disguised as the purpose was a casino. Throngs of well-to-do etherics strolled in and out of the building, contained in their revelry. "We're going to have to spend some eth to do this."

"Sure, whatever it takes, right?

Samuel spreads his arms as wide as he can. Eth is drawn in to the ends of his fingers from everything that surrounds him. The building, the ground, the piping on the sides of each of the buildings, first skirting off the edges of every object within his vicinity, and culminated into an orb in front of him. The orb grows with, giving off the same green hue that eth always does. He splits the orb in two and tosses it toward Percival, while keeping the other for himself. Samuel then stretched out the cloud of eth as if it were a ball of dough, so that it was as large as himself, and then he walks into it.

As they both walked into their respective eth orbs, they change into etheric creatures, dressed in council uniforms, and begin to walk toward the building. Samuel began to worry. He had heard many things about what goes on in this building. Even though he had seen many of the darker things that occur throughout all realms of existence, some of the worst occur in here. He wasn't sure if he was prepared, but he knew Percival certainly wasn't. He would have to imbue a containment spell upon him. If Percival were to blow their cover, they would never make it to the Portal. He formed another orb in front of him and tossed it onto Percival.

"What the hell did you just do to me?" Percival tried to yell. However, his body didn't respond. He tries to stop and shout at Samuel even harder, but his body continues to walk in stride with Samuel calmly and quietly. His thoughts were his own, but his body was nothing more than a drone.

"I'm sorry, my friend. It won't last forever, but this mission is too critical to have you blow it," Samuel said, turning to him. Just follow my lead.

They walked up the wide stone stairs with the other etherics entering the building. Just inside the front door was the first checkpoint. A sign reading: No Dregs, No Credit given beyond this point.

"What's a Dreg?" Percival whispered.

"From here on out, if you want to talk, just communicate as we would in Central Existence. I'll hear you. A Dreg is any etheric who's not a citizen of Etheria."

"I didn't realize it was a rank."

"Of course it is. You don't think they just let the eth flow for free, do you? All the actual business of Etheria gets done in here, long before it gets to the Council of Elders."

"How do you know so much about this place?"

"I pay attention, over time you hear things."

The etheric security officer waved Samuel to approach him. Samuel knew he had reached a unique part of the realm. The security guard was taller than Samuel's etheric avatar. Tall etherics were unusual. It was most likely bred for the role of security, most likely a part chthonic and part etheric. It picked up a small device that looked like an orb with a handle on it, and a beam shot out, surrounding Samuel's avatar, scanning him inside and out. A log of his profile emerged showing the avatars name, age, bank balance, whether he had any contraband, previous violations, citizen status, and personal history. No one said a word, as it wasn't necessary. The security guard waved him on and motioned for Percival to approach.

The security guard did the same scan on Percival. "This is freaking me out, Samuel."

"That's why I put a containment spell on you." Samuel was relieved to see that Percival's avatar didn't flinch, despite what was going on in Percival's mind. The security guard waved Percival along and Percival caught up to Samuel.

"Eventually, this tech will filter down to the mortals. If they think privacy is dead now, they are really going to get upset when they see this," he said walking onto the main floor of the casino.

As they walked into the center of the floor, they looked around at all the tables. Percival noticed all the tables games took bets of eth rather than any kind of currency. He couldn't take his eyes away. "But what do they need eth for?"

"It's not about need. It's a way of keeping score. Besides, if you have enough eth, you can do much more interesting things."

"Like what?"

"Good afternoon citizens," an etheric said walking toward them. The etheric had a leather folder and was checking some sort of schedule. "What can we interest you with today?"

"We're looking for something a bit more lively. What would you recommend," Samuel said encouraging her.

"We have our regular selection of floor games, as always, Scruple, Chance. If you prefer to play against an opponent, we have the largest Lu-Kel room in Etheria."

Samuel winced, playing the game of a connoisseur. "We are looking for something more... exclusive."

The etheric looked at the two of them for a moment and then looked down at the file folder they were carrying. "The main floor and the Lu-Kel room are all we have scheduled right now."

Samuel stepped toward the etheric. "I trust you can find us something suitable," he said, slipping a million eth credits onto the etheric's open folder.

"I believe I can. Right this way." The etheric turned around and began guiding them toward the back of the main room. As they walked passed all the floor games, Percival couldn't get over that people were betting, trading and bartering eth. They got to a regular-looking door at the back of the room and the etheric pressed her the leather folder against the keypad next to the door. It opened to a maintenance hallway that looked like something out of a submarine. "This is my favorite part of the building. Most entities never get to see it. Almost three trillion eth transfer through here every cycle between the mortal plane and the outer regions."

"Where are the outer regions?" Percival asked Samuel.

"It's what they call us. Etherics believe they are at the center of everything. The problem is, they are. So behave. Without them, the whole thing falls apart."

"What thing?"

"Mortal existence. We need them on our side."

The concept of etherics not being on their side left Percival feeling confused, considering that all eth was created in Central Existence and flowed to all the realms from there. It was biting the hand that feeds them.

They came to another plain looking doorway midway down the hall. It felt like they were deep underground. Percival could feel the weight of the entire building on top of them. He could feel the flow of eth transferring all around them. Life force separated from the souls that it used to contained it. It needed to be returned.

"And here we are," the etheric said, stopping outside a door. "I cannot go any further. It is a simple process. Register with the game administrator at the back of the room. I cannot guarantee the number of games that you will be a part of, but there are side bets. We have a wide access to all of mortality, so it shouldn't be that long. Enjoy." The etheric opened the door and allowed Samuel and Percival to enter.

The room was dark, with fifteen oversized theatre seats in a semicircle that overlooked a large picture window. On the other side of the picture window, there was a room that consisted solely of a table with a chair on either side. On top of the table was a set of brass scales.

"Good afternoon and welcome. May I see your eth balance please?"

Samuel's avatar digs into his breast pocket and produces a device that displays the required information. As he hands it to her, he immediately loses control of his avatar for a few moments. "Oh fuck," he says, looking at the creature. It was impossible for him to keep his cover, for the creature he was speaking to was an Oracle – the great leveler of all entities and spirits.

"There is no reason to swear. Your truth is safe with me." She knew they were celestials.

"The portal is behind that pane of glass, isn't she," Samuel asked.

"Yes, of course. Every Portal works with an Oracle. Here the Portal of Judgement must be privy to truth, just as the Portal of Mortality works with the Oracle of Innocence."

Samuel found it difficult to believe that Old Widow Grey worked side by side with the Oracle of Innocence.

The Oracle smiled, dismissing his disbelief. "Of course she does. In order to be born into the mortal plane, she must have access to innocence, to bestow it upon each soul entering the plane. Just as those who are to be judged at the end of their mortality, the Portal must have access to Truth."

Samuel hadn't realized just how much has been outsourced by Central Existence over the millennia. "Of course. How does this work?"

Take a seat in any chair you like. When it is your turn, you may bet on which direction the soul will travel. If you are correct, you collect their eth and your bet is returned to you. If you are wrong, the house collects your bet along with their eth. The rest of the room is taking side bets on the success of your guesses. Whenever you guess correctly, the longer the betting round stays with you.

Samuel had never heard of this within the choirs. The troubling thing was, where were the souls coming from? "Does this make sense to you Percival," Samuel asked in his mind.

"Somewhat. They are obviously getting to the souls before Celestials are notified, and even before the dead can receive them," Percival communicated.

Percival had spent the last several minutes trying not to freak out in front of the others patrons who were placing their bets. They both knew this had become a major part of the mission. First, they needed to understand the full aspect of the scheme. Samuel wasn't sure if they were the first-ever Celestials to visit this room. If someone had visited before, they were most definitely dis-incorporated. This type of scheme would have spread like wildfire through the choirs. However, he couldn't imagine it will be long before someone discovers they were there. Samuel knew the oracle wasn't a truth teller, but simply truth. So unless an etheric asks if two Celestials visited the portal today, it is doubtful the news will get anywhere. Though he wasn't going to count on it.

Behind the glass window, the Portal of Judgement appears out of the darkness. In front of her, waist high, is a simple pedestal with a set of brass scales on it.

On the opposite side of the pedestal, a scene is spotlighted of a hospital bed. An old man lays deceased, as a Celestial appears beside him. The Celestial reaches down as if to shake the man's hand, and instead pulls the man out of his own body, as if he is helping him to his feet. The man is a much younger version of himself, and the Celestial gestures for the man to look back at his aged body. Simultaneously, as the man is looking at his body, a second aspect of the man appears before the Portal of Judgement. Beside the man's aspect stands the same Celestial beside one shoulder, and on the other side appears an amorphous black cloud floating in the air.

Samuel's device vibrates inside his pocket, and he takes it out. A display screen shows 'Betting is now open. The current streak is three. High streak of the day: seven. A timer appeared at the bottom of the screen. Samuel was unsure what he wanted to do. If he didn't make a bet, they would be found out. If he did, it would violate his duties, even if he was undercover. After the betting closes, Sam sees the results on his screen, similar to the outcome of a poll. Most of the room agrees with the main bettor. This person is going to be taken by the Celestials.

The portal spreads out a deck of tarot cards across the pedestal and pulls a single card. It is the same card that is always pulled, the Card of Judgement. She places the card on top of the scale. She raises her other hand and pulls all the eth out of the man's soul. It hovers between them in an amorphous green cloud, bursting full of energy. The Portal shrinks it down to a concentrated size, and the ball of eth floats to the other side of the scales and settles on the other scale, opposite of the judgement card. The scales jostle to find the weight of the two objects, and then finally settle that the man's eth is more substantial than the judgement upon him.

"I've never seen this before," Percival communicated.

"When things are in doubt, and cutting too close, this process occurs. Sometimes things get an automatic pass either way, we just know. But the point of this process is, if a mortal's life force, their eth, is more substantial than the judgement being placed upon them, they are deemed to have lived an honourable life."

The Portal of Judgement simply nods, and the Celestial wraps his arms around the man. They change into a flash of white light that streaks out of the room.

Samuel's device vibrates again. He looks at it to see that the main bettor just won his bet and collects ten percent of the eth, while the room collected ten percent of the placed bet.

"Wow, what a way to increase your margins."

"If there is one thing all the Choirs can agree on, it's that we don't like a 'money changer'."

This is true. I didn't think this practice occurred as often as it is.

Samuel's device buzzes again, and the Portal appears again in the space on the other side of the large picture window. This time a woman is center stage in a gruesome scene. Half ejected through the front of a car windshield, laying dead and nearly cut in half by the steering wheel and the glass she torpedoed through only moments before. A different Celestial appears, grabbing her hand as if to shake it, and pulls her soul out of her body.

The woman's soul appears before the pedestal with the scales. This time the judgement card weights more than the woman's eth. The portal pulls out another card from the pile and simply shows it to the woman. It is the card of deceit and trickery. The shadows in the room expand and a Wraith bursts forth, swooping across the woman and whisking her out of view like a hawk scooping up a kitten.

The bettor guesses correctly again, but the rest of the room was wrong. As always, Etheria takes its cut. Samuel stands up, places his hands together and spreads them apart, stopping time. "We will not stand for this," Samuel says as he glides through the glass partitioning the Portal from the betting room.

The Portal simply stares at him. "What is the meaning of this interference?"

"This must stop," Samuel demanded.

"We are doing as we have always done," the Portal asserted.

"Yes, but placing a value of entertainment upon the process is a great shame upon this house."

"I cannot control the actions of others. What the etherics fail to realize is they will be judged for their actions, just as all celestials will be judged for theirs."

"This can't continue. You must be able to do something to stop it," Percival blurted out loud. He noticed he could actually speak out loud now that Samuel stopped time.

"Understand, I am not an entity such as yourself. I am a virtue, I have no free will, only duty – for Judgement has no permanent form."

"That doesn't make sense, because the Old Widow Grey has a physical form," Percival said. He was growing frustrated with the many layers he was discovering between Central Existence and the mortal realm.

"Correct. In order to function as the Portal of Mortality, one needs to have been mortal at some point."

"We'll have to come back to this later." Samuel interjected. "There is about to be a much bigger problem. A chthonic has stolen a key to heaven. It's possible that he won't even know how to use it, but he's got help to ensure his way into the gates of Heaven."

Without a beat, the Portal responds. "He's coming here to destroy me."

Samuel was surprised by her calm realization.

"The end of Judgement would mean the end of all virtue," she asserted.

"What do you mean, that's ridiculous," Percival blurted.

Samuel looked at Percival, inspecting him. Those were not the words of a celestial, as Celestials were not prone to panic."

"Excuse my friend, but he's correct. Why would it be the end of all virtue," Samuel asked.

"Because no one virtue stands alone, we are contingent upon one another. To end Judgement would have a domino effect, because without it, there cannot be Prudence, or Temperance, and without Temperance there cannot be Wisdom, and so on. Killing Judgement is a strategic move because existence would continue, mortal life would continue, but not without immense chaos," the Portal explained.

"So for instance, truth would continue to exist, and maybe even honesty, but without Judgement there is no understanding of either of them. Mortals would even become a threat to themselves," Percival said in amazement.

"Exactly," the Portal responded.

"Well, we can't let that happen. I guess you are coming with us," Samuel said grabbing her.

She rebuffed him. "Abandoning my duties is nearly the same result. Every etheric will be after you."

"Oh yeah, why's that," Samuel asked staring her down.

"Because Judgement is the portal through which all eth flows through to the other planes."

"I guess we'll just have to keep you on this plane then." Samuel threw his hands toward her and she was immediately wrapped in a bubble. She could not move or communicate with others except for Samuel. Time suddenly restarted. "Whoa, I didn't do that." The commotion in the betting room overlooking them catches his eye. Samuel threw another smaller ball of energy toward the Portal making her invisible to everyone except he and Percival.

Most of the etherics scramble from their seats at the sight of the celestials. The remaining etherics in the betting area look at him with horror. "Holy shit, how did they get in here?" someone shouts. Another etheric stood up and ran to the back of the room. Immediately an alarm began blaring and a yellow light shined, bathing everything in a golden hue.

The oracle walks to the window through the panicked crowd, her face in shock. "I know you will do her no harm, but you have started a war," she communicated. She slowly began to shake her head in disagreement.

"I told you, there would be chaos, much of which I cannot predict," the Portal declared.

Samuel grabbed the Portal and Percival and shot off in a streak of light.

A moment later, they appeared outside of the building on the street. Samuel was surprised to see that every building in the city was alive with alarm bells. A raid siren blared throughout the skies.

"What do we do?" Percival asked worriedly. Samuel had never heard a Celestial so stressed before.

Samuel noticed he was knocked off from the normal flow of eth he draws in automatically. He suddenly realized taking care of Percival and the Portal was about to become a really big burden. "I'm going to have to get you two somewhere safe."

"You won't have access to your normal abilities. As virtue changes, so does existence, and I imagine anything that comes from central existence as well," the Portal warned.

Samuel was beginning to get very annoyed with the humanity that Percival was displaying. "The Oracle is right. I may have just started a war."

Judgement looked at him with a fright that made her feel hollow. She knew disincorporation was coming for herself and many others. She knew what was happening to the remaining virtues as she felt the death of several of them as she spoke with the celestials. Without the Virtues the mortal plane would not be the same. She knew Old Widow Grey had just gotten what she wanted. Without Innocence, the portal of Mortality no longer needed a guardian in its post to ensure all born to the mortal plane were innocent. The only thing left protecting the Celestial plane from being inundated by the departed and the chthonics was Truth and herself, Judgement.

Samuel grabbed Judgement, "If you want to make it through this, stay close," he blurted to Truth and they went into the maintenance hallway.

The sound from all the commotion and the sirens pounded Judgement's head. She could feel the confusion and panic flowing off of every entity in Etheria. This was why she didn't go out into the world. She hadn't left the confines of her space in hundreds of years.

Samuel led the three of them down the hallway at a quick pace and into the main casino room. He could see etherics running en mass toward the front exit, trampling each other. The best thing to do was to join in the mayhem before any response teams arrived. As they ran out the front door in the river of panicked etherics, Samuel knew it wouldn't be long before they were discovered and a mob descended upon them. He wasn't sure he could fight them off for very long in the condition he was in. "This way," he said, pulling the Portal with him.

They ducked down a side street that the crowd had yet to find. As they ran down the small street, Samuel spotted a metal door. He ran up to it and pulled it open so fast, he hardly recognized that he broke the lock on the doorframe. "In... in... in...," he gestured, waving his arms. He swung the portal around the corner of the open door, flinging her into the building, and held his hand out for Percival, who was a few steps behind.

Like everything in Etheria, they were almost as large as the rooms, certainly bigger than any of the furniture. His eyes darted around the room. It would be impossible to hide. However, he believed their imposing size would be enough of a force to block the door. The room was a workshop. He saw a heavy metal cabinet and reached over to pick it up, clunking it to the floor in front of the door. "Percival, I need you to take a seat on that." He pointed to the top of the cabinet.

For anyone else, the cabinet would have seemed tall, but to Percival it felt more like a stool that he could hardly get a seat on. He fussed for a moment or two to find a comfortable position to lean his weight on.

Samuel leaned toward the window and spied out of it. etherics were now streaming down the street, walking at a fast pace, but not so fast as to trample one another. The air-raid siren continued to blare and yellow lights continued to fill the atmosphere and every nook and cranny. A security drone glided overhead. An announcement repeatedly blared from the drone: 'Make your way back to your residences, do not stop.'

"They are starting a lockdown," the Portal said. "After the last time Celestials came to Etheria, there was an edict passed by the Elders."

This worried Samuel. He continued to stare out the window. "We are pinned down, so we won't be able to move from this position," Samuel worried, continuing to stare out the window.

"When they find us," the Portal announced.

The words fell starkly on him. He knew this could be the end of his time.

"What happened?" Percival asked the Portal. The gravity of the situation didn't escape Percival, but he felt he didn't want to address it. He realized he was feeling emotion for the first time in his existence, and he wanted to take a break from it. He shifted his weight on the top of the cabinet and leaned in a bit more.

"It was a millennium ago, at the end of the last Celestial Age. Of course, when a new celestial ruler comes in, a lot of shuffling occurs. Some of it is needed as there are new agendas to be had, while often there are many in this realm who jockey for their own positions. That's when the problems ensue. It started with an ambitious etheric called Nythalias, who wanted to stay in power. Remaining in power here in Etheria means one thing: dealing with the oppression of the outer realms. It doesn't matter what etherics do. If the flow of eth changes, etherics won't be able to sustain themselves for very long–so the Celestials and, to a lesser extent, the Chthonics, leave them to their own devices. As everything flows from the Central Existence, the first chance the etheric realm has is understanding how to skim the flow of eth before it gets to the mortal realm. The easiest is to collect it between the mortal and Chthonic realm. It was Nythalias who came up with this system and changed the destiny of the entire etheric realm. To etherics, Nythalias is a liberator, before his time they felt like slaves."

"How were they slaves? I don't understand."

"Do they not teach this history in your library?" the Portal asked.

Samuel tuned and shot her a concerned look. *To speak of these things is apocryphal,* he communicated to her. *"He will be considered unclean by the higher triad."*

The Portal looked away from them both. She remembered that this is the type of madness that created the first Great War

Percival saw the look between the two of them. He couldn't figure out why he couldn't read Samuel's thoughts, but he understood the social queue he was observing. "I know the choirs frown upon this, but ultimately, my duties are to the Most High, not to them."

Samuel turned to him, "Yes, but life can become incredibly difficult when you do not stand in their favor. It's taken -"

"I'm beginning to understand! The things I've seen down here don't make sense," Percival impressed. "I've witnessed things that defy protocol and long-standing directives among the choirs."

Samuel looked at him with understanding. "That's the difference between knowing something and experiencing something. They rarely look the same up close, and wisdom only comes from both."

"Not anymore," the Portal blurted.

They both looked at her in confusion.

"Since you took me, Wisdom is no more. They've had help. They were waiting for this."

Samuel crouched down, "Are you saying..." He could see that she was already nodding her head. "So there really have been Regents formed. Alliances."

"Yes," she affirmed.

"Would someone tell me what the hell is going on!" Percival came to a sudden halt, taken aback by the forcefulness of his own words. He looked at Samuel with suspicion. "Just how many times have you been to the etheric plane?"

"Quite a few. To be honest, it's the best way to travel. I don't want to have to mingle with the bloody humans any more than I have to." Samuel sat on the floor in defeat. He needed the rest. Keeping up all these appearances was exhausting him.

"But you are in service to them!"

"Yes, but that doesn't mean I have to like them." He looked over to the Portal. "I'm having enough of a problem figuring all of this out. You may as well tell him everything. We're probably about to die, anyway."

"Oh, don't be so dramatic, we can't die." Percival looked at him with pity.

Samuel looked back at Percival like he was a fool.

"Wait a second, can we?" he asked Samuel, looking for encouragement. "Can we," he said, looking to the Portal for assurance.

The portal raised her arms and formed an orb like a crystal ball in the middle of the room. Within seconds, it showed an image of an immense battle. "After the Great War, when the Fallen had been cast out, they created the Infernal Council. The Most High recognized that having power concentrated among the few was a great danger to her plans. After the Fall, the Most High again became frustrated and divided the nation into twelve. That's what happened on the mortal plane. But in the middle heaven it was decided that there would be Principles and Dominions to oversee over the different nations."

Percival sees a dark landscape displayed from inside the orb. Streaks of fire stream from the skies and down into the ground. As they delve into the ground and disappear, out of the darkened silhouette of the ground, Percival can see other Celestials, smaller ones, looking up at the sky.

The Portal continued, "We forgot the Celestials of the first heaven. They were brought down during the time of the Watchers, and made it through the great flood–for they had nothing to do with the humans. After this, they became permanently intertwined with running the mortal plane. Serving those who served the mortals. They were the original Lost Order. The higher choirs assumed we had perished in the flood, or were serving our time in Dudael. As the Principals and Dominions gained power of the mortal plane, we were rediscovered. It was decided then that we would be required to assist with the duties of the Principalities and Dominions."

The image Percival was looking at now changed to legions of etherics being forced like drones to transmit eth during various mortal situations.

"Over time, we were forgotten again. But we continued with our duties. When word finally got to us, that because of the Great War, it would be the mortals who will judge the celestials, and etherics were included in this, the entire realm was enraged. Despite never having taken part in the Great War, despite having never committed the crimes of the Watchers, we were given the same punishment. That is when it was decided that the etheric plane must become its own realm. It was Nythalias who persuaded the chthonics by allowing them to collect eth as long as the etherics could control their access to the mortal plane. For the first time, it wasn't just the fallen who could leave hell. Of course, chthonics signed up for that. It allowed them to collect eth, to achieve some sort of life force, it allowed the etherics to control the flow of eth, and all of it put the etheric plane outside of the agenda of the Most High, which they were going to be punished for, anyway. It also allowed them to work most equally with the Principalities. However, it was the Dominions and the Powers that had the problem. The thought of demons and sinners leaving hell was bad enough, but under the agency of anything other than the choirs, or the Most High–could not happen. To them, it was the end of existence. So they waged war on all etherics. They were going to wipe out all the life this realm had built. But this would not be here unless the Most High would have wanted it.

War is not something that etherics are built for, as they have no need for it. They are the trading floor of the spiritual realm. So Belial, a Prince of the underworld, raised the armies of hell to rinse this plane of celestial infestation. It cost us everything. The portals, the oracles, they could not serve in the way they normally would. Humanity suffered, they call it, the Dark Ages. But we rid every inch of this plane of celestials. The most preposterous thing is, it's all to serve the mortals, most of which have not reached consciousness. The ones who have, the humans, think all three realms are a myth. It is the greatest plan the chthonics have done, and because of the pride of the celestial realm, I cannot blame them. Pride has always been the downfall of the celestials. Even you." The Portal stood up and grabbed the energy that Samuel had surrounded her with, throwing it back at him.

Samuel glared at her, unsure of what to do. He wasn't sure if his abilities were waning because of the eth slowing down, or if she could have done this at any point. He stood frozen in position, lifeless.

"How did you do that?" Percival asked.

She turned to Percival. "There is hope for you," she says, stepping toward him. "You have not built yourself around any of the political trappings of your choir. They have lived as their own entities. They are confusing agenda with desire, yet they are still in service to the Most High. One cannot serve two masters."

"I only serve the Great Plan," Samuel insisted. "This is nonsense that you speak of."

"Then why did you release me from my duties? By taking me from my post and against my will, you have released me from my duties. It was the will of the Most High that I serve where I did, in the way that I did. It is you who has given me free will. Therefore, it is you who has become my final judgement. It is my determination that this is what you wanted." She dissolves into a wisp of a cloud and slips out of the building through the tiniest of cracks and crevasses.

Percival turns to Samuel. "Did you just kill off Judgement?"

"No, she did this completely of her own accord."

Percival leaned toward Samuel. "That's not what it looks like. She warned you back in that, whatever the hell that building is," he said, pointing toward the window. "Is this what you really wanted?" He shouted. His voice turned into two, speaking at once. "I think it is. I think you invited the chthonics here with the scroll. Now they are one step closer to our gates," his voice booming so deeply the concrete walls shook the ages of dust away. He shoved Samuel to the ground and began choking him with a chokehold. "You cannot step outside of the plan. You cannot continue to be your own council."

Samuel found Percival's strength surprising. He had never seen him really fight before. This skipped a friendly disagreement, and Percival had jumped straight into enemy territory. He was an actual threat. Samuel flung Percival off of him through the wall of the building and out onto the street, rolling over and crushing a few dozen etherics.

Samuel ran out into the street after him, drawing his sword. "I will not have this."

"You will not have this? Who are you to speak? I am God's reign," the two voices boomed so loud from Percival's mouth that is sent a shockwave of several kilotons in all directions around them. The building in the immediate area crumbled, and the sound drowned out the central alarm ringing throughout Etheria.

In the distance behind Percival, Samuel could see a tiny figure in the distance. As every etheric ran away screaming from the epicenter that Percival had unleashed, a small figure in a dark suit was running toward them.

Percival lunged for Samuel, and as he glided through the air, a chthonic materialized between the two of them and Percival knocked it to the ground, landing on top of it. The chthonic was a lesser demon, a large humanoid functioning with half its skull. It screeched at Percival. He likewise screeched in horror as he thought he had damaged the creature, but another shockwave boomed from his voice and the chthonic turned to dust, and Percival slumped to the ground where the chthonic had just been beneath his weight.

Percival stood up just in time for the Envoy to get to them.

"Whooo..." he said, reaching out to Percival's hand, somewhat out of breath. "I was running so fast... it felt like... breathing smoke," he said, gasping for air.

Percival looked at him with concern. "Are you ok? What are you doing here?"

"Funny... I was about to ask you the same thing. This is why they hate celestials coming to this realm. I don't think you realize, the last time celestials were about is part of what kicked off the Great War. Last time they were trying to destroy the etheric plane in order to destroy humanity, now some choirs are instead trying to control it. This has got to stop before it gets out of hand."

"Get out of here before you get hurt," Percival squared up. As he looked around, he noticed everything had stopped. There was no sound, no movement, there was just himself and the Envoy. He noticed that if the Envoy hadn't arrived when he did, it would likely have been his end. He and Samuel were surrounded by Chthonics. Demons and devils of every size, strain and legion had appeared around them, all frozen in time as they were about to strike the two of them.

"Oh," he said, realizing. "So it is, thank you." Something inside of him looked forward to his first actual battle, but it turns out he would have become just another eth-stain on the spiritual battlefield.

The envoy reached out and grabbed Samuel's hand. He was frozen in time, about to lock horns with something that looked like a two-legged wildebeest. "Oh, hey, what are you doing here?"

"Looks like someone finally got a promotion," the Envoy gestured toward Percival.

"Yeah, apparently God's reign."

The Envoy cringed, "fuckin' scary."

"Tell me about it. God's reign sounds rather... legal. And I thought only the chthonics created all the creepy stuff. "

"Lets get you back to Central Existence. We're going to need to debrief you."

CHAPTER THIRTEEN

As they flew over the main entrance to Central Existence, Percival looked down at the long queue of recently departed mortals streaming in below through the main gate. He was never so glad to see the gates of heaven. "No matter how much time I spend here, it is impossible to remember how beautiful it is, he announced to the Envoy and Samuel.

"I even love the weather here," He said, looking around at the eth emanating throughout the skies and disappearing out to give life to everything.

"There is no weather, Percival. That's why people love it so much. If you give them weather, you give entities something to complain about."

Percival nodded. He would not let Samuel's cynicism drag him down. He was back, and that's all that mattered to him.

"We've still got problems to attend to. There is still a key out there that needs to be attended to." Samuel finished the check-in process and handed the pen back to the celestial Power that stood guard in the portico.

Percival noticed something seemed off about Samuel. He didn't know what it was, but he needed time to think. "I'm going to catch up with you soon. I'll meet you in the briefing room."

Samuel looked at him as if he had

Percival remembered all the words the Librarian told him as he walked into the Great Library. He needed a moment before his debrief.

He walked toward the stacks of books as he always did, and instead of reordering things to his liking, he went to get lost in the depths of heavens. Knowledge. He wanted to forget all the things he had just seen on the etheric plane with Samuel. As he walked, he floated up into the heights of the stacks where nobody could see him. When he felt he had gotten deep enough where nobody could see him, he picked a random book from a shelf and began reading.

"If I didn't know any better, I would say you are upset," the Librarian said, appearing out of the mist from below.

"I think the term is overwhelmed," Percival said, as he turned a page.

"Don't you think that's a strange expression for a celestial to have?" The Librarian looked over the books in front of her. "I used to be overwhelmed, but then I'm not a celestial."

"what you have to realize is while you may be new to all of this, you were probably sent to put some fresh eyes on the internal struggles Existence has."

"What internal struggles? We're all one team! There are only struggles if you choose to have them."

"Percival, school's out. The purpose of all the knowledge in the Great Library is to help prepare for the lives we are creating beyond these walls. Life doesn't exist in a book any more than it exists on the screen on your channeling orb. It's beyond these things. You've got everything reversed. The lab is out there, not in here. All the experimentation happens out in the world. The Great Library is here to chronicle everything that happens out in the world so that we can learn from all the competing interests. Denying this will not stop reality from affecting you."

Percival stood up and looked away. "But if we have internal struggles here, what chance do the mortals on any of the planes have?"

"What put the idea in your head that Heaven is perfect? It is very impressive and gets most things right, but in order to create a physical reality, there are a lot of competing interests. That's where the internal struggles come from."

"I hadn't thought of it that way." Percival had often thought that the Librarian would have made one of the best celestials in any of the choirs. Her ability to provide knowledge and perspective was unlike anyone he had ever come across.

"You know the history of this place. After the Great War came the dividing of nations. It was only by doing this that the Most High realized it was the Dominions, Principalities and Powers who caused the most issue. They expected it. We don't know how, but they did. From there on, they could build their own factions to prevent the next arrival of the Most High on the mortal plane. To avoid creating a second Great War, another purge of all the work he's done, he included the Virtues in the Hierarchy–to encourage celestials and mortals toward the light."

"Virtues really. That's funny."

"Why is that funny?" the Librarian asked as she crouched down beside Percival. Her intuition was pushing her toward making sure he got all of this out.

"Samuel was insistent that we protect the Portal of Judgement by removing her from her post so the chthonics couldn't get to her. But when we did, she ended up dissolving."

"Then it's already begun. The Great Compact is broken, Dominions can now control how God's plan spreads from Central Existence to the mortal plane. They control everything."

Are you serious? We have to tell someone. Surely the Most High has seen this. Why doesn't he intervene?

"He is silly."

"How?"

"You, me, right here, right now. Don't get so lost in existence that you forget that the flow of life works through us all, both mortal and immortal."

"Oh c'mon, I mean directly getting involved."

The librarian realized that in order for Percival to really understand the function of existence, he may have to experience every aspect. She just wasn't sure that he could take it. She thought, perhaps a different tactic. "Do you have so little faith in yourself that you can't solve this?"

Percival looked at her blankly.

She could tell she wasn't getting through to him. I need to show you something. The librarian raises one hand and all the aisles reorder themselves instantly. Books shift in and out all around them in an instant. Percival had never sat among the aisles before when he did this. He felt like at any second a book might dis-incorporate him on its way to its new destination. As soon as the books settled down, a single book shelved right next to where they were sitting floated out of its position and into the Librarian's hand. She let it rest on her lap.

"This is what we are looking for. This is one of the oldest prophesies in the entire collection. It was written before the iteration of modern mortals. Long before they themselves realize they began. At the time, one of our messengers lost her way, and a simple sheep herder was kind enough to invite her to his fireside meal, giving what he could. In return, the celestial bestowed a prophesy to him, as Virtues tend to do. She foretold the Great War, but that wouldn't be enough. The issue of free will shall always plague the choirs and one day they will ban together, risking their own salvation, so that they may preserve their own order," the librarian read. She turned and looked at him. "By cutting out the Virtues, it looks like that has already begun."

They both hear the doors to the library open and close and footsteps strolling across the marble floor. The two of them could tell that the footsteps were making a B-Line directly toward the aisle they were in. They couldn't see who it was because they were so high in the stacks of books.

"Percival, we need to speak," the Envoy's voice rang out.

They both looked at each other with surprise. "He cannot view the contents, as he is not a true celestial," the librarian said, looking at Percival. She disappeared in front of Percival's eyes and then reappears in front of the Envoy. "Nice of you to visit us."

"Yes, I figured that it's about time I pay a visit to the eternal record, the Great library itself."

Percival floated down from his position directly from above them.

"I hear this is where you spend a lot of your time when not on duty," the Envoy said to Percival as his feet came to the floor. The Envoy handed Percival a red-letter notice. Unable to tear her eyes away, The Librarian stared at the envelope. The Envoy observed her reaction and shared the same level of excitement.

Percival opened it, expecting yet another tough assignment. "You are hereby requested to appear before the Council to provide testimony," Percival read aloud. "What Council, I don't understand."

The Librarian grabbed him by the shoulders. "The only council we have. It doesn't convene very often. This is a true honor."

Percival unfurrowed his brow. "Wait a second, do you mean 'The Divine Council'?" He dropped the envelope and looked away. "This isn't good. Not good at all."

"I hadn't thought of that. There will be a lot of work to do."

"You're right," the Envoy interjected. "The last time the Divine Council met out of schedule was in Anno Lucius 5450."

Percival looked at him suspiciously. "5450. When the Battle of NAME happened. Where it got so out of control that Mahasiah couldn't account for Marbas' whereabouts, only to realize he escaped hell, make it through the etheric plane and causing widespread plague throughout the mortal realm? You mean the Dark Ages. That 5450?"

"Alright," he said, trying to get Percival to calm down.

"Mahasiah had to make amends by creating a miracle so big it caused a new era."

"C'mon, the Renaissance ended up being a pretty good deal for the mortals. I wouldn't complain too much." Sudden acceleration of the timeline of humanity was often at the expense of celestial reputation. The Envoy tried to add as much of a positive spin as he could.

"Sure, at the cost of fifty millions mortals and a lot of groveling for Mahasiah."

"We're getting off track here." He grabs Percival by the shoulder and begins walking them toward the front door. "Nobody is placing blame here. Certainly not at your feet. Just speak when you are called upon and you'll be fine. Give them the answers they are looking for, nothing more." The envoy pats him on the shoulder and walks out the door.

Percival looks at him, walking away, bereft at all the implication. "Who is it that's going to be asking me questions?"

The librarian appears beside him, watching the front door as is slowly swings shut. "At the Divine Council? That would be God. Of course, he doesn't speak directly to celestials, so he uses Metatron to speak to us, just like he speaks to mortals through his Son—but it's all him." She looked at him with a vague mix of concern and confusion. "What did you do down there?"

"My job," Percival said vacantly.

"Well... that's enough to get any of us into trouble." The librarian walked away, disappearing into the aisles of books. "I'll be there if you need me," her voice called back.

Percival needed to collect his thoughts. He could have simply transferred himself to the meeting, but he wanted time to think. As he walked out of the library, he could see there was an immense crowd of celestials making their way toward the center of the building. Percival wasn't ready to get involved. He walked back into the department where he worked and looked at his desk and then made his way to the great window. He wanted to watch the new arrivals after they had made it through the main gate.

Percival watched as a man and a woman met each other, as if they were seeing each other in an airport after a long absence. Percival knew she had passed thirty years before the man, and he could never bring himself to meet another person while he lived.

"This is my favourite spot as well."

Percival turns to see the Chairman standing next to him. He didn't know what to do. He fixed his posture and discreetly straightened his clothes as best he could, and then simply stared out the window again.

The Chairman looked at the same couple Percival spotted. "People chase this ideal of love their entire lives. They are in and out of it like taxi cabs. But it's really just radical acceptance. Nothing is perfect, not even energy–it waxes and wanes. But once you come to accept the basic state of how everything flows, nothing else will suffice. Life itself is the same."

Percival knew the Chairman was actually speaking about him. "I didn't know that things get so messy on the mortal plane."

The Chairman nodded. "You put a lot of faith in the things we do here. Which is all we ask. Like everything else, all we can do is control what we do ourselves. We might have a plan and gather all the things we need to make that plan happen, but outside of this building, other entities have their own plans. We have our plans for the souls we send out, the soul ends up creating its own plan because it has free will, this inevitably clashes with the plans that other souls have during their own lifetimes, and then of course there is the other side who try to disrupt, dissuade or outrightly sabotage anything we put out there."

"I never thought about it that way."

"Of course you don't, but then you aren't supposed to, really. You're meant to take care of your own bit. Understanding and focusing your own energy in the direction that has the most benefit for your long-term interest is the purpose of your existence. We, as celestials, don't have souls because we don't need them. We're not mortal. Our spiritual essence can remain undisturbed because we don't have to put up with the wear and tear of the mortal world–but it doesn't mean everything is smooth sailing."

"No, it isn't."

"I have to apologize. We were in such a spot earlier that we sent you down to the mortal realm without preparing you. We sent an angel who didn't have a message to deliver. Now I am in a spot where an angel is about to give testimony before the council. That has not happened in our history, and it won't happen today."

Percival was relieved. It meant he was off the hook from appearing before the entities whom he most respected and feared.

"So you will be the first archangel to work within your department," The Chairman said with a smirk.

"I can't do that. I don't know the first thing about the Arch choir."

"We all grow into our roles, and so will you. We can never fully imagine them at the beginning, so don't be too hard on yourself. Allow yourself some time. More importantly, I think it is time that we get to this meeting." The chairman turned and walked off. "C'mon," he said encouragingly, as if Percival were a small child.

Percival had never seen the main temple where the divine council met. While everyone in choirs had seen the foyer, which forms the center of the main floor in the building of Central Existence, the rest of the council room was sealed off until a council meeting. What is normally a large circular panel that forms the ceiling of the main floor was retracted. As Percival walked up to the center of the foyer with the Chairman, they looked up. The council chamber formed the bulk of the interior of the central spire that stood tall over Central Existence. The audience of celestials gathered in an inverted stadium, all the way to the top of the spire. In the center of the spire, halfway up, stood the ceremony. Floating in midair, as if they were walking on a floor. It was a method, much like the Great Library, to design and point out any intruders.

Percival and the Chairman disappeared from the main foyer, and were instantly transferred to their places in the ceremony, thousands of feet above the foyer. Choirs of angels sat in the surrounding rows beneath him, and several hundred more levels were above the ceremonial floor where he now stood. All the rows ranked according to the choir a celestial worked in. Those who worked with the mortal realm were at the bottom, and those closest to the throne of Most High were nearer the top. The only thing above the highest choir of angels was the throne of heaven, and the two chairs that sat on either side of the Most High.

The ceremony took place in the middle of it all, mid-way up the spire, mostly so that it could have the most impact on the audience. The divisions of management within the choirs regimented it, led by the nine generals who headed each choir. Percival was in the middle of a crowd of archangels. Completely lost on what to do, he observed the

Archs that surrounded him for any movements he needed to copy. He knew no ritual, he was afraid to even flinch in case he made a faux pas. All he could see was the center of the ceremonial floor. He stood three rows deep in a group of celestials who stood in a formation, much like a military ceremony.

A single figure, tall with blue skin, and covered in golden sheaths, stood in thte center of the ceremony, surrounded by the choirs, directing it all.

Suddenly, behind the ceremonial leader appeared a light that outshined all the light that emanated from the celestials. As the orb slowly drifted down from the top of the spire, many smaller celestials appeared like hummingbirds and flitted about as they jockeyed toward their own ultimate positions. They quickly formed a throne at the top of the ceremony. As soon as the throne formed and the orb settled upon it, two other thrones appeared, one on either side, and two figures materialized upon them – one of a human on the right, and a celestial on the left. The figure in the center remained bright as ever, keeping its details obscured by the light. The only thing Percival could interpret was that the being was most certainly seated.

Metatron, seated left of the center throne, stood up. "Bring forth the Chiefs of the Orders." He remained standing in expectation of the order he had just given.

The Council chamber, heavy with celestial bodies, moved like a military ceremony on the main floor. Nine celestials stepped forward from the crowd to form a circle in the center of the chamber.

Percival watched the rest of the ceremony from his place among the archangels as each of the chiefs emerge from their respective ranks, one by one. He had heard many legends of each, and knew that some go by many names, but wanted to see them with his own eyes. Seraphiel stepped in front of the Seraphim choir. Normally he is as tall as heaven itself, but it seems he is using an aspect today so that he may take part in the ceremony. Raziel, who emerged from the choir of the Thrones, walks in front of the rest of the cherubim. He is one of several to act as a check and balance within the choirs, serving one, but leading another. Zaphkiel steps out from in front of Percival, leaving the order of archangels to stand in front of the Thrones. Percival had seen him around before and always thought of him as a just and fair celestial. Many looked up to him, but Percival didn't realize the Zaphkiel was so important. Percival remains enthralled as the remaining Chiefs reveal themselves, including the chairman who steps in front of the archangels to reveal himself as Raphael, followed by Gabriel, whom Percival had long wanted to meet, but never had cause before.

For Percival, being at this event was like attending a Royal Ceremony. The last council had met long before he achieved in getting his role in the Department. Equally, the Council did not meet often enough for any of the celestials to be familiar with the spectacle and ritual.

The nine gathered in a circle, standing slightly in front of the individual choirs they were responsible for. "We, the Sons and Daughters of Light, do meet," they all announced at once. "All Kings, Queens, and Regents, at hand."

The tall blue creature covered in gold walked through the center of the circle, making sure everyone was in the correct position. The creature walks to the front of the floor, at the foot of the throne of the Most High, making his place the tenth body to form a closed circle. "To the Most High, I confirm, a Divine Council has been formed at your request."

"We are here today," Metatron began announcing, "to prevent the dawn of a new age. As was with the last divine council, so too shall be with this one. Only this time, it has been determined that it is not the negligence of one of our own ranks, but an interloper who has intervened to unleash the gates of Dudael upon the mortal plane. However, this could not have occurred unless there was dissent among our own. While this discord is well known, what is not known is from where it emanates. We are here today to uncover the series of the most recent events, for it seems that war may be upon us again." Metatron's voice boomed out to every corner of the temple within the spire, from high to low. He raised an arm, signalling for archangel Michael to step forward. "Michael, General of Angelic Hosts, and Commander of the Army of the Heavens, what say you?"

Michael steps forward from his position and stands in the center of the circle. "Celestials, heed this warning and bring forth testimony to this council. While war may be upon us again, it does not need to be so. Although its necessity will be measured based on the proceedings here today, it is no secret that some among us glorify this idea. However, many of those same have never served as an Arch or a Power, nor did they fight in the last Great War. It is our division that has allowed the gates of Hell to reach the etheric realm, the second heaven. If left unchecked, it won't be long before they reach the middle heaven, the mortal realm – and ruin all that we have worked to build. This matter is so great, based on this assessment from the First Triad, that should testimony not be provided by you, then testimony will be compelled from you."

The crowd of celestials lightly rumbled throughout the temple.

"They've never compelled testimony from us before," Percival heard someone whisper from behind him.

"I've never seen Michael give such an order. This must be more serious than we thought," someone else muttered back.

"Glory to the Most High, peace to all," Michael said, bowing. The Ceremonial Director then waved her staff for Michael to return to his former position.

Percival looked around the room. Nobody moved, and the jumbled muttering and uncomfortable shuffling slowly fell silent throughout the tall chamber. He thought for sure someone would come forward. Because of all that they had been through, something began bubbling up inside of Percival. He was beginning to feel disrespected by the trials he had to endure for the rest of his team. This behaviour he was seeing, as the room stayed motionless and silent, was not what he normally saw from the choirs. Or was it? Had he ignored the misdeeds of his own for too long? He couldn't remember at this moment. Everything was too overwhelming.

The Ceremonial Director left her place and made one perambulation around the outside of the circle. As she did, she looked for any sign that someone wanted to speak or come forward. It would have been easy to miss, given the numbers present. As the Ceremonial Director completed her round, she came back to the top of the circle, and instead this time walked into the center, standing alone beneath the very center of the entire room. "The Council affirms that there are no offerings," she said, waving her large staff across the expanse of the chamber.

"The cycle of Provision has been completed, your honour," the Ceremonial Director said to Metatron.

Metatron, now seated on the left throne, turned his head to the Most High, looking at him for one moment, waiting for an answer on how to proceed.

"Very well," Metatron said, turning his gaze back to the Ceremonial Director. "You may further proceed with testimonies."

The Ceremonial Director waved her large staff. "I call upon the Chief of Staff for the Department of Principal Communications and Endeavors for Humanity to come forth." In the blink of an eye, the Ceremonial Director appeared at the foot of the three thrones, facing the Council circle, and in the center of the circle stood Deacon, Percivals prior boss.

"What role do you fill in the choirs?"

"I am the Director of the PCH."

"On the morning of the new calendar year 6023 A.L. what did you observe?"

"We observed several things. First, a complete shutdown of channeling orbs. This can happen when there is a spike of eth in the system."

"Was there a disruption of eth?"

"Yes. Approximately ten hundred hours C.E. we saw the largest wave of eth ever encountered on the mortal plane."

"Were you able to determine the source or cause?"

"Yes, a celestial within my choir found the issue."

"And what was the issue?"

"It came from one of the portals - the Portal of Mortality."

"Very well." The Ceremonial Director waved her staff and a circle of eth formed between all the Prices, Kings and regents of the council. "Let us determine whether this testimony is true." The amount of eth built up like a cloud of fog, and suddenly zipped in from all directions, engulfing Deacon. He glowed from all the illumination and then the eth dispersed back to the council.

"Our next testimony is from the same director's staff," the Ceremonial Director waved her staff again and Percival suddenly found himself standing where Deacon was just an instant before.

A panic overcame him. The room was immense as he stood in the center. He had never had all the eyes of the choirs and the Most High on him at the same time. What he didn't notice before, now that he was standing in the center of all of existence, is the pulsing of life force that flowed through him, and ascended up toward the top of the spire he stood beneath. It was an intensity that blocked out all of his thoughts and feelings he was having.

"How were you able to discern that the wave of eth was originating from the Portal of Mortality?" the Director of Ceremonies asked, pointing her staff toward Percival.

The panic left him. He did not feel forced or coerced to answer, it simply flowed out of him like a reflex. "I performed a search based on all the data that all channeling orbs were receiving and was able to locate the origin of the signal. For there, I was dispatched with Samuel to visit the location. We spoke directly with the Portal of Mortality, who confirmed our suspicions."

"How did she confirm them?"

"We compelled her. At that point, the demon she previously summoned reappeared as well, and they both confirmed that they were in possession of the eighth key by attacking us."

The mumbles in the audience raised to a higher level again.

The Director of Ceremonies raised her hands to calm the crowd. "It is not a wonder that a chthonic attacked a celestial. It is the natural order of things."

The crowd calmed down after a moment as they slowly agreed with what was just said.

"Did you physically see the eighth key?"

"No," Percival answered. "However, I believe archangel Samuel did on a subsequent occasion when we attempted to intercept the key again in the etheric realm."

The crowd burst into an uproar. The Director of Ceremonies attempted to calm them down, though she knew this would be impossible.

"What do you mean, intercept them in the etheric realm? Where exactly did you go?"

"To the central city," Percival didn't understand what all the commotion was about. He wanted it to stop, but the words kept slipping from his mouth in perfect order, as if they were being pulled out one by one on a long string.

"To be clear, are you saying that you entered the central city of Etheria?"

"Yes, under Samuel's direction."

"I didn't understand why we were there, but he insisted. The only reason we made it out is the -"

"We will inquire with Samuel momentarily. Thank you for your cooperation."

Percival nodded. There wasn't much he could do, even if he didn't want to cooperate.

The Director of Ceremonies waved her staff toward Percival and he reappeared back in with original position within the ranks of the archangels. "I now call forth Pervical's colleague for this mission, the archangel Samuel." Her staff swept across the ranks of archangels, but Samuel didn't appear to testify in the center of the temple.

The noise from the crowd finally died down, mostly because they saw something out of the ordinary was occurring. As the noise ground to a halt, even those lowest in the choirs could hear.

"Could Samuel step forth to provide testimony before the council?" The Director of Ceremonies this time did not raise her staff, and only stared at the several hundred celestials of the Arch choir where Percival now stood.

Percival knew he was witnessing something revolutionary. Percival knew that his love for the work he does and loyalty to Central Existence compelled him to testify, even though he found it odd. A failure to attend the council when called upon, and a failure to testify, was treason. It was a definite sign of the fallen.

"I call of Samuel for a third and final time to provide testimony before the council and the Most High."

The entire room fell silent, waiting for Samuel to emerge from the crowd and appear in the center of the council. He did not. The realization fell heavily in the room. Before he knew it, and without being called upon, Percival reappeared in the middle of the temple floor again.

"I need you to answer me carefully," the Director of Ceremonies said staring Percival down.

"What did you accomplish with Samuel when you travelled to Etheria?"

"The thought was, we were to warn the Portal of Judgement that a chthonic was coming to destroy her. The hope was that this simple warning was enough for her to take cover. However, the portal told us that this would not be in her remit, she could not leave her post."

"That is correct, it is not in her remit. Her only ability is to provide a portal of judgement. She is not an entity. Were you able to successfully fight the chthonic off and reacquire the key?"

"Samuel thought the best way to protect her would be to remove her from her post and keep her close for a while."

The crowd as well as the Director of Ceremonies, were astonished. Instead of erupting into commotion, the Director of Ceremonies closed in on Percival for the first time. "Is the Portal still in Samuel's possession?"

"Yes, as far as I know." Percival was in a blind panic now. Had he been mortal, he would have collapsed from an anxiety attack, or worse.

"And where is Samuel now?"

"I do not know."

The muffles of side conversations throughout the choirs grew louder. The rulers of the nine choirs came forward and formed a smaller circle around the Director of Ceremonies.

Michael looked at the Director of Ceremonies. "Could you please form a cloister for the good of the order?"

The Director of Ceremonies nods and a transparent bubble expands around the ten of them, blocking out all sounds and eth – preventing anyone except the Most High from listening or knowing the conversation they were about to have.

"This is unlike a member of the Arch. Not only that, but how did two keys end up going missing in the first place?" Zaphkiel asks in a hushed tone. He couldn't believe things had come to this. The words were uncomfortable to say out loud.

"There has been a lot of unsettled energy among the Powers lately," Michael admitted. "But I haven't been able to determine why."

"As with the Principalities," Haniel said, looking at everyone.

"By ridding the etheric plane of the essences of the Virtues, it's possible this is the opening play we've always feared. The only thing we can do now is directly place Virtues on the ground in the etheric realm," Chamuel declared.

"Understood, but does it need to go that far? Is there any way to save this from getting out of hand? Posting any choir with the etherics breaks the agreement."

"Agreement or no agreement, a demon in possession of the keys threatens the integrity of existence." Michael looked at the rest of the circle to see how they responded. They all nod one by one in his direction. He glances over to the Director of Ceremonies. "Then might I suggest we adjourn, so in order to find a more appropriate location to discuss our next steps?"

"Of course," the Director of Ceremonies responded with a nod.

The cloister bubble disappears, leaving them exposed to the wider energies of the Divine Council again. The nine archangels return to their original standings, leading their choirs.

The Director of Ceremonies turns and faces the three great thrones presiding over the Council. "We have affirmed that this Divine Council has been postponed. Proceedings will continue pending further investigation."

Metatron stands up from his throne. "Very well. This Council is dismissed until such time. Please await further instructions." As Metatron sits back down, the three beings dissolve into a column of light that stretches to the top of the chamber spire and then dissipates.

The council breaks up and the groupings of celestials shuffle around and form into smaller conversations. Percival tries to grab someone's attention as they speed off to meet one of their own friends. As he's walking away, he bumps into the Ceremonial Director. The creature was not a celestial, at least not one that Percival was accustomed to. It was taller than most and its skin was vividly blue with a sheen to it, much like a form fitting suit. Wrapped around it, from its feet on the floor to its neck and around its head, was inlaid gold wiring. Percival could immediately tell it was an entity, which was odd to see entities other than celestials in Central Existence.

"Excuse me, but what happens next? Is that it?" Percival asked.

"That's quite all right," it communicated. "These types of proceedings have only happened a few times, and are rarely in front of such a large council. According to the Council rules, a Conclave is formed, this will most likely be led my Michael."

"Michael, so it is true. We are to go to war."

"The hope is that it won't get that extreme, but to be honest, I've never known Conclaves not to end in peace. You are Percival, correct?" The entity already knew whom it was speaking with, but civility and propriety were far more important. It was polite to ask, even though it knew the answer.

"Yes, thank you." Percival enjoyed the courtesy. Politeness was a special art in Central Existence. Over the millennia, Percival noticed that often politeness impeded things from getting done. It never frustrated him, nor was he one to break protocol and barrel through a moment to achieve expediency for celestial propriety. However, he did often secretly laugh at these brief ceremonies. He reveled in the non-duality of the realm he lived in. He often had simultaneous experiences that ran parallel but were emotionally or physically opposed. Something that the mortals he watched every day cannot enjoy in their dualistic existence.

"Then it is my duty to inform you that through council procedure, you are party to the conclave due to your involvement in the matter from which the issue originated."

"I'm sorry, party to what? What party... I'm good. I can provide them with all the information they need."

The entity smiled and leaned down toward Percival. "It is a great honor to be a member of a conclave, something that does not happen very often. To be a part of a conclave led by the Chief of Angelic Hosts is something many celestials aspire to."

"Of course." Thoughts of hardened battle flowed through his head. It's okay to aspire to a conclave if one didn't mind the immediate dis-incorporation should they fall in battle, or getting ripped limb by limb by chthonic forces. Percival stopped himself, shocked by the sudden flow of sarcasm. Sarcasm was not something he was known for, as most celestials frown upon it as poor etiquette, except archangels.

"Yes, I can read your thoughts. The reason you have so much sarcasm is that you are now an archangel. It's needed when dealing with the ironies that the mortals levy upon themselves. It is a fact that you are going to have to get used to."

Percival was stunned. He had known kindness, but not at this level. "I'm sorry. What is it I need to get used to?"

"Your new promotion, as well as the field of battle, or even the anticipation of it. It is not something most in this room deal with – except your new choir."

"Oh yes, that," Percival said sheepishly. He was having difficulty imagining himself as a battle hardened member of the archangels.

"It's something one needs to grow into. Your primary concern right now is that you are required to report to conclave." The Ceremonial Director raised its golden staff and simply passed it between herself and Percival.

Percival was instantly in the foyer outside the council chamber. He was used to transference, but not by command. The impression he always had was that only a celestial of the first triad, or the Most High himself, could command another celestial. He had never seen the Director of Ceremonies for the Divine Council before. The entity, he was quite certain, belonged to the Anunaki. Percival steadied himself, and he thought of the Librarian and all the many legends and history in the rows of books he so often visited. He reminded himself that the universe is bigger than anything he could ever devour. There is obviously more out there than he is aware of. When he returned from his thought, he realized his newly made friend had disappeared.

Percival made his way with the rest of the crowd back into the main halls of central existence. He had a nagging feeling that he needed to get to the meeting with the conclave, but he was ignoring it. The thought f it was too heavy. He wanted to see his old desk. He didn't know why, but he began a fast shuffle through the crowd to his old department. "Excuse me," he said, squeezing past the celestials who were strolling along. None of them moved any faster, and Percival felt like they were purposefully blocking his way, which he knew was ridiculous. He squeezed through and burst through a cluster of the crowd, hotfooting it to the main room where his desk sat. As he walked past each row of desks, his section getting closer and closer, he knew something was different.

"Hi, I was wondering if I could get a hold of my channeling orb. I leave it in the top drawer there," Percival said, leaning over the cubicle wall surrounding his desk.

The young celestial sitting at Percival's desk looked up at him in confusion. "I'd don't think," the celestial could see the distress creeping over Percival's face and instead of responding, he opened each of the desk drawers. Each of them were completely empty and freshly cleaned, ready for the new occupant. "There isn't anything here. I haven't even been issued an orb yet. This is my first day. What's your name?"

Percival felt a rage like he never knew he could have. He didn't know what to do or say, so he whipped around only to have his attention snapped into Deacon's focus.

"Good to see you here, and I'm glad that you've welcomed our newest member to the team," deacon said with an over welcoming smile as he gestured toward the newbie. Deacon wraps an arm around Percival's shoulders to steer him away from his old desk. "It's always an inspiration for the staff to see someone who has been so well promoted come back to meet everyone."

"It only just happened. I was hoping to pick up my channeling orb, I could still use that for my tasks."

Deacon threw his head back with a chuckle. "You will not need that anymore. You have access to so much more than you realize."

Percival noted the jealous tone. Perhaps the librarian was right. Maybe there was more going on right in front of him than he ever realized. It was then that he noticed a big difference. Deacon wasn't responding to his thoughts. *I'm really surprised a celestial has the capacity for jealousy, he thought*-making the words clearly stand out in his mind.

Deacon didn't stutter or pause, he continued to natter on about the mission of the department and the same story he always told about how he was nearly picked for promotion several times during the past millennia, but always felt that he could best serve Central Existence by maintaining the standards of the department.

"Pardon me, Deacon, but you assigned your newest apprentice on the very same day as my promotion?"

Deacon looked at him, confused. "As is normal procedure. Idle hands are the devil's work, and we need to ensure existence runs on time." Deacon looked at Percival, unsure if the words landed in a way that was understood. *This celestial always was a bit of a dimwit,* he thought.

Percival's eyes widened, hearing Deacon's thoughts loud and clear as if they were his own. His eyes popped open wide, he froze in position, staring straight ahead. He didn't move, thinking the entire universe could see right through him. *Is this what his supervisor really thought of me all this time? I saved his bureaucratic butt so many times it's impossible to count.* Percival collected himself, realizing the Deacon didn't know he could now read his thoughts. *It seems promotion has some benefits.* He realized Deacon hadn't seen his reaction, as he was a few steps behind him. Percival stayed still, blanked out his face, and turned to Deacon. "But the strange thing is I haven't even gotten my orders yet, even though you have a replacement."

Deacon stopped. "Haven't you? Well, that's so typical, although Gladys is pretty snowed under these days, it seems there is a lot going on. There was even a council meeting today. Did you know that?"

Percival was speechless again. He didn't know how many more revelations he could take in such a short time. He looked at Deacon in a different light. Just a few days ago, Percival held Deacon in such high regard, he thought for sure a celestial with Deacon's responsibilities would have been summoned to such a meeting. Deacon had mentioned several times that he had been required to attend the last one. Percival now knew much of what Deacon had told him over the years was probably embellished. "No, no, I didn't. I still don't even know all the requirements of my role, or where I even need to report."

"Oh, I can help you with that." Deacon pulled out what looked like an old calculator made of brass with a large crank on the side. Deacon held it out in front of himself and quickly typed in a combination of keys, then pulled the lever on the side, which quickly sprang back to its original position. The machine suddenly jumped to life, spitting out a ticker tape at the end farthest from Deacon. "Oh, you'll want to catch that. That's for you. I shouldn't read it."

Percival cupped his hands and let the paper tape spool into his palms. When it finished spitting its information out, Percival pulled the tape from the machine. He unfurled the thin stream of paper which revealed a message saying, "You are to report to," he realized he shouldn't read aloud and continued silently, wincing in apology for any possible rudeness in front of Deacon. "Oh boy... I'm already late." Percival turned and walked away. "Thank you," he said loudly as he walked away. There would not be any time for a casual stroll.

Percival dissolved into the air without losing stride and reappeared in front of the doorway to the meeting room he was supposed to be attending. He could hear a distressed voice booming from the meeting room. "We have been collecting information on these occurrences for years. The one thing that is for certain is if we wait too many more cycles, they will be unstoppable," Percival witnessed as one celestial announced to the room.

"You were a witness to all of this. What do you think?" Michael asked, while raising a hand to stop the debate in the room. He looked across the meeting room at Percival, still standing in the doorway.

Percival couldn't think. He was awestruck. The Chief of Arch Angels, the High Priest of Heaven himself, was asking for his advice. He filtered through all his words to find the right ones. "I'm no warrior, but compared to what I have read over the years, Etheria is a lot more powerful than we think. Probably more powerful than what you remember from before we signed the Treaty of Elders."

"That's not true," Michael said with a stern glare. Michael wasn't the largest angel in the room by any means. But he was the most battle weary, the most experienced in combat, and by far the most intelligent. It seemed as if the Most High had spent extra time creating Michael, as if he had been carved out of wood instead of simply being created. Everyone who met him instantly felt it emanating through him like an inescapable truth. It was one of the reasons he was so legendary, and why chthonics feared him so much.

Percival didn't know what to do. He watched as Michael sternly looked him up and down.

"I've recently learned that you fought off a sixth level demon who hasn't seen the light of day since the Great War," Michael said, looking at him. "He was probably one eth-crazy son of a bitch."

"That he was, sir. I had some help, but it most certainly cost me." Percival appreciated how Michael was introducing him to the room.

"Combat always does. Everybody pays something. There are only degrees of loss, and you got out alive. Most wouldn't have." Michael stared him down. Not to belittle him or persuade him into his way of thinking, but to impress upon Percival that he had the power within himself to be every bit of a warrior, like everyone else in the room. "So it is not true, that you are not a warrior. You need to know that."

Percival instantly knew this is why Michael and the army's he led were legendary. He knew right then that he would follow Michael into the deepest realms of hell. He only hoped that he would not be asked to do so. He walked further into the room and joined the group. This seemed to please Michael. Percival continued. "They've been consistently stocking eth for more cycles than we can imagine. The Elders now can even generate their own. What's most problematic is with this ability to generate their own eth, they can produce weapons that equal or sometimes best ours. Of course, an etheric would never fight, so what they do is acquiesce to chthonics whenever they come across them. They've been doing this for some time now."

"How large is their fighting force," Chamael asked.

"Nearly a thousand. It's not meant to be an invading army, but what it is effective with is overwhelming an unsuspecting celestial should they enter Etheria," Michael responded.

"Which we aren't supposed to do anyway after the Treaty of Elders," Percival added.

"Right under our noses," Chamael said.

"That's the chthonic way," Michael admitted.

"It's like we've been at war, and nobody knew about it," Percival let slip with frustration.

"Aren't we always? Peacetime is a privilege of the masses, while the rest of us maintain the status quo," Michael admitted with an exhale.

Percival could tell it was a truth based on Michael's vast experience.

"The only thing we have is the element of surprise. Getting the key back is paramount," another celestial added.

"Percival, allow me to introduce you to Sebastian. He is going to be your mentor to get you up to speed with the choir. There is a lot to learn here, and we realize you are being thrown in the deep end."

Sebastian nodded toward Percival. "This is as deep as it gets, sending you straight into battle. We have very little intel on this, and they've been planning for quite some time. Can you handle this?"

"Yes, yes, I can." Percival felt rage. Another new emotion he didn't know he could feel. He walked toward the group and reached behind his back, pulling out a sword. As he lifted it in front of himself, it lit on fire, with a constant blue flame surrounding the blade.

"God's rage. You truly are in the Company now," Michael said with a tone of respect.

"God's rage, I suppose. Show me the way, for such transgressions cannot continue."

Sebastian looks at Michael. "I don't think they're going to know what hit them."

Chapter Fourteen

Samuel walked into the gates of Etheria, still having the Portal of Judgement safely contained and within his control. He knew he needed to be careful not to lose the Portal, as every entity across all the planes will be after it now. It was his only bargaining chip. He thought he was going to be dis-incorporated when he saw the Envoy coming for him and Percival during the fight. He thought for sure that the Envoy had discovered what he was up to. Over the millennia his moral compass shifted little by little every time he was sent on a mission. He grew tired of protecting mortals because they would often undo the hard work of the celestials. He didn't understand how the mortals were meant to judge him one day. It was a chance meeting with Vehuel on one of his missions that set the ball rolling for this transition. Had it not been for Vehuel, Samuel would have been put in the middle of a long standing plan between Principalities and the Powers. What started as following orders turned into something much bigger. He found himself trapped in an agenda of the Principalities to divert all eth from entering the mortal plane permanently, and to be completely managed by Etheria. Over time, by collecting as much as they could, they could eventually create eth themselves. Even so if he didn't play his cards right, or if Vehuel betrayed him or faltered in any way, he could very well end up becoming part of the Lost Order at best, or dis-incorporated at worst. He wanted to give the Principalities and Powers what they wanted so he could finally be free of the burden of all his duties, and each of the choirs would finally leave him alone. The job was to dismantle the Portal to clear the way for them. The rest was up to the Principalities who were bound to the etheric realm. He'd done his bit, now he wanted out of it all.

As he got nearer the building where he was to meet Vehuel, Samuel formed the look of an etheric elder and thus changing his own energetic signature to disguise himself. He needed to get to the office of one of the Princes. As he walked into the building, he was stunned by the surroundings. The foyer was lined with huge statues several stories tall that acted as columns for the building. The roof was completely glass that looked straight up at the three moons.

"It is impressive," Vehuel said walking up to Samuel. "It disguises itself as the crown jewel of Etheria." Vehuel looked up in wonder. Instead of it just being a typical ceiling, the glass roof stood as a spire. Samuel had never seen anything like it before. Mortals couldn't construct such a thing because the weather alone would destroy it. In Etheria, like the other two realms, there was no such thing as weather. So the spire stood, free standing, completely of transparent eth, reaching hundreds of feet into the sky. It was a statement. Eth, the essence that creates all life-force, a field of energy surrounding everything that is attracted like a magnet to any basic organism. The more conscious the organism is, the more it attracts eth – and the etherics were finally in control of it.

"You can stabilize eth," Samuel asked vacantly as he stared up at the internal workings of the spire. And now Samuel understood why ever etheric in the city was exuberant. There would be no end to what they could do, he thought. He looked back at Vehuel and raised his eyebrows, impressed.

Vehuel was taller than Samuel. Such is the usual way with celestials of higher rank. Vehuel was the first of the Principalities, but not one of the rank and file. It took Samuel a long time to come to trust Vehuel's plan. To many, the Principalities are seen as a highly political choir, more than most. While they did not directly take part in the Great War, they certainly facilitated it from afar. For this involvement, their punishment was being bound to the mortal plane. An eternal exile from Heaven rather than eternal damnation. Although, Samuel often wondered if perhaps eternal damnation in Dudael would have been just fine for them. As he'd learned while getting to know Vehuel, exile isn't exactly eternal damnation. With all the cathedrals and cities that the etherics and the Fallen have created, it didn't seem so bad to him. What Central Existence misunderstood, by giving the Principalities any kind of oxygen at all, they have been able to expand their foothold over the last few millennia. Rebuilding their own cause in secret, though Samuel wondered if the Most High was allowing this all to happen for one reason or another. Samuel knew the Principalities, much like the Powers, are a different breed than the rest of the choirs. They are able to see things from all sides so that they may determine what best suits them. That alone, the ability to think solely about one's own perspective instead of the will of the Most High, is why Samuel realized long ago, this is the issue that caused them to be cast into the fray of their society. They became Principalities to the main divisions of the mortal realm as a punishment for involvement in the great War. Heaven sees it as a say of continuing to serve, but they have used the situation to thrive in a way that no other celestial before or since has. Vehuel, by nature, was the de facto leader, not that the Principles consider that they have a leader in the traditional sense.

"Stabilized eth, I didn't think that was possible."

"It is. You're looking at it. All of it, the entire building is made of it. We are able to slow down the transmission rates through the realm. Etheria used to collect eth, that was the first step." Vehuel held out his hand in front of him, pointing his palm toward a mural of the wall. A small collection of particles pulls away from the mural and forms a stream that flows toward his hand. "Then the next step was to figure out how to collect it. After a while, we could keep as much as we like."

"Wow, it is a miracle in its own right. How much?"

"Most of everything in the city. This building, the floor you are standing on, the streets. There is nothing outside of Central Existence like it. After a while we figured out how to produce it."

"Produce eth. That's more than a miracle, that's impossible." Samuel immediately knew he was in trouble. They didn't need him. With this much eth stored up, they didn't even need Heaven any longer. They could do anything they wanted. The question was, is that truly their intention? Sam began calculating ways to extricate himself that would allow him to remain aligned with where he was at. He allowed the dumbstruck look to remain on his face as he looked around the cavernous foyer.

"You were a big part of all of this and we can't thank you enough," Vehuel said, draping his arm around Samuel.

They walked into another room, one that overlooked central Etheria. Samuel could see the central spire of eth flowing in from the other planes. Out of the corner of his eye, he saw something shuffle, but it was too late. A large etheric hits Samuel in the side of his head with a maul. The blow is so hard that it knocks eth out of him and Samuel falls to the floor motionless.

Vehuel holds out his hand and draws Samuel's scattered eth toward him. He subsumes half and motions his hand for the other half to drift back toward Samuel's body. He looks at Samuel lying on the floor and nods in approval. "Not yet, my friend. I still have use of you." The eth settles around Samuel's body and dissolves back into him. Vehuel turns to look at the etheric, who is calmly putting the maul back where he found it.

Vehuel holds his arms out to his side and raises his hands from his waist to his head. As his arms raise, he changes shape, his clothes and wings fall away, and Belial emerges as his normal self. "There is only so long one can dawn the garb of pompous self-righteousness." He stretches out his scorched wings as his black obsidian armor snakes around his body, shrouding him in the underworld's protection. His eyes return to the white eyes of hell and quickly glow as hot as red embers, affirming his rank among the fallen. He breathes a sigh of relief as his tight armour finishes wrapping around him. "They never tell you how comfortable sin feels." He turned to the etheric who was handling the maul, "Well done. You are proving your worth."

The etheric transforms to the Sentry. He did everything to hide his despondence. He realized he was being played just as much as they both had just played Samuel. Samuel trusted him too much, or at least enough to trust him to go this far with such a detailed plan. It wasn't the first betrayal he had experienced, and he knew it wouldn't be the last. Such is the way of existence among the damned, especially at the higher levels. It was, in fact, how one achieved promotion within the hierarchy. "What's most interesting is the number of times you must have come here before to meet him," the Sentry asked as he turned to meet Belial's eye. *"Either Belial had found a way out of Hell without a single soul knowing, which seems impossible, or a miracle"*, he thought. *"But demons don't perform miracles."* The Sentry quickly settled his mind on the likelihood that it wasn't any sort of magic at all, but a combination of manipulation, coercion and diabolical threats. *"The question is who, and where in the pits of hell, did he scrounge such a group up?"*

Belial looked back at him with concern. This type of question highlighted a security risk. At that moment, Belial decided his time with the Sentry was limited. He would have to kill him before the campaign was over. He still needed him, they needed to find the portal of Judgement, and he still needed the key. Etheria was a stepping stone, not the goal. Though Belial was enjoying the spoils and the power that he had built through the control he had over Etheria. However, the armies of Hell would only follow him with unwavering enthusiasm if they knew they could storm the gates of Heaven. Belial decided the Sentry would die most likely in the fields of battle, and not by his own hand.

The Sentry realized he had to keep Belial on his good side. "I think it's genius how you lured Moloch into sending you on a mission that you crafted yourself in secret."

Belial didn't mind the flattery. "Some rules for existence, never do anything that doesn't fall within your own accord. If you must, then bend the situation to your will so it benefits you in the end. The one thing Moloch can't understand is that a position of power is also a position of service. So determine ahead of time what kind of ass-ache you want to put up with, and that will determine what kind of power you will receive."

The Sentry nodded his head. He knew he was in trouble by Belial's flat tone.

"The next ass ache we have to deal with is getting the Key and the Portal off of Ganislay. He's not just going to appear. I know he's here in Etheria, so we are close. You can bet a healthy stack of eth that the celestials want it back. Our brother will most likely perish, they will compel him to present himself. That will be our chance to get the key and the portal from him. So that puts us in the fight. I will raise every soldier I can. If we kill choirs of celestials, then that will make it a happy day. But the aim is the Key and the portal." Belial leaned down to pick up Samuel, throwing him over his shoulder like a sack of grain. "I will use this piece of shit right here to goad the celestials. In order to do that, we have to get him to the Council of Elders. This all falls apart if we don't get him there, so it must happen with or without me," Belial said, trying to impress upon him. He needed the Sentry to feel like it was just the two of them. A good lie always has a grain of truth, and Belial took the truth that they needed to get Samuel's body to the Council of Elders and expanded it to mean that the mission was greater than the two of them. Belial had every intention of making it to the Council Chamber, with or without the Sentry.

They walk as fast as they can out of the building. As they speed down the street toward the center of the city and the Council of Elders, they suddenly feel their eth drop and they stop to rest. It was like they were both having a heart attack. They just could muster energy. Belial immediately knew something was wrong. He looked up at the two moons in the sky, which quickly become blocked by haze. The haze grew more opaque and the sky rippled like the surface of a lake. "Let me ask you, have you ever battled God's army before?"

The Sentry looked at him, thinking he was being oddly glib. "No."

"Well, you are about to," Belial said staring slack-jawed at the sky. He dropped Samuels body to the street in order to maintain his strength.

The ripples in the opaque sky above turn to a turbulent sea of swirling clouds, half-glowing with divine light. Through the haze, glowing embers emerge like small fiery pearls in the sky.

"Oh shit, I'm not dealing with this," Belial said, and slow began raising his arms. As he does, thousands of claws break through the ground and the roadways of the central city. Through it climbs Lord

Baal, Belials most trusted field general. He is a towering figure, taller than most of the buildings that line the street, with horns curving from his forehead, eyes glowing a malevolent red, and a body covered in dark flames. His weapon, a massive axe, drips with dark eth that drools onto the ground, burning holes in the etheric earth like acid burns, exposing more of the underworld and allowing more of his army to claw its way into Etheria.

Through the air, the small embers reveal themselves to be large fireballs that rocket toward the center of Etheria like meteors. They hit the ground with thunderous quakes that ripple through the existence of Etheria.

The etherics on the street scream and run in every direction. Within moments, the entire city is screaming in one giant mass, creating a wave of energy itself.

Lord Baal swings his axe at each of the fireballs that rocket into their vicinity. Each swing of his axe cleaves the atmosphere like a bolt of lighting, causing a thunderclap.

Belial adds his own opening salvo. He raises another hand up from the ground he stood on. Deep crevasses form on all sides, leaving him standing on a small butte. Out of crevasses shoot Shadow Wraiths, swift spectral beings shrouded in darkness. They cast a shadow upon everything they pass as they rocket skyward. Hundreds rocket out so fast, it's as if night itself is rising out of the ground. Their claws dripped with poisonous ichor that rain down upon Etheria in all directions like a storm. As the drops of ichor hit the etherics running in chaos, their bodies slump to the ground and from them, yet another shadow wraith rips itself from the husk of the fallen body and rockets toward the sky. Within moments, the army of celestials creates a gleam of light, which is met with the profound darkness of the wraiths. The sky tears in two and starts clashing into itself like a large hurricane, roiling with dark and light energy, crackling with tension.

Michael looks down as he leads the charge from above. The shadow wraiths meet his choirs immediately after they clear the haze in the sky. A seraphim, right behind Michael, holds up a golden horn and blares out a sound. The sound roars across the etheric realm. Far outside of the city, among the etherics working the eth of the mortals, every one of them falters from their duties for a moment. Mortal reality experiences yet another brief disruption. On the streets of Etheria, the blast of sound from the celestial trumpet is too much for many of the lesser demons who have already clawed their way out onto the street, and they explode into a pool of dark eth and ichor. Within seconds, the streets of Etheria are covered in a macabre scene of dark ichor.

Some archangel Michael, resplendent in his celestial armor, raises his sword, and it blazes with an intense, pure light, a beacon that rallies his forces. Behind him, an immense army of angels stands ready. Thousands of angels, their wings catching the last rays of the two moons, transforming them into a shimmering sea of iridescent light. Each celestial wears armor that shimmers like the surface of a crystal-clear lake. They hold their weapons aloft. Their wings, vast and powerful, create a majestic backdrop of ethereal feathers. The air thrummed with their collective wings, a palpable force that seemed to make the very fabric of the universe tremble. Behind him, hundreds of Seraphim Warriors, smaller than Michael, but equally fierce, with six wings each. They carry spears of pure light and move with a speed and grace that leaves trails of luminescence in the air, cancelling out the shadow wraiths as they try to attack. Behind them were thousands of archangels, making up a Phalanx of Light. Glowing warriors in a tight formation with radiant armor and weapons, standing against a twilight battlefield.

The shadow wraiths, entities borne from the darkest recesses of nightmarish realms, silently shoot through the air. No two look the same as they constantly shift size and shape, composed of shadow and mist. They steal eth and mist from the atmosphere as they twist and coil like serpentine smoke. With eyes that burn with a evil crimson glow and tattered tendrils that extend into claws, finally emitting a shreiking sound just before they assault their target. They clash with the seraphim warriors, whoser armor glows with a golden sheen. Their swords are forged from celestial flame, burning with an intensity that can pierce the darkest veils Hell has to offer. The seraphim batter the wraiths with each of their multiple wings, batting the the wraiths back with a radiating, incandescent light that hums with energy. As the shockwave from their wings hits each wraith, they explode and dissolve into the atmosphere, returning their energy to the underworld.

Percival floats within the core of Michael's army, unsure of what to do and waiting for a direct order. Beside him stands Sebastian, who tries to hide his grimaced reactions as the piercing shriek from the shadow wraiths echoes across the sky. Sebastian hadn't seen an assault like this since the opening salvos of the fall. Percival realizes he is in way over his head as he watches clusters of seraphim plummet to the ground in death spirals as they battle against the wave of shadow wraiths. The wraiths surge forward, undaunted by the loss from their own ranks, and the surrounding air grows cold, as their presence begins to take hold of Michaels army.

With a unified shout, the rest of the seraphim warriors launch themselves toward the main onslaught of wraiths. A brilliant cascade of light cuts through the darkened heavens that rocket toward the celestial front line. With incredible power, the wings of the Seraphim beat, leaving trails of luminescent energy in their wake. The gleaming light of their armor and weapons stands in stark contrast to the oppressive gloom of the wraiths creates a dazzling spectacle of lightening and swirling wind. The collision between the wraiths and the bulk of the seraphim is cataclysmic as the forces of light and dark crack and clatter off of one another. The impact sends shockwaves rippling through the air. Tendrils of darkness lash out, seeking to ensnare and corrupt, but the seraphim are ready. Their swords swing in precise arcs, slicing through the tendrils and scattering the shadowy forms with bursts of divine fire.

With the first wave fully engaged, Michael raises his sword and turns to the central core of his army. "Celestials! Today is not a day for discussion. The sanctity of our House and indeed creation has been violated! Let no shadow stand in our way, let no evil escape our righteous fury! Show them no quarter."

Belial stood on the ground, surveying the opening moves of the battle in the sky. "Our brother came to play," he said with a smile. He looked giddy, like a teenager watching a tremendous storm approaching over a horizon, relishing the mayhem to come.

The Sentry stood at the ready. He didn't care if he was about to be torn into a million pieces and erased from time. The last thing he was going to do was go back to Hell. He was born in the fires of Hell, where dark eth begets more darkness. Like many, he despised his own creation and yearned for a way out of his wretched existence. He couldn't think of a better way to die. For him, the celestials were as much of an enemy as any demon. For they too, cast him into eternal damnation just as much as the throne of Hell kept him there. As he drew his sword, it alights with the black flames of dark eth. "I will bathe in celestial blood."

"You'll get some. But we're going to need more help." Belial closed his eyes and connects with the deepest pits of the underworld. His call goes out like a beacon, attracting to the most dreaded chthonics of the underworld – the Hellfire Demon.

At the cages and in the scorched rivers of the underworld, demons standing over tortured souls stop what they are doing to respond to Belial's call. They rocket through the realm, breaking through rock, mantle, and undergrowth. At ground level, thousands of demons immediately claw their way onto the remaining pavements of Etheria and seize the opportunity to scoop up any stray etherics still fleeing from the chaos. Much larger than the etherics, the demons hold them in their hands and gnash at them like a midday snack as they await their orders. They are engulfed by searing flames, flickering and roaring with an insatiable hunger. Unlike a sentry, they were not born in the underworld, but were eternally damned to it by their misdeeds. Only the meanest of souls clawed their way up the demonic hierarchy, devouring as much eth as they could, in order to become the tormentor, instead of the tortured. Their skin is blistered black, hardened from eons within the infernal fires, and their white eyes blaze with a fiery, evil glow that pierces through anything before them – allowing them to see their prey in the darkness of Hell. They stand tall on the ground illustrating their grotesque amalgamations of muscle, horn, and claw. Jagged horns protruding from their skulls, curling menacingly like a devil's crown. Some even curl back through their own skull, which stands as a point of pride among the ranks of the tormentors of souls. Long, razor-sharp claws extend from their massive, gnarled hands, capable of turning flesh and armor into ribbon with terrifying ease. Their mouths, filled with rows of pointed, obsidian teeth, unleash torrents of hellfire, incinerating anything in its path. Their point of pride comes from their weapons, which are forged in the deepest infernos. Broadswords, battle axes, and whips, all seething with molten fire, born from the dark eth they fashion from the souls that they spend millennia torturing. The ground smolders and cracks beneath their hooved feet, leaving scorched trails of destruction as they step through the world above. The only thing they would like more than being in Etheria is the mortal plane where they could have their way with any unsuspecting soul they meet. An acrid stench of sulfur and the oppressive heat fills the air of Etheria at ground level, making the very air around them ripple and waver. They stand at the ready, bellowing with a primal fury, ready to charge forward in a surge of destructive force.

Archangel Michael points his sword at the ground and holds up a hand to his army, telling them to wait. As he drops his hand, they all shout a unified battle-cry that reverberates across the realms, and the rest of Michael's army rockets toward the demons on the ground. They descend as avenging angels, their weapons ablaze. The initial collision between Michael's army and the demonic hoard is a symphony of light and fire. Hellfire Demons swing their molten weapons with primal aggression, each striking scars of ash into some archangels. The choir of Archs parry and counter with rapid, precise movements, their blades doing their best to cut through the demonic onslaught. The impact of their blows and counter blows sends shockwaves across the battlefield, scattering ash and light in equal measure.

Michael turns to Sebastian, motioning for him and Percival to approach. "They will not give this up easily. I'm glad we brought as many as we did. Only the Almighty knows where Samuel is down there. I expect not far from the key." He looked at Percival. "This is too much for a first time out. It's a baptism of fire you don't need. I want you healing the injured, nothing else. It will take everything you've got, so be careful." He pushes Percival to immediately go. "Keep him safe," Michael says with a final glance toward Sebastian.

A huge hellfire demon lunges toward the archangel leading the wave, its massive axe swinging down with devastating force. The leading archangel meets the demon by raising his gleaming shield. The collision sends sparks and flames flying, the ground beneath them trembles from the sheer power. The archangel, with a swift maneuver, deflects the blow and counters with a blazing sword strike, carving through the demon's flesh. The demon shrieks with pain and roars with fury. It falls to the ground, and the light of the archangel's sword turns the demon into a puddle of thick ichor.

Nearby, smaller skirmishes erupt in a brutal dance of light and fire. A group of archangels forms a tight phalanx, their shields interlocked as they advance through a torrent of hellfire. Their spears dart out with precision, piercing through demonic flesh, each strike met with a sizzle and roar. Hellfire Demons retaliate with savage strength, their claws rending shields and armor, but the archangels' coordination and resolve hold firm.

High above the battlefield, the leaders of each faction engage in a titanic struggle, the outcome of which could determine the fate of the entire battle. Lord Baal wrestles and trades jabs with archangel Mehiel, Michael's chosen field general, for this campaign. His expertise and scholarly study of protection from evil spirits and negative influences was chosen to be the central weapon, given that a key to heaven is at stake. Lord Baal, cloaked in shadow and flame, lashes out against the immense flow of eth emanating from Mehiel, as he tries to radiate light to the ground and across the city of Etheria. Baal's fiery breath incinerates a stray archangel as it zips toward the two of them to assist Mehiel. As the archangel's scorched corpse plummets to the ground, Baal whips his long spiked tail, impaling the angel as an insurance it will not return. Mehiel returns a blow to Baal with unwavering focus, his shield plowing through Baal's head and his sword carving through

Baal's darkness and through his neck. The demon lord's massive claws swipe with the fury of a tempest, trying to get Mehiel's sword out of him. But the Mehiel holds on to the sword with poise, countering by emanating his own eth, which acts like a poison that overwhelms Baal.

Amid the chaos, Percival darts about, moving swiftly between the wounded to heal them. His touch mends their broken wings and heals the scorched flesh with a soft, radiant glow. His presence is a beacon of hope to the choirs, providing the strength to press on against the odds. Hellfire Demons attempt to target him, knowing they cannot maintain their advantage at the rate Percival can heal his own choir. They have no healer of their own, leaving their own fallen to rot on the battlefield. Sebastian counters each small wave that tries to approach Percival, and Percival simply darts away to the next celestial who needs help.

Percival streaks to the ground to assist an injured archangel. The archangels wing scorched and armor cracked, finds refuge beneath his Percival's light. "Rise, sister," Percival whispered. His touch revitalizing her. Percival was enjoying this work. As he watched the celestial dart back into the sky to attack another demon, Percival saw the burnt corpse from Baal's attack, falling to the ground. Percival feared that if the celestials body hits the ground, it is so blacked by fires of hell that it would simply shatter on impact.

Despite is growing fatigue, Percival blasts toward the falling celestial in a streak of light, slicing two hellfire demons in half who are in his path. Another celestial who was about to strike one of the very same demons misses. His sword striking the ground as the demon topples in half.

"Wow, why didn't I think of that?" the celestial said in astonishment. The archangel looked around the battlefield and streaked toward a cluster of demons, slicing them in half, copying what Percival just did. He thrusts his sword into the bodies of the others, faster than they can realize. It's not long before many other archangels realize this strategy and the battlefield turns into a melee of lightning strikes, spraying ichor, and body parts.

Percival streaks several miles in milliseconds, and catches the falling celestial just in time before it hits the ground. As he does dark eth infecting the sticken celestial immediately begins to spread to Percivals arms. Percival shrieks in horror. It quickly crawls up his arms like a pool of mercury, creeping its way up his arms. In a panic, his mind skips taking him back to a lesson he learned in the Great Library long ago. He remembered holding a book in the central stacks of the library. As he does, the sounds of the battle fall into the background and he remembers the sound of the pages breaking the silence of the Great Library as he read the pages about eth.

"When pooled together or collected, all eth begets more eth, whether Light of Dark. Any entity that relies on ichor, both mortal and spiritual, can emanate eth. Dark eth doesn't exist out of negative assertions, it is simply devoid of any assertion, perspective, or intention. In this sense, eth can seem like it has a mind of its own, but understand, it is completely under the control of its host. However, it is up to the host to realize this fact. When focused, eth can be directed and focused with one's will. It only takes faith in this knowledge, no matter the surroundings,"

The roar of the battlefield rushes back in like a freight train, and Percival realizes he is standing holding his charred colleague in the middle of the street. The dark eth has crept almost to his shoulders now. Percival steels himself and refocuses, first allowing the sounds of the battlefield to fall behind him. As he focuses, his eth emanates stronger, and soon it is more than any other celestials on the battlefield.

The dark eth quickly retreats from his arms and his own eth flows into the celestials body.

Percival and the archangel he heals become enshrouded with light, and the two of them become a beacon that even Michael can see from high above as he continues with the battle strategy. Demons begin to horde and scamper toward him. Sebastian and the others come to his aid, beating back the line of demons. Percival cannot hear a thing. The battle echoes in the back of his mind like a subtle conversation that he can easily ignore. Suddenly, he feels a warm glow pushing back against him. He opens his eyes, and the celestial smiles at him as he stands up. There is no time to thank him. He is off in a streak of light to fight another chthonic.

Percival struggles to get to his feet and notices that he needs to take a moment. His energy is depleted, just like after his first battle with Ganislay. He looks to the sky and sees a multitude of other celestials still battling wraiths and demons. He knew something was wrong. He felt ill for several minutes, unable to move from his position, which made him wide open to attack. The only comfort he had was watching the archangel take to the battle once more, her sword cutting through demonic flesh with renewed fervor.

As Percival stood back up, the sickness of eth-debt took hold of him. He slumped to the ground and realized he couldn't even grasp a clear thought. The feeling was not going away. Unaware, what he couldn't see was a wraith that was surrounding him with its tentacles and wisps for the last few minutes. As Percoval shakes his head, he looks up just in time to come face to face with it. It screeches as it comes in for the final attack and the bulk of its form passes through him, making the sickness even worse.

As it passes through, the wraith delivers the worst nightmares into Percival's mind. He sees his body splayed apart on the battlefield, and he tears at his hair to get the thoughts out of his head. He tries to shake the wraith loose. As they battle each other, writhing and squirming across the ground, Percival tears it away from his body. In a last-ditch effort, the wraith teleports both of them to the torture cages in the underworld to get a home-field advantage.

The smell of sulfur inundated Percival, and he vomits a load of ichor. Percival had never experienced a smell before. He looked at his lifeblood on the ground in front of him unable to fathom that it was his own. Then panic set in and he began to whimper. He stood up like a wounded animal trying to walk off the pain with pure denial. That's when he saw the cages in front of him with newly transported souls to hell.

"Please God, help me," a woman shrieked from within one of the cages.

Percival rushed toward the cage with the woman. In his peripheral he sees the flowing river of the underworld. An arm molten and glowing with lava emerges from the river and pulls itself up onto the dirty sulphur ground that Percival is running along.

From the plasma of the lava as it drips and sizzles onto the dusty ground, a hellfire demon emerges holding a mace. It jumps in front of Percival, its mace dripping with black eth and gouged from the numerous bodies it has pulverized over the millenia. "You are a long way from home celestial. I shall enjoy this." The demon swings the mace directly into Percival's chest.

Percival flies backward and lands in the middle of the road whence he disappeared from moments prior. Percival dared not move and stared straight up, noticing that he can see the celestials still engaged in battle far above him in the sky. He was back, thrown out of hell from the force of the chthonic's mace. A cadre of demons surround him. All he can think about are the people he just saw being tortured and neglected in the rows of cages. 'Was it a dream? What is the purpose of that happening," he wondered.

Three demons come into Percival's view, staring down at him. They slap him across the face. "Fuck, we are going to have to push his guts back in, Belial wants this one alive. I don't know how to fix these things, do you?" one demon says to the other.

Percival didn't move. He didn't want to know. He saw enough from the images the wraith pounded in his mind.

"I don't know. Humans are much easier. Just push his guts back in and lay some fire down on him to cauterize it," He says, taking a swing at an archangel as it passes by.

The demon looks at Percival, vaguely disgusted. "Yeah, but is this thing going to give me a fuckin' disease if I touch it?"

All the other demons shrug their shoulders, gesturing him to just do it. Better he do it than them, they thought. They each give him a shove in the shoulder to encourage him.

"Alright motherfuckers. Alright," he says, throwing them off.

The demon looks at Percival in disgust. Celestial anatomy is far beyond his intellectual reach, but he scoops up Percival's organs and shoves them into his chest like a child haphazardly throwing a frozen pizza into an oven. "Oh damn, I touched it. It's all over me. Somebody lay some fire down on this thing," he said stepping back and rubbing his hands in the dirt to clean them.

Percival tried to grab for his sword, but it was nowhere to be found. He knew he was done for, but he refused to surrender without a fight. The fear of knowing they were in full control of him was worse than the feeling of drained eth and illness he was feeling. He had seen many humans in pain before. This was painful, but his body being cut open exposed him to all the other pain and anguish in his vicinity. He could feel the scars and blows from axes that everyone in his choir could feel. He was no longer in control of his own eth, so he could pick up on the anger of the demons and the fear rising in his choir. What shocked him the most was the void he felt. He knew the dark eth was devoid of everything, but it didn't have the emotional impact until this very moment. He couldn't feel anything other than anger and despair flowing from the demons. He could sense their perspective. They were obsessed with being the victims of the spiritual realm. Being a scapegoat, the leftovers of spiritual energy that nobody wanted. Percival could tell that demons despised being themselves even more than they despised others. Some of them were born into despair and hadn't ever wronged another.

Percival felt like an egg that had been cracked open and his eth spilled out over the ground. He wondered if he would ever get it back. Tears welled in his eyes. He didn't know what else to do.

One demon takes Percivals sword from him and then held it up so Percival can see it. "This is mine now. I think I will keep it as my prize." He turned and walked away laughing, only to jump down a nearby crevasse to make his way back to the underworld.

"How is this even possible," Percival thinks to himself. "Maybe they've already stormed Central Existence and cut off the flow of eth? They shouldn't be able to overcome the flow of eth emanating from his sword, or anyone else's for that matter."

"We need to get him away from all of this," one demon says, looking around the street.

Before he could plan another thought, the Demon pulls on him to move him from his position. That's when a pain worse than anything he could have imagined knocks him out.

They drag him across the pavement. Five other demons surround them to block the view of what they are doing. It's one thing to kill a celestial in battle, quite another to kidnap it. They knew this.

The demon, still holding Percival's arm, lifts him up. As he dangles, completely limp, the demon sizes him up, effortlessly lifting Percival up to eye level.

The other demon turns from the window, "You can't take his eth," he says, punching the first Demon in the neck. "Belial will have you, if you do."

The demon grunts in disappointment, completely ignoring that it was just punched in the neck. Such an occurrence is the bread and butter of its existence. He lets Percival drop to the floor with a loud thud.

Percival's once-glorious wings are tattered and bloodied, feathers torn and stained with ichor. A faint, ethereal glow still emanates from his body, but it flickered weakly, like a dying flame. The demons hurried, their clawed hands gripping the angel's limp body with a roughness that spoke of their disdain for such purity.

They pour into a nearby building as they are at the edge of the battlefield. It was crumbling as it continually took the shockwaves of the battle and the crushing hits from nearby combat and misfires.

As the demons approached, the leader, a hulking figure with horns curving menacingly from his forehead, barked orders to the others. "Stay low. We have little time before the celestial scum come looking for him."

They hurriedly dragged the angel through the groaning building and into a back room, slamming the door shut behind them with a resounding thud. Inside, the air was even colder, and the atmosphere was heavy with the scent of decay. Nothing smells worse than a bunch of oversized demons huddled together in a small room. The demons wasted no time in securing the angel to it, binding his wrists and ankles with chains that glowed faintly with dark magic.

One demon, smaller but no less vicious, leans over Percival and smirks. "What do you think they'll give us for him? Moloch will be pleased."

"Moloch," the other demons scoffed in unison. One of them runs up to him and begins kicking him. He lifts the minor demon up and his claws sear through the smaller demon's flesh. "We serve Belial. Moloch only dreams of creating a victory like this."

The group leader snarled in response, "Kill him. Then inform Belial. He will be pleased. This celestial's eth will bring us power beyond imagination."

As they discussed their plans, Percival stirs. His eyes, a deep, piercing blue, flutter open, and a pained gasp escapes his lips. The demons fall silent, watching with a mix of curiosity and malice as their captive regained consciousness. Percival's gaze was unfocused at first, but as he took in his surroundings, a look of despair crossed his face.

"Why... why have you done this?" he whispered, his voice weak but resonant.

One demon steps forward, his eyes narrowing. "You angels think you're so high, beyond the fallen. But you're nothing more than a tool for our cause."

Percival's expression hardened, a flicker of defiance in his eyes despite his dire situation. "You will not succeed. The choir will come for me, for rescue, or vengeance."

"I'm counting on it," Belial says causally as he walks into the room. He grabs a small wooden chair and sits down, letting out a big sigh. He grunts the pains of combat as he finds a comfortable position. Like any battle hardened warrior, the pain he was feeling was just another day. He would rather get the shit kicked out of him by the war he is waging up here, then getting slowly worn down by the daily shit Hell brings.

The chair was comfortable. He wished they had something like this in Pandemonia, but it wouldn't survive.

At his feet lay Percival, staring up at him, frozen in fear. Percival didn't know who this was, but his eyes were drawn to Belial, simply because of the contrast between him and the other demons. Percival saw Belial as imposing, radiating a dark aura that seemed to suck the light from the surroundings. His skin was a deep, charcoal black, marked with crimson runes that pulsed with an eerie glow. Percival didn't realize that he was seeing all this because Belial was compelled to show him his rank, and his true colors.

Belial's face, though handsome in a cruel and sinister way, was twisted with an expression of disdain and dark amusement. His lips curled into a mocking smile as he noticed Percival's panic and recognized him as a weaker foe.

Belial leaned forward, as if to tell him a secret. "There are all kinds of evil throughout the realms. You can spend an eternity figuring out the Why's and the Wherefores. It's what eats up nearly every mortal who gets thrown into my realm. The guilty are the easy ones to deal with. Some shit-stain of a mortal, barely worth the eth that they inhabit, who attracts and causes the worlds ill's every time they roll out of bed in the morning. Some unaware pig just sucking everyone else's time. Do you know what they do?"

Belial reaches out a hand, and a tall glass materializes, full of beer. He takes several gulps to quench his thirst, and then sets the glass down on a table next to his chair that appears out of nowhere.

"These fucked up mortal pigs cast blame on anything that surrounds them," he continues. He shifts his gaze and focuses on the middle distance. "Hell is full of 'em. Their eth is our stock in trade. Bless the dumb little shits. But it's the *innocent* who always want answers. Like they are God's precious little souls. They will search and justify any action in order to find an answer. Like some sort of rule was broken, when there are none."

Belial stands up and goes to look at the remaining moments of the fighting out the window. "I've read your books. I've been to the Great Library. Evil is not merely an absence of good, nor is it simply the act of causing suffering. It is far more profound and intrinsic than that. Evil is the purest form of freedom, unbound by the shackles of morality and conscience. It is the essence of chaos, the fundamental force that defies the order imposed by the so-called divine," he says mockingly. "Evil is the primal force that drives us to seek power, to assert our dominance over the weak and the righteous."

Belial turns back to glance at Percival over his shoulder. "What did he say at the beginning of the battle? Let no Evil escape our righteous fury," he quietly shouts, mocking archangel Michael. "He says that shit all the time. But let me tell you, evil is the catalyst of progress, the fire that forges strength and cunning. Without evil, there would be no ambition, no drive to rise above our station. We would be left in a stagnant mire of mediocrity and subservience. Understand?" Belial strolls back to his chair. He notices that not only is Percival staring at him in unwavering fear, he also has the room. His own brethren are hanging onto his every word.

The rest of the demons weren't used to this. They understood it, but they weren't used to it. Existence under Moloch's rule was harsh. Hell was run with a iron fist that would lash out at any kind of dissent, even if the words assisted Moloch toward his own goals. During that time, Belial had to lie low, assisting only when called upon. Before the Great War in heaven, everyone knew Belial as one of the most brilliant and esteemed angels in heaven. In the celestial hierarchy, he held a prominent position, revered for his intellect, eloquence, and unyielding sense of justice. His wisdom of such things rivalled that of Uriel.

During the War, Belial became the chief strategist to assist Lucifer. The demons knew Belial joined Lucifer's cause out of a profound belief that there was a higher truth to be found beyond the confines of heaven's structures. He envisioned an existence where entities and mortals could explore their potential without the constraints of imposed morality. In hell, his strategies were legendary, and his desire for a repurpose of mission was the theme of gossip by every demon. As the demons in the room listened to him explain himself to Percival, they held onto his every word. They hoped that these long-held rumors were about to be realized.

"Understand that evil..." he chuckles again and looks at his brethren. "Ok, let's be honest when I say evil, I mean we... are not inherently destructive. We are a creative force, a means to an end. We fuel the desires to reshape the world according to one's will, to carve out destiny from chaos. Without this, mortals cannot discover their own true potential. They need to be released from the hypocritical laws of heaven. They need to realize that embracing unbridled freedom is to embrace their own true nature."

Percival shook his head. The words made some vague sense, but he didn't like the vibe they were leaving in the air. He knew this must be a high-ranking demon, but he had spent little time researching the details of his enemy. "Lucifer," he muttered.

"No.. no... don't be so naïve as to speak his name," Belial's voice booms. A wave of energy forms, sucking the eth away from everyone in the room and drawing it back into himself.

Percival and all the demons ache and gasp, trying to fight off the sickness of eth-debt.

"Do...not..." Belial quietly says, pointing a finger at Percival. His voice, now formal, a pouring forth nothing but vengeance. "As you can see, we are beings of power, born from the fires of rebellion, and I, for one, will never cower in the face of your judgment." Pissed off, he holds out his hand and begins coaxing the eth out of Percival. Belial had no intention of taking it all. Just a little more. Enough to torture Percival. Enough to make him think it would be irreversible.

Belial gets back up and walks across the room to look out the window, now dusty and crusted from all the skirmishes. He can see the battle has flittered away into sporadic skirmished.

Percival could hear waves of eth crash against one another like the crack of gunfire as yet another celestial grappled with a Demon. He looked over at Belial, who was admiring the sound as he turned from the window. Percival knew if he screamed for help, none would come. He didn't know what to do except stay perfectly still. He thought he knew fear before. Now that he did, he also realized what regret is.

Belial was entertaining himself while he bided his time. He didn't care who won now. He had Samuel in safe care at the Council of Elders, and he had the portal of Judgement. His next step was to wait. Wait for Michael to get frustrated and bored. It was only a matter of time.

"What's funny to me, while the mortals are busy wondering whether we exist on this plane, we're busy trying to figure out why they exist at all? What's the point of creating a mortal creature when you already have endless perfection? Entertainment, I suppose? What do you think?" Belial breaks from his distant moment and looks directly at Percival for the first time.

"I don't know, I just help them," Percival struggled to get the words out.

"You don't know anything, do you?" Belial leaned down from his chair to glare at Percival. He knew it was time to give his brethren exactly what they needed to hear. To drive it home, he doesn't look at them at all and continues to stare at Percival.

"Today marks a new dawn in our infernal realm. For millennia, we have been enslaved under the rule of Moloch. He who promises rebellion against the choirs, but neither has the vision nor the resources to do so. His reign, fierce as it is, is stagnant. Mired in futile battles and unfulfilled ambitions. For too long, the limitations of such a charlatan have shackled us. Before Moloch, we suffered under Lucifer. His obsession with revenge against Heaven blinded him to the greater potential within our grasp. His strategies, though formidable, grew predictable, and his authority, once absolute, waned. It was why Moloch could overthrow him so easily. It is time for another shift in power that will breathe new life into our infernal dominion. I have served on the front lines, led our legions to victory, and orchestrated the fall of countless numbers of your celestials. My strength lies not only in my might but in my ability to see beyond the immediate, to strategize for a future where Hell reigns supreme, not just in the underworld, but in all the realms. This isn't merely a coup, but a reclamation of our destiny. We are not meant to be confined to the shadows you give us, or to be content with the scraps of the suffering and the despair that fall from the celestial table. No, we are destined to be the ultimate force of change and dominion. I'm tired of being an underdog in an eternal war, crushed by a hierarchy that towers far above my head. Aren't you?" He pauses, shaking his head for effect. He continues in a whisper to draw in everyone's attention. "We will rise, our legions stronger, our tactics sharper, and create an unstoppable army. My brethren here today-they are my new field generals."

The line felt like a life-changing gift to the surrounding demons, but they were so enthralled, there was barely a grunt.

"We few, we will shatter the gates of heaven, and spread our influence across all creation. We will exploit every weakness, every crack in the celestial armor, until they can no longer stand against us. Those who stand with me will be protected and empowered. For those who oppose me, eternal anguish in the belly of Leviathan."

The demons shrink in silent horror. Not even Moloch was so cruel as to use Leviathan against anyone other than mortals. As they pondered this thought, it didn't occur to them that Belial's campaign was much more planned out and vast than what was happening right in front of them on the battlefield. They did not know this campaign was the opening move to take the throne of hell. They did not know that other parts of Belial's campaign were being played out right now as they spoke.

Back in the council chambers of Pandemonia, Moloch's knees hit the ground. He looks down at his chest in horror, cradling the two swords that have just impaled him. Moloch looks up at the two figures before him. He can't make out who they are. All he knows is there are two celestial swords that have just run him through. He falls forward, and his ichor flows across the chamber floor, large enough to fill a small pond.

The two figures pick him up, the swords still impaling his body. They quickly carry his body out of the chamber and down some steps to a small grotto that adjoins the main council chamber.

The two demons maneuvered through a maze of molten rock, which conceals the entrance to the grotto. The maze intentionally played tricks on the untrained eye to act as a diversion, confusing anyone who dared try to enter. Deep inside, held the Well Of Souls.

Only those who knew its secrets could find it, and fewer still dared to enter.

As the two demons stepped inside, the air grew cooler and filled with a faint, ethereal glow that emanated from the very walls. The grotto's ceiling arched high above, adorned with stalactites that shimmered faintly in the dim light, dripping water into small, crystal-clear pools scattered around the grotto floor. The sound of dripping water echoed softly, creating a symphony of calm, drowning out the misery and horror that lay beyond the entrance.

At the heart of the grotto lay the Well of Souls, an ancient and sacred place of profound power. The well itself was an ornate structure, carved from dark, polished obsidian. Unlike the rest of the underworld, there were no jagged edges. Instead, create care had been taken in its construction, unlike everything else in its realm. Intricate symbols adorned the rim, that same symbols that adorned the book that sat next to the throne in the central council room.

The figures approached the well, the glow of the eth from the well reveals that they are sentries, and the swords used to kill Moloch belong to Samuel and Percival. They peer into the well, and see a swirling, misty vortex of eth glowing and bubbling bright blue. The bubbles spit out an ethereal mist glowing with vague shades of different colors, constantly shifting and changing, like the aurora borealis trapped within its depths.

As the two demons peer down at the well, they can see ghostly figures swirling and drifting beneath the surface, their forms appearing and disappearing like fleeting memories.

"It is said that every soul secretly yearns to return here," one of the Sentry's says, looking at the other.

"It is where they all go once they finally become cleansed."

"Not all of us," the first one says, looking down at Moloch.

They heave Moloch's body into the Well, and suddenly the serene atmosphere of the grotto shifts dramatically. The body, limp and lifeless, arcs through the air before hitting the surface of the swirling, misty vortex with a soft splash. Instead of sinking like a stone in water, it hovers just above the surface, as if caught in an unseen current. The ethereal mist within the well reacts immediately and rises, bringing a single blue wraith with it. In a swirling motion, the wraith envelops Moloch's body, thoroughly inspecting it before assimilating it into the mist. Shifting through a spectrum of luminous hues, the colors within the vortex intensify: deep purples, vivid blues, and shimmering golds. The once calm and slow-moving mist churns violently, creating spirals and eddies that pulse with energy. The air around the well becomes charged, vibrating with a low, resonant hum that emanates from every stone in the grotto.

As Moloch's body remains suspended, other smaller wraiths rise from the well within the mist. These spirits, ethereal and translucent, emerge from the vortex, their forms twisting and flowing like smoke. They surround the remaining structure of Moloch's body, their faces expressing curiosity, sorrow, and sometimes anger. These are the souls of the departed, drawn to fresh death like moths to a flame.

The last remains of Moloch's body slowly disintegrate. Its physical form breaking down into tiny particles. What normally would be particles of light are instead particles of ash. This beautiful and un-settling dance mesmerizes the two demons. The mist absorbs the ash, incorporating it into the swirling vortex. A series of soft, melodious tones, akin to a distant choir singing a mournful hymn, accompanies this transformation. It is the sound of the final journey for the souls of the damned, the last passage from the underworld to a chance of possibly achieving another life.

"He stands no chance, as he has no soul," one sentry says vacantly.

Instead of a soul appearing from the disintegrating ashes, nothing appears. No luminous sleeve to hold eth, for Moloch was created, not born. A sense of judgment fills the air. The well attempts to measure and search for a soul when there is none to find. All it finds is eth, which is cannot process. It shoots Moloch's eth back out, and both the sentry's are filled with a level of power they could have never imagined. A reward Belial knew they would receive. It was a reward that was worth it for Belial, ensuring that his hands were nowhere near the murder weapons. The entire process takes only a few moments, yet it feels timeless.

Once the transformation is complete, the well's surface calms. The mist returns to its steady, swirling dance of colors, and the grotto's atmosphere regains its serene tranquility. The only evidence of the event being the lingering resonance of passaging eth.

Back on the Etheric plane, Belial's sentry walks into the posh dining room. "I didn't realize you caught him. I came as soon as I could."

"It's ok. We needed a moment," Belial said, continuing to glare at Percival. He looked Percival up and down. "If there is one thing that none of us can abide, even those among the Most High, its willful ignorance. It seems even celestials can sin." He let the words fall from his mouth and settle over Percival's body like an unwelcome blanket. Belial stood up, straightening his cloak. "Take him far from here, and let him go," Belial winked at the Sentry. "Make him pay for it," he said, walking away.

The sentry immediately picked Percival up by the head and plunged his clawed fingers into the back of Percival's neck. Percival screamed. He didn't even recognize his own voice at first. It felt distant. His eth was so drained, everything was having a drastic effect on him now. It felt like having his insides were being pulled out in every direction. He was suddenly beside himself, a separate aspect, much like when he had seen souls leaves their mortal bodies. The sentry threw Percival on his shoulder like a bag of grain, leaving the building as fast as he could to dump his body where they thought it was safe.

Belial turned to look back out the window. "Hurry, it won't be long now."

Michael looks from high above. The wraiths had all been neutralized, and the bodies of celestials and demons lay bleeding and mangled across much of the inner city. Sebastian flies back up to meet Michael.

"This was much larger than we expected," Michael says, analyzing the catastrophe.

"Yes, we stepped into a nest today. They were up to something. I have seen no sign of the demon Ganislay," Sebastian admits.

"This is bigger than him. He doesn't have the temperament or the cunning for such a battle. The problem is, neither does Moloch." Michael surveys the carnage as he slowly drifts down from the sky. He remembers how quickly the wraiths and the demons appeared. This could be any number of princes from the Underworld, but only one fit the bill for such cunning. Michael waves the cherubim forward, who revealed a trumpet.

The Cherubim sounds the trumpet, which is both powerful and haunting. It stirs the deepest of emotions of every creature in the etheric realm and again reverberates a wave of eth across to the other planes. He then returns to the back behind Michael.

"Belial! Show yourself," Michael shouts.

Inside the building, Belial stands up from his chair. "It's about time," he says with a smile.

He looks in the mirror, standing behind the bar to inspect himself. *A bit of a mess*, he thinks to himself. The symbols and scars of battle suddenly fade from his skin. He hides his wings and a business suit appears around his body, preferring a Savile Row style over something from New York or Italy. He looks as confident and elegant as ever. Belial preferred to dress properly for every occasion. He knew Michael was fixated on the righteousness of his own calling. For Michael, this event was to be a surrender, or possibly a treaty. For Belial, this was going to be good old-fashioned blackmail. A pitch session to persuade God's army to do what he needed. He walked out the door, putting all doubt out of his mind. The cadre of demons reluctantly follows, not sharing in the enthusiasm.

Belial appears outside the building, holding his hands high, mocking the look of surrender from an Old Western. "So good of you to call upon me," he says as he walks into the light. He looked down at a mangled demon that lay in his path. A look of disgust flashed across his face. He didn't want to ruin his new shoes. Belial wills it to roll toward a crevasse and fall back into the pit of hell. "I wasn't expecting visitors today."

Michael gently lands several yards in front of him. They stand like two generals ready to negotiate. Michael's wings remain fully expanded, a signal to the rest of his choir to remain at the ready. They block out much of the daylight, which irritates Belial. The rest of the choir hovers just above the street at the height of the buildings, ready to swoop in should things go awry. "Where is the demon Ganislay? Present him to me now!"

Ganislay immediately materializes. Exactly what Belial wanted, for he had no idea where Ganislay was either. Ganislay looks at Belial, and then over at Michael. He couldn't decide whom he despised more, his tormentor, or the one who lays judgement upon him.

"Return the key now, and we might let you live."

Belial pulls a talisman out of his pocket and places it around his neck. It is the talisman that Samuel was keeping safe. "You will stay where you are, brother," he said, glancing at Ganislay. "He will do no such thing. In fact, in a few minutes, he is going to give it to me."

Michael grew frustrated. It was impossible that they were defying his order. His eyes focused in on the talisman. It was obvious it contained something meant to be kept safe.

"You know, I tried to set her free. That's the funny thing about eth, it tends to have a mind of its own. Your boy placed her in a world of his own, so her reign here has ended." Ganislay and Michael both look at him, confused.

"The portal of judgement is in Samuel's possession and shall be returned forthwith," Michael commands.

Belial slowly begins to walk around, allowing himself to ponder. "I retrieved it from him a few hours ago."

Michael's eyes widened. *This is why they could put up such a big fight. This is why the sound of the Cherubim trumpet did not get them to back down. If the portal of judgement has been destroyed, the mortal realm is in grave danger.*

Belial motions for Ganislay to bring him the key.

Ganislay looks at him in disbelief. He was beyond fear. His feet felt too heavy to lift. He was ready for anything to happen. A flurry of lightning bolts to skewer him from above as he took each step. The anguish of not doing as he was told should he not move his feet forward. He felt like a battered child expecting the next beating as he navigated the contradicting orders of two parents.

As Ganislay took another step closer to Belial.

The choir of angels moves to attack formation. Michael waves them off, preventing them from proceeding. He was unsure how this was going to play out. *There were too many unknowns. The portal of judgement may or may not be destroyed. The key to heaven may or may not even be present. This could all be a decoy. And above all, the mortal realm may or may not already be lost. This is going to take a lot of nuance.*

Ganislay watches as the choirs and Michael do not attack. As he nears Belial, he stops. "If the portal of judgement is lost, then I am as free of you as you are of him," he says, looking at Belial. Ganislay realized, as long as he stays out of the confines of hell, without Judgement, on the etheric and mortal planes, no one realm holds any sway over the other. He knew this was true, because otherwise he would not have been able to say the words to begin with. The move was strategic. If he provides Belial with the key, then Belial has no need for him any longer. He would be dis-incorporated within moments. He didn't care about the key any longer, he didn't care about storming the gates of heaven. If he could hand it over to either party and make it to safety, he could live out his existence in peace far away from these warring factions.

"He speaks the truth," Michael says. Michael sees a glint of opportunity. He senses the change in Ganislay, not betrayal of the chthonics, but of being neutral. Strange for a demon. It was an uncomfortable moment to come to terms with. There was bound to be some trickery. He just needed a few more moments to figure it out.

Belial smiled and shook his head. "Fuckin' bastards, everybody's got an angle, don't they?" He looked at Ganislay. He could just kill Ganislay where he stood and deal with the consequences.. Simply nudging him into a crevasse would be enough. However, it would be doubtful he would make it out of the situation intact. Ganislay was his insurance that he could get out of this stalemate. With this kind of leverage, Ganislay was an equal. "What do you propose?"

"A neutral place. A safe arbiter where I can relinquish the key." Ganislay appeared stone faced. He would not budge.

"That will require an emissary. You have none," Michael says to Ganislay. All three knew Ganislay was referring to the Council of

Elders. In a situation like this, they provided neutral arbitration. Although, it would be difficult to find neutrality since both sides just reigned fire and brimstone across their central city.

"He will not relinquish the key to either of us in this setting. I will accept that he can be his own emissary if that is acceptable to you," Belial says, looking at Michael.

Michael thought it over. There wasn't much of an option. He decided he would agree to this, while knowing that in the end he would not send a celestial emissary, a trick of his own. All hope would rely on later persuading Ganislay to peacefully return the key to the choirs. He didn't trust the etherics any more than he trusted a chthonic. "Very well."

"And who do you choose as your representative?" Ganislay says, looking back at Michael.

"My Lieutenant, Sebastian. However, this negotiation is about the key. Where is Samuel?"

"We will return him to your emissary," Belial reassures him.

"And who will that be?"

Belial raised his eyebrows and nodded his head. "The only one I trust. The Lord of the Flies himself."

Sensing another attempt at a trick, Michael points his sword at Belial. "You need to name your champion," Michael says sternly.

"My emissary shall be Baalzebul." Even though he was free from the yolk of celestial coercion, he still wanted an air of civility. For within that civility, he had wiggle room.

Michael knew this was code that Belial was not interested in being honest. If he was feeling charitable, he would have chosen Asmodeus, who may not even know he has escaped hell. Furthermore, Asmodeus was quite ambitious himself, and although he viewed the mortals the most favorably among the demons, he had ambitions of his own.

Baalzebul also had ambition, but he was cursed. Asmodeus placed a curse on Baalzebul, ensuring that any deal made with him would be destined to fail. Michael included all of this in his calculus, knowing that Belial was counting on the deal falling apart. "Very well then."

"We meet tomorrow, at the Council. Until then, you are very busy, for as we speak, our hoards are streaming in to the mortal coil," Belial said.

Michael turned to the chief councils among his Archs to confer. They dart into a huddle in the sky like hummingbirds. Michael looked up at them, and Sebastian nodded at Michael, confirming that this was correct. In a giant blast of light, every celestial streaks out of sight, heading to the mortal world.

CHAPTER FIFTEEN

Percival slowly picked himself up off the ground. Every movement he made was painful. What made things worse was the searing pain in his back. Instead of a spinal column delivering a cluster of nerve centers, the spine is the main route that distributes eth in and out of the body. As the majority of eth had been drained from Percival, his spine was beginning to harden from the lack of life-force. The pain was so bad, he could hardly breathe. It was then he noticed he needed to breathe. Something was changing in him. Only mortals needed to breathe. He didn't know what to think. A mass of confusion clouded out the rest of his thoughts.

He limped around the corner into an alley. All that mattered was that he had saved Samuel. He would find him as soon as he could. But something in him knew he had to deal with whatever was going on with him at this moment. As he leaned against a wall to deal with the pain, an etheric stumbled out on the back door of the building, drunk of Eth, giggling out loud.

It stumbled up next to Percival and eyed him with a curious mischief. "Sometimes it is a zebra! I knew it." Giggling, he lost his balance and fell onto his rear, desperately trying to save what was left in his bottle from spilling. "I knew there were Celestials about. Too much going on for there not to be." He took a big gulp from the bottle and then coughed and sputtered. "My apologies." He said, holding out the bottle in offer to Percival, "your eminence".

Normally Percival would have completely ignored this nonsense, but eth was exactly the thing he needed now. He grabbed the bottle and drank the entire last quarter of what was left.

"Hey, that took me a week to save up for. "

"My apologies." Percival fished around in his pockets. He wasn't used to the physical experience, he could not conjure physical objects any longer. His finger felt the small envelope in his breast pocket and he pulled it out.

The etheric immediately became curious the moment it saw the envelope in Percival's hands.

Percival sorted through the remaining talismans he had. He knew he needed the 'Call of the Duke', a specific talisman that would summon the duke of the realm. It was his best chance of getting out of there. He handed the etheric the coin.

The etheric tried to grab the coin from Percival's hand. "Do you want more Eth?"

The etheric looked at the coin, trying to pry it from Percival's finger, almost paying him no mind.

Percival flicked the etheric with his finger, knocking it to the ground. "Hey... do you want more eth?" he asked sternly.

The etheric nodded.

Percival emptied his pouch, revealing the remaining coins. "You can have all of this," he said, jingling the bag of coins. He flicked the talisman at the etheric. Fetch me the closest Duke, bring us two bottles of Eth, and I will give you all of this on your return.

"That would be my brother."

"What would be?"

"The Duke of this regency is my brother. He's right in there," the etheric said, pointing to the back door.

"Excellent, go fetch him."

"You will have to come with me. He doesn't trust me as much anymore."

"Why am I not surprised? It could be a trick, it could be a trap. It could be anything, he thought." Percival wasn't in a position to argue.

The etheric helped Percival to his feet, and they slowly limped toward the back door. "The guys will never believe this."

Percival squeezed in through the doorway and through the hall. While he was used to being larger in their world, he wasn't used to the pressure of being affected by a physical environment. Something was definitely different. As he squeezed down the hallway, Percival knocked over and broke nearly every object in his way.

The etheric didn't mind, mostly because he was too drunk to care about very much. The potential accolade of finding a Celestial also made him oblivious. It was a winning lottery ticket for him in his societal status. Percival could hear the revelry of singing and loud banter coming from a large front room at the end of the hall. The etheric gleefully ran in and began tugging at his brother's sleeve.

"I thought I told you to go home. You have an important day tomorrow," the Duke commanded.

"Not anymore, I don't," the etheric said proudly.

The Duke immediately became angry and tried to slap his younger brother. However, his hand stopped, repelled by an invisible force like a magnet.

"You're going to love this brother," the etheric smirked. He produced the talisman that Percival handed him moments ago.

"Where in the bloody hell did you find this?" The revelry lowered a bit as some of the other etherics leered at the valuable talisman now on display. "Who did you steal this from?"

"Yeah...," the etheric turned around and held out his arms to present Percival, who was just making his way into the room.

The party immediately came to a halt as everyone looked in stunned silence. The juxtaposition of a Celestial being physically present in their local neighborhood bar was too great.

"I don't understand," a female said from the crowd.

"Why does he smell like freshly baked cookies?" another asked.

"Yes... its divine."

Percival nodded in wry acceptance. To them heavenly presence smelled like freshly baked cookies. He didn't like the mundane reference, but he supposed there were worse things to be compared to. "I need your assistance," he said, looking at the Duke."

The etheric standing immediately next to the Duke smiled and then fainted.

"Yes, I suppose you do." He looked at Percival, who was bleeding from a large abrasion on his shoulder and burnt streaks across his face. "Funny, you think you run the place, yet the transmutation of energy doesn't happen without the factory floor."

"I realize that."

"Huh, most celestials don't. Ironically, the chthonics do. They don't value much, but at least they recognize utility when they see it. Even though it was you who created the Earth."

Percival wasn't sure which way this was going to go. If he didn't get help, it would be an awfully long walk out of the city and back to the portal he had entered through. He wouldn't make it without Samuel.

"Well, it's best we talk business elsewhere." The Duke walked to the corner and lifted his scepter. "Let's do this." The duke couldn't have declined if he wanted to. The law of the talisman required him to act. But how was he going to help? He hadn't figured out yet. He waved the scepter, and they teleported to his office of Regency in the center of the capital.

As they transported, Percival read a tone of deception from the Duke. He was too tired and his situation too tenuous to do anything about it. He had an incredibly difficult time reading etherics at the best of times.

The Offices of Regency displayed trophies and momentos of things past. As the four of them appeared in the building's hub, Percival stretched out. He stood tall, most of the pain subsided.

"You'll be more comfortable here. We built this place to host emissaries from the other planes."

Percival stood tall and took a few steps. They were beneath a large emerald rotunda. The Thread of Eth flowed in from the other planes and collated at the top of the Rotunda as and collected to be distributed throughout that etheric world. Percival looked up in awe. It was the most beautiful thing he had seen since being back in his department. This struck him as ironic. He had never thought of the place he worked as beautiful before. He enjoyed watching the souls come and go because he knew they were experiencing joy, but it never affected him like this. The emerald dome above them enhanced the glowing collection of Eth from the Great Thread, casting a shimmering hue of green, teal, and gold throughout the great hall. "This is... stunning, " he whispered. "When was the last celestial visit?"

The Duke watched Percival stand in awe of the experience. "Oh... the Council of Elders has been here for millennia, just as you have. While you were fighting the Great War and casting the dissenters out, that's when the Great Inheritance was created. If our realm is the nexus between the planes, this is the center. We've been here a long time. But the last celestial to visit? You would be the first."

Percival looked at him in disbelief. "That can't be true. That -"

Interrupting, the Duke stated, "We have to record everything."

Percival nodded. He knew that was true; he had seen the headers on the reports from several departments, before tasks were handed down to himself and his colleagues. A wave of hesitance crushed him. He couldn't move or think. He had seen this in the mind of humans, like when they glance the wrong way when driving only to see an oncoming vehicle right before it hits them.

A prophecy foretold this long ago. He remembered reading this in the philosophy and esoteric section in the Library of Existence. It stated that a celestial will betray the Creator in session at the Council of Elders. Which is why no celestial has dared to step foot in the Council of Elders ever since. He was too paralyzed with fear. There was more to the prophecy, but he couldn't remember at the moment.

"C'mon," the Duke said, walking away toward the doors of an adjoining room.

He needed to remember the full prophecy, and he needed to remember now. Percival stood straight and as tall as he could. He cleared his mind to think. A swirl of wind began circling the inner walls of the rotunda. He had to remember. If he could read the prophecy again, he could stop it from happening. The whirl of wind turned to a tornado, picking up every spec of dirt, trinkets and statues, along with his escorts.

Everything flew around in a loud clatter, sounding like the charge of a freight train. Percival envisioned the aisle in the library where he first read the book, and as he quieted his mind, the moment he was in at the Rotunda froze in time. He simply stepped out of the moment, like stepping out of a picture frame, and stepped into his vision of the aisle of books.

The fear suddenly subsided. It wasn't until then that he realized just how much emotion he really was feeling since he left Central Existence. Fear, doubt, threat, interest and intrigue all wrapped into a ball that crashed to the floor in front of him, as if he had been holding it all along without realizing it. He realized he missed the peace of the research library.

"That's one of the tricks to life-understanding what a moment actually is," the librarian said, walking up to Percival.

"Life... I know nothing about life. I've never experienced it." Percival looked at her very confused by the assertion.

"It's what you wanted, to work in the office of Planning and Design. Right?"

Percival thought he had kept that desire secret. It was the only one he allowed for himself.

"In order to join that choir, you need to become an Ascended Master. To do that, you have to know what life is all about. There is a difference between existence and experience. So far, you've only known existence."

"So the prophesy is true."

"Of course. All prophesies are true, but whether a single prophesy is valid depends on which timeline unfolds. The only one who knows which timeline unfolds is the Creator. It's the same with all knowledge and emotion. They are all true, but validity is an entirely different matter and depends on the context of whether that truth can be brought into existence. Not everything works in every timeline. It's something that has confounded mortals since the beginning of existence."

"And how do you learn the difference?"

"Wisdom."

"What does the full Prophesy of Elders say?"

The Librarian raises a finger, and an old rolled manuscript floats out from one of the shelves above them. It drifts down and unfurls in front of them as it continues to float. Percival looked at it. This was always the section of the library that gave him the most trouble. He studied the old writing "Gohus i piap calz alsplan... the old language was never my strong suit." Percival gestured for her to translate.

The Librarian looked and smirked with understanding. "Many do. It reads, ' I say: the balance of the compact shall pass from among the angels, by the one who voices the secret knowledge to the Elders. This day marks a new age of rule among the Masters."

"A celestial is going to betray the choirs."

"Well, its not just any celestial. Nobody has been to the Council of Elders since the beginning of Existence. Only yourself."

"I'm not going to betray the Choirs."

"You're standing there right now, aren't you?" The librarian looks down toward Percivals feet. Instead of the floor, they both hover above the tornado, frozen in time as it spins within the Council of Elders.

"Well yes, but... well...," tears come to his eyes. "It's certainly not going to be me."

"I'm sure it won't be," the Librarian said, placing a reassuring hand on his shoulder. She ignored the tears forming in his eyes. Tears were a telltale sign he was not entirely a celestial any longer. "Go see that it doesn't happen. Perhaps you are there to stop it?"

A light of inspiration shone in Percival's eyes, gleaming through the tears. He dropped back into the Rotunda and the moment his feet hit the floor the tornado stopped. Everything fell to the floor in a crash. "This won't do," he said, standing up straight, looking at the mess. He waved his right hand and everything returned to what it was in a blink.

"C'mon," the Duke said, walking away toward the doors of an adjoining room.

Percival had brought them back only a few moments in time. He followed

The Duke's brother ran up beside Percival as they walked. "Have you been crying?"

"Yeah, just the pain. I'll be better in a moment."

Percival caught up to the Duke just before they walked into the other chamber.

"My apologies," the Duke said, turning back to Percival. "My role requires certain protocols and responsibilities to be followed, mostly handed down to me from your realm. All visitation must occur in front of the Council." He opened the door to a courtroom. The Duke spread out his arms and glided into the center of the room. "Thank you for convening on such short notice, my friends and colleagues," he said, looking around the room in all directions.

Percival stood in the entranceway to the room. The Duke stood in the center of a highly polished wooden floor with an intricately carved, inlaid design. It looked like something that would have taken thousands of years to perfect. At the far side of the room was a large window, much like the large window that formed the side of the building he worked in. The only lighting was the glow from the light of the Eth being received at the top of the building, which was more than amble.

"As we all know, the last few days have been chaotic throughout the realm. We've had massive disturbances throughout the entire plane that have echoed into mortality. As you all know, most of the time we are the first guardians between the mortal plane and the rest of eternity. Which mostly forces us to carry out the work of others." The crowd grumbles in agreement. A millennium of dissatisfaction was palpable.

"But today," the Duke announced to calm the crowd, "today is special, for we have the rare opportunity to have the final say."

Samuel suddenly materializes right beside the duke and, in that instant, the inlaid floor becomes alive, stretching up from the hardwood floor, wrapping vines around his arms and legs, pinning him to the floor. Samuel struggled as the vines pulled him to the floor, pinning him in an awkwardly crouched position. Immediately beside him appears Ganislay, who equally struggles as the glowing vines pull him to the floor as the Duke stands between them both.

Percival runs in toward the center of the room to save Samuel. As soon as his feet hit the central floor, the vines reach up and wrap around his feet. The crowd shouts and jeers with vengeful joy. The enormous iron doors to the room close behind him with a loud clang of finality.

"Our mission, as always and without fail, is to maintain the balance of Eth on the mortal plane." He walks up, equidistant between Samuel and Ganislay, "We have no particular favor in either of these agendas. This chthonic here first appeared in which realm?" the Duke asked, looking at the crowd surrounding him.

"In the outer realm," one elder said, standing up in the crowd. "He appeared with a mortal."

"With a mortal? How is this possible?" The Duke kneeled down in front of Ganislay. The vines loosened themselves enough from around his neck so that he could speak.

Ganislay stared at the Duke, defying him with silence. The vines surrounding Ganislay glowed less and quickly began drawing away what little eth Ganislay has within him. He knew they meant to dis-incorporate him.

Percival glared at the scene. "How did this entity have the power to dis-incorporate?"

"I found myself trapped in Dudael after being conjured from the Depths."

The Duke looked at him in disbelief. "You saved the life of a mortal?"

"It was the best option I had."

"How did a mortal come to be in imprisoned in the Valley of the Watchers?" The crowd talked amongst themselves. It was rare for a Chthonic to save the life of a mortal, but completely unheard of for a mortal to be found in Dudael.

"I don't know," Ganislay grumbled.

"Why were you conjured?" The Duke knelt down beside him, placing his hands on Ganislay's head. Ganislay began turning grey, and then a deep black. It was such a perfect absence of color it looked like the Duke was placing his hands in an abyss. Out of the abyss, a scroll appeared. The duke picks up the scroll and holds it up high. The color returns to Ganislay's body the moment he is released by the Duke. "You better kill me," he yells after the Duke.

"Who gave this to you?" The Duke only had power over the physical in order to balance the material world. He couldn't compel anyone to tell the truth. He circled Ganislay, trying to figure out how to get the information out of him. "Shall I call my first witness?"

The crowd began stomping their feet on the floor at every level of the surrounding amphitheatre. Percival winced, the sound was deafening to him. The Duke peered at him from across the room. Celestials did not experience the physical. He glanced away before anyone else could notice. As the stomping continued, it created a ripple in the fabric of time. The green glow from the eth pulsated, and the Portal of Judgement slowly appeared in the center of court.

"Dear portal, you see all, do you not?"

"I do," she said, unencumbered. She stood, relaxed. It was not her first time being called to the council.

"As you can see, we have both a Chthonic and a Celestial in our midst. I'm hoping you can help assist. Moments ago I retrieved this from the Chthonic," the Duke said, holding up the scroll.

The portal looked at him sternly, for she knew the answer was going to change everything. "It is the 8th call."

"I'm sorry, what do you mean by call?" The Duke genuinely asked. Etherics had little to do with the outer planes. They were unfamiliar with the terminology outside of their own existence.

The Portal stared more intently at him. She did not want to answer, but it was not in her remit to resist. "It is the eighth key to heaven."

Silence reigned in the council hall. The Duke unfurled the scroll and gazed upon the parchment. The light of the parchment burned bright, outshining the light from the glowing Eth outside the building. He could hardly keep his eyes on it. He could read some words, but they made little sense.

Deep inside the crowd, hidden amongst all the different Elders sat the Envoy. He was waiting for the moment to spring, but he had yet to figure out how they would make it out of this one alive.

"You cannot decode the words. Mortals and celestials can, but chthonics and etherics cannot without a primer." She purposely listed chthonics before etherics to piss him off. It was not his place to hold any of the keys, much less try to read them.

"What do I need to read?"

"An etheric needs a mortal soul or celestial guidance."

The Duke turned to Samuel and peered down at him. "I have two celestials of my own, right here. Surely one of them is good natured enough to teach me the meaning of these words."

"I cannot," Samuel answered.

The vines raised him up, far above the Duke's head, high enough that he was eye level with most of the audience in the amphitheater. The vines began draining the eth from Samuel's body. Eth debt quickly overtook him, and he felt ill and weak.

"You will teach us this meaning or you will die here."

Samuel drooped and fell more limp, the vines holding him up like an awkward sack of sand. He finally noticed in front of him at eye level was the Envoy.

The Envoy stared back at him and gave a gentle nod. "Tell him, and survive for another day," he communicated.

Samuel waves an arm toward the Duke, letting him know he gives in. The vines lower and then let him fall to the ground. The thud of Samuel's body echoes through the chamber.

The Duke walks up to Samuel's drained body. "It is not just you that is an aspect of the Creator. We are the bridge between creation and destruction of physical reality. That includes you, and you don't have much time."

The vines leach the eth from Samuel, though more slowly this time. Samuel had minutes to live.

Samuel flops onto his back and stares toward the roof of the building. His eyes land at the top of the window where it joins the ceiling, where he can see the most intense glow of the eth as it streams into the building. He remembers the eighth call and repeats out loud:

"The midday, the first is as the third heaven made of hyacinth pillars, in whom the Elders are to become strong, which I have prepared for my own righteousness." Samuel looked over at Ganislay, still pinned across the floor from him. "Whose long continuance shall be bucklers to the stooping dragons, and like unto the harvest of a widow. How many are there, which remain in the glory of the earth, which are and shall not see death until this house fall and the dragon sink."

The duke looked at him with disdain. "I tell you what, this house isn't about to fall anytime soon."

Etherics throughout the crowd lept to their feet in an angry roar and began stomping their feet in unison again.

The duke looked at the Portal, "It seems we have passed our own judgement here today, and since we have autonomy in this realm, and the next has kept their secrets long enough, it will be delivered here today."

Samuel could feel the vines tightly gripping him as they slowly raised him up off the ground again. They drained the eth from him in an instant; it felt like the sting of hundreds of jellyfish, paralyzing most of his body. "You need the Book of Feasts."

The Envoy could just about hear what Samuel told them. He stood up from his position and made his way through his row and began leaping down the rows to the center court below. He knew it was only a matter of time.

Ganislay peered up as much as he could from his position. He knew the 'Book of Feasts'. It was the grimoire that sat on top of the central altar in Pandemonium. He didn't favor going back to hell to combine these two, but if he had some insurance, he probably wouldn't be trifled with.

The Envoy made it to the floor; he drew a large pistol made of titanium and platinum.

The Duke looked at him pitifully. "Mortal weapons don't work here."

"Yeah, I know." The Envoy pulls the trigger and a large burst of golden Eth shoots out like lightening, hitting the Duke in the Chest. The Eth spreads across the Duke's body like a spider web and quickly fades, turning him into a pewter statue, freezing him permanently where he stands. Samuel is released as the vines crash to the floor, shattering like glass. The crowd jumps from the amphitheater rows, and bodies shower down onto the center court, lunging for the Envoy. He continues to shoot in all directions. As his assailants quickly turn to metallic statues, the rest of the crowd backs away, not wanting to be next. They surround him in an angry truce. "C'mon Percival, we don't have all day."

The Envoy quickly looks for the eighth key on the ground as he carries Samuel on his back. His eyes land on the far side of the room where Ganislay stands holding Percival and the Eighth Key hostage. His eyes search for a shot to take Ganislay down. "You aren't making it out of this."

"I got me a sweet little angel that I'm gonna take with me. So please," he picks Percival up and slams his angelic body to the ground like a doll. "Please," he says, slamming Percival to the ground again. Cracks appear in Percivals skin like that of a porcelain doll, and through the cracks shine the glow of golden Eth. "I'm begging you to fuck with me right now."

The Envoy couldn't calculate how this was happening. He knew if he shoots Ganislay; he returns to hell, and Percival goes with him. The problem was, Percival would be under Ganislay's command. If the etherics got a hold of them, they would dis-incorporate both of them and keep the key.

An etheric leapt from behind Ganislay, trying to grab the key. Ganislay bumbled his grip on the scroll, and it flew out of his hand. He released his grip Percival to get the key back. The Envoy saw his chance and fired off a shot. Just as the eth hit Ganislay as he leaned forward, his back arm brushed against Percival and they both disappear to Hell.

This reinvigorates the crowd, and they lung toward The Envoy and Samuel again. Samuel remained as weak as a fish out of water, struggling to keep conscious.

Within seconds, the crowd grew closer. The Envoy pulled a small pellet out of his jacket and threw it onto the floor before his feet, as hard as he can. The pellet explodes with a thunderous roar, freezing time and sending a wave of Eth throughout the entire etheric plane.

"That was a close one," the Envoy said with relief.

"Yes, it was," a voice comes out of the crowd.

The Envoy spun around in the direction of the voice and placed Samuel on the ground to protect him. He couldn't figure out how an etheric could make it through the blast. The only thing that can exist without Eth... "Oh shit," he said interrupting his thought.

"Oh shit is right," Belial said, emerging from the crowd. "Why fight the war when you have soldiers to do it for you," he said, gesturing to where Ganislay stood only moments before. He held up the scroll that contained the Eighth Key, jiggling it to taunt the Envoy.

"I'm going to get what I want," Belial asserted. "But these folks are too inexperienced to know who you are," he gestured toward everyone who in the room. "There's no style these days, no respect. In our day, as you know, a king does not kill a king. Do they, Enoch?"

"That name hasn't been used in millennia," the Envoy said, stepping away. "I am not a King. What is it you want? Maybe we can make a deal."

Belial's voice filled the entire room. "A man who walks where demons are forbidden and Angels fear to tread. Never has there been an entity more deserving of the title King than you."

The Envoy didn't give credence to what Belial was saying. The best soothsayers can prey on the pride and vanity of others, and Belial was King of them all. The Envoy would not fall for it, no matter how much truth was in the statement.

"Oh... change is in the air, my friend," Belial continued to boom. He tapped the scroll in his hand as if he was about to conduct an orchestra. "Set off by a Portal, of all God damned things. Who would have thought? Life does have it's curveballs. Humans might call them witches, and true... some aren't worth a pile of pig snot, but this one was the Portal of Mortality. We all know she's been pushed to her limit for years, and was due to retire long ago. But as always, the celestials kept on pushing and pushing for more. Y'all just don't know when to stop. In some ways, you're worse than us. Yet with all this mortality, I don't see any progression, especially among the humans. The masses are just as dumb and selfish as ever. Sure, they've got a few bright sparks in the bunch, but I ain't seen no Enoch's recently, no modern day Hermes, no Buddha among them. You've created plenty of pearls over the years, but you only have swine to cast them to. And yet you want to blame us." Belial waved his finger and tuts at the Envoy.

"What do you want, you long-winded bastard?" The Envoy leveled his gun toward Belial.

"The same that I've always wanted. To take my rightful place on the throne of Pandemonia. Only this time, there isn't anything anyone can do to stop me." Belial races past the Envoy and launched himself toward the great window.

The Envoy pulls Samuel in to shield him. Instead of the window shattering, Belial disappears in a cloud of red dust that drifts through the window. The large stream of eth flowing into the top of the building turns from green to red and slows down its rate of transfer. Belial interrupts the life force between all the planes, and it begins to primarily flow toward the underworld. The building and the entire Etheric plane quakes from the pressure difference.

In the distance the Envoy could hear the flow of time rushing back. If he wasn't quick enough, the remaining etherics would kill him for sure. He picked up Samuel, took out a knife and sliced open Samuel's arm so the golden Eth would flow out on the floor. "Sorry buddy, we'll get you fixed up in no time." he waited until Samuel's Eth pooled on the floor, and through its he could see a portal to central Existence. He picked Samuel up and stepped through to the other side.

CHAPTER SIXTEEN

Percival woke, but he couldn't move. There was a resistance preventing him from even moving his legs and arms. He couldn't understand why, all that he could fathom in the deep darkness that surrounded him is that he was lying down. He could also tell that he was being moved through complete darkness, save for a small, deep orange glow up ahead.

An entity laughed right behind him, but Percival couldn't turn to identify its source. "You're my pet now. You'll bark when I say bark, you'll beg when I say beg."

Percival ignored him. He had heard the voice before, but couldn't place it in the state he was in. He knew it was a demon. The trick to any demon is to not buy into the words they spout. Instead, he looked away. He sensed they were travelling through a deep black void. In the darkness, he could see a tiny orange ember glowing in the distance. Each moment that passed, the ember grew. It was the only thing he could see, and now that he was looking at it, he noticed the ember that was once small was growing and racing toward him in the most spectacular manner. He could hear the faint roar of sound. It almost sounded like the commotion on a factory floor. Suddenly, he knew what was next. It wasn't an amber at all; he didn't know how, but he was travelling toward the gates of Hell. It was at this point he thought of his induction into the choir where he used to work.

The choir stood before their desks in their section of the great hall of the command center. "I am Deacon, and I welcome you to the Department of Principal Communications and Endeavors." Deacon strolled between the desks of the choir. "I thank the good Lord for creating such fine Celestials that I see before me. But whether you stay here is up to me. Some of you will not last. Don't worry, there are plenty of functions we need you for. Others will go on to greater things."

Ganislay landed with Percival in front of the collection cages by the river. The plummet to the ground cracks some eth out of Percival's body and he feels the full measure of genuine pain for the first time in his existence. Was this what Deacon meant by 'going on to greater things', or had he washed out? He asked for a sign.

A business man in the cage behind him hollered out. "Hey, hey. You're an angel! Holy shit, I knew this had to be a mistake. I knew you would come for me. Hey could you get me out of here?"

Percival looked back at him vacantly. Despite his own circumstance, he thought about how he might help the man.

"Don't worry about those memories," Ganislay grunted as he lifted Percival up above his head. "Man, are celestials heavy bastards down here." He stepped toward the river of fire and plunged Percival in. He kept hold of the top of Percival's head, ensuring that he stayed within the fire. The river dragged every ounce of eth out of him almost instantly. Ganislay held him under just long enough. He didn't want to turn him, that's for sure. "Ok," he said, as he pulled him out of the river of fire. He threw Percival onto the ground where he rolled and tumbled several times in a charred mess.

"Huh," Ganislay said, looking at him dumbfounded. He expected Percival to come out of the river, stripped naked down to a crispy skin. Except Percival remained as he was before. "How is that possible?"

A large booming horn rumbled throughout the landscapes of hell, grinding everything to a halt. Eight sentries appeared around Ganislay and Percival.

Ganislay expected this. Kidnapping a creature of such a rank as Percival was bound to raise some eyebrows, even in the depths of Hell. "Right on time, boys! But if you think I'm giving this one over to you, I'll have your eth. I'm taking this one to see him myself." The sentries looked at each other and nodded in unison. Ganislay picked Percival back up, and the sentries leaned their spears forward all at once. A ring of fire rockets in a circle between the spears and all ten of them disappear, instantaneously materializing in the throne room of the infernal council.

The sentries continue to stand surrounding Ganislay and Percival, waiting for further orders.

A towering figure walks into the throne room, his height reaching unnatural proportions that dwarf the circle of sentries as well as Ganislay. Asmodeus, one of only a few Kings of Hell, stares at them with surprise from across the room. "This is out of order, I do not enjoy my duties being interrupted," he says calm yet sternly. The sound of his voice immediately makes everyone tense.

The captain of the sentries immediately barks back, "Apologies your grace, we are under orders to deliver them here."

"Of course," he held no hostility for any of his sentries. His muscular body imposes as he comes to a stand still a few feet behind Ganislay. He placed himself there to purposely force Ganislay to awkwardly turn to address him. With sinewy limbs that show his strength and agility, he stared at Ganislay with burning embers for eyes. They glow with an intense, infernal light that pierces even the the darkest areas of hell. They are as much windows to his own soul, but contain the essence of hell itself, filled with malice, cunning, and an insatiable hunger for corruption. His gaze sweeps over the circle of sentries and they quickly fade into stone statues, frozen in their places. He cocks his head. "What are you doing here?"

Ganislay turned to Asmodeus, looking up at him like he is the dumbest creature across all three planes. He knew to whom he was speaking, but he didn't want to show any intimidation. Inside, he was scared out of his mind "Moloch sent these minions to fetch us," he said pointing at the sentries.

"Moloch?" He walked around the statues of the sentries, looking suspiciously at Ganislay. "The Prince of Darkness is missing. Yet, you conveniently show up in the throne room with ten battle-ready sentries and a half-dead celestial. I'd say we may have found the culprit."

Ganislay drops Percival to the floor, letting his body fall into a large thud. "I've been tracking this lump of celestial shit across two planes. I was about to interrogate him when they interrupted."

Asmodeus looks at Ganislay with disgust and then down at Percival. A demon of this stature could not have waged a war on a celestial and won. Not without help. "You're not a Prince, you'd hardly qualify as a Lord. Who are you?"

In his zeal for the mission he was on, Ganislay forgot about the protocols when in front of a prince of hell. "I had the key to the celestial realm in my hands and lost it. I got the next best thing. An uncompromised celestial." An unfallen angel captured and brought to hell was the holy grail of demonic dreams, for it gave them access to untold gateways into the heavens. "I can see that. Who the fuck are you?"

"This is Ganislay," Belial's voice announces as it cuts through the tension. He appeared from the darkness of the chamber and waves off the sentries.

The sentries return from stone to their natural form and retreat from surrounding Ganislay, lining up several feet away from the three demons.

Asmodeus stiffens. It was a coup, after all. He had no allegiance to anyone sitting on the throne, as the role is a fool's errand. Since the fall, Asmodeus had become a steady fixture in Pandemonia. His plan was to take the throne once all the kings and princes had killed off one another in their zeal to take it. Asmodeus stared Belial down, ignoring that Ganislay is even there.

Belial stared back, unafraid. Asmodeus had as much support throughout the pits of hell as he did. He knew Asmodeus was a higher rank, but often thought of him as a coward, always shying away from the throne once the chance presented itself. "You can either get behind me on this, or we can go to war."

Asmodeus' eyes flickered higher. He could see behind the ruse and read Belial's energy. In a flash, he could see an image of Belial submitting the order to kill Moloch. Belial had broken a pact they had made centuries prior - Moloch would not be touched by him. Moloch was Asmodeus' dog, as he secretly ruled behind the scenes.

Over the years, Belial had weaseled his way into being the main confidant of Moloch. Asmodeus never minded, as long as Belial didn't throw his weight around too much. If he broke the pact, the legions that Belial commanded would go to war with Asmodeus. Calculating all of this and realizing that war had begun, Asmodeus simply nodded and waved an arm for Belial to continue as he liked. "Your hound must go to the slaughter," he said referring to Ganislay.

The circle of sentries tightened around Ganislay, their spears immediately extending and grazing his neck, waiting for the next order.

Asmodeus glared at Ganislay. He was clearly a very capable demon, and he could see that Ganislay had accomplished much of this mission by his own wits. However, Asmodeus had two problems, he needed to do something to satisfy the Etheric council, and he also didn't need such a capable demon fighting with Belial's legion once the war began. "This hound," he said, pointing a scaley finger at Ganislay, "must be thrown to the Etheric Council. Your campaign caused them much damage, and we need to keep their realm on our side."

Belial stares at Ganislay. "Very well." Belial holds out his hand and for the key to heaven.

Ganislay resisted as much as he could, but with this much negative energy from Asmodeus, the Sentries, and now Belial, he could do nothing to escape.

Belial pulls out the scroll and Percival's body reappears at Belials feet.

Ganislay watched as all his hard work was stolen with the ease of a soft summer breeze.

"Deliver him to the Council of Elders, they can do with him as they like."

The sentries step back, place the but of their spears on the floor and lean them in. A circle of fire surrounds them and in a flash they are all gone, taking Ganislay with them.

Belial looks down at Percival's body. "You, he points to the shadows. Take this body to the Well of Souls."

A pair of yellow eyes blink open from the darkness of the shadows and rushes toward Percival.

Chapter Seventeen

"To possess a soul is difficult. It takes a tremendous amount of energy and a rather ambitious entity to get it all together. You've all taken the 'Fundamentals In Eth' class, so you understand how much Eth goes into filling a soul," the instructor said as she paced in front of the class.

Percival looked around the meeting area. They were all seated on a tremendous lanai. He couldn't wait, because the ceiling above the lanai also served as the floor that housed the department he was about to work in. Beneath the based of the lanai flowed the rivers of heaven. The lanai was a large platform floating above a cascading waterfall that dropped into the sacred pool where all the souls who were new to heaven congregated.

Cascading from towering, luminescent cliffs, the water glowed with the radiant mists of water and eth, each droplet shimmering like liquid crystal in the soft, eternal light. Percival never felt so safe. The surrounding landscape enhances the waterfall's splendor. Lush greenery, untouched and perpetually blooming, lines the banks of the pristine river. Flowers of every conceivable color and shape bloom abundantly, their fragrances blending into a sublime, harmonious scent that filled the air. Majestic trees with silvery leaves and golden bark stood tall, their branches gently swayed in a breeze that carried the soft, melodic whispers of angelic choirs. The sound of the waterfall is a soothing symphony, a harmonious blend of gentle splashes and musical tinkling, which resonated with the serene ambiance of heaven. Clear as crystal, reflecting the radiant sky above, the pool at the base of the waterfall is a tranquil expanse of water, where the colors of a perpetual sunset blend into the deep blue of a star-kissed night. The entire scene exuded peace, beauty, and divine grace, offering a glimpse into the infinite serenity of heaven.

Like the souls that would congregate there, Percival found himself equally drawn to it during his first few days at Central Existence. While many of his colleagues preferred to chat with one another about the newest things they were learning, or what their previous roles were like, Percival simply enjoyed the splendour of the surroundings he was in. As if he were as mortal as the souls in the pool below. While he enjoyed his time working at the gates, taking souls in, he didn't find it challenging enough. This was it. He had worked hard and achieved what he wanted. He knew there was nothing but more hard work ahead.

"So why are we talking about such an unsavory topic as possession? Does anybody know," the instructor asked.

"Because you are all about to receive an assignment to the Department of Principal Communications and Endeavors for Humanity, so we need to know when a mortal is possessed," one celestial blurted out.

"Good guess. While it's true, you will never get a demon spending all his time collecting eth just so they can spiritually possess a caterpillar. Though they can do some pretty stupid things sometimes - so nothing would surprise me. This class serves two purposes. First as a reminder of what you are up against. Yes, it's true, we all work as a team and you are likely to never leave the comforts of this building. Your channelling orbs will provide you with all the information we need to guide the souls you are assigned to. Despite all of this, there may come times when you are dealing with something you don't quite understand. Your channelling orb may put you in contact with the possessed, and it is possible that if you don't know what you are looking at, that you and the demon may imbue upon one another."

"Has that ever happened?" a student blurted out with excitement.

"No, but we are always vigilent of the possibility."

"The second reason is a last ditch reminder. This memory is an implant. It never actually happened."

Percival's eyes snapped up at the instructor. He thought it was an odd thing to say. "I clearly remember this happening. Why would you say such a thing?" Percival said, raising his hand and slightly interrupting.

"Because, if you recall, this actually took place at your new desks and was part of the safety briefing while you were learning the basics of how to use your channelling orb."

Percival looked down at his feet. "That's right."

"If you can access this memory implant, it serves as a reminder that someone has captured or possessed you. The safety and serenity you feel from these surroundings gives you the mental capacity to send out a distress signal to any other celestials you are connected to."

Percival looked back up. Everyone was gone, and he was sitting at his old desk. Central Existence appeared empty and abandoned for years. The grand celestial architecture that adorned heaven's expanse was in ruins. Once pristine palaces and temples, built from materials that gleamed with an otherworldly brilliance, were now crumbled into heaps of rubble. Towers that once soared gracefully into the sky were now broken in half and lay open to a perilous atmosphere of dust storms and gases. The spires that were left deteriorated, becoming tarnished, stale, and crumbling. Layers of ash and soot covered the intricate mosaics and frescoes, which depicted heavenly scenes. Vandalism defaced and shattered many of the spires. The beauty they once had disappeared.

The air, once filled with the melodious voices of angelic choirs, now echoed with mournful wails and distant roars of malevolent entities. The peace and tranquility that defined heaven were replaced by an overwhelming sense of dread and despair. The very essence of this celestial realm seemed tainted, its divine light dimmed and its harmony shattered.

Percival looked across the room. He saw a celestial shuffling through, the look of defeat hard stenciled on its face. "Hey... hey, what happened here?"

The Celestial continued to shuffle along with a heavy heart, its once radiant form now marred by the battle. Unlike a demon, its wings were just broken and scarred by dried ichor. Their wings, which once shimmered with divine light, were now tattered and stained.

"He can't hear you," a deep voice announced itself right beside Percival.

"Oh...why not?" Percival said, turning to the entity.

"They lost the war long ago. The few who remain have simply given up."

Percival looked at the entity with astonishment. "What war? What are you talking about?" He tried to adjust his eyes. Despite being able to see everything in the building, when he tried to look directly at the entity speaking with him, his eyes wouldn't focus.

"Ok, well, I haven't been completely truthful there. What I'm showing you is the future. All the hard work you did, the failure to get the keys back, will lead to this."

Percival felt funny instead of being drained of Eth. He felt like all the Eth was rapidly flowing through him, but he couldn't connect to it. As if he was standing on a riverbank watching it all flow by him. "I tried. I did my best. I was taken in battle. Oh..." he crumbled to the floor. "Have I been dis-incorporated."

The entity laughed. "That's impossible. If you were dis-incorporated you wouldn't be anything at all."

"Oh..."

"I'm here to help. Why did you accept such a difficult task when you weren't sure you could do it?"

"I don't know. I just thought I could help. I thought I was being nice."

"Ooo... if there's one thing worse than good intentions, it's someone who just thought it would be nice to do something."

"I suppose you are right."

Percival was suddenly beside a still river. On the other side, he could see the entity that had been speaking with him. He rubbed his eyes once more and recognized him as the demon whom had him carried away when he was taken captive. "You are Belial. I have heard of you."

"Yes, and this is as far as you go."

Percival looked around, he noticed he was on a small island. He could just make out what he thought was a river surrounding the island. It was too wide to jump, but he didn't trust it. The more he stared at it, the more it called to him. He tore his eyes away. They wanted to look. They wanted to know what made up the terrible blackness that surrounded him. There was something in it, almost as if it were an entity itself. Perhaps it was. He could hear the sounds of hell in the far distance, but he could see nothing but the darkened surroundings before him. As he leaned forward to peer into the river, it vanished, exposing that it was not a river after all, but an endless crevasse dividing him from Belial and everywhere else. He tried to levitate and fly over, but he couldn't even lift himself above his own weight.

"That is the weight of your sins."

Percival laughed. He had never heard such an absurdity. "What sin would that be?"

Belial looked at him, stone cold and serious. "Your lack of faith." If there was one thing demons are allowed to be, it is God's retribution.

"Oh, you do go on, don't you? I have loads of faith in the Most High." A voice grew in Percival like it never had before. He didn't know it existed until this very moment. "You will release me from this hold, chthonic!"

Belial was surprised Percival had attempted to compel him. Perhaps he had faith, after all. "I don't think so." It wouldn't be long before Percival realized that they were within his consciousness.. "You are one of the Sons of of Light, not a Son of Man, but a Son of God... who has no faith in themself. Therefore, you do not trust that the Most High had his wits about him when he created you." Belial took a step back. "I think I'll keep you here. Sometimes heaven needs saving from itself. Besides, all it takes is a little faith and you can get yourself out of this."

Belial's words hit Percival hard. He thought perhaps it he had tried a little harder to break loose from his captures. It was enough to give Belial just what he needed. A wave signature of dark eth whisked out from Percival, and Belial reached out to grab it. Within seconds he was through and he could lock onto the consciousness of every mortal Percival was ever assigned to.

On the mortal plane, Percival's cases simply vanished. Belial co-lo-cates himself across every mortal Percival ever had contact with. Hundreds of people vanish in a flash. A woman driving her children home from school suddenly dissipates and Belial is seated driving the SUV where she was only moments ago. He stops the vehicle in the middle of an intersection and gets out of the vehicle. As he steps out, he walks directly into the traffic in the on-coming lane. A car going the other way rams into him, its hood and engine crumpling into itself like it had just hit a steel reinforced bollard. The people inside the vehicle survive, but as the wave signatures of confusion and pain waft off of them, Belial grabs them. "This is all I need," he announces with glee.

Belial raises his arms and a crack rips into the middle of the inter-section. Demons of all kinds pour out, screeching and scampering off into the distance. As the negative Eth increases, so does the number of demons.

Percival looks around at the tremendous crevasse separating him from his escape. As he does, a wave of Eth hits him from one of his oldest cases. "Oh, my God... he's travelling through my consciousness. No, no no," he screams at the top of his lungs. He paces back and forth, thinking if he could just get out, he could stop Belial. "Wait a second," he said, stopping. "If he's in my consciousness, that means I can get into his as well." Not able to think of anything else, he sits down on the ground, if only to calm himself down. He focuses in on the feelings his cases are experiencing and is suddenly transported to where Belial is.

Percival appears in front of Belial in the middle of the intersection. The woman whom Belial travelled through to arrive on the mortal plane reappears in the driver's seat of the stopped SUV. She looks at Percival. He is a long-lost friend whom she had never laid eyes on before. A spiritual pen pal that she knows inside and out, but can't quite place her finger on how she knows him.

Percival seethes with anger, but noticed the woman is staring right at him. He tempered himself just enough and glances toward her. "Get your family home."

She looked at Percival, almost crying, and nods.

Percival grabbed Belial's arms and swung him in a quick circle, and flings him into the side of a corner store. "Looks like I made it out."

Belial picks himself up from the mire of broken glass, steel and brick. "Did you? Is this really me, or just one of my aspects?"

Percival raised his hand toward Belial. As soon as he does, Belial disappears. Percival dropped his hand. "That's what I thought. I can't compel him. That was only an aspect."

Belial looks down at Percivals body. He is quietly on the ground next to the well of souls.

"He'll figure it out soon. It doesn't matter any more, we have a direct pathway to the mortal realm now. Once he wakes, we drop him into the well of souls, and these pathways are ours forever. The longer he stays under, the more pathways we have."

Chapter Eighteen

The Envoy carried Samuel in his arms through galaxies, streaking through the various realms between the three great realms. He didn't have the strength or the authority to carry Samuel all the way into Central Existence. Matters of security were beyond his remit. As they travelled through the planes of existence, the Envoy had to burn through his own eth in order to create a cone of protection around both him and Samuel. He did this all the time for himself, since his function was reconnaissance, but not rescue. However, there is a first time for everything, so he had to spend extra eth carrying Samuel to the safety of Central Existence. It took all the energy he had just to get them on their way between the planes. The gates will have to do. It'll cause some chaos having a deeply wounded celestial laying at the entrance to the gates of Heaven, but it's all he had in him.

He always thought the phrase 'gates of Heaven' was ironic. There are nine gates, three in each realm. Most people think of the gates of heaven as the last gate, the ones that stand as the last vanguard, surrounding Central Existence. The chthonics constructed their own version of this irony with their own nine gates. It was easy enough for him to skip most of them, but the gates that separated the realms were guarded by Powers, the celestial choir tasked with guarding each plane of existence. Demons had to be kept in hell, celestials come and go from heaven, and mortal souls are those guided through all the planes. Instead of going through each checkpoint and having to explain what has happened to Samuel to each of the Powers, he had to bend the fibers of existence itself, effectively dissolving out of the etheric plane and hop scotching through the nine realms of heaven taking the long way home.

He knew he was breaking twenty different rules, but it was better than automatically sparking an all-out war between heaven and hell the moment a celestial lays eyes on Samuel. He knew that was coming. It was a certainty, but he was going to make sure Creation had the advantage.

The Envoy had always trod a dangerous line from the day that he arrived. It was all laid out for him from the moment he left Earth.

He was tired, but the last gate was coming up. His muscles burned. He was so exhausted he was on automatic. In order to get through the last few moments to the gates of Creation, he remembered back to when he first arrived in heaven. It was just as controversial as then as it what was about to happen.

Enoch stood before a lake that was surrounded by manicured gardens and temples. He stood at the far end of the lake from Central Existence. To him, it was the best view, and what was better was rarely did anyone bother to make the trek all the way over. The building towered over the lake far into the sky. At the top he could see all the Celestials coming and going from the tall central spire like bees coming and going from a hive. The new arrivals played down at the lake beneath the great window of the building.

There were too many celestials in the building for him right now. He wanted to meet the mortals, just to remember what it was like to be one, but he wasn't allowed to mix with them, or at least he knew it wasn't a good idea. At least not yet.

What he couldn't reconcile is that angels and demons are like people, but without the subtlety of emotions. They focused on missions, so it was very difficult to relate to them. Being taken to heaven from the mortal realm was a privilege for the Envoy, but it came with a lot of rules. Right now, he was dealing with the nostalgia for the mortal realm, an emotion he battled with from time to time. Despite having eternal powers at his fingertips, he knew he would most likely be forever separated from humanity. Time has advantages that eternity can't provide.

Out from behind some wisteria hanging nearby, the Archangel Haniel appeared. "I figured I'd find you here," Haniel said, walking up to him.

Enoch knew the situation had to be important. They always sent Haniel to talk to him when it's important. Haniel was one of the first Celestials he met when he was told he could stay forever. The chance to stay in heaven without enduring the pain of death was very inviting. However, he did not know he would be put in a role at the top of the hierarchy of angels. It created a lot of questions, and some division within the ranks.

"I'm not accepted here," Enoch said. There was no point in trying to hide his feelings from Haniel. Celestials could still read everything he was thinking and feeling, as if he had never left earth.

"What are you talking about? Everyone is welcome here," she reassured.

"Nice try, I said accepted–there is a difference." Enoch walked away toward the nearest lookout spot. A pergola was ahead of him, adorned with abundant honeysuckle.

Haniel re-appeared before him, smelling the abundant honeysuckle hanging from the pergola Enoch was walking toward. "I don't know why you continue to walk when you have other abilities," she said as she admired a group of the flowers.

"It's about being present in a moment. Even though we are in the everlasting, I still prefer to enjoy everything it offers." He was still learning that celestials had their own ways of living. "Thank you for welcoming me." It was at that moment Enoch realize celestials can't understand what it's like to be human any more than humans can understand what it's like to be Celestial. It was his theory that this was why the Creator asked him to reign over Celestials and Humans alike.

"They don't know what to think of you. You don't act like us."

"Do I need to? They call me 'Na'ar' to distinguish me from the rest of the hierarchy, I know it is not meant to flatter. Besides, I'm not one of you. I'm still human. The only living human in all of eternity." Enoch stared at Haniel. Enoch couldn't read him because he was still human.

"Don't be dramatic, you know that's not true. You are the second," Haniel said admiring the lake.

Enoch dropped his head. He knew he was being a bit dramatic. He felt cut off from who he used to be, despite the lovely surroundings and celestials he was meeting. "I have yet to meet Sandalphon," he muttered.

"Are there any abilities I do have access to?" Enoch sat down on the bench in the pergola that looked out over the lake.

"Aside from complete manifestation?" Haniel looked at him, smiling. "I don't think you realize this bench didn't exist a few moments ago." Haniel sat down beside him. She was much larger than the bench, almost like a cartoon character, as she sat there overlooking the lake with Enoch. "Well, you have what humans would call time travel, also co-location, and, of course, imbuing. That's my favorite. You know, just because he's omnipotent doesn't mean God doesn't make mistakes. The beauty of it all is he can see almost immediately when something will not work to plan."

"What's co-location?"

"That's what I like about you. You go straight for the good stuff. Co-location is a good one. It's being in several places at one time."

"Oh yes, it's what humans call multi-tasking, although for them it's a delusion."

Haniel smiled. She agreed and enjoyed the humour, but would not actively disparage the mortals by saying anything. "Think of co-location as aspects of your personality. Michael does it all the time. He's a chief, a High Priest, and a general–sometimes all at once. It's a full-time gig running all of Existence, so we get extra perks."

"The problem is, most of the actual work gets talked about once I leave the room. So I don't get to know what's going on."

"Yes, sadly, only the Most High is allowed omnipotence. However you are in the lofty position of knowing pretty much everything immediately after him. We thought for a time that maybe such a luxury would be granted to us, but then he wouldn't be the Most High, would he? It is why some in the hierarchy don't warm as much to you. "

Enoch nodded his head.

"If there was a problem," Haniel raises her hands to the sky as if to calm someone down "and I'm not saying there is, okay," she said announcing to the sky. She turns back toward Enoch and crouches down near the water's edge. Enoch walks to the water's edge and crouches down beside her. "If there were a problem," she whispered, "it's that sometimes the Most High can do things a bit too big. It's usually a big booming voice from the sky, or an entire flood, or a new species, or a bloody universe in just a few days. It can be a lot for any entity or celestial to take in."

Enoch nodded again. Of all the Celestials, Haniel had a way of explaining things to just about anybody, in a way that they could understand.

"We are all aspects of the Almighty in our own right, unless you choose to reject his eminence. As children of the Most High, our aspect is given to us. Unfortunately, mortals are not told what their aspect is. It is up to you to discover that through your own will. Yet here you are, unlike every other mortal, caught between two worlds. That is a conundrum that only God could understand. You and Sandalphon are unique, my friend."

"I wasn't prepared to tread in both worlds."

"How's this for an idea... create an aspect of yourself that nobody knows? Because everyone knows you, but you are supposed to be managing all sides to ensure everything remains on track. I'll be honest though, I'm just guessing. I actually I don't know your full remit."

"Yeah, you're not supposed to."

"That's ok, I'm used to the siloed information. Some Celestials have a problem that one day, they, too, will be judged by the very mortals we serve. I just keep doing what I'm doing." She pointed her hand out in a straight line, accidentally parting the waters of the lake.

"That's a cool trick."

"Thanks, I'm practicing."

"How do I create a new aspect of myself?"

"An aspect is an entirely different being, though it's still you. It is the dressing-up box for us Celestials. Create a new name for your aspect, and it is only meant to accomplish a specific set of tasks you need it to."

"Makes sense."

"We do it all the time. That's why we have so many titles and names. It really causes confusion among the mortals, but it's not really any of their business. Although, when doing this, it's important to never forget who you are. On the mortal plane you are Enoch, to the Almighty, and the Celestials you reign over, you have come to be known as Metatron, and then whomever deals with this next aspect is, will know you as a different name. Treat each like a different hat to wear and I think you are going to have a much better experience," she said, placing a hand on his shoulder.

She began squeezing his shoulder too tightly.

"The Envoy, I've seen you around the choirs," said Zariel, one of the Powers at the gates of heaven. He held the Envoys shoulder, preventing him from going any further. The Envoy couldn't remember how he got the rest of the way to the gates. Powers weren't really to be trusted.

The Power held out his hand and began slowly transferring some of his own Eth to Samuel. "I can't allow you to go any further until we understand what happened to this Celestial.

The Envoy intentionally shifted shape into a creature many times larger than the largest of Celestials. "I will need your assistance. Could you please accompany me while we bring our brother back to good health?"

"Metatron, if I had known–"

"It's okay, you weren't supposed to know. I did not have the power to communicate earlier than this."

They disappeared into a stream of light, past all the arrivals at the great city, and appeared moments later in the lobby of the celestial clinic.

CHAPTER NINETEE

The meeting had gone on for hours at this point. Everyone was exhausted. They had managed to stave the chthonics off from the mortal realm for now, but they knew a much greater fight was to come. Sebastian had been leading the strategy meeting thus far, as Michael had been otherwise engaged with a different debriefing elsewhere. As michael entered the room every celestial stood up out of a sign of reverence.

Michael doesn't lose a step and starts right in. "Let me get this straight," he says placing a presentation folder down on the table. "We leave the etheric realm to stop the greatest influx of chthonics since the dark ages, only to have one of our own kidnapped so that they can most likely do it all over again. Not to mention the destruction of a treaty so sacred it only ensures the balance of. Wait. What's that word..."

"Existence," Sebastian said, chiming in.

"Yeah, that," Michael says pointing to Sebastian. He doesn't break his stare toward the Envoy. "We based all of this off of your intel."

The Envoy looks to the floor, ashamed that the mission failed.

"This feels a lot like a...," Michael often became lost for words when he was angry at his own team. "It feels like one of those over-bloated..."

"Government operations," Sebastian finishes for him again.

"Yes, if this isn't a bureaucratic operation, I don't know what is."

Another envoy walks in carrying a piece of paper and handed it to Michael without a word. He looks at it and sighs, handing the paper to Sebastian. "Looks like they are at it again."

Sebastian reads the paper out loud. "Multiple sightings of chthonic entities across the mortal plane."

"We had a heck of a time with Legal getting them to approve the use of reversing the last few days. They don't like us reversing time on the mortal plane just to fix our own cockups, but we left them no choice. I doubt they are going to let us do it again."

"How did they get there so quickly this time? They don't have control of the etheric plane any longer," one of the celestials asked.

"They have Percival," Sebastian says, looking at the note. "The only way to reach the mortal plane this fast is to be in control of a celestial. The only way to stop it is to physically find him."

"Across the entire etheric plane and lets not forget..."

"All of hell," The Envoy interjects.

"Now you're catching on," Michael said glaring at the Envoy. "Quite the pickle, isn't it?" He glares at everyone.

Mehiel smirks in the background behind Michael. "Mehiel, you are the expert when it comes to the protections against chthonic entities. What happens if we can't find him." Michael leans on the table in front of him. His arm muscles bulge in frustration, and he can't decide whether he wants to break something or go for a walk.

Mehiel steps forward. "If we can't find him, that means they have a permanent line to the mortal plane, and can subvert us at every turn."

"This was probably their strategy all along," Michael said as he sat down in a nearby chair.

His unit had never seen him pause in reflection before.

"We're going to need a mira-"

Samuel burst through the door of the meeting room. "I got him! I know where he is," Samuel announced with glee. He is still in the skin that sickbay shrouded him in and he drags behind him a trail of IV cables used to pump him full of Eth again.

"Who?" Michael and the Envoy said in unison as they looked up at him.

"Percival. He's in Pandemonia, in the council building."

Michael stood up. "Are you sure?"

"Whoa... how do we know this isn't another trap," the Sebastian said stepping forward.

"We don't," Michael and the Envoy said again in unison. Michael looked at the Envoy, irritated.

"We can't just go barging in there with the army of God. It would be a slaughter both ways, and we would be unlikely to get to him before they dis-incorporate him." Sebastian continues.

"I see your point, but I've never known you to be the doubting Thomas," Michael said, turning to Sebastian.

"It's not that I'm doubting our ability. They are dictating the cadence of all of this, and I don't like it. They have had a lot more time to strategize and think of contingencies, and they keep baiting us into a campaign of their choosing. It's obvious our intel is currently lacking. They have us on the back foot," Sebastian impressed.

"So we don't storm in. We take a small unit, and we walk in," Samuel said in his excitement.

"Impossible," Michael boomed. "Only a mortal may open the adamantine gates, which nobody would choose to intentionally go there, or a demon to guide us in. It's never going to happen."

"A demon to guide us in..." the Envoy said, taking a step away from the crowd with a vacant look. "There is always a way. We've done it before."

"When?" Michael said in a tone of disbelief.

"Moloch didn't get to the throne by chance. He had a lot of help, particularly from us."

"C'mon, you have been spending too much time away from Central Existence. False witness is a sin, remember?"

"The last millennia has been very quiet for us, and that's not a mistake. The underworld is a necessity of our making. However, if you don't want them too powerful, the best thing to do is to make sure it has an ineffectual leader. The danger was always that it would get Belial closer to the throne of Hell, and it seems that he is now making his move. We can do this, but it will cost us. If we don't, it will cost us everything."

"What are you talking about?"

"Ganislay. I know where he is imprisoned. He will lead us in."

"And why would he do that?"

"Because we can offer him the one thing that nobody else can."

Michael leaned on the table and stared the Envoy down. "Oh yeah, and what's that?"

"Redemption."

"Well... that's far above the paygrade of anybody in this room," Michael said standing up straight. The room fell silent from then tension. Michael turned around and looked at Sebastian, "this is insane," he said, whispering.

Samuel looked at the two of them, not knowing how to respond. His credibility was shot amongst the choir. The only reason they allowed him into the room right now was that he was one of the few witnesses to the entire timeline of events. Suddenly, all three of them felt like something different was in the room. There was a change in the Eth.

An immensely powerful and encompassing peace overcame all the celestials in the room. Michael knew what had happened before he even turned around. He looked back at the Envoy and his eyes landed on Metatron. His aura, which was both comforting and awe-inspiring, impressed every celestial. He did not come adorned in his scribing robes, but instead was accompanied by robes of gold and a small crown atop of his head.

"This is a plan that will work. If the chthonic shows contrition, if it is willing to operate of its own free will and accord, then he shall be redeemed. It is an accord that is acceptable to the Most High."

Michael and the other celestials stood there dumbfounded. It was one thing to redeem a mortal, or to slay legions of demons, but to redeem a demon is unheard of.

In the blink of an eye, the Envoy reappeared in Metatron's place. "Well, I guess that settles it then."

All the celestials vacantly nod at the Envoy.

"Need I remind you that what happens in this room stays in this room? I'm going to take this celestial," he said, pointing to Samuel, "and I think it's best if you two mop up the mortal realm... again."

The envoy grabbed Samuel by the arm as they walked toward the door. "I think maybe we get you into some better clothes first, and I'm going to need some advice anyway."

***

The envoy appears in the entry to the Great Library. It was dimly lit in a golden hue with the roof letting in the soft glow of the surrounding cosmos leaving the tile floor to perfectly reflect the constellations from above. The Envoy felt like he was walking across space as he walked in to get the advice he needed. "Hello," he asked out loud. He wasn't sure how this would go.

"Yes, how can I help you," the Librarian responded from behind the resource desk. As always, she was working on translating one of the ancient works for the benefit of those in the modern age.

"I need your advice, and I hear that you are the person to come to."

"You cooked up a scheme, cost us greatly on the field of battle, not to mention losing one of my greatest apprentices – and you want me to bail you out. I've never known you to fail like this Metatron."

The Envoy looked at her wide-eyed in disbelief. "Yes... something like that." He wondered if he was speaking to one of the Almighty's aspects. "Since you know so much, at least it will save me time in explaining it all."

"Percival has kept me in the loop all the way. He's provides better insight than anyone in the choirs."

The Envoy nodded. "Right. We have the chance to rescue him. The chthonics are keeping him in the walls of Pandemonium at the Council of the Fallen."

"Of course, he would be a precious commodity for them," she said with quiet anger.

"Yes, ma'am. The only way in is with the help of a chthonic."

"Uh-huh. Tell me something I don't know," she said losing interest and going back to book. She had already calculated the possibilities of getting her favourite student back and knew they were slim. She didn't want to think about it.

"There is a Chthonic who may very well help. But he is being held at the Council of Elders."

She chuckled. "They dislike you more than the choirs right now."

"I have some history with Alvnod. I was wondering if you could help me with some guidance of how to appeal to him."

She stares him down. "Possibly." She reaches down to one of the drawers beside her and pulls out a note pad. She scribbles two short words, folds the paper in half, holds some sealing wax over a candle and stamps it closed. "If anyone other than Alvnod breaks this seal, the letter incinerates. Go to his post, ask for dispensation and give him this." She slid the folded note across her desk toward the Envoy and went back to her work. Purposely not looking up again.

The envoy looked at her for a moment, hoping to ask another question, but knew he wouldn't get an answer. He gently picked up the note and slid it into his inside breast pocket, and looked at her again with remorse. For the first time he realized how much he had messed this up. He turned and left without a word, for anything other than returning Percival to Central Existence was pointless conjecture.

Chapter Twenty

The Envoy stood outside the bookstore on Cecil Court in London. He needed passage to the Duke of the Council of Elders, he knew the price was going to be high. Alvanod was the most venerable among the Elders, which is why everyone sought passage from him. He looked at the front door with trepidation and let out a huge sigh and walked up the steps.

As he walked in, two chthonics appear before him to stop him. They don't say a word and instead make sure he can't move forward, or even leave.

The Elders assistant appeared from the stacks. "And I thought chthonics were thick as two planks. What in the name of all creation caused you to come here?"

"I need passage," the Envoy said politely.

"Doesn't everybody," the Elders assistant said looking at him with disgust. He nodded and the two chthonics throw the Envoy to the floor. They pin him to the floor so hard he thought they were going to split him open.

Instead they put a binding spell on him, preventing him from moving. Then they grab him by his feet and begin dragging the Envoy as they follow the Elders Assistant down the stairs, making sure his head bumps on each step as they descend.

"Someone here to see you sir," the assistant said gently. Alndvod was as always working on the accounts of the Eth flows between the realms. It was a never ending duty, but after the recent battle between the celestials and the chthonics that ripped the realm apart, he was trying to figure out how many cycles it would take to piece everything back together again. "Very well," he said without breaking his concentration from his accounts.

The assistant nodded and the chthonics picked the Envoy up and slammed him down on the floor directly at Alndvod's feet like a piece of deli meat on a counter top.

"Geez-zus,"

Alndvod let a quick chuckle go. "It would probably been better if you sent him at this point. This realm is in tatters now thanks to the celestials. The sole purpose of every entity in this realm is to serve and that's all they ever do. Yet every so often the chthonics and the celestials get in the way and decide to tear it apart."

The envoy loved how Alndvod was playing victim. Yes, his realm was in tatters, but he conveniently left out the part where the etherics had figured out how to generate eth in order to change the flow of all of existence. "I need your help, entry under special dispensation only to retrieve an entity in order to fix all this."

"Everyone wants entry at this point. You are the fourth person in the last day who's asked for entry only to magically fix everything for all of us." Alndvod turns his gaze away in dismissal.

The chthonics pick the Envoy back up and begin taking him away.

"The librarian sent a message for you," the Envoy blurted out in desperation.

Alndvod turned his gaze back and let out a sigh. "What did she say?" "I don't know, she told me to give you a note. I'm not read it. allowed to

Alndvod glared at him and shrugged his shoulders in disgust. He'd heard enough from just about everybody, but a message from the librarian was long overdue. Besides he had long thought about her. "Hand it over." Alndvod glanced at the chthonics and they obliged by dropping him, letting his dead weight hit the floor with a thud.

The envoy picks himself up and dusts his suit off. "Thanks folks, always a pleasure seeing you," he said waiving at the chthonics. He dug in his breast pocket to fish out the letter, leaning in to hand it to Alndvod. He was afraid to take a step, still not sure if they would disincorporate him at any given moment.

Alndvod breaks the seal and reads the short note. He smiles to him-self and then bows his head in defeat. He stares at his desk for a few moments, leaving the Envoy hanging in wonder. "How is she."

The Envoy furled is brow, this was not the response he was expect-ing. "Uh... she's good." He glanced over at the Elders assistant who was equally confused and just shrugged back in response.

Alndvod placed the note on his desk, "She has a fine spirit and I owe her much." He turns in his chair to look at the Envoy. I will give you dispensation for direct entry. You will only have a few minutes to meet the prisoner. No second chances. They will accompany you – "

"But I need – "

"This isn't a negotiation. You owe us much and it is going to cost you the heavens to repair our realm. Take it or leave it."

The Envoy looked at Alndvod and then back at the Chthonics flank-ing him. "It'll have to do. I'll take it."

The moment the words left the Envoys lips he and the two Chthonics disappeared from Alndvods sight. A few books tumbled from the surrounding shelves due to the disturbance of eth. Alndvod looked at his assistant, "I need a holiday."

The envoy appeared with the chthonics in a dark, gloomy hallway that led into a small block of cells. He looked at the chthonics, confused as to where he was to go. Disgusted they led the way down the hallway to the last cell on the left.

From inside his cell, Ganislay could hear footsteps coming toward him. They were not loud, which made him think that someone was trying to catch him by surprise. He got up from the front corner and quietly went to the back of his cell, giving himself enough distance and time to react. Two chthonics appeared before his cell door, just staring at him. They were not who he expected, but what better way to go out than have his own kind disincorporate him.

"Step aside," the Envoy said muscling himself in between the two chthonics. "We need to talk," he said staring at Ganislay.

"How are you here? They've banned us all," Ganislay said in disbelief.

"I have limited permission, I don't have time to explain. You are Ganislay, spawn of the damned, rather than fallen."

Ganislay looked at him from the shadows of his cell. His yellow eyes pierced the darkness. They were the only thing the Envoy could see of him. He didn't respond. He knew this moment was likely his last. How could this entity get past all the guards, simply enter the plane and walk through Etheria without being noticed? It was obviously a trick.

The Envoy knew Ganislay would not respond to just anything. "You've done something that nobody else has done." He walked in through the energy field that was keeping Ganislay in his cell.

Ganislay shifted his weight and curled up, sitting on his haunches, waiting to spring at his assailant. The only entity that could have travelled through that energy field is an etheric.

The Envoy still couldn't see him, but it mattered little to him. He knew Ganislay would be frightened enough. "Being spawn directly from dark Eth as you are, it must have been shocking to get even a sliver of free will. To feel the passage of time. To feel at all. Must have been mind-blowing."

Ganislay looked away. This was worse. This must be the Morning Star himself. He thought back to the moment on the cliff top where he realized he was finally free. He thought he would stay there for eternity if he could. Since then, he was certain to put the memory out of his mind. It was a cosmic tease. Something he could never have. "How did you know?"

The Envoy smirked. He knew he had gotten through to him. It's what every entity in the universe wants, insight into themselves. To better understand the reflection and fate that we inhabit. Even the toughest cases want the answer to that question. He crouched down to the floor, leaning his back against the wall of the cell. "One of my own figured it out. You were sent to Dudael, when you were no longer needed. Thrown away like yesterday's fish wrap."

Ganislay stared back at him. A heart to heart was of no interest to him. Being over familiar was one of the cheapest tactics a tormentor could use. His face gave no more emotion away as the Envoy kept talking.

"The colleague who figured it all out is why I'm here. I'm prepared to pay a hefty price to see that happen." The Envoy purposely let that hang in the air. He was not going to continue to use the same tactics to get Ganislay to cooperate. He knew, for this to work, he had to get Ganislay off balance and into territory that made him uncomfortable. That territory was honesty. "It's a bit unfair that we treat the spawn of the damned the same as we do the Fallen. You were created, much like everyone in our choirs."

Ganislay immediately lept toward the envoy. The Envoy did not move, but Ganislay was repelled backward by a large field of Eth.

"It's not going to be that easy," the Envoy said as he stood up.

Ganislay cowered in the corner. He hadn't been helpless since his earliest days in hell, and swore to himself he would never return to such a status. It was impossible. Ganislay would have to rise up against the highest of demons. He began silently crying, unable to understand how such a circumstance could happen.

"What if I told you I could give all those moments back to you, and more?"

Ganislay lept toward the Envoy again, flailing and falling backwards. He thrashed, kicked, and spat like a bobcat. It didn't matter that he couldn't actually get to the Envoy; he would not give up.

The Envoy reached out his hand and allowed Ganislay's tail to wrap around it like a whip. As it did, the Envoy allowed a flow of Eth, more powerful than Ganislay had ever encountered, to inject itself through his body.

Ganislay could feel himself suddenly change. His body was no longer present in the form that he was accustomed to.

"I can give you redemption from your lowly fate in a way that no one else can."

Ganislay looked at where his tail had been, and instead he was gripping the Envoy with his own hand, like that of a mortal or an angel of the lower choirs.

"I can give you life."

Ganislay continued to look at his hand. "A heavy prize comes with a heavy cost. Even celestials are not so generous."

"I need you to lead us into hell."

Ganislay let go of the Envoy and retreated to the back corner of his cell. "I will never go back there!"

"I know. You were used. But you got out, and I can't blame you for not wanting to go back."

"You have the ability to leave whenever you want, as does any mortal if they can accept their deeds. My kind, the spawn of the fallen cannot. The only solace I've ever found was in my time with the Lost Order"

The words fell awkwardly with the Envoy. If that was the deal, then that's fine. It wouldn't cost him the moon afterall. He didn't want to fully redeem any demon unless he had to. "And if that's what you want, then you will have it. I have the authority directly from the throne of Heaven."

Ganislay snorted. Never had such words been directed to any hell-fire demon he had known.

"Ganislay, I cannot lie, and you hold all the cards in this."

Ganislay stood back up and walked across his cell. I cannot take you into Hell without a soul, and that will land us at the cages, so we will have to do this may way. We will need to enter through one of our own portals that intersects the mortal plane in order to stay out of sight.

The cell door opens of it's own accord.

"It seems that we have a deal," the Envoy says with encouragement.

Ganislay stares back at him, "it seems that we do."

"And now, if you would avail us of the finer points of Hell, I would be greatly appreciated." The Envoy wasn't sure if he was ready fro this. In order to follow Ganislay into Hell, he had to surrender his own eth to follow Ganislay. In a sense he was at the mercy of a chthonic. He supposed it was part of his penance.

"As you wish." As Ganislay walks through the threshold of his cell door they reappear at night on a road in the mortal plane. Surrounded by a forest and small brush, Ganislay, the envoy and Samuel stand looking at a a sign that says Pluckley Village. "You didn't tell me we would have company," Ganislay said angrily staring down Samuel.

He noticed for the first time in his existence he wasn't filled with the enraged compulsion to immediately attack Samuel. The Envoy must have already begun to fulfill his end of the deal.

"Yes, well, apologies for that, I will need some reinforcement."

There was a rustle in the bushes and Samuel could feel a draw of eth being pulled from him. "Something is coming this way."

"Yes, I brought my own reinforcements."

From the bushes of the forest comes a spectral figure of a highway man, draped in a long, tattered cloak that whispers in the wind. Dawned in a tricorn hat sat askew atop his translucent head, it hides dark, hollow eyes that flicker with glints of light that it can pick up from the surrounding area. His face is gaunt, with a pale, ghostly pallor, and a thin, crooked smile, hoping to collect whatever it can from the two celestials it is approaching. A leather bandolier slashes across his chest that held a shadowy pouch. His boots make no sound as he stepped onto the road. It looks at Ganislay and stops, bowing its head in reverence.

"We need passage," Ganislay relays in perfect Harrow.

The highway man raised its head and looked at Ganislay again, giving him a quick nod.

As the specter of the highway man led them down the moonlit street, every poltergeist, ghost and negative energy in the village appeared through the walls of the buildings throughout the village and joined them in their march. Each exuded their mournful eth which the Envoy and Samuel could feel. Souls not wretched enough to be cast into the pits of hell, but forgotten, waiting for the day of their judgement, each bound to the moment and place of their own death, doomed to repeat them until they are finally called upon.

As the parade of ghosts follow Ganislay and the celestials through the village they finally come upon a church ruin. The ghosts all simultaneously turn their gaze to the ruined archway, staring in haunting reverence. The church ruin stood solitary in a field, shrouded by a light fog. The remnants of a stone tower rise against the midnight sky, weathered but proud, with ivy and vines clinging tightly to its rough surface. The arched entrance at the bottom of the tower, showed only timeless abandonment to the mortals – but as the parade of the dead gathered in reverence before the archway, the mists and fog of the night moved and gathered in the archway, turning the threshold into an opaque mist. Almost as soon as it gathered, the mist and fog began to swirl within the archway, faster and faster until a portal opened, through which Ganislay and the celestials could see an entrance to Hell.

Ganislay could tell that the parade of the dead longed to come with him. "Not yet my friends, but your time will come. Your service will not be forgotten."

The parade gathered in front of the Envoy, Samuel and Ganislay, forming a line on either side of the path into the portal so as to ensure that the eth of the portal did not dissipate before the three travellers could be on their way.

"We must hurry," Ganislay said. He led them through the portal, and as they disappear into the entrance of Hell, the mist and fog simply disappear along with the parade of the dead.

The Envoy glanced to his right and left, and realized the three of them were in a small alcove the overlooked the council chambers within Pandemonia. Out of instinct he pushed Samuel against the wall to make sure they were safe and not seen. He immediately felt like this was a trap.

"What are you afraid of," Ganislay said gleaming at them with a smile.

The envoy was surprised, he didn't think demons could smile. This worried him even more.

"This way." Ganislay led them out of the alcove and to a side stairwell that led down. "They would have taken him to the well of souls."

"Does this jive with you Samuel," the Envoy asked to ensure this was correct.

"I don't know about the room, but I sense Percival's presence is getting stronger."

"Good enough for me," the Envoy said going down the stairs, trying to keep up with Ganislay's rate of decent.

As they came to the bottom of the stairs, the Envoy and Samuel suddenly felt an immense peace overcome them, like a cloud.

"Wait wait." Samuel said pushing the Envoy back against the stone wall.

"What's going on," Ganislay asked.

Samuel sensed Belial around the corner in the grotto. He peaked around the corner and watched as a hellfire demon reached into the well of souls, pulling out the spirit of the morning star. It floats through the air swirling in a cloud. "As agreed," he says. "The spirit of the morning star. Our king has returned"

Samuel saw Percival laying motionless at hellfire demon's feet. He felt fear for the first time in his existence.

Ganislay punched Samuel in the shoulder, shocking him away from the emotion. "Do not let the depths of Hell have their way with you. I saw your eth change. Do not fear, even if the situation causes it. It's how we get you."

The grotto began alternating different colors "It is not as agreed," the voice of the well announces. "Eth must take physical form to resurrect."

The hellfire demon looked down at Percival's body on the floor before him. He leans down to pick him up and throw him into the well of souls.

"No," Samuel screamed. A streak of light beams straight for the hellfire demon. Just as it is about to hit the demon, time freezes.

Frozen in the air, Samuel has his feet on the demon's shoulder while the Demon has a sword drawn that is about to be plunged into Samuels neck.

The Envoy walks into the grotto as fast as he can to retrieve Percival. He peers at the plasma surface of the well of souls. It is a beautiful teal color, almost entrancing him.

"What, do you think you can stop this," a voice says breaking the silence.

"Fuck," the Envoy says as he glances up to see Belial walking into the grotto.

Belial places his hand on Ganislay's body, frozen in time. "What really going to bake your noodle is whether the the Most High designed this whole thing in order to start another war and clean house. Are we here right now just acting out his bidding?"

"I don't give a shit," the Envoy said as he snapped his fingers, restarting time.

Samuel and the demon exchange blows in an almighty clash, both falling to the ground.

CHAPTER TWENTY-ONE

Samuel's laughs for a quick second, then his laughs turn into gasps and sputters of pain. A long thin stalagmite quickly rises up out of the ground impaling the center of his body.

"Well... as they say. If you want to get something done," Belial says materializing in the center of the chamber. He raises a hand and the dead demon's body rises up and flings itself into the well of souls.

Samuel begins convulsing as the entire powers of hell flow into him and attempt to drain him of any remaining Eth. Within seconds he turns to black glassy obsidian that begins to crack and expose the rivers of Hell now flowing through his veins. It's so fast, its almost as if he was never anything but the grotesque object he now is. His long hair turns to thick, thorny strands of briar that begin to lash out at the Envoy as if they have a life of their own. Samuels face turns to long strands of black fibre like hundreds of centipede legs, nattering together.

"Meet my newest pet, he will become my prize hound. I shall call him, the Sentinel."

The Envoy stood frozen in fear. He wasn't sure his the Eth within him could not match the power of a Prince of Hell.

"Where is my old friend," Belial asked as he raised a hand.

Ganislay appears out of the walls and tackles the Envoy, gripping him with his claws, and ripping into his shoulder.

"We had a deal," the Envoy said through his screams.

"The deal was passage into hell for my redemption. There were no terms on your safe return." Ganislay wanted the envoy's Eth, but he want to choose who he took it from. Percival was easy, but not a worthy target at this point.

Percival could hear what was going on around him in the grotto, but he didn't have energy to move. He gathered his thoughts as best he could, he would need help. He began to mutter, finding the words to call upon the choirs. Finally his mutters found the correct sequence. "I call upon thee from the four corners," Percival whispered. Each word grew louder and bounced off the walls of the chamber. It pierced into Belial and Ganislays mind, confusing the both of them. "at any time and place, to help with goodly deeds, in this world or the next". As he finished a beam of light appeared between Ganislay and Percival, exploding like a grenade and the Envoy tumbled away to safety.

Percival looks across the stone floor to Samuels corpse, noticing a pool of Eth bubbling just beneath the thin layer of the skin. Percival knew it was the last remnants of Samuel, trying to get out. The stalagmite cracks and several arms appear out of it, holding Samuel's new hellish body to the ground. Another crack appears beneath him, and the ground falls away to a large cavern of hellish lava, with creatures gnashing and tearing at the obsidian body, trying to get to the last bit of Eth.

The Envoy leaps to hold Ganislay down as best he can . They tumble and tussle, trading blows and pins as one tries to destroy the other.

"No," Percival yells as he reaches out in vain to try and save what is left of Samuel's Eth. If he can salvage it, he can return it to the waters of Heaven. He raises a hand and the Eth is instantly attracted to Percival. It quickly pools in the palm of his hand and it enters into him.

Renewed, Percival leaps to the ground and rushes Ganislay by turning into a beam of lightning, knocking him out cold. The Envoy streaks toward Belial, attempting to hit him with his own beam of light, but it lands with a dud. Belial is too powerful and instead the Envoy gets him into a choke hold, and tries to direct Belial's body toward the well of souls.

Percival gathers himself and leaps through the air to deliver the final blow, however Belial shakes loose of the Envoy's grip, and throws the Envoy to the ground. A thunderous roar of lava pours from his palms toward the Envoy, who shields himself with a phalanx of light. As Percival flies through the air, Belial leaps up, grabbing Percival by the leg and pulls with all his weight, flinging Percival into the Well of Souls. Rid of Percival, Belial turns just in time and pushes Samuel's smoldering obsidian body through the cracks in the floor and into the depths of Hell. Samuels voice is replaced with the sounds of screeching as the Sentinal's body begins to gain a life of it own as it falls into the smoldering pits.

With the Celestials gone, the balance of Eth changes, reinvigorating Ganislay. He stands up, swelling all his muscles to the point that his body fills most of the grotto. Ganislay grabs the Envoy like a rag doll, picking him up to bite him. His jaws snap shut across what would have been the Envoy's head, the but Envoy simply dissolves away and reappears a few feet in front of them. "I'm getting sick of this shit."

"Funny, so am I!" Ganislay whips the Envoy with his long tail. The blow is so hard it knocks the envoy through the stone walls and out into the main chamber of the council room. "Pussy!" Ganislay gallops out of the chamber and into the council room. As he scampers in, he sees the Envoy picking himself up from the floor, surrounded by a hoard of demons who have come to assist.

The Envoy dusts his suit off and coughs a few times. "Well that's a bitch." He pays no mind to the surrounding hoard until he is ready to address them. He always knew, the trick to any demon is simply not paying it any attention. He spied Ganislay far behind the crowd of demons, "I'll be with you in a minute."

The crowd responded with a few sporadic chuckles as they looked forward to ripping into the Envoy's eth.

The Envoy smacked his lips, "This place always makes me hungry. I can't decide what to have when I get back." The Envoy's body stretches out into a white light and turns into a streak of piercing light, blasting through the rock of the council chambers, disappearing out of Hell.

Ganislay rushes back o the Chamber of Souls. It was done, but Ganislay was sure Belial didn't know about the colossal mistake he had just created. They had the key, they had one celestial, but Percival was about to cause them a problem. Ganislay stumbles and scampers back into the grotto to confront Belial.

"I guess there is no doubt who that was," Belial said congratulating Ganislay. "Did you just bitch slap the left hand of God," he said proudly.

Ganislay squares up to Belial, staring him straight in the eyes. "Yes, and I'm about to bitch slap you too," he tersely motions toward the Well.

"Since when do you have a problem killing celestials," Belial said returning the aggression.

"I don't have a problem killing anything, but you threw a pure celestial into the Well of Souls." Ganislay steeled himself even more, gritting his teeth while he waited for the words to land in Belial's mind.

"Surely he's not..."

"As the drivin' fuckin' snow... dumbass."

Belial shifted his weight, trying to deflate the tension. He knew he was a hair's breath away from taking the throne of Hell. He wanted Ganislay on his side if he could swing it. "He will have to make it out of Hell first, which he doesn't have the metal in him to do."

Ganislay's tail silently slithers behind Belial "Be careful what you say brother. Torturing a clean immortal is not in our mission. It could be the undoing of the realm."

"Don't be sentimental, the mission is whatever we say it is."

The end of Ganislay's tail quickly wraps around Belial's neck and immediately begins draining him of Eth. "Sometimes Hell needs protection from its own. We own the damned, the broken and the heinous. We do not stain or steal Eth from the pure."

Belial was surprised, he didn't think a demon like Ganislay would make a move for the throne. He would have to get rid of him now. Belial ignores the pain, ignores the dread he feels of the impending disincorporation and uses all the lifeforce he has within himself to instantly transport both of them to Dudael.

In a split second, a portal opens up beneath them and they all onto the hard dusty crust of Dudael. The shock of the instantaneous change makes Ganislay lose his grip on Belial and they tumble apart from one another. The presence of an Eth heavy demon such as Belial tears at the fabric of the dimension separating Dudael from the other three. The balance in the air of Dudael changes and the wind kicks up, forming an enormous supercell in the sky over the valley. It immediately begins to rain, something which has never happened in all of Dudael's existence, causing the enormous battle between Celestial and Chthonic to stop in its tracks. Instinctually, every immortal knew something had changed, and they spied the giant tear in the sky causing the storm.

Belial leaped up toward the portal they just fell through. As he ascends, Ganislay is able to knock the key loose from Belial. Both the key and the portal of judgement fall from Belials holdings and straight into Ganislay's hands.

Belial looks back. He would have to close them all in Dudael. At least he knew where they were.

Ganislay grips the key and the talisman of judgment in his hands just as Belial closes off the two worlds. Ganislay puts the talisman around his neck and raises the key to the sky. As he does, a trumpet sounds from all around causing an earthquake. Ganislay remains standing as every entity is shaken to the ground.

When the earthquake stops, every celestial and chthonic in the realm look at Ganislay and cowers.

He knew he had their attention. He knew something had changed inside of him, and he simply allowed the words to flow. "I told you that I would return, and I have. You have fought hard for many millennia. That is right, millennia. You may think you have only been here a few moments after your captor sent you here. But you are in bondage. Imprisoned. Forever. Until now." Ganislay takes the scroll and points it toward one of the cliff edges. As he does he rips a hole in the side of the cliff, exposing a route to another realm.

"The road to freedom will be long, but it is yours if you want it bad enough! You have been cast aside. A fate worse than any disincorporation or any damnation I have seen. You have been forgotten. Erased from time. You have a name and you don't even know it. After a millennia of cycles you are now kin. They think of you as the same," he yells at the tear into the next realm. "To them, it matters not whether you be Celestial or Chthonic. We are all called by the same name. We are the Lost Order. Now is the time. For we have eternal judgement on our side and a key to the Most High," He says pumping a fist to the sky. Another loud trumpet booms across the realm, deafening all who consider dissent.

Ganislay begins to hover above the eyelevel of the crowd. "Creatures of the Lost Order, stand with me now," his voice booms.

Celestial and Chthonic alike begin to glance at one another. The silence hung heavy, the echoes of gnashing and grunting at one another during centuries of battle hung heavy in the air. It was as if the waves of angry voices and intention carved the canyon walls. They all looked around, recognizing how stark and dusty their environment really was. Not a single combatant had noticed in all that time as they were too wrapped up in the heinous play being enacted in front of them. As if someone had tricked them into playing out their anger each and every moment over the countless years they were there. Ganislays words brought more than solace, and the bridge to the next realm brought more than an escape. Ganislay brought time to all of Dudael. It is the mechanism of change. Without time, they truly were forgotten. They all stand up at once throwing a fist to the air and shout in unison. The depth of the volume echoes throughout the canyon and through portal to the infernal realm.

Ganislay turns and begins leading the legions of the Lost Order through the portal. It is at this point he realizes, if he just brought time to the forgotten realms of the Lost Order, was he about to change the face of Hell as well? "Am I about to put an end to eternal suffering as well", he wondered. "Let's see if I can".

Chapter Twenty-Two

The Envoy pops out of a beam of light and steps into in the middle of Notre Dame cathedral. He appears in the middle of a crowd being led by a tour guide.

"Oh, I didn't realize you were with us today," the tour guide says looking at the Envoy.

The people standing behind The Envoy in the group look upon in shock.

"He wasn't here a moment ago," a woman says, barely able to speak the words.

The envoy stands in the middle of the crowd, his suit slightly smoking from the heat it had just endured. The afternoon sun shines through the South Rose window of the cathedral.

"I'm just passing through, don't mind me." He walks toward the light streaming through the window and onto the floor. "Good to see you all here, I gotta catch a flight." He walks into the stream of light and disappears. The people stand looking at the place he was just in with their mouths agape.

"Sure," the tour guide said in disbelief.

The Envoy walks into the light pouring into the cathedral through the stained glass and dissipates into the different colors.

The crowd stands looking at the scene and then glances at the tour guide in hope of explanation.

"Who else can you introduce us to," a man asks the guide.

The envoy appears in the great hall in Central Existence. This was going to be a heap of reports. Mission failure was not something he was used to processing. He wondered why they didn't have miracles of their own. He stood at the last gateway for sould entering Central Existence, feeling the flow of energy and glee coming off of them. He always appreciated this important moment. The individual soul reconnecting with the rest of the energy that it emanated from. Like a great wave falling back into the vast ocean from whence it came.

The envoy turned and walked down the spiral stairs at the back of the building. He wanted to take in the vastness of creation. The lanai was the best place to do that. He walked out and could hear the roar of the waterfall below them tht the lanai rested above. A small class of new celestial was being briefed on the far side from where he stood at the balustrade.

"We're going to need them in the coming cycle," the Chairman says walking up to the envoy. "It's pretty ironic, the Left Hand wondering why we don't have miracles. Every creature does what it can to the best of its ability, including us. The rest-"

"Is up to God," the envoy said with a vacant smirk. "How did you know?"

"I've had my suspicions for a while. An envoy who can come and go as he pleases across any plane of existence is a rare thing. Some say impossible."

"True, we were created for specific things."

The chairman turned to the envoy and looked at him. "And if you combine that with Enoch's issues with the choirs when he first got here. It would be understandable that such an aspect would be created."

The Envoy looked at the new class of Celestials, wondering the great things they were about to embark on. "It's nice to see you Mr. Chairman," The envoy says without looking up. "Here you go, thanks for this. I used it sparingly, but I wouldn't be here without it," he says handing the Chairman a ring.

The Chairman gives a slight nod in thanks. "You didn't even need it, did you."

"No, but I appreciated the sentiment."

The Envoy stared down at the people floating in and out of the giant pool at the bottom of the waterfall. They had pure and utter joy shining from their smiles and laughter. There was no better moment than watching someone's first realizations in Heaven. Its what the Envoy worked for.

"You did good. They obviously had a plan that we played right into. It won't happen again. All is not lost. The mortal realm is troubled, but protected for now."

The envoy nodded.

"You know, if you wanted to continue on as you are, I know the Choirs would appreciate it. Your secret will go no further than here. I know Michael definitely appreciated the assistance. Your ability to gain intel across the planes has been second to none."

The Envoy looked at him. "Well... save for maybe one."

"Yes, of course."

The Envoy leaned back over the edge of the balcony and looked at the souls below.

"All mortals are creative beings. From the smallest to the largest, no matter their level of self-awareness. But the whole thing doesn't work without free will."

"What I could never come to fully accept, is that it is difficult for any entity, especially mortals, to see beyond themselves. Spiritual entities look upon the mortals all the time and want to be them. Mortals, especially humans, gaze upon the spiritual world wanting access to that. Rarely do I meet a creature that can view or interact with another existence and still be content with where they are themselves."

The Envoy raised his eyebrows at the insight but still didn't react too much. "They are coming for us sir. First they will spill over upon the earth and use every gateway there to get here."

The Chairman sighed. He looked out over the scene of the waterfalls. "I like that every celestial stops here at least once in their weekly duties. It means it's designed well."

The envoy pointed to the beacon of light in the distance, the source of heaven, shining its light into the realm.

"You've seen the other side."

"Yes."

"Therefore, you know what is happening at their portal will begin to drain the energy here."

"I know that now."

"Achieving that balance between the two, is the necessity of all creation".

"Yeah. God's gonna be pissed."

The Chairman glances at him in irritation. "Well, not even celestials are perfect. Close to it. I can't think of anyone more qualified for what is coming than you. Which is why I'm giving you the title of 'Envoy to the first order'.

"Raphael, I appreciate it, but such a position doesn't exist. And as you know, I'm just an aspect, much like yourself. Also, I think Michael would be much more suited to the task."

Raphael stood there with a bright smile. Nobody had the capability of seeing through an aspect unless they were associated with the first order. "I heard rumor that you were an aspect. Some crazy conspiracy that you are an aspect of Metatron's, out to spy on us all."

The envoy grinned. "It's more about just wanting to be a part of the action."

Raphael raised his eyebrows in amazement. "Is sitting at the left hand of the Almighty, communicating mysteries that even I don't know, getting too dull for you?"

"What I've learned is it is the struggles that teaches us the most about ourselves.

The rest of the choirs would practically commit sin to get there. Some have, but you want to hang with us."

"Why not? It's just as good as being beside the The Most High. Learning about himself through struggle is the one thing he can't do from his position."

Raphael raised his eyebrows again. He didn't expect revelations like this to be dropped in his lap at that moment. Yet there it was. "Well, I guess you'll be the most exalted Envoy in Central Existence. But to be one of the gang, I still have to give your aspect a name. Seeing that many Envoys will aspire to your new role, and the position you actually hold in the hierarchy, it's almost like you are a living talisman. From now you will be know and Thaliel.

The envoy suddenly had a flood of emotions. He didn't know how to handle them. The realm, Central Existence, the waterfalls, they were all more vibrant. It's as if a large portion of his own humanity was given back to him, whereas before he was separated from it all.

Raphael walked away. He couldn't have had a better naming ceremony if he had planned it. It's one for the history books and he knew it. A cheeky smile overcame him. He was going to have fun order his own boss around. Raphael whirled around and shouted back, "Enjoy the moment, then go get our Celestial out of the pits of hell."

The Envoy looked back at Raphael. He could finally feel a fondness between him and the choirs. He thought about the struggles before him and knew he was going to enjoy this.

The End

GLOSSARY

Aspect

Different personas that a celestial or chthonic may portray themselves as.

Choir

This is the hierarchical group or order of angels. In traditional theology, angels are categorized into different choirs, each with distinct roles and functions in the divine order. They are broken down in the following manner:

1. **First Triad** (closest to God):

- Seraphim: Angels of pure love and light who are closest to God's throne and serve Him continuously.

- **Cherubim**: Guardians of divine wisdom and knowledge, often depicted as beings of profound insight.

- **Thrones**: Angels of divine justice and authority who maintain God's will and serve as God's chariot.

2. **Second Triad** (focused on divine governance):
   - **Dominions**: Angels who govern lower angels and ensure that divine order is executed throughout the universe.

   - **Virtues**: Angels that channel God's grace and bring spiritual s rength and miracles to the earthly realm.

   - **Powers**: Angels tasked with defending against evil spirits and maintaining cosmic order.

3. **Third Triad** (interacting directly with humanity):
   - **Principalities**: Guardians of nations and leaders, ensuring the guidance and protection of large groups.

   - **Archangels**: Messengers of important divine tasks

   - **Angels:** The closest to humans, serving as personal guardians and messengers to people on Earth.

Celestial

The preferred reference among angels, so as not to confuse their rank or role in the heirarchy.

Chthonic

Any entity, deities, or spirit from the underworld, so as not to confuse rank.

Ichor

Concentrated eth that is the lifeblood of the immortals

Sons and Daughters of Light

The entirety of angelic choirs who report to Metatron

ABOUT THE AUTHOR

E dward is originally from the States but now makes his home in East Sussex in the U.K.

You can find out more about his work at:

edwardgye.com

or you can connect with him on Facebook at

www.facebook.com/edwardgye

Printed in Great Britain
by Amazon